MY LIFE AS A CADAVER

A Survivor's Tale

Karl Schoenberger

OSIRUS PRESS

Osiris Press, San Francisco
My Life as a Cadaver, 2nd Edition
Copyright © 2014 Karl Schoenberger
All Rights Reserved
ISBN-13: 978-1491253120
ISBN-10: 1491253126
Library of Congress Control Number: 2013919907
CreateSpace Independent Publishing Platform North
Charleston, South Carolina

Dedicated to Alexandra Levine,
who patched me up and sent me on my way

One

A hideous sound assaulted him in the dark, a furious insect flapping its wings on his eardrums, summoning him from ink black slumber. He looked at the digital clock on the nightstand to see 3:07 AM glowering at him in red liquid crystal insolence. His throat vented a staccato voice midway between shout and croak: "Shit, shit, shit!"

Slowly he came to realize the noise was the shrill chirping of a mobile phone commanding him to cast off the warm, sweet swaddling of his down comforter and hoist himself out of bed. It would have been less painful had he been roused by the sobering ring of his landline phone. The effect of this sharp electronic noise was a thousand times worse than the abuse Pavlov perpetrated on his dog. The dog did not have to overcome the will to resist the stimulus. The dog did not wake remembering a dream vaguely involving sex with a woman who had green eyes and long black hair. The dog did not experience the raw, sickening evisceration of the gut that extreme sleep deprivation perpetrated on him now. The dog just salivated. Colleagues urged him to change his ring tone to something more euphonious but he did not know how to do that and never got around to learning.

The coroner searched for the little silver handset with a sweep of his left arm and in doing so knocked off the top of the lamp. The base of the lamp remained erect on the bedside table, but it was decapitated, shade and light bulb assembly cast to the floor and waiting to be crushed when he stood up to gain equilibrium, reaching for the phone in the dark. It was a $17 lamp his wife purchased long ago at a gigantic Scandinavian furniture store. He knew from experience that what he needed to do next was to pick up the top and gently thread the two parts back together. The pigtail of an energy-saving bulb cast frugal light on his hands as he hurried to flip open the phone before the call was lost. He recognized the voice on the other end.

In a congested bark he answered: "What the hell do you want, you idiot! Do you have any idea what time it is?"

"Sorry, Leo. It's a funny case, maybe a homicide, the kind of thing you said I had to wake you up for." The half-hearted apology oozed from the receiver. "And you're supposed to be the second AME on call tonight anyway. I'm just doing what you told me, Leo, because Dixon is already out on a case and you're the backup on the list. Maybe you forgot."

Behold Wilson Dubrovnik, the morgue assistant taking his turn on the graveyard shift, he thought, just doing his job.

"It's a hit-and-run in the Inner Mission and the cops want someone of your expertise to double-check the body *in situ* before signing the certificate. The inspector told me specifically to get you here pronto so he can get back to bed. He said there are strange anomalies with the body."

Wilson's voice betrayed the same combination of naiveté and impetuousness that made the coroner consider him the Jimmy Olson of the Medical Examiner's Office, earnest, stubborn, too often clueless. Wilson was in every sense of the word the department's *diener*, the lowliest of living creatures in the morgue, who was telling him now he had better get dressed and jump into his car and drive to Hill and Sanchez.

He coughed out a long mournful sigh. "I'll be home soon, my love," he said toward the other side of the king-sized bed. It was empty, however, as he knew it would be. Missing was the shallow depression she left on the mattress after hopping up to make coffee on nights like this.

It did not take long for him to crawl into yesterday's checkered boxer shorts and pull on his white shirt and brown suit. He reached into his pocket for his keys but they slipped out of his hand and dropped to the kitchen floor as though they were attracted by magnetic force.

When he stooped to pick them up they escaped his fingers again. Cursing, he clutched them tight as he opened and slammed shut the front door and unlocked the garage. He shook his head vigorously, jowls flapping as he slipped behind the wheel of his gray humpback Volvo, a relic he rescued from the junkyard twenty years earlier. The car had 347,915 miles on its third engine and sported a rusted fender Alice had nagged him to get fixed for as long as he could remember.

Coroner was not his official title, it was his name. For years his colleagues had referred to him behind his back as the coroner and when he first got wind of it he was not sure whether it was a term of respect and endearment or biting satire. He chose to consider it in a positive light because he understood he was generally well liked. The name was somehow appropriate. Technically there were no coroners in San Francisco, only medical examiners. The term coroner carried an association with the old-fashioned county coroner system, where the modern science of forensic pathology was not necessarily the rule. He knew his courtly, informal style did not fit the mold of a straight-laced medical examiner, however, and he accepted the name without insult or injury. He was the coroner, if they wanted him to be.

He met no resistance motoring down Van Ness Avenue toward Noe Valley, listening to a repeat of the same National Public Radio newscast he heard last night on his way home from the morgue: Bob Edwards was chatting with David Gergen about the trial of the Washington sniper suspect John Allen Muhammad. This was followed by a cute holiday commentary by a man who encountered ancient ghosts in caves while camping under a full moon in the Grand Canyon. The coroner jabbed the button to quash the babbling radio, prefer-ring the silence of the abandoned thoroughfare. All they do is recycle the news, he thought, yesterday's news. The news industry was going bankrupt and he was losing his respect for the journalists he knew. It had been years since he fraternized with newspapermen in confidence at the M & M to swap stories, sometimes to leak secrets in the body of a murder victim for the greater public good.

He ignored the nuisance of untimed red lights at the deserted intersections but made it a point not to exceed the maximum speed permitted by the law, as was his custom. He opened all the windows so the chilly air would slap him awake. His body jerked when he wondered whether he remembered to put his black leather tool bag in the trunk before leaving the office earlier in the night, forgetting he was on call. After angling down Market he chose Dolores as his route to the scene. The coroner took great pleasure in gliding up and down its fluid slopes past the sentinel palm trees that laced the grass median strip evoking the Mediterranean ambience of the old Spanish missions.

He anticipated this would be just another routine call like so many of the countless traffic accidents in his career. He will rule out premeditated murder, document the manner of death – mangled by steel, sliced by glass, crushed by wheels – then perform all the perfunctory tasks. A feel for the pulse, a penlight in the pupils, a jot on the death certificate. He was a highly accomplished, veteran forensic pathologist, he growled to the palm trees, why did they bother him with routine chores like this? He knew why, of course. The law says someone has to do it, and it was his duty tonight. He would make quick work of it and be back in his bed before it got too cold.

Two

He found a lit-up squad car and Wilson's motorcycle at the accident scene. Two patrolmen and one plain-clothes cop were milling about swaying their flashlights at the pavement. He saw Wilson straining to rise from a squatting position to greet him, almost extending to his full six-foot-three-inch frame. The scene was frozen as though in pause mode, gray figures on a backdrop of darker gray. They were waiting for him to emerge from the Volvo and go through the motions of taking charge. Wilson slouched toward him. He looked as though he was ready to keel over into the gutter. Poor bastard, he thought. *Dieners* are supposed to be short, wiry and tough, well adapted to going long hours without sleep and loving it, getting high on it like medical interns staying alert beyond reason. I have spoiled the boy, he thought. If this case was more complicated than it seemed he would be up for overtime, maybe a double shift. If it was run-of-the-mill they could both go home soon and sleep until Monday.

He saw the body sprawled out on the street in the supine position with clenched fists, curious fists, poised to smite a mortal enemy.

"White male, approximately 50. No identification – we're estimating the time of death at around two-forty," one of the uniformed officers said as he sidled over to him. In the parsimonious light shed by the patrol car and the street lamp on the corner he noticed the cop had a protruding gut hanging over his gun belt despite his otherwise lanky frame, like a thin man who swallowed a bowling ball he could never digest.

"We're a little puzzled, Leo. Maybe a little suspicious about the circumstances," said another cop, this one wearing greygray slacks and a blazer, necktie askew, his flashlight dancing at his feet. "Usually in a hit-and-run you find the guy all doubled up like a shrimp or face down with his butt in the air but this guy looks like he's been laid out for display. I'm thinking there could be some foul play here, maybe."

The coroner recognized homicide's Lieutenant Inspector Robert Villaragosa, a veteran of the police force he worked with on a dozen murder cases in the past. Serious, a straight arrow, but not known as a particularly zealous crime stopper. He was coasting toward retirement, the coroner figured, and it was rare to see him out on the street at that time of night.

"Hello, Bob," he said, nodding in respect. "What got you out of your pajamas on this occasion? You and I should be at home getting our beauty rest."

"These guys thought I should see it before they zipped him up," Villaragosa said, motioning toward the pot-bellied patrolman and his partner. "I'm working on a crime pattern, Leo. Bunch of homeless guys have been getting rumbled, beat to a pulp by hooligans over the past eight months, a few fatalities. We've seen cases where they run them down on the street and leave stolen cars abandoned up the block. All in the name of good fun."

"Hadn't heard about it, Bob. News to me. Find the car that done this?'

"Not yet. That's hard to do at this hour. We could get a crew to sweep the neighborhood for bloody bumpers in the morning," he said. "But it'd be good if you could help me get an opinion about whether this looks out of the ordinary."

"I dunno, I'll take a look-see," said the coroner, shaking his head and running his hand over his face as though he was wiping off a cobweb. "Bums have always been easy targets for miscreants. For vehicles too."

"The case I'm working, it's different, Leo. It isn't a Zodiac but it's random serial murders. Racial hate crime doesn't appear to be involved. It's equal opportunity assault on victims nobody would care about when they're gone."

The coroner grunted. He had been tied up in the futile Zodiac investigation for a brief time along with the inspector thirty years ago, random serial killings that terrorized the City, still unsolved but long forgotten. It became a media circus until the press got bored by it. He could see the wisdom of avoiding sensationalism.

"Ever seen *A Clockwork Orange* Leo? It's more like that. The profile is snotty-nosed white kids coming in from the suburbs to score drugs and seek some entertainment along the way. The supposition is that they get hopped up on crack or ecstasy and go on a rampage, pulling guys out of the bushes at the park and their cardboard boxes under the highway. They kick their teeth in, crush their ribs.

"It's happening on a regular basis. We picked up a few suspects and they're not our local gang bangers. We didn't have enough evidence to hold them and their dads drove up from Sunnyvale with lawyers in tow to take them home. It seems to be a one-upmanship thing in the high schools, about who rolls the most in a single night. Bum-bashing Junior Olympics. Fucking vicious."

The coroner yawned and stared at the inspector in mock disbelief.

"You mean to tell me kids are more vicious these days? Hasn't bum-bashing been around since time immemorial?"

"By the way, have you seen the dog-boarding they're doing at the park these days? It's the new thing," Villaragosa said. "Saw it a few Sundays ago on JFK when I was there on business."

"Dog boarder," the coroner said. "They got dog kennels in the park now so their lazy owners get a break from bagging shit?"

"No, Leo, it's like this. Guys on skateboards are out there with their dogs. You wouldn't believe it," he said. "The dog's on a leash pulling the skateboarders around. The dogs go wild and the rider says mush, mush until he hits a curb and goes flying. Couple of nights ago one of them landed in the bushes face-to-face with a bum named Buck Pomeroy. That's why I was there poking around. They got Buck to the emergency room just in time – he fits the pattern exactly."

"I've seen lots of homeless men with blunt trauma at the morgue," he said. "How come I haven't heard about this case? That's what I'm supposed to be doing, Bob. Let's work together on these sorts of things. I'm supposed to be a forensic pathologist, licensed to kill. Do you think these tire marks are fresh?"

"You're the best, Leo. But we're keeping a tight lid on it. The chief and the mayor want us to get a hold on the particularities and get some, uh, conclusive evidence and some suspects before it gets leaked to the press. They don't want homeless activists organizing protests, you know. We need to nail the kids in the act, not scare them away. It's been a need-to-know basis. Sorry they left you out of the loop."

"Okay, okay. So who's been doing the autopsies? Young Dixon? Pretty hard to stanch the rumor mill at the ME's office. Can't imagine how the staff didn't tell me." He paused to think, "Is it Du Goyle?" He didn't need an answer. That sycophantic ass, he could only conclude, was violating departmental protocol to play the slimy game of politics.

"Sorry Leo," Villaragosa said. "That part of it's been out of my control. And yes, the skid marks are fresh in my estimation."

They eyed each other for a good seven or eight tense seconds before the coroner let out a belly laugh.

"Things are so fucked up at the ME's office I don't care anymore. Only a matter of time before I'll be laid out on the slab myself," he said. "So let's get to work. What's going on here that you think fits your pattern?"

"That's the problem. This one is a little different – most of it doesn't fit the pattern because this man wasn't torn up by boots and brickbats, just an isolated gash on his forehead and lacerations on his face. It could be an ordinary hit-and-run as far as I know, but I had a hunch," the detective said. "Sorry to drag you down here, but something's out of place with this body. Maybe you take a closer look and tell me if you see anything unusual."

"No problem, Bob. Someone had to be here anyway, and it's my fucking turn," he said. "What's he doing with his fists like that? Was he grasping something?"

He sat on his haunches to examine the body. The cartilage in his knees protested with a crack and a momentary jab of pain. Squatting was turning into an occupational hazard. He fumbled with and dropped his Maglite, cursing when he picked it up. Then he dropped it again.

He scrutinized the man's face and hands, the blood oozing from a single gash on the left brow. The tire marks on the pavement veered away as though to escape after the collision, or so it seemed. The coroner took a second look at the man's face and noticed a remarkable similarity to his own. He had a habit of identifying with the victims, but not like this.

"Did you say he didn't have a wallet? Who took his wallet?" The coroner looked over his shoulder with barely concealed suspicion at the pot-bellied cop. His partner stepped out from the shadows.

"No sir, we checked. It wasn't there. That's why we figured he was homeless. But it didn't look right, so we called homicide. Turns out Inspector Villaragosa lives just a few blocks away on Jersey and he got here right away."

Was this guy the one who filched the victim's wallet? He made a mental note to watch the officer's mannerisms before drawing any conclusions.

"You sleeping in your clothes these days, Bob? Got a fireman's pole?"

"Naw, I'm just naturally quick."

The beam from the coroner's flashlight was growing pale, flickering, batteries running low. No point in changing them now. He did not see much blood pooling under the head but there was a fair amount spattered on hisß face. He saw lacerations and abrasions consistent with having been shoved along, face down, across the pavement by the offending vehicle. This is getting interesting, he muttered to himself.

Three

The dead man was lying with his neck cocked in anticipation. The eyeglasses should be mangled and scattered on the street, he thought. If the mortal wound is on the forehead why is he lying face up instead of with his face in the gutter?

"Are you sure you didn't move him?" He glared at the uniformed, wallet-snatching suspects, both of whom shrugged in innocence and shook their heads.

He put on his white cotton gloves and felt the man's arms, ribs and legs, and found no obvious signs of broken bones. He looked closely at the wound on the forehead, which was deep but seemed too small and narrow to be caused by a bumper or a front grill. A blunt instrument, perhaps, but that seemed out of place. More likely a wallop on the edge of a curb causing a fatal concussion, but it was very odd he was not facing down. Maybe the man struggled to get on his feet and crumpled onto his back. His eyeglasses, however, were improbably attached to his face. He slipped them down the man's nose and shuddered for a moment as he pulled out his penlight for a cursory look at the pupils. The eyes were so familiar. He touched the jugular. He checked the pockets of his torn and faded blue jeans and found a clump of bills the policemen had missed.

"Let's note the cash in his left pocket," said the coroner, as he counted it before putting it back. "Thirty-seven dollars and some change. It wasn't robbery. Just homicide." He made a satirical sign of the cross. "Let's fill out the form, Wilson."

"What do the skid marks tell you?" he asked the patrolman, who was helping him out by aiming his flashlight on the face of the dead man.

"Looks like the driver slammed on his brakes, then blasted off," he said. "If it was an intentional hit he wouldn't need to slow down. He'd just clip him on the hip and send him dancing without a moment's hesitation. Unless he wanted to stop to see the damage. It's not entirely clear. I'm going to do the chalk and take pictures before we leave."

"Wilson, why don't you shoot us our own set of pictures while we're at it, just to get this closed expeditiously. I'll get the camera out of the back seat."

"No need to do that, Leo, I already took them," he said, pulling out and pointing to his mobile phone.

"That's your phone, you numbskull. I'm talking about cameras, not wireless devices. What did you do, phone the stiff and ask for a mug shot?"

"But it's a camera too. A lot of cell phones take pictures now, and with better resolution than your old camera. I can send them as jpegs to you and they'll be in your inbox when we get back to the morgue."

The coroner shook his head in confusion. He did not want to embarrass himself by asking Wilson to remind him what a jpeg was in front of the others. The tall cop with the bowling ball midriff snickered anyway, but it was either too early in the morning or too late at night to care. I'll call the guy, Brunswick, he thought.

"The witness didn't see anything, just heard the screech," the second patrolman said. The name patch over his shirt pocket said Mahoney. "Thinks he saw a light-colored sedan racing away down Sanchez when he rounded the corner with his dog, but who knows. We've seen lots of drunk drivers doing this sort of thing."

"You got a witness? Where is he?" said the coroner, squinting through the beam of light. He thought he recognized the cop, yes, it was a sergeant he had worked with last month. He was not the kind of cop who would steal a wallet from a corpse.

Mahoney pulled out a pad of paper, which the coroner could see was filled with narrow lines of writing in the legible hand of a copious note-taker. He copied down the name and address on a blank page and ripped it out. "Can't guarantee you'll get anything useful from the old codger," he said. "He heard the noise and saw the body and called 911, but he was pretty much incoherent. A bit senile maybe, so we sent him home. I think his little dog was taking him out for a walk and I had some concerns about his presence of mind, if you know what I mean."

He groaned and turned full circle to examine the intersection. Sanchez descended here from a moderately steep grade from the north, then flattened out at the corner with Hill Street, which was one-way to the east, two-way to the west. The driver might have hit the man as he crossed the street while speeding down the hill, then slammed on the brakes too late, then turned a sharp right onto Hill without looking back. He wouldn't have turned left because it was one way in the wrong direction, but on the other hand what would he care about a traffic violation when he had just killed a man?

He turned to Villaragosa. "Doesn't look totally cut and dry to me. The shape of it says hit-and-run, but if you don't mind I'd like to take a look at that file of yours on the homeless predators. I'll keep it locked up, out of sight of our ass-sucking Deputy M.E. He'll never know I'm hip to the secret case."

He was answered by a quick nod and a wide grin.

"Sure, I'll tell the duty officer to hand it over. I'll do better than that. Go check out our Mr. Pomeroy at Mission General. He just got out of the ICU. Fractured skull, brain trauma, broken jaw and serious damage to his scrotum, the details of which I don't need to mention. He's conscious, begging for a drink. I talked to him yesterday and he's got a pretty good yarn to tell.

"But me personally, I'm planning to be out on the golf course after I have a little nap, seeing as how you're leaning toward the accidental view of this," the inspector said. "Let me know what you find in the autopsy."

"We're not supposed to cut on weekends but I'll take a closer look, maybe later this morning. I won't need to dissect his brain to get a general idea of what killed him," he said, looking at his watch and wincing.

"What do you think, Wilson?" He guffawed when he saw the *denier* snap his head back to attention, roused by the sarcastic bite of his boss's voice. The coroner savored the sweet revenge for his own rude awakening.

"Whatever you say, Leo," he said. "But what about those kids? Isn't that something we should . . ." The coroner cut him off before he could finish his sentence.

"You're going to call homicide and ask very politely if we can borrow Inspector Villaragosa's file soon as dawn cracks and the rest of the world wakes up, amongst other things you'll need to do," he said. "First you're going to brew a pot of your famous mud." He dropped his anemic flashlight and stooped to pick it up from the pavement.

"I don't reckon this is murder in the first degree here, boys, but it could be an interesting case. A vagrant with a wad of bills in his pocket. There's a puzzle to it," he said in a satirical voice that echoed the tone of a pulp crime novel. The others got the joke and grinned, everyone except Wilson, who handed him the blank death certificate with due solemnity.

The coroner filled in the particulars and scrawled his signature. Estimated time of death, 2:20 a.m. Manner of death, struck by vehicle. Cause of death, blunt trauma to the brain, pending autopsy.

"I don't know why he died, with a relatively superficial wound like that. He'd almost have to try to die. Could be suicide, and the hit-and-run driver was doing him a favor. Murder? Doubt it but who knows. Sergeant Mahoney, can you write this up before your shift ends?"

"That's the rule," he said. "I'll call for the wagon." While Mahoney went to the squad car to speak into a squawking radio the assistant medical examiner thought he saw Officer Brunswick staring at him disrespectfully, almost smirking, as though he were watching a bumbling idiot. It was a sensation the coroner experienced more frequently in recent years as his authority started to wane. He crossed the street to his car, and midway through the intersection he turned to face Brunswick in a feeble attempt to salvage his dignity.

"Which one of you bums tampered with the evidence and put the spectacles back on his face?" They did not appear to know whether he was joking or casting aspersions but they laughed anyway, in a charitable way.

Four

It was nine-fifteen already when he woke with a groan, rudely rousted from sleep for the second time that morning, dreamlessly this time. Grumpy and disoriented, he reached into the void for answers. What was he doing at work, sleeping face down on the desk of his private office, and feeling an impetuous hand shake his shoulder?

"Bug off, Wilson. What in God's sake do you want now? Can't you let a man sleep?"

It came back to him quickly, however, how he parked his car in the lot under the freeway before dawn, so exhausted that he nearly dozed off for a while behind the wheel, with the motor still running and the radio chattering softly.

He recalled dragging himself out of the gated enclosure and squinting into the dazzling sunlight that shone with such intensity it turned the grubby sidewalk into a clean carpet of grayish white. He walked into the glare, taking the long way around to the front of the Hall of Justice, past the cheerful McKay's hamburger outlet on the corner that always struck him as at odds with the row of seedy 24-hour bail bond shops across Bryant Street. He mounted the stairs and saw that the building was empty of the usual cast of criminal justice extras that swarmed the lobby on weekday mornings, the swaggering cops, the squirrelly defendants, the bug-eyed criminal defense lawyers in discount store suits. He wondered why he took the detour. He felt particularly annoyed by the sound of his heels shattering the silence of the marble corridor. He fought off a sense of dread as he exited the back door of the grand lobby and walked down the open-air causeway that led to a large bunker-like building in the back housing the San Francisco City and County Medical Examiner's Office. He was surprised to find his Sanchez Street victim stretched out in the cold room, ready for him to inspect.

He recalled doing a cursory examination of the body, thinking the man would have to wait until Monday to get his rib cage ripped open, his organs sliced and his brain placed in a pickle jar.

He recalled his wonder when he took a close look at the face. Behind the bent and blood-flecked spectacles there was intelligence in the eyes, even in death.

The corpse before him was a nameless man who had been run down in the middle of the night, who was probably homeless, who was staring at the coroner as though it was a game of who-blinks-first. This was a dead man with an expression he had never seen before. He was missing the slack jaw, the glassy gaze and the repose of absolute stillness. His facial muscles, the orbicularis oris and oculomotor, were animated as though he was ready to rise from the surface of cold stainless steel at any moment.

He recalled that rigor mortis had not set in, yet the man's hands were locked into pugnacious fists, just as they were at the curbside where he was found six hours earlier, poised to punch his way out of darkness. The man intends to go somewhere, he remembered thinking, but he is not yet ready to leave. The man wanted to talk. He wanted to smoke one last cigarette and pause midway in his journey to tell the story of his life to a stranger.

Now that he was fully awake, the coroner could see rusty-haired Wilson clutching something under his arm. "I got the file from homicide, Leo," he said. "Nicki's in today and says she'll get us a report on the serum samples by ten." His freckled, acne-scarred face was beaming. "Very good, Wilson," he said. "But I did notice there was no damn coffee made when I got here, which was exactly why you found me dozing just now. However, I am feeling munificent this morning and I shall refrain from breaking your neck for countermanding your orders."

"Shut up, Leo. The jar was empty, honest. I was going to go out and get the beans but things got busy all of a sudden," he said. "You seen the body yet? The transport crew dumped him in the cold room before I got here."

"Yes, I have seen the body," he said. "Got a good look at him. He and I are old friends now. We earnestly discussed Pythagoras and Osiris. It was divine."

Wilson shook his head and shrugged off the coroner's sarcasm, as though his boss's mind was beginning to slip. He placed the file on the desk and skulked out of the room, announcing his mission to fetch a large cup of coffee from the cafeteria for his master, pronto.

"No cream, no sugar," Wilson said before the coroner could say what he always ticked out at this point in the script. "Black as the night."

The battered brown cardboard file case on the desk, identified by a thick black Sharpie as "EI-012XM bumbash-2003," contained a dozen manila folders containing typed-up case reports and handwritten notes on pages torn from yellow legal pads with underlined and circled words and arrows pointed at selected passages of apparent significance.

The coroner's eyes were stingingly dry and had difficulty focusing on the pages. It will require some lubrication to navigate this day, he told himself, but he would wait to find the flask at a more respectable hour. He put the files back in their brown case and secured it with its elastic string, which he noted was frayed and about to snap. He knew he would suffer all day from the effects of sleep deprivation. He had gone to bed past midnight, after an interminable day at the morgue working on a thankless euthanasia case with cops and lawyers and bereaved family members nipping at his heels.

Just as he was about to go home they rolled in a six-year-old boy in a tiger costume who had just been shot in the neck one block away from the Castro Street parade. A man with a 22-caliber handgun snatched his mother's purse, and the boy leaped at him, growling ferociously in her defense, an act of extraordinary courage that reminded the coroner of the blurry line separating fantasy and reality in a young child's mind. No, not only in the mind of a child, he corrected himself.

The line confuses us until we die, with its porous distinction between what we'd like to imagine and what we are supposed to recognize as real. He made an effort to block the tiger boy from breaking his heart when he finally crawled into bed, way past his bedtime.

Since the department suspended weekend autopsies last year for budgetary reasons, Friday's work was hell. It was supposed to be done by the end of the day, which generally stretched well past midnight. Then the following Monday was a madhouse from the weekend carnage, the Saturday night gang warfare, the wife murders, the suicides, and the heart attacks men had in bed with their young mistresses, not to mention the peaceful slipping away of elderly souls. A bullet was still lodged in the tiger boy's neck but the forensic exam would have to wait until Monday. No rush in this case. They got the guy who did it, a crack addict who was tackled by a bystander as he tried to ditch his gun. This was a holiday weekend, and the coroner knew Monday would be one of those Mondays when the morgue seemed more like an abattoir than a pathology lab, thanks to the budget. And it was the day for his annual performance review, to be conducted by the department's martinet, his nemesis, Horace Du Goyle. The coroner yearned for the old days when his work was calm, deliberate and genteel.

He strolled over to the examination room to find the corpse biding his time, eyeglasses still affixed to his nose, covering that peculiar gaze. While he was napping at his desk, Wilson had stripped off the clothes and spread a sheet over him. At the death scene he noticed a slight depression about the size of a nickel visible in the balding area on about 9:15 degrees on the top of the man's skull. He thought it might be related to the trauma above his left eye, but it was curious that there was no sign of bleeding, bruising or contusion at the spot. He put the gloves on and probed the same area with his fingers, and found three more dents under the hair toward his left temple, too well aligned in a square to be anything other than the archeological remains of a craniotomy. Someone sawed a hatch in the skull and done something inside before putting it back on and sewing up the flap of the cranial muscle sheath, revealing only burr holes as clues. Most likely this fellow had a malignant tumor in the left hemisphere of his brain that some old-fashioned neurosurgeon, handy with a drill and router, excavated from the white matter, prolonging his life until he got to the corner of Sanchez and Hill early this morning.

Hot coffee always jump-started the coroner's neurological capacity for critical thinking at a time like this. The jumbo cup that Wilson brought from the Coffee Chain Café, kitty-corner to the Hall of Justice, immediately produced beneficial effects. Wilson explained in his apology for the delay that the cafeteria was closed on weekends because of the cutbacks and he knew how much he despised McKay's mediocre coffee.

"No, this is better," the coroner said. "And it's pronounced *mac-kai*, not *mac-aye*. How many times have I told you?" McKay was his Scottish great-grandmother Nellie's clan on his mother's side and he held the hamburger franchise in contempt for bastardizing his ancestors' good name.

Chain Café's coffee met his approval because they sell large quantities in a short period of time, and that means it is usually freshly brewed, unlike the sludge at the bottom of the cafeteria urns, and certainly better than the bitter black paint Wilson and the others made in the morgue's pantry. Before drinking, he inhaled the aromatic fumes of dark tangy Arabica bean brew.

The surgery on the mottled dome of this man's head must have been a long time ago, maybe twenty years past, he concluded, because they rarely hacked up skulls like this with the technology in use today. He wasn't up to speed on the subject, however. He could not keep up with the torrent of new information in the field of medicine. His JAMAs and Lancets stacked up unread on his living room floor. It was hard enough just to follow the forensic pathology literature. Yet he imagined that today, after scanning the brain into walnut slices with an MRI, they would work up a three-dimensional image with some kind of computer animation technology, then snake their way in with a tiny scope to see what it looked like and to snip off tissue for the biopsy. Occasionally he found radioactive pellets implanted next to tumors in his autopsies that he understood in some cases obviated the need for blasting a person's head or body with gamma rays. He did not see telltale tattoo marks on the dead man's head that would have guided the barrel of a medical cyclotron, but the evidence of a craniotomy suggested this homeless man had been given traditional treatment for brain cancer. In an earlier life, before he took to living on the streets, he must have had a job, a health insurance policy, a brain worth saving.

The corpse's mousey-brown hair was asymmetrical and grew like dried corn silk, suggesting damage to the follicles from radiation or chemotherapy. The hair was much thinner on the left temple than the right, consistent with the hatch on the left of the skull and the probability of radiation therapy. The important question, he reminded himself, is whether an old brain tumor might be related to the cause of the man's death.

He dictated his observations into a micro-cassette recorder purely out of habit, for there was no one left to transcribe tapes anymore – it all had to be micro-chip memory now but it helped him organize his thoughts. Wilson or one of the other assistants would rig up the electronics for the autopsy.

He paused to consider the clues. An old codger summoned police to the scene after finding the man sprawled on the northeast corner of Hill and Sanchez Streets. According to police, the man did not witness the accident but heard the screech of tires followed by grinding gears and the roar of an engine as he rounded the corner during a pre-dawn walk with his dog, which yelped hysterically at the sound.

The victim's forehead presented a remarkable gash oozing blood when the coroner arrived at the scene. The blood was partly congealed and left a pattern of dried red-black and glistening crimson streaks on his face. The severity of the wound was not consistent with fatal blunt force trauma. He wondered why this man, superficially in fair health with an athletic build, aged about 48 to 52 years, had expired so easily. He did not mention the weird sensation that he was looking at himself on the slab.

The coroner turned to probe the body and again did not detect broken bones. A close view of the face revealed mild to moderate lacerations and abrasions on his nose and cheeks, apparently caused by scraping across the pavement face down, but then why was the body found face up? Skid marks on the street had matched roughly the dog-walker's auditory account, fitting the scenario of a hit-and-run traffic fatality: A car careening around the corner, too intoxicated or reckless to brake in time and avoid knocking the pedestrian off his feet, then slamming on the brakes after feeling the soft impact and hearing the thud. He imagined the terror as the man raised his fists to the blinding headlamps, too late to dodge and the car coming too fast to avoid the irrational impulse to fight for survival.

Did he see his life flash before his eyes, as survivors describe their experiences after leaping into the abyss from the Golden Gate Bridge?

A surge of memory, a torrent of images and sounds unfolding in vivid detail and chronicling all his hopes and loves, achievements and lost opportunities. The corpse lingered between vigor and void, perhaps taking a thoughtful look at the world he could not bear to leave behind. Eyebrows rueful mouth chagrined, he had an important commitment to make, a promise to honor, a lover to embrace. The man was not homeless; he was on his way home. This was the least dead of all the bodies he remembered examining in his 30-year career.

The coroner did not believe in the afterlife and he had no tolerance for mysticism, yet he could not help himself from imagining this man hovering in confusion over his own body, inspecting himself in sadness from a bird's-eye view and at once looking upward, trying to penetrate a shroud of twilight before surrendering himself.

The coroner felt the jugular for any faint quiver of pulse that could explain the corpse's mien, and he probed the dead man's diaphragm for signs of breath he knew he would not find. He guffawed unprofessionally at the loud *brapp!* of escaping gas. The man's heart is stopped and the bellows of his lungs were still, but his bowels have not given up the ghost.

He saw many corpses jerk on the slab with a final discharge of neuroelectricity, he heard death rattles in their throats, and he once observed in utter astonishment a crash victim with devastating head and back injuries to sit up and put his legs on the floor. The fellow was pronounced dead on arrival, but after standing he strutted toward the door of the morgue, reaching frantically at the waist of his hospital gown for a missing mobile phone. He was an investment banker who traded mortgage-backed securities, and in his first delirious words after returning to life he asked about his pending deal with Fannie Mae. Fannie who? Would that be his wife's name, the coroner replied. No, the man was not expressing concern about the welfare of his loved ones, who all perished instantly in the head-on collision. A blasphemous resurrection, he thought, as he re-examined the strange eyes of the man before him, perplexed by their animation.

Under the glare of the halogen lights he noted the eyes were splayed, pointing at different places on the ceiling. Both eyes were hazel brown. The left eye was more dilated, and it strayed as though it was the diseased stem of a plant hungry for photosynthesis at the same time it strained to stay in line with its mate. The eyes made the face slightly off kilter. He saw the vulnerability of a once arrogant man.

The police seemed relatively certain the man was homeless, one of the countless indigents who prowled San Francisco's neighborhoods after midnight, foraging in garbage receptacles for discarded food or the currency of aluminum cans and plastic bottles. That assumption was supported by the unkempt and strangely asymmetrical hair, the stubbly salt-and-pepper bum's beard, the ragged dirty blue jeans, and the fact he had no wallet or identification on his person.

They were wrong, however. There was an alcoholic stink about the corpse, bourbon, but nothing approaching the signature fragrance of an unshowered street dweller. Cursory evidence of his medical history did not fit the assessment. The body had an aura that betrayed disorientation but not homelessness.

The coroner removed the pants from a large ziploc bag Wilson left on the rack under the examination table. He counted the money stashed in the man's pocket, a twenty-dollar bill, three fives and two singles, plus forty-nine cents in change. Perhaps he had a streak of good luck panhandling, or recently cashed a General Assistance check? No, the money reflected his status; he was not indigent. He felt a hard lump at the waistband, stuck his finger into the little fifth pocket of the dungarees and fished out a key. The cops missed it at the accident scene, and so had he. It might open a locker at the bus station or a post-office box where he collected mail. It could open the front door of the man's house. He zipped it up in a small plastic bag and dropped it under the flap of his suit coat pocket. It was a house key, he was fairly certain, but until he discovered the man's identity, the door it opened would remain a mystery. The body was waiting for a loved one to file a missing person's report and come forth to claim the remains. He could not say why, but he did not think this would occur. With the backlog of marginally suspicious deaths and unsolved homicide cases in the pipeline, this particular corpse, toe-tagged "John Doe 03-Z39," might have to wait a long time before he was honored with a name.

The San Francisco ME's Office had a fairly good track record identifying the dead when it got around to it. Last year 158 John and Jane Does came to visit the morgue, according to the data he himself compiled and passed up the chain for the office's Annual report. All were eventually identified by way of DNA testing and forensic diligence, but that was not always the case in the recent past, as he knew from personal experience. In all but a few cses the departed were presumed homeless men. He recalled a recent NIH article that estimated an average of 400 corpses a year go to their rest unidentified. Too many morgues out there are denied the resources they need to do the job properly, or they are mismanaged. Too many of them still run under the old county coroner system where political hacks run the show instead of medical doctors. He vowed years ago he would never allow such inhumanity on his watch, but his influence was waning. No, he had to admit, it was all but gone. He was a relic of the past, and the precepts of his calling were already obsolete.

This man is not merely dead, and he is not sincerely dead, he mused. A vagabond worth $37.49, with a curious gaze and a mysterious house key hidden in his pocket. The coroner resigned himself to the likelihood that forces out of his control would take the dead man out of his hands. If he is lucky, the deceased will be afforded the glory of serving mankind as a cadaver at a teaching hospital, a considerable step up in prestige from the pauper's crematorium. He had a friend who worked as a body broker. His job was to shop around for cadavers with interesting conditions and provide them to teaching hospitals.

He might call him on Monday and put him on notice, or maybe not. No, he definitely would not. He felt protective of the corpse. There was an inexplicable affinity he had never felt for one of his silent clients, a spell cast by the man's eyes, perhaps. He felt a duty. He did not want the autopsy botched by a clumsy second-year medical student doing a clerkship at the county hospital. "This one is mine," he said with a soft grunt. "I am going to listen to his story and give him back his name. I will hear his story and that will bring him back to life." The coroner curled his hands into fists.

Five

He caught a wisp of Nicki's perfume and knew she was standing behind him well before she tapped his shoulder and spoke.

"What was that you said, Leo? There you go again, talking to yourself like a madman."

"Good morning, my love," he said, not bothering to turn and abandon the corpse. "What brings you in on a lazy Saturday morning? Never mind, don't tell me because I have a job for you. This fellow here needs his fluids checked out before I can decide if I go home or fiddle around here some more. He's a mysterious bird. Seems he died after a relatively moderate bang on the head and I want to know why."

"Your wish is my command, Dr. Bacigalupi," she said. "Might as well do your bidding since I got to be here anyway. It'll help kill the time."

"I don't suppose the case is going to warrant a full-blown autopsy and inquest on Monday unless we find some indication of foul play, but I'm probably going to do the full nine yards anyway, just because I said so. Don't need an excuse to do the right thing."

He turned to greet her with a weary grin and did his very best not to linger in the appraisal of her milky skin, plump lips and dark eyes, making his best effort to dispel the surge of uneasiness she aroused in him. He chose to focus on a gray stain on the floor next to his right shoe.

"We have to take into account the very unlikely possibility he was assaulted, or maybe he prearranged his own death," he said. "My friend over in homicide was poking around at the scene thinking he's maybe a victim of something more than just a bad driver. I have my doubts but we got to check it out anyhow, we have to, what, eliminate the negative before we hold on to the affirmative? It's the scientific method."

The coroner felt suddenly smaller than his subordinate and wondered whether he charmed her with his witty remarks or revealed how foolishly he was under her spell.

"Roger, Leo," she said, snapping to attention with a tense smirk. "I'm also supposed to recheck some results on our little tiger boy. God, what a fucking unmitigated tragedy. I have a nephew that age."

She padded quickly toward the door, toward the warmth outside the room.

"I'll be back in a while with my vampire kit," she said.

The cops could have cut corners and saved everybody a lot of trouble by having the corpse rushed off to Mission General, where he would be declared dead on arrival, a simple case of vehicular manslaughter. They did the right thing, though, and left him with a puzzle that only he could solve now. The man might have fallen prey to miscreants, or jumped off the curb in despair, but in the current political chaos at the San Francisco City and County Office of the Chief Medical Examiner the case would not merit a proper investigation unless he intervened aggressively. He could not say why it mattered but the thought occurred to him that the demise of this anonymous traveler could be his very last case.

The coroner was one of five assistant medical examiners, and despite his vast experience and seniority he had been passed over twice for the deputy position and taken out of running for the top job. The current deputy was threatening to add injury to insult by working tirelessly to finds ways to force him out – his salary was too high, he booked too many hours of overtime for the staff, he was arrogant, cocky, and displayed contempt for authority. Last year's annual performance evaluation also noted he had grown slovenly in appearance and slow in his work. He had a drinking problem, it said, and he rejected instructions to avail himself of the county administration's Employee Assistance Program. Ha! The EAP was a setup, he knew, a counseling program designed to usher employees out the door. There was no doubt about it, he was marked for a coerced early retirement. He was stalling for time and clinging to his station, very much like the vagrant on the slab before him.

He stepped out of the chilly room, walked down the sullen hallway to his glassed-in office in the lab room and slumped into the chair at his desk feeling heavy and dizzy, fighting off the urge to surrender to sleep. It would have been so easy to turn around and drive home to his own bed. He felt old beyond his years, and only intended to take a little catnap before going back to work as he rested his forehead on a pillow of file folders stuffed with paperwork and topped with the report from homicide. His body was under deep water but his mind was still buzzing around the events of that morning. It was his custom to review the details and consider his next step before pausing on a case, and he had an inkling this case was going to prove very important to him. He straightened up and pinched the back of his neck until the pain pulled him back from the edge.

Six

The sound of activity on the other side of the venetian blinds helped him get back on his feet. He usually enjoyed working on Saturday mornings because he could do what he wanted down here undetected by bureaucratic sonar. He could go at his own pace and think more clearly without Du Goyle breathing down his neck.

"Leo, I've got something!" It was Wilson on the other side of the glass flapping a crinkled piece of paper in his oversized paws. "It was stuffed in the bottom of his jacket pocket. I felt it when I was tagging his clothes. The cops must've missed it when they patted him down at the scene."

With a grin hungry for approval, he approached the door and handed the paper to the coroner for inspection. It was a printout of an email message, or rather, the second page of the message, because there was no header at the top that would identify the sender or time of transmission. It started mid-sentence:

" . . . totally horrid, but I'd rather be disappointed in a person and make a fool out of myself than mope around wondering. You sounded uncertain on the phone. I guess I surprised you, but I don't care what you think, I have to see you and get this over with. I'm taking the first shuttle out of Burbank in the morning and when I knock on your door you can either let me in or tell me to go away. We've hurt each other so much already. I'll understand."

It was signed "C."

On the obverse, a faintly scribbled line, evidently in the dead man's hand, read: "C, exburbank 879 4915."

The sloppy 5 might have been a 6 or a 3, he thought. The handwriting had a Parkinsonian look to it and he imagined fingers clutching a pen and the pen defying the writer's will.

"So he has a lady friend, does he? And she's on her way this morning," he said. "Or so it seems." Wilson was leaning over him trying to decipher the handwriting for himself, crowding him with his big frame. "Wilson, why don't you go to the lab and find Nicki for me."

The coroner reached for his cardboard cup because coffee helped him think, but it was empty. He continued thinking without the coffee. The deceased was going to meet a woman this morning, which explained the air of expectation in his death mask. Of all the clues so far, this barely legible note was his best bet in finding an identity for the supposedly homeless man. John Doe has a Jane out there whose name begins with the letter C. She is on her way, or here already. She would lead to a significant other if she wasn't one herself, and if they find her someone will come forward to claim the body.

"Do me a favor and fetch me an evidence bag for this *billet doux*," he told Wilson as soon as he re-entered the room. "And then I want you to get on the horn with the airlines. We need to find a female passenger who booked a flight from Burbank to San Francisco this morning and whose name begins with C. Probably blonde and blue eyes."

"How do you know it's a she? Is that the flight number or a phone?"

"Men don't write notes like that, Wilson, especially over the Internet. They don't use words like 'horrid.' And that's a phone – seven digits is too many for a flight number. I want you to call this number. Let's find out who sent the email to him, and who the victim called or planned to call. It might not even be the woman's number. Maybe he was going to call a plumber or his dentist for all we know. This woman doesn't sound like next of kin, more like a spurned lover – or a lover who spurned him – but she's coming to town and she can give us a name. We'll work from there."

Wilson shifted his feet uncomfortably. "The phone call is going to be easy," he said. "But finding a passenger by the name C, that's going to be really tough, Leo. Which name would that be, the first or the last?" His voice quavered, his slack jaw tightened. The coroner sensed Wilson feared he would spend the rest of his day engaged in an impossibly absurd task. It was already three hours past the end of his grave-yard shift. It was Saturday, however, and the morgue is not staffed with assistants over the weekend. Wilson was the only option.

He could see he had to persuade the *diener* that the case was worthy of overtime, even if that persuasion involved a minor act of deception, because he could no longer authorize the extra pay. Everything was supposed to go through Du Goyle, who had the power to approve or deny retroactive overtime claimed, after the bloody sweat work had been done.

He knew from experience Wilson would work like a yeoman and that if you pushed him hard he would yield flashes of true brilliance. He knew Wilson did not want to let him down after everything he learned from his master, not just the rudiments of forensic pathol-ogy or forbearance for the grunt work in the morgue, but in the art of improvisation, without which, the coroner liked to say, a scientist is condemned to mediocrity. Wilson possessed formidable computer skills he mastered as a young boy doing naughty things with his second-hand Macintosh, to which he confessed when the coroner interviewed him for the job. The FBI arrested him at age sixteen for breaching security at NASA's Ames Research Center, but dropped charges when they realized they could use him to learn about the legions of prank-sters they were unsuccessfully trying to outsmart. The accommodation didn't last long. Wilson had a problem with getting focused and his resume was blotted with years of menial jobs. He had a high school equivalency degree and a short stint at SF State, where he flunked out his sophomore year. He was hardly qualified to sweep or change light bulbs at the morgue. "Perfect," the coroner told him on the spot.

"You'll start on Monday. But only on the provision you get your college degree. Go to night school, take classes at City College on your days off. Major in computer science or dog catching, I don't care. If you screw up again on your education you're out the door." Wilson was the best hire he ever made.

The coroner watched television sparingly, but he had seen enough crime-stopping forensic pathology shows to be annoyed to the point of rage by the outlandish scenes where a young genius flails away at a laptop and within seconds cracks codes, and pulls up confidential data on members of secret criminal societies in Buffalo plotting to destroy the world, replete with photos and the names of the plotters' former girlfriends. Wilson was plodding, typing with his two index fingers, talking to himself out loud as he plowed though screen after screen in an accelerating blur of data. Eventually he almost always delivered, however, amazing the coroner with information he culled from opaque government agencies, hospitals, banks, genealogical societies.

"This case may seem marginal, but if we want to identify the bastard it may be tough to crack," he said. "And you know how I feel about names. They all deserve the dignity of a name."

He may be going to seed, depressed and drinking a little too much, he told himself, but he still knew how to manage people. He also protected them up the chain of command, for instance, when Du Goyle was conniving to fire Wilson for rank incompetence last year after the *diener* misplaced the heart of a gang-shooting victim.

It suddenly occurred to the coroner that he had not changed out of his worn brown suit, shiny on the seat of his pants, in weeks.

"Shouldn't I check on the fingerprints first? Then the phone number and the airlines? Looking for C's flight itinerary sounds like a real long shot, a needle in a haystack. Are you sure they'd cooperate on a case like this?"

"Possibly no," he said. "How about that multitasking thing you're always talking about doing when you're not paying attention to anything. Look, for all we know there's someone out there who signs emails with the letter C and bashed the victim on the forehead with a brick bat after luring him out to the street with a love letter. A spurned lover exacting revenge in a crime of passion. Or nothing at all. This could be the handiwork of a Shiite terrorist in drag wearing a burqa who pushed him off the curb into harm's way. Or a Christian fundamentalist…"

The coroner thought he must learn to control his sarcasm. It weakened him.

"I'm in charge here, and because of the peculiar circumstances I haven't ruled out foul play, at least as an excuse to get to the bottom of this. If the airlines don't cooperate tell the assholes we're in touch with Homeland Security on a possible terrorism plot to blow up the Golden Gate Bridge. Airlines freak out when they hear the T-word."

"That sounds crazy, Leo. What if they bust us for, well, I don't know, faking it?"

'Impersonating a spook? Why, it's our patriotic duty to find this girl, my lad, and I'll take the heat," he said. "I'm going to get assassinated one way or another, sooner than you think, so I might as well go down with guns blazing. Let's start things rolling with the letters F for fingerprints, T for teeth and C for the girl. And when Nicole's chemistry is done I might start probing a little deeper to see what actually killed him. It wasn't just a cut on his forehead."

Seven

The tissue was stiffening now and the eyes that had startled him with their post-mortem animation were not nearly as remarkable as they were at dawn. Still unusual, but the pupils did not emit the same glow. They suggested a fugue state, as though the corpse was still figuratively alive but slipping away toward a coma and beyond, not yet glassy and not without a glimmer of sentience, playing a last game of possum, perhaps.

He lifted the sheet for a cursory look and noticed for the first time small bruises on the abdomen. Nicki's report on the plasma showed a dangerously high glucose level, 620 milligrams per deciliter, enough to poison him. That he was a diabetic on insulin therapy was the only explanation, he concluded. Too thin to suggest the Type II variety, adult-onset, the scourge of the morbidly obese that had attained epidemic proportions in America. Type II diabetes caused premature heart failure, kidney disease and blindness. If it is not too late, an adult-onset diabetic can shed weight or take oral medication to stay out of trouble. John Doe's blood sugar, however, suggested Type I juvenile diabetes, a terrible chronic curse on children, who must spend the rest of their lives shooting up with insulin in a relentless struggle with their metabolism to ward off the fate of long-term, deadly complications.

He must ask Nicki to run the test for ketones. The saturation of glucose in the victim's blood ruled out the scenario of confusion and diminished consciousness that comes with extremely low blood sugar, which might have caused him to stumble into a car.

An insulin-dependent diabetic ordinarily would have a certain amount of bruising on his belly from injecting insulin by syringe, with attendant lumps of hardened tissue. The skin was clear, however, save a zigzag pattern of dark moles. On closer examination he found three round marks of faintly reddened skin with indents the size of small buttons and tiny puncture holes in the middles, one showing a bit of scab. The other two looked fresher. They resembled bug bites, but no, this diabetic was using an insulin pump, he concluded, leaving the traces of the tiny catheter that infused insulin into the subcutaneous tissue to be absorbed into the capillary system. He had seen such marks before on a nine-year-old diabetic girl who wore a pump and died of asphyxiation in a fire. Her rainbow-decorated pump fell out of its pouch and dangled from the thin plastic tubing still attached to her belly, clanging on the side of the gurney as they rolled her into the morgue. Her blood glucose was 91 mg/dl, perfectly normal. Insulin pumps are good, very good, he reflected, but they do not save you from asphyxiation or blunt trauma to the brain.

If the corpse had used an insulin pump to manage his illness, it was very odd he was not wearing it during the night. He may have detached the pump to shower or to change the infusion set and forgotten to reattach it, distracted by the anticipation of meeting his lover. Perhaps he had a bout of absent-mindedness on his way out the door, hurrying to do a midnight errand. Was he off the pump long enough to propel his sugar over 600? Or did the horror of oncoming high-beam headlights goose his liver with norepinephrine, forcing it to release stored glucose?

Evidence of the pump conclusively eliminated the possibility of homelessness.

Indigent diabetics do not use insulin pumps. They present ulcers on the bottoms of their feet and gangrenous toes when they finally enter the morgue. Insulin pumps cost upwards of $5,000 and are unattainable to most people without respectable health insurance. The mystery cadaver before him had more than a woman friend who sent him email and boarded a plane to visit him. He had a home and probably a family. He had an employer and colleagues, high school classmates, pets, credit cards, a mortgage and a car parked somewhere in the neighborhood where he was found dead. His belly said this. His eyes said this.

Whoever he was, he was a creature of disease. Evidently he survived a brain tumor and managed his diabetes for many years. In the category of far-fetched, maybe a gang of rampaging suburban punks killed him and stole his insulin pump. Maybe he had good reasons to evade the woman whose name began with the letter C and snuff himself out, leaving no trace of identity. No, he believed his personal corpse would not do such a thing. It was inconsistent with his post-mortem affect. The man had to have been exceedingly stubborn, intent on self-preservation, the coroner surmised. That would be why he was not ready to let go yet or, or at least had second thoughts about dying. He had other reasons beyond the lizard-brain instinct to survive. Beloved children, a passion for his unfinished work, an unquenchable nameless desire, the gathering scent of a woman he wanted to love all over again.

Then he heard it, a whisper puncturing the fragile screen separating reason from rhyme. He thought he saw the corpse's jaw move infinitesimally, and bent over straining to hear John Doe utter his last raspy testament, whispering as only a corpse can whisper. It was not the rattle of a meaningless sound, but a word. Distinct, but so faint it was inaudible – as though it was spoken in a frequency only dogs or orca whales could understand. It was a name, the coroner knew, a name.

Eight

He left his basement sanctuary to refuel at the Coffee Chain Café, taking the stairs instead of the elevator to get the blood flowing in his brain. He ßslept poorly ever since he lost Alice, and today he felt a steady state of exhaustion that he feared he might never escape. If he tried to fight the monster in bed it would torment him with grief, make his neck taut, tangle his bed sheets around his feet, ruin the cool puff of his pillow, cause his sweaty crotch to itch madly.

On his way to the café he passed the little watch shop wedged between two bail bond boutiques that he had passed a thousand times without paying attention, but today he noticed that nearly all the timepieces in the window and mounted on the walls of the shop were frozen at 9:15. Perhaps the proprietor set the time to give optimum aesthetic balance to the clock faces, arms outstretched to embrace the vastness of time itself.

He sat on a stool facing the window for a panoramic view of the street scene in front of the stately gray Hall of Justice, grateful to be drinking Ethiopian roast as he watched trucks and busses rumbling down Bryant Street. The caustic scent of diesel wafted on the breeze. He took great pleasure in watching a young couple with a stroller, a thin gawky father and a fleshy handsome mother, and hoped they were on their way from a day-rate parking lot to the Metreon to spend a happy family day and not bound for a courtroom to face the man's arraignment on drug charges. They passed an elderly woman wearing a ragged black wool coat and red beret who was speaking into the air and gesturing with a shaky raised arm. I can only pray she is not sleeping in the rough, he thought, another soul slipping through the cracks.

He noticed for the first time the logo on his cup, picturing a mustachioed little man in shackles stooping over a coffee bush, framed in a red circle crossed by a diagonal line. "Coffee Chain Café," the letters on the paper cup read, "All Organic & Slave-Labor Free."

He half-listened to a man belting out the day's newspaper headlines on the sidewalk a few yards away. "Petaluma Cat Woman on the Lam, read all about it," he warbled, "Thirty Big Rigs Crash in a Hailstorm on Donner Pass! Get your final edition here. Get your Chronicle, hot off the press!"

He guessed by the man's disheveled appearance that he was a wily street entrepreneur who put two quarters into the slot of a newspaper box and borrowed the whole stack to sell.

The coroner reviewed the results of Nicki's serology tests on the midnight corpse: Blood, urine, bodily fluids. No narcotics or banned substances such as crack cocaine or morphine-type alkaloids, but the corpse did have a blood alcohol of 0.127 g/dl, well above the legal limit for automobile operators. The inebriation would not be as dangerous for an ordinary pedestrian, but combined with other effects of his health condition it could make him tipsy enough to lose his balance.

He heard a shout and looked up to see a scuffle ensuing between the newspaper hawker and a plainclothes cop who flashed her badge before snatching the bundle of contraband from his canvas satchel. Taking the job a little too seriously, he thought. The other patrons sitting along the window booed and hissed at the officer as she flipped open her phone to call for backup.

The man yelled at the top of his lungs: "Help, police!"

Nine

Motley, gaunt Buck Pomeroy looked up from his bed to see a strange man in a brown suit approach on tiptoe.

The coroner had great difficulty locating the patient at the county hospital until he barked and flashed his CME office ID at the third-floor nursing station. He found the man in a post-operative ward in a room shared by seven other patients, their beds lined up three feet apart with no curtains for privacy. He was a male Caucasian, approximately 70, gray-bearded with jaundiced eyes. Long tangled dreadlocks spilled from the right half of Buck's head. The other half was clean-shaven and had a line of staples marking a long gory incision. He had three IV tubes in his arm and he said, "Who the fuck are you" when the coroner sidled up to his bedside.

"Not another cop," the patient said. "I've seen enough cops today. Or was it yesterday? "

"I'm here to help, Buck, maybe to keep you out of the special ward I work in. It's a lot worse than this one. Nobody checks out," he said. "I'm a friend. Tell me what happened to you."

"A doctor?"

"Yes, I'm a doctor. My name's Leo. I got your particulars out of the inspector's file on cases like yours, but I don't work for the cops. My job is finding out what kills people, hopefully so the next guy doesn't have to die. You can speak to me in confidence."

"They jumped me in the park," Buck blurted out on cue. "Four or five of them, killers, a pack of wild animals." Then he froze, his blood-shot eyes narrow, expressing both peevishness and fear.

The coroner nodded his most sympathetic nod. He knew he was out of practice with bedside manner but he considered himself a competent listener. "Go on," he said in a soft but authoritative voice. Buck did not need any further prodding.

"One of them grabbed my arm and this other guy spit in my face and started punching me in the head, then they pushed me over and they started kicking the shit out of me and they were laughing and calling me scum and shit. Parasite, they said, fucking parasite filth. I thought I was going to die. I'm a fucking decorated veteran and I got wounded in the leg in a firefight in 'Nam but that was nothing compared to this shit. These guys were taking pleasure in it. Little mother-fucking monsters howling and hollering. Laughing. Then they held me down and spread my legs and this big asshole started kicking me in the balls, kicking and kicking, and I screamed for help until I blacked out."

"You're very lucky," he said. "The inspector told me a flying skate-boarder landed on top of you and called 911."

"Fuck that! It was my buddies that saved me, not the skateboarder. They said he got scared and split the scene. It took them a half-hour to get the cops and an ambulance to come." Buck started to weep at these words: "That's how we stay alive in this shitty country of ours. That's why I'm here to talk to you now. These guys would die to cover my ass and I'd do the same for them. We get beat up and spit at and crapped on but we have something they don't have, we have fucking valor."

Buck shut his eyes. The conversation was over.

When the coroner returned to his office he reached for the flask hidden behind a fat folder labeled "DNA – Inconclusive" in the filing cabinet. He took a quick snort, felt the sting of vodka on his raw tongue and placed the flask in his jacket pocket. He was disappointed that the flask was filled with Stolichnaya and not Jack Daniels, but it was satisfactory, and after the strong coffee the effect was both soothing and bracing. It was the flask Alice gave him for his fortieth birthday, made of sterling silver and bearing his monogram, *LBD* on the fine leather cover. Would she regret the gift, he reflected, if she saw him now?

Fortified, he went down the hall to check on Wilson, who was supposed to be calling the airlines, dialing the woman's phone number, and trying to match fingerprints in the federal IAFIS database all at the same time. He looked over Wilson's shoulder and watched him scrolling through a Web site hosted by the San Francisco Coalition on Homelessness.

"That other stuff hasn't checked out yet, Leo. No callbacks, busy signals, disconnected phone lines, you know. A United Shuttle guy is supposed to get back to me with all their C passengers from Burbank this morning. The other airlines are not so cooperative. Put me on hold until the line goes dead."

"That's what they pay themselves to do," he said. "What the hell are you devoting your short attention span to now?"

"Homeless shelters," he said. "I'm sending jpegs of the death mask around town, places in the Tenderloin and the Mission, soup kitchens, churches in the area. There's a Presbyterian church a couple blocks from where the body was found, but they apparently mostly do music stuff, not sanctuary."

"That's all fine, except you're wasting our time. The guy isn't homeless. The cops may think he's homeless but C wouldn't think he's homeless if she sent an email to his computer. We have his house key, for Christ's sake."

"He could be a Presbyterian," Wilson said. "Or he volunteers at a homeless shelter."

"For all we know he's a devotee of Zoroaster," the coroner shot back. "Let's concentrate on the fundamentals, the fingerprints and the girlfriend. We'll allow the Presbyterian minister to say a few words at the funeral. The point is this guy was on the grid. He had an email address and access to the Internet. She won't find him at home this morning so we're going have to find her. The phone number, did you call it?"

"Yeah, but the number at the end looks like either a three or a six and of the two combinations, neither one panned out yet. It's either dead lines or wrong numbers, or a man picks up. Are you sure C couldn't be a man?"

"She's a girl. I know these things, Wilson, trust me," he said. "Occurred to you that number is a five? Looks like a 5 to me. A shaky five all excited about a lady friend."

He asked himself what he was expecting to prove in the pro forma autopsy Monday. What did it matter what the specific cause of death was, when it was already clear the man was mowed down by a car and not dispatched by a derringer or a samurai sword. He had a predisposition for untimely death with his medical history, and a blunt-force blow to the head would be compounded by an already-damaged brain. The coroner needed a sound reason to conduct a full-blown pathological study to trump Du Goyle's peevishness.

There are so many less fortunate than this man. The corpse appears to have cheated death at least once and enjoyed the gift of more years than he might have prayed for. There were innocent victims of homicide who died under uncertain circumstances whose cases were never resolved. Rape victims whose bodies spoke out with damning DNA evidence from the men who committed the post-coitus strangulations, but these outrages were redressed only if the perpetrator's genetic profile was on record, and not even then. Too many cases are left open until nobody cares.

Leo Bacigalupi told himself that it was his mission as a pathologist to unveil the secrets of every corpse he examined, poor or rich, nameless or famous. He was powerless in this case, however. The man would have to take a number and wait in line Monday like everyone else. He, for his part, was off the hook and could go home now and sleep.

After all, what did he expect to prove by spending his time tracking down the man's identity? Why did he feel such curiosity about the mysteries of the life that predated the banality of the man's death? What if he started to crack open the corpse and found he was still alive?

He cringed. There it goes again, the rude assault on his cochlear nerves, the shriek of his mobile phone.

"Wilson, you've got to fix this ring tone for me or I'll kill you," he said, out loud, heaving a sigh. He flinched when he saw the caller ID warning him Du Goyle was on the line.

"Oh, hello, Horace," he spoke. "What can I do for you?"

"Christ Almighty, Leo, what the hell are you doing at the morgue on a Saturday? I heard you were sticking your nose into the homeless case, but this one's off limits for you – it's a special investigation we're working on with homicide, confidential. They told me your boy filched the file this morning."

"He's not homeless, in my estimation," he said. "He's just lost, Horace, wandering."

"Leave the speculation to Dixon, why don't you. You're off the case. Dixon will perform the autopsy Monday according to protocol, not you, so give it up. Go home. This is a piece of an important investigation we're working on and it doesn't concern you. Forget about him. Return the file to homicide and go home, Leo. That's an order."

Today the DME is using his best bitchy teenager voice, the coroner thought, vaguely effeminate but exceedingly belligerent. The man could be charming and chatty, even likable when it suited his purposes, and then turn vicious the next moment. Du Goyle was volatile and dangerous.

"I am not paying overtime to Wilson or anyone else you've roped into this," he continued. "And don't forget your performance review's on Monday, ten aye yem sharp in the conference room. You dodged out on the last appointment but you be here Monday or there will be consequences."

How did he know? Leo trusted Nicki, but one of the other lab techs might have called Du Goyle. Or the duty officer in the inspector's office after Wilson picked up the file. Du Goyle has spies. He took a deep inhalation and let the air whistle out through clenched teeth. He was not going to be intimidated by the threat of "or else" this morning.

"He's not homeless, Horace, and he's not nameless. We just don't know what to call him yet," he said. "We're on the trail here and it looks more important than you may realize. He doesn't fit Villaragosa's pattern, if that's what you're talking about, but there's a key and a girl-friend who can identify him when we find her. It's my duty to proceed."

He knew his nemesis would not buy his flimsy excuse for staying on the case. He was not certain he could justify to himself his personal interest in the corpse. It had to be the mirror of the dead man's eyes.

"Your duty is to do what I say and I say drop the case," Du Goyle said, screaming like a colicky dog. "Drop it or you're in a greater shit than you already are. I will see you on Monday. Ten *aye yem!*" A click on the other end of the line ended their little chat.

"What did he say, Leo?" asked Wilson, looking worried, red eye-brows raised.

"He said it was okay. He said keep up the good work. I'll get a com-mendation from the police commissioner and a dispensation from the Pope when I solve the case, he assured me."

The coroner strode toward the door with a limp, affecting wounded bravado under fire.

Ten

He took time out for lunch before plunging back into the fray. He sat at his desk and dined on a chocolate bar with peanuts and caramel from the vending machine in the canteen, snickering to himself over what Alice would say after so many years of nagging him about the importance of a nutritious mid-day meal. He chased it down with a quick nip from the flask. He had to stop this drinking if he was going to keep his job, he realized. He wanted to brave it out despite the unrelenting pressure to oust him, to prove himself capable of prevailing over the conspiracy against him, to persevere. Alice would want him to go on doing the job he loved until he eased comfortably into retirement. He would face Du Goyle on Monday and outsmart him again.

He stuffed the flask deep into the desk drawer when he heard another yell from the other room. Why did Wilson have to yell all the time, going out of the way to get on his nerves? He went to the main room to see what the fuss was all about.

"Charles Barlow! I got a match on his prints and his name is Barlow, Charles. A taxi driver," said the ebullient slave of the morgue, grinning over the top of his computer monitor. "I found him in the county database, all ten prints. He got his permit in 1979, age 25."

"You're brilliant, Wilson. Simply brilliant," the coroner said. "Let me see that photo." The record was linked to a fuzzy image of the taxi license that had been scanned into the database.

"He has a ratty beard and dark brown hair down to his shoulders. Look at the daggers in those black eyes of his," he said. "I don't think

I'd want to get into the back of a cab with this fellow behind the wheel. Looks like Charles Manson, or Osama bin Laden's nephew. He's one of those *kamikaze* cab drivers who terrorize our streets of San Francisco."

The birth date on the license profile was July 9, 1952. Height five feet eleven inches, weight 177 pounds. Address on Laidley Street in the Mission, not far from Noe Valley on the flank of Diamond Heights. Shave the beard, crop the hair and Photoshop a balding pate on the top of his head, then age him at about 25 years, and Charles Barlow is our specimen, the coroner concluded. He measured the corpse at 182.6 centimeters, five feet and seven-eights short of eleven inches, not precise but close enough. Fingerprints rarely lie, not all ten.

"This looks like our friend," he said.

Now the quest would begin in earnest. He told Wilson to check the phone books, city directories, the Internet people-finder sites, LexisNexis court documents. "We got his birth date on that license. Check with DMV, get his medical records and invade the fucker's privacy for me. Go for it, Wilson. Tickle those ebony keys on your computer there, just like they do on TV."

He went to his office and fired up the computer on his credenza, thinking he might as well pitch in – he took classes, he knew a thing or two about working the Internet. Pecking away, he tried over and over again to get a key-word combination in the search engine screen that would match the taxi driver's date of birth and vocation to his corpse. All the Charles Barlows approximately that age lived in places like Indiana and New Jersey, not Noe Valley.

"Charles Barlow is a mystery man," said Wilson, yawning when the coroner hovered over his shoulder. "He didn't leave a trace. A lot of dead ends with this birthday. This is going to take a long time. What do we do now?"

"We'll change course then. Let's focus on the girl. We need to get her, Barlow Charles's girlfriend," he said. "Any luck on that phone number?"

Wilson looked helpless. The coroner spotted Nicki. There she was, voluptuous Nicki. What was she still doing at the morgue? Hanging around to torment him?

For years Nicki had been a mild distraction and he quite inappropriately and unprofessionally had a very hard time keeping his eyes off her pleasing hindquarters. The problem got worse after Alice died. He was aroused by Nicki at the same time he felt protective of her, perverted and paternal in one act of indiscretion. He once arranged to have a lab assistant disappear after the fellow touched her and made lewd comments. She had been working at the morgue for thirteen years and the coroner observed her body ripen over time. At twenty-five she was high bosomed and slender, a fetching siren in a white lab coat. At thirty-eight she had matured into a rounder and more womanly specimen. Her breasts hung lower but in pleasing symmetry with her fuller hips. Her gate gait swayed fluidly. By the time she is forty-five she will be perfect, the coroner reckoned. She would age beautifully, the way Alice did, with the collage of imperfections on her skin saying she was totally real, with the furrows on her brow showing how much she knew of pain and sadness, and with the lace of crow's feet around her eyes revealing a lifetime of joy and laughter. Toward the end, Alice wore the scars on her bosom with such lightness and grace that it was impossible not to desire and love her, deeper and deeper. I must stop thinking about her, the coroner told himself, or I cannot do my job.

"Hey, Leo. I took a close look at him," Nicki said as she entered the room. "Did anybody notice that he sort looks like you? It's in his eyes."

"Oh shut up, little Miss Dracula," the coroner said. "I'm tired and broken-down but I'm not dead yet. Give me a few more years."

Wilson's voice broke in. "I've been calling the number all day and called it again a few minutes ago, Leo, all three combinations," he said. "No luck yet." The coroner held his tongue. Phone work was not Wilson's favorite chore. He did not concentrate on the task and lacked initiative. It was painful for him to make cold calls and interact with strangers.

Nicki wafted toward them, graceful yet purposeful.

"Hey, it just occurred to me, Doc," she said. "You guys have been barking up the wrong tree calling that number. You're so wasted you're not thinking straight, and you forgot something very important." The coroner was caught off guard. Wilson wrinkled his nose like a frightened rabbit.

"First of all, that's unmistakably a five. No other way to read it," she said, pointing to the page on Wilson's desk. "And she's getting on a plane at Burbank airport. Burbank is in Southern California. That phone number wants to have an area code in front of it, and it has to be from somewhere down south where people don't torture themselves driving to LAX if they can help it. Somewhere like San Fernando or maybe San Gabriel Valley."

She paused as both Wilson and the coroner stared at her blankly, and affected the intonation of a LaLa girl *"Like, you know, Pasadena or Van Nuys. Whatever."*

It took a moment for this to sink in, before the coroner broke free of a mild stupor and took stock of the situation.

"Wilson, you numbskull! Sometimes I wonder whether you know the difference between fecal matter from shoe polish!" He looked up at Nicki expecting a chuckle only to see the tension in her facial muscles, and looked down at Wilson to see an undisguised expression of humiliation. *There I go, I've done it again.*

"Look, I'm sorry, son, it's partly my fault. You're very good at what you do with these damn computers, now let's transfer that to the telephone and get the job done." When he saw the relief in the *diener*'s face, he continued with a snort of deep exhalation.

"Could you, *please,* get a list of every area code in Los Angeles and in neighboring counties, and every patch of the god-forsaken Southland desert from Pomona to Riverside. And start dialing. Nicole, dear, send me an invoice for extraordinary brilliance and valor under fire, payable on receipt in Leodollars."

Nicki gave him a mirthful smile, a smile that suggested forgiveness for an old besotted fool.

Area codes in hand, they both dialed. The receiver slipped through the coroner's hand and banged on the linoleum floor. He picked it up with two hands, sensing the others pretended not to notice. He hit two disconnected lines and got through to one angry wrong-number lady. Then Wilson raised his head, pulled off his headset and said: "It's 626, Leo, listen to this!"

He dialed the number again on speakerphone mode. It rang five times, then clicked.

"This is Christina. I've been waiting for your call. Please *do* leave a message after the beep and I will call you back. Promise!" Her speech emoted a low, sultry purr that lingered like an audible perfume until a robotic voice broke in: "The mailbox is full. Please call again later." Followed by static on the line.

Eleven

Leo Bacigalupi paused to look at the chair behind his desk. It was upholstered in bile-green Naugahyde, ripped and peeling. He never before noticed how sad this chair was but decided it was perfect for a civil servant in his circumstances.

He sat his tired buttocks down, propped one foot on the desktop and hooked his reading glasses on his nose to thumb through the homicide folder. Then he read the fallen taxi driver's police report for a second time. A review of the basic information yielded no additional insights but the way the patrolman described the scene was unusual. Missing were the misspelled words and jargon of the usual unintelligible prose that most cops pound out at the end of their shift, tired and anxious to get out of the precinct station. With a keen eye for detail, its author, Sergeant Mahoney, had turned routine blotter material into an excerpt out of a satirical pulp novel. He had the name of the red-collared dog that the witness was out walking in the middle of the night, "Shorty," and its breed, Cocker Spaniel. He noted that the witness was a white male estimated in his late 70s with short-cropped silver hair and a bottle-brush moustache, and that he was wearing "garish purple striped pajamas, flannel, under a black silk robe." He mentioned the house slippers, the man's high-pitched Southern drawl.

Most law enforcement personnel would ridicule an officer for writing in this way on an incident report, but Mahoney probably would be impervious to the razzing. He must have been amusing himself in his writing to relieve the boredom of onerous paperwork, the coroner deduced.

His description of the scene brought to life the ambiguity of the death, making the coroner want to revisit the corner of Hill and Sanchez for another inspection. The details he documented with such precision – the position of the body (face up, legs splayed, fists locked), the weather (dewy, faint mist, 50 to 54 degrees), the tread width on the tire marks (195 mm) were impressive but they did not explain the bigger picture. Mahoney mentioned he called Villaragosa because he had heard about the serial bum-bashing case the detective was investigating, but on the report he remained an objective observer, drawing no conclusions.

Mahoney mentioned other odd details. A broken sugar skull a few yards away, the kind of ghoulish confectionery many people of Mexican heritage used to celebrate the Day of the Dead. The two halves of the skull "glistened in grainy white on the sidewalk," he wrote. "It's possible the sugar skull was stolen from a front porch in the neighborhood and broken in a manner consistent with the monoculture's seasonal rite of smashing pumpkins."

The coroner's next step was to check on Wilson, whose lips were moving as he hunched over reading the small Arial font on his computer screen. While he waited for the airlines to find a passenger named Christina he shifted his focus to tracking down the dead man's identity using the myriad of exotic online resources available to the ME's office. There were plenty of Charles Barlows out there, but most had walked the earth before the twentieth century. None were born on July 9, 1949.

The two of them were engaged in a weary discussion about the lack of matches for Barlow's profile when the coroner detected Nicki's scent and felt the light brush of her hair on his cheek. She was leaning in to get a look at the computer when she let out a sound that was half giggle, half guffaw.

"It's pretty obvious to me you fellas are doing it all wrong again. You're working with the wrong birth date," she said. Her sharp edge excited the coroner, even as he knew the woman was about to say something that would make him feel stupid. "Take another look at the picture you printed out and tell me if you really think that baby-faced boy just might be younger than his snarly black beard would indicate."

"I don't get it, Nick," said Wilson, shaking his head.

"It's elementary, my dear Wilson, you have the wrong birth date," she said. "The other day I took a cab and struck up a conversation with the driver. He said it was his first day and that he'd been wanting to drive a cab for years but didn't qualify for the license until he turned twenty-five. This Barlow lied about his age on his application, and that's why you can't get a match for the DOB." Returning to the lab in triumph, she looked over her shoulder to catch the coroner's eye, smiled impishly and affected a little wag of her tail. Oh my God, she knows, the coroner thought, and she is teasing me. She is in complete control.

Could it be possible that the dead man not only lied about his age but also the name on his taxi license application, that he had been someone else before taking on an entirely new identity?

The coroner left it to Wilson to do the heavy lifting in the hunt for Barlow, but he had learned some simple internet search skills from his computer training course last year that he could try out. He opened Bamboozle.com, the search engine Wilson recommended, and pecked in the Boolean key words "Charles Barlow" and "San Francisco."

Laced throughout the search results was a journalist by the name Raul Barlow who had hundreds of matches, mostly newspaper articles with datelines in Asia. An article republished in an anti-terrorism blog titled *Jihadi Notes* caught the coroner's eye. It was originally printed in 1985 on the front page of a Connecticut newspaper, a story about how the reporter parlayed a dead baby's birth certificate into a false identity, which he used to obtain a passport and purchase a handgun. "They would string him up by his thumbs and water-board him if he wrote that today," the *Jihadi Notes* blogger mused. He went on to say he dug around and unearthed old records that revealed the FBI and the ATF investigated Barlow, and when they decided the reporter had been sympathetically covering Puerto Rican terrorists involved in a local armored car heist, they advised the U.S. Attorney's office to consider prosecution. Evidently the case was never closed, and the blogger speculated that Homeland Security may have rediscovered Barlow and placed him under surveillance. "Who knows to what lengths they go to protect the American public?"

Intriguing, the coroner thought, but irrelevant to my own investigation, and I cannot waste time on this kind of digression when Charles John Doe Barlow is decomposing in the other room. The corpse was playing cat-and-mouse with him, dodging identities and hiding incommunicado on the World Wide Web.

His computer froze and he spewed a torrent of the best profanity in his considerable vocabulary. He once broke his right thumb toe by kicking a filing cabinet when he lost ten pages of a report this way, after resisting the urge to throw the monitor on the floor. It was not necessarily the level of equanimity to which the coroner normally aspired. Pathological computer rage, as he called it, must be common among men his age. He was about to yank out and reinsert the power cord in the wall socket to reboot the machine when he decided to do what he did best, when he was not torturing himself at the computer or examining flesh and bones for clues in the morgue: Old timey investigation on on shoe leather.

He refilled his flask and headed for the door. Even in the basement he could see it was already dark outside.

He saw comely Nicki on her way out, tossing her backpack over her shoulder and pulling a brown ponytail out from under the strap. Undoubtedly she packed up in haste because she knew she would not get paid the time-and-a-half if she stayed past the end of her shift. Smart girl. Wilson pleaded exhaustion, justifiably, and the coroner sent him home to sleep it off.

"Go have yourself a personal life, Wilson," he said. "Meet some girls, go drinking with your chums, work out at your fitness club. Take your mother bowling. Then we're going to crack this case Monday."

"If you say so, Leo."

The morgue was under the spell of a peculiar silence, corrupted only by the humming of fluorescent lights. He checked the cold room and saw that Wilson left the corpse in the open. He rolled Mr. Barlow through his hatch on the wall and made a mental note: To be carved later and under the circumstances not necessarily by me, dammit. He took the lonely key out of the evidence baggy, placed it into the left pocket of his brown trousers just in case he got lucky, and departed.

Twelve

The coroner arrived at the curbside scene at 10:02 pm after stopping off for a drink and a bite to eat at John's Grill, where he was with the bartender, Rick Zeppo, for seventeen years. Zeppo was a true cocktail artiste, but it was his night off, so the coroner settled for beer to wash down his fried calamari, just one modest pint of Anchor Steam. He was ready now to scour for evidence.

It was wet and cold and an uncharacteristic thick mist was wafting down from Dolores Heights. He squinted at the pavement, which was dimly illuminated by the anemic streetlight on the corner and the soft glow from living room windows along the block flickering with the bluish hue of cathode ray tubes. The contorted chalk outline of the body was smeared but still instructive. He heard, or imagined he heard, a foghorn moaning in the distance, filling the air with an eerie pulsating whisper. It was improbable, he thought, to hear a foghorn so far away from the channels under the Golden Gate and the Bay Bridge. "I am not hearing this," he mumbled.

It was a deep bass woolen sound, the lowest voice of an enormous tuba held in exhalation for a full measure before trailing off. The horn repeated itself, louder now, then softly receding, reverberating in the damp air.

He pulled the flask out of his pocket and took a long draw to soothe the gathering pain in his head, the kind of pain that comes from a long, jagged day without sufficient rest. He considered how odd this was. He could not remember ever hearing the sound of a foghorn in the Mission District. It was relatively rare even in his neighborhood on Russian Hill. He thought they used other navigational aids these days, the Global Positioning System, sonar, electronic echolocation technology. He occasionally heard the irritatingly high-pitched pinging travel faintly from the Bay, the newest technology for guiding pilots past rocks and through the channel.

This foghorn produced tinnitus in his entire body, penetrating up through the asphalt in a vibrato under the rubber soles of his wingtips, rising up his leg bones and all the way up to the nasal cavity. San Francisco's foghorns were a tourist attraction, historic and beloved like an endangered species. He wondered whether the sound was resonating from his aching head, bellowing a return to memories of a forgotten past. He shivered, wishing he had brought the tattered trench coat that hung on a peg at the office.

It was necessary to concentrate in order to complete his task. He would check out the scene, go home to get a good night's rest, and then return to the office for a short while to defy Du Goyle with a few preliminary cuts, and tap out a persuasive report recommending that he should personally perform an inquest on Monday. It was a preposterous idea, however. Du Goyle would stand in his way, and doing anything would increase the odds of his being crushed like an inconvenient insect. After thirty years of selfless unstinting service to the City.

He caught a glimpse of motion over his left shoulder and when he turned he saw a shadow of a man wearing a black beret darting around the opposite corner of the intersection. He had the unsettling feeling he was being watched, even though the man in all likelihood was going about his usual nighttime business.

Back stooped and nose close to the ground, he prowled up and down the curb near the chalk lines. He knew the area had gotten a thorough going over by Mahoney, but anyone can miss stray details. When the coroner arrived the first time, he placed his attention on the body, not its environment. Slipshod work on my part, he reproached himself. His head began to ache again as he duck-walked around studying the black stains and chipped concrete along the curb.

He got down on one knee and inspected a crevice in the concrete with the tip of his index finger, where the sidewalk had been pushed up by the roots of a large camphor tree. With the impact of the car, something could have flown off his person and lodged here, he postulated. Now his tooth started to hurt again, taking his mind off the headache. He first noticed the pain at the beginning of the week and meant to call his dentist, a jovial and talkative fellow who wore plaid pants and a white belt. It emanated from somewhere on the left side of the back of his mouth, but he could not determine exactly which molar it was, top or bottom. The pain came suddenly like blunt needles poking his jaw, and then it subsided.

He stood up and took a suck on the flask to deaden the tooth and dampen the chapped lips that were puckered with the sting of the vodka. He wiped off the drips with the sleeve of his brown suit jacket.

The skid marks here were short, he detected by the beam of his flickering flashlight. The black traces of burned rubber on the pocked surface of the street struck him as odd, unlike the marks he saw at a typical hit-and-run scene. Usually they are more or less parallel to the curb, and longer, because the driver would see the pedestrian and slam on his brakes before impact. These marks pointed toward the curb, not straight ahead, then took a quick jerk to the left, leaving a second set of screech marks consistent with rapidly spinning tires. He considered the possibility that the marks were going uphill, not down, which would suggest the driver swerved over from the opposite lane with malice of intent. Recalling the mention in Mahoney's report of fresh tire marks up the street, he wondered what that might mean. It crossed his mind that there was a chance, however remote, this was more than vehicular manslaughter, perhaps something along the lines of what Villaragosa was talking about.

The first responders asked all the right questions, and now it was his job to ask the unspoken questions and answer them. The probability was that a drunk driver lost control of his car, hit Barlow and then sped off in a panic. If he had something more solid than speculation, protocol would dictate that he summon police inspectors back to the scene to review the new evidence. Perhaps his imagination was getting the best of him, he thought, and he should dismiss this line of thinking until he got a good night's rest. The cops would only get in the way of his examination and dismiss him as a bumbling old fool.

He recalled the false identity article written by the other Barlow, Raul the journalist, and pondered whether the dead man also had a secret life, that of a sleeper agent. Perhaps he met his assassin. No, that was the wrong Barlow. As an objective forensic scientist he had no room to indulge in paranoid conspiracy theories, fun as they are, yet he could not shake away a heightened sense of drama and urgency he felt. He drained what yet was left in the flask down the gullet. "I do my most inspired work when I am a little high," he explained to the camphor tree.

His eyes were fully dilated and dark-adapted now, giving him the nocturnal vision of a raccoon. As he was rotating his head for a panoramic view of the death scene, a flash of silver reflected in the meager beam of his flashlight caught his attention. It was on the edge of a storm drain a meter down the street where the skid marks pointed. He approached it cautiously, as though it would scurry away if he moved in too quickly. On closer examination it appeared to be a broken bracelet, face down, with part of its chain dripping down into the grate toward the abyss of the metropolitan sewage system. The coroner dropped his flashlight and picked it up again. He reached under the lapel of his jacket for the thin white gloves he kept in the left breast pocket. They were always there, and he never dropped a piece of evidence when he wore them, just as he never dropped a surgical tool in the theater. When he did not find the gloves he was tempted to go back to the car to look for them, but the excitement of the discovery overtook him. He heard himself speaking out loud, but then his voice was drowned out by the forlorn echo of another confused foghorn. Two long blasts, one short, followed by two long, then a pause, a silence that was louder than noise.

The coroner steadied his hand and snatched the bracelet from its resting place on the grate, sighing in relief as he clutched it tight and cautiously backed away from the pit. He scrutinized the red emblem embossed on its face that, he recognized immediately as an image of the Staff of Asclepius. A snake coiled around a staff between the words Medic Alert. The obverse of the medallion was etched with tiny print that he could barely make out without his reading glasses: "CNS Lymphoma, Seizures, Diabetes Insulin-dependent."

"Christ Almighty! Matches our Barlow, no mistaking," he bellowed at the fingers of fog slithering down the hill. The fingers did not reply.

The coroner reminded himself to take a calm and sober approach to the evidence. He would not have known about the seizures by just carving him up. The burr holes gave away the craniotomy, but he would not see evidence of seizures when he slices the brain into thin crosscuts. An expert would have to scan him with an MRI and examine the white tissue for signs of epilepsy. Even that would be inconclusive in explaining the cause of death. A seizure could have caused him to jerk and dance into the street, just as a tailspin into severe hypoglycemia could have caused him to wobble off the curb. His blood sugar was significantly elevated by the time they tested the serum at the lab. He taxed his knowledge of endocrinology and recalled that in cases of extreme low blood sugar there is a bounce-back where the body juices itself with norepinephrine to trigger the release of glucose stores in the liver. The Somogyi Effect, it was called, a name that struck him as being somehow sinister despite its life-saving capacity.

He was disappointed to see there was no name on the medallion, but there was a telephone number, "Call Collect: 209-634-4917," and a 12 digit number below. He fished his mobile phone out of the sticky plastic holster on his belt.

"This is Dr. Leo Bacigalupi from the San Francisco Medical Examiner's Office. We have a deceased person here but do not have a make on his identity. He was wearing one of your bracelets, Ma'am. Can you tell us what information you have on him?" He spoke the ID number into the phone, twice. After a long wait while the operator consulted her supervisor – he wondered for a moment whether he was connected to a call center in Mumbai – she came back on the line and asked for his call-back number. Standard procedure. He tapped and scuffed his feet on the asphalt waiting for the phone to chirp, answering "Bacigalupi here" out of habit.

A jolt of electricity traveled up his spine and raised goose bumps on his neck when the woman's lilting South Asian voice pronounced the name: *Raul Charles Barlow.*

He banged the top of his head with his free palm, the one that was not crushing the cell phone to his ear, and regretting it immediately when his left temple throbbed with pain. The operator gave him Barlow's updated address on Liberty Street – just a few blocks up the hill from where he was standing. "That's all we have on file, sir. No emergency contacts, doctors or health insurance. It seems the account was updated a year ago but I can't release that information without authorization."

"I need that information," he barked. "Let me speak directly to your supervisor, immediately. This is a homicide case, an emergency."

It was not long before a man's timid voice came on the line. "How can I help you sir?"

"I need to get the previous version of your medical profile for Raul Barlow, before it was updated. It is urgent. I am a medical examiner, a forensic pathologist, and I need you to authorize the release."

"I'm afraid I can't do that," the man said. "We don't have access to the data here. You'll have to call the main office in Modesto when it opens on Monday."

He snapped the little phone shut tight. He wondered whether he should wake Wilson and tell him to get the Modesto Police Department on the line, but he quickly realized what a stupid idea that was. This most likely was a case of vehicular homicide, not a chain saw massacre. He must wait patiently until Monday to unlock the black box that would reveal the next of kin, his physicians and details of his health history.

"Raul Charles!" He felt the spittle drip down his chin as he yelled. "Barlow fucking Barlow Raul Charles! The hack from Asia, the identify thief! It was right in front of my Goddamned eyes and I dismissed it." He was deeply annoyed by the voice that echoed the air.

Instinctively he spun 360 degrees, watching for a sign of the man wearing the beret, but if he was out there he was well hidden. He listened for more blasts of the foghorn but none came. Only a ping and then another ping that seemed to come from all directions to warn ships in the bay of potential disaster. Only the white noise of a sleeping city, a faint stew of klaxon, humming electrical transformers, grinding transmissions of midnight buses and trucks, yapping dogs. All condensed and quieted by winding sheets of fog that sneaked down the hill from Barlow's house.

Thirteen

The climb up Sanchez made the old injury in his left knee creak painfully with bits of floating cartilage. The pumping of his head sent blood to his rotten molar and made the tooth and the surrounding palate throb. He could have driven to the address the lilting voice on the phone gave him but he wanted to retrace the steps that Barlow took on the way to the accident.

There they were, the second set of skid marks Mahoney described in his report after diligently measuring and matching them to the marks down at the death scene. The coroner wondered whether he was walking on the wrong side of the street, which would depend on whether Barlow's place was east or west of the intersection. A car might have hit him and carried him on the hood across the street and dumped him on the other curb.

The victim could have crossed the road on his own volition, perhaps on his way to the all-night liquor store he noted at 24th and Sanchez. That would account for the informality of his dress and the wad of bills and the single key in his pocket. He might have been so agitated by his phone conversation with Christina that he forgot to reattach his insulin pump when he hurriedly changed from pajamas to street clothes on his way out the door. He wasn't going out anywhere special last night, just taking a quick dash to get a bottle of something, whatever newspapermen drink these days. Scotch? Sh ch ? His throat parched at the thought.

He was scaling the hill, distracted by these considerations, when he heard the clack-clack-clack of a woman's heels rushing down the hill and producing a Doppler effect on the sidewalk across the street. The maker of the sound emitted a gust of air, a chill that crossed the street, tingled his skin and emptied his lungs of breath. He turned to see the back of a woman's tan coat and spray of long frazzled hair trailing her head like black streamers. He could not see her feet, for they were hidden in a low puddle of mist as she tromped down the sidewalk. He thought he heard quiet and plaintive sobbing, a muted wail of bereavement. He found himself frozen on the spot, unable to act on an urge to run after her, comfort her, to rescue her and to beg for forgiveness. He had taken a sacred vow to heal the living, but it was also an oath that said, first, do no harm. The affairs of this woman were none of his business, probably generic man trouble, he consoled himself.

He looked up the hill to his destination, and when he glanced over his shoulder to follow the woman's progress, she had vanished. The street was empty and silent until a siren broke the calm. He judged it to be coming from the southeast, and he recognized the signature of a medical emergency vehicle, one of the old McCoy Millers he heard so often racing to Mission General.

It was not difficult to find Barlow's bungalow. It was wrapped in cedar shake siding on the north side of the street, where Sanchez goes over the crest of the hill past a towering pine tree, zigzags to the left and then right, and continues its descent onto Liberty. Winded and wheezing, he knocked on the door, at first softly because of the hour, then with greater authority. He dug his thumb into the button of a silent doorbell. The place was very familiar, he did not know why. Barlow could have a roommate, which he somehow doubted, but if he did, that person could not protest being woken late at night for the ill tidings of Barlow's death. The gathering scent of night-blooming jasmine greeted him on the front stoop, but his rapping on the door went unanswered. There was no stirring inside, no sound of approaching footsteps. The house was dark, save a soft glimmer of light from the back of the room seeping through the reed blinds on the window.

He opened the little plastic zipper evidence bag. He removed the key from the evidence bag and slipped it into the lock.

With the sound of a well-oiled click, the door drifted open on its hinges, revealing Barlow's crypt and its odor of curry, sandalwood and sweaty gym clothes, the odor of a man who lives alone. A small lamp on a desk across the room beckoned from behind a folding rice-paper screen that partitioned a workspace from the rest of the living room. On the surface of the desk, to the right of the lamp, an open laptop computer rested purposefully. It was warm. He tapped the space bar and watched an eruption of gently scattering stars animate the screen. "He has not let go yet," he said aloud and listened to his hushed and shaky remark bounce off the walls in the twilight of the room. "Barlow did not turn off his computer because he is not done writing his story." He sat hesitatingly in Barlow's battered oak captain's chair.

This was the den of a writer, a scribbler, a blind housekeeper. Cobwebs decorated the corners of the ceiling and a thin layer of dust slept on every surface in the room. The coroner was excited to see fresh elbow prints smudged into the film of dust atop the desk, marking recent activity. An eight-and-a-half by eleven-inch notebook, spiral-bound, sat open behind an empty coffee mug, stained milky brown at the bottom. The dust was not broken in the perimeter of the notebook; it had lain there undisturbed for several days. Not so with the mug, this had spirals around it.

He saw an open cardboard box under the desk filled with notebooks of various makes and sizes.

Four wooden bookshelves approximately seven feet tall lined the opposing wall, but their shelves were sparsely filled, giving the impression that what was once a substantial library accumulated over many years had been culled down to the essentials, the other books left behind or donated or perhaps burned in the small fireplace across the room in an self-inflicted auto-da-fé, for remorse was a sentiment betrayed by the dead man's eyes. An ugly steel filing cabinet imposed itself from the corner behind a couch that displayed Hopi designs in its faded upholstery. Boxes on the floor spilled documents over their sides, and stacks of old newspapers teetered, ready to collapse at any moment. A mission oak dining table, a small Japanese tea chest, a blood-red Persian rug lapping the dark hardwood floor. A paper lantern dangling from the ceiling. A television, a stereo, a phone.

It took some time for him to adapt comfortably to the pall of the room's amber light. He hesitated to turn on the other lamps and spoil the ambience of Barlow's mood when he walked out the door for the last time. He saw a dusty unsealed envelope on the floor near the entrance and, rising to open it, found a note written in feminine longhand that read: "Raul, please call me on my cell phone, please, I'm worried about you. We haven't talked in so long and I wanted to check up on you because your brother said you're holed up here like a hermit crab. You're not replying to my emails or phone messages and that really has me worried. I'm in town for the weekend & going back to Reno Monday. Call me, please. Love you, Sasha." There was no postmark, no stamp, no return address. Whoever Sasha was, she evidently slipped it under the door when Barlow was not home. But he had seen it, opened it and no doubt read, only to leave it on the floor. It seemed the deceased had been incommunicado for some time before his last night.

He turned on a rubber heel, making a squeak on the floor. "Quiet down there," he whispered to the offending wingtip. Then he spied a bottle on the kitchen counter and tiptoed over to inspect it. A fifth of Jack Daniels, two-thirds full. He was sorely tempted to siphon off a jigger or two for his empty flask, but came to his senses just in time. It would violate the strictures of his trade to tamper with evidence, liquid and unnoticed as it may be. It would dishonor the dead. On second thought, perhaps it would celebrate the dead to toast him in fealty with a promise to bring the intimate stranger back to life.

Two bedrooms and one bathroom lined the dark hallway, but he decided to put off examining the smelly sheets, the dirty clothes and the toothpaste-smeared junk in the medicine cabinets one usually finds in the homes of people who die unexpectedly before they could tidy up. First he would take a bite out of the writings of Raul Barlow.

He thought he would start by looking inside the computer and get right to the email list to learn who Barlow had been talking to online. He presumed the message from C, the one they found on his person with the first page of the printout missing, would be at the top of the queue and might offer a fast track to the man's state of mind. He tapped the spacebar and a box popped up asking for a password. He thought for a minute. How about Dolores, Liberty, Barlow, Christina, Japan? I could strike out all night, he thought, feeling the beginnings of computer burn well up. I will have to return when I have more clues.

He picked up the notebook on the desk. It was open, after all, inviting him to read the scrawl that traveled across the page. This is better. Electronic writing was too easily edited, he believed, susceptible to the recasting and deletion of the truest first thoughts. Mechanical font does not reveal the writer's character. With handwriting it is far more difficult to redact the raw words and sentences and replace them, censor them, gussie them up. He withdrew the reading glasses from his breast pocket and positioned them low on his nose.

There was one long entry in the notebook. The other pages were blank.

—

9:26:03
Aurora
v

Aboard a train on my way home from Berkeley, tired and bored by the day-old news in this morning's Chronicle, I shifted my gaze to the window, blackened by the tunnel, and examined the reflection of my face and of the shadows of the other passengers. When we stopped at 12th Street the doors slid open and I saw the image of a tall woman wearing a white gypsy dress step aboard. The woman didn't lose her balance or reach to grab a stainless steel bar when the train lurched and tilted into motion. She walked straight toward me. I lowered my eyes to the newspaper to avoid gawking and making her feel uncomfortable. I sniffed a delicate trace of jasmine as she sat down next to me and released her breath. I felt a quickening, a shock of recognition in my chest. I looked up and found myself whispering "Christina?" Her head jerked slightly.

Then I saw it in the profile of her face, the imperfect nose, the milky cheeks, the generous lips, and the raven raven-black hair. She turned, head pivoting gracefully and independently from a slender torso. She spread an unforgettable smile and sized me up with her eyes wide open, her pupils dilated to large black circles. I had made an ass out of myself.

But her expression was forgiving. She didn't cross her arms or look away as women do on trains, and I got a full view of the outline of her breasts, her shoulders, her smooth neck and throat, without feeling intrusive. These weren't Christina's eyes. This woman's irises were hazel brown, not green with the tiny flecks of chocolate. Yet she cast a beguiling spell of familiarity.

"No, I'm not Christina," she said, "but I love the name." Her gaze was constant, unblinking and intimate. "Who's Christina," she asked. "Who are you?

———

The coroner could see a speckled pattern of light brown stains across the page. He imagined a cup slammed on the desk and coffee spattering out like blood from a fresh wound. He could not help wondering where Barlow purchased his coffee and which blend he preferred, dark or mild. It seemed to him a writer would have idiosyncrasies pertaining to the coffee he drank, the way he made it, all superstitions of the craft. Was that a special cup he used every morning, some sort of talisman? Did he wash out the mug before re-using it or let layers of light brown film accumulate at the bottom to add an oaken age to the flavor? When he resumed reading he noted an increasingly bold and more confident stroke of penmanship that etched furrows into the surface of the lined paper. He touched the page and felt the indentations like a blind man reading braille.

———

I sat there agape, unable to say a word, as though I were having one of those petit mal seizures that used to paralyze my arm and tongue. "I'm sorry," I finally managed to say. "I didn't mean to bother you."

She watched me for a moment. "It's okay," she said. "I have the feeling this Christina is someone very important to you. You're looking for her."

"No, it's just that you remind me of this woman I knew. I was just a little surprised."

Her smile said *surrender your weapons – you're my prisoner now . . .*

"Don't waste your time on me with a pick-up line like that, mister," she said in a teasing voice, silky, flirtatious and totally in control.

"Sorry. My name's Chuck." I said, wondering why I identified myself with a name I hadn't used in more than forty years. "And you? I know your name isn't Christina."

"Most people call me Kat, with a K," she said. "That's not my real name. My real name is Aurora. You can call me either one."

"Aurora," I said.

The train emerged from the tunnel into the morning light, and we were silent until we passed the West Oakland station and descended into the big bore that would take us deep into the muck at the bottom of the Bay, leaving the bright sunlight flickering at the rear of the car. When the windows were black again I turned and saw a pale mask in the glass, my own.

"We broke up in an ugly fight," I said, "I was an idiot, but why am I telling you this?"

Yes, why was I confiding this to an attractive woman in a pressurized tube one hundred and thirty feet under the surface of the bay, a total stranger? Christina was always on my mind but I had tamed the thought of her, packaged it neatly where it would cause me the least amount of pain. The yearning for what I'll never have again. But this young women woman brought to the surface raw emotions I thought I'd managed to lock away. Hopeless yearning, fantasies. We'd arrive at Embarcadero Station in a minute and the conversation would be over, anyhow. I'd be left in the seat alone.

"You should be talking to her, not me," Aurora said. "She might be waiting to hear from you."

"No… We're out of touch. I don't know where she is, she doesn't know where I am, and it's better to leave it that way." My words must have sounded hollow to Aurora. I did look for her. I wasn't lying; I was just coping. I was excited but wary, maybe terrified by Aurora because I didn't want to go down this road again, – it was self-destructive and it makes me the loneliest man in the world.

The train burst out of the tunnel, horning its way toward the platform. She saw the anxiety on my face and said, "This isn't my stop. Is it yours?"

I shook my head.

"Maybe I could find her, but she doesn't want to be found. She's too young and she's too smart to want to hear from me. I'd be a total nuisance and it would be too awkward, like I was stalking her or something and being creepy. Women don't want to hear from their old lovers after they've moved on to another life. I know that and I'm not stupid enough to try it again."

I told her how many times I tried to find Christina in Los Angeles and backed away whenever I got close. At one point I was pretty sure I had her current phone number, but I hung up when a man answered the phone.

I was relieved when Aurora didn't make a motion to get off at Montgomery.

"She might be flattered if you contacted her," she said. "You don't know what she's feeling, so don't sell yourself short. How about you, Chuck? Does a strange woman answer your phone?"

"I moved after getting divorced, and my number's unlisted because I like my privacy," I said. "It'd be pretty hard to find me unless I told you how. I don't have a cell phone and when I go online I don't chat. I've done all of that shit already and I don't run around naked on the grid anymore to glorify high technology for a news publication. I don't work for anyone and I don't answer to anyone, just myself, no bylines, no panel discussions, no public persona. She won't be looking for me. And she probably couldn't find me if she tried."

Aurora studied my face like a subway therapist.

"You are possessed! You're impossibly in love with her and you want her so much you're hiding from her," she said. "It's okay to want someone you can't have, Chuck. You can keep it the way it is but you have to tell her, she needs to know this, you need to know it yourself."

When the wheels screeched to a halt at Powell I was certain I'd have to watch this unbelievable woman get up with a pleasant nod of the head, alight on the platform and walk away with the same stride and the same long black hair swaying from side to side as she disappeared into the crowd.

"I usually get off here, but I can go to the next stop to transfer if you don't mind. I just have to catch the N-Judah to Parnassus," she said. "This is too interesting. Where do you get off?"

"Twenty-fourth, but don't go to any trouble on my account." I had sand in my throat. I felt like clutching her wrist before she vanished.

"I'm late for my shift at the hospital, but there's nothing I can do about that now. They can't fire me." She was younger than Christina.

"What do you do up there?" I shoved the pile of newspapers off my lap to the floor.

"I'm a medical resident. In cardiology. I have a passion for hearts," she said.

"You are about to get off . . . can we talk again?" I said, knowing what the answer would be, but I had to try. "Get some coffee or something? Can I take you to dinner?"

I expected her to laugh in my face, but she didn't. She frowned.

"I am not your Christina," she said as she washed my eyes with a warm ocean tide. "Be patient, Raul."

Aurora paused, then leaned in close and put her mouth on mine. We joined in a warm salivating kiss that lasted for eternity in the span of three seconds. My lungs heaved with a rush of cool air, my heartbeat jumped and fluttered, then stopped. I was ready to die now.

Then she strode to the door, turned toward me, and with the gravity and precision of a surgeon she nodded her head.

I looked down at my hands, numb and stupid. Did I hear her say Raul? I didn't tell her my name was Raul. She couldn't have known.

—

The coroner placed Barlow's journal on the desk exactly where he found it, unsure what to make of the words the dead man left behind. They were truly consistent with the expression on the corpse's face, of a life cut short before realized its greatest desire, a plaintive voice that is as impermanent as the hand, the pen, the paper.

Fourteen

The coroner's head ached with a pang of guilt as he leaned back in Barlow's captain's chair, which squeaked in protest under his weight. He did not know what to do next. He wanted to inspect the house for physical evidence, but it might be a better move to return to the morgue and the body for an unsanctioned autopsy before Du Goyle got in his way. That was the best he could do for Barlow. Name him and carve him before he lost control of the body.

It was too late, however, to stop reading.

In the skein of mild inebriation, he rationalized his decision to violate protocol. If there was foul play, Barlow's written record could shed light on his enemies, should he have any. A jealous husband from a tryst with a married woman? A goon from Reno collecting gambling debts? What kind of man was Barlow and what might he have done to place himself in harm's way? It was conceivable that federal anti-terrorism zealots were hounding Barlow because he wrote the primer on the dead-baby method of false identity theft years ago, the one the coroner found floating in the Internet Saturday in his efforts to name the corpse. No, that scenario was irrational, bordering on paranoia. Whatever the coroner's prying eyes detected, however, it might bring the corpse back to life, if only for a fleeting moment in his own imagination. Understanding Barlow, he thought, might stop the throbbing pain in his head and jaw.

The Senior Assistant Medical Examiner of the City and County of San Francisco felt woozy, on the verge of being overtaken by sleep.

When he was a very young child, there was a picture of the Sandman hanging on the wall above his crib, an old man with a long grizzly gray beard and a conical hat set against the starry night sky. His mother used to try goading him into taking his naps on time by invoking the Sandman, who would come to take him away to the comfort of slumber. She never realized how much this idea terrorized a two-year-old boy, who imagined a frightening old man crawling out of a sand dune to reach over the rails of his crib and snatch him away into darkness. He hated the Sandman in the picture and he defied him by learning how to fight off the naptime monster. He was a tired and stubborn boy.

The sun was rising now and it pierced the bamboo shade covering the eastern window, casting a bold pattern of thin horizontal black-and-white stripes on the opposite wall.

Somewhat wobbly, he struck out for the bathroom, turned on the light, and rifled thought Barlow's medicine cabinet until he found a plastic bottle of acetaminophen, Extra Strength 500 mg gel caps. He took four, drinking from the tap with his palm and splashing water on his face.

Back in the front room, he studied the file cabinet, the boxes of mysterious papers and the books on the shelves. When he scanned the books his eyes were drawn intuitively to a red volume wedged inconspicuously on a side shelf titled *Red Horse Hill*. The mottled cover and the battered spine suggested it was a much-loved book from childhood.

He opened it. The copyright page said the book was one of the publisher's Young Reader series, printed in 1958, written by Stephen W. Meader. When the coroner flipped through the pages he found a shallow cavity in the middle, a square hole cut crudely and lined with tattered edges. It seemed to be the handiwork of a small boy who wanted to hide something, a key, a cereal box decoder ring, or a juvenile love letter, but the secret compartment was empty. "Nothing," he said to himself. "Absolutely nothing." He put *Red Horse Hill* back where he found it.

Now what? His instinct told him to dig deep into the cardboard box under the desk and pull one out to see what it had to say. The date on the cover of the one he chose was August 1980, and it was so old and fat with heavy handwriting that the pages were puffed and wrinkly.

―――

Sailing to the Lost Isles of Langerhans

It was a blazing hot afternoon and I was sweating profusely with all the windows buzzed all the way down, frantically looking for another place to pull over to relieve myself for the fifth time that morning. San Francisco is a tough place to find a public restroom – I have no idea how the homeless get by without pissing in the alleys. But it's an even worse place to find a parking spaces when you really need one. My fallback was to stop at a hotel and dash into the lobby for relief, then find a water fountain or a place to buy a soda, maybe two sodas, because they went down fast in this weather. Problem was, the rides off hotel taxi lines are usually shorts, and aren't worth waiting for, unless you think you're going to get lucky with an airport. Better to play the dispatcher between toilet breaks, but I was still losing time and money with every pit stop. I thought I was going to lose my mind. There was a white zone in front of a Chinese restaurant and I grabbed it. I didn't care whether they yelled at me in Cantonese for using the facilities without ordering a plate of garlic bok choy. It was an emergency.

Back behind the wheel of my battered yellow Plymouth Volare, I made up my mind to take time off and get out of the city as soon as possible because pissing and drinking and pissing again was making me miserable, making me angry, making me crazy. I feared the stress of driving the cab and the stress of living with Satomi was going to kill me. I started seriously smoking again, not rolling up the occasional Drum tobacco on Zigzag paper anymore but actually buying packs of Marlboro Lights, something I'd vowed never to do again. Each one was going to be the last, and I imagined the "light" version was less harmful than the regulars. I was deluding myself, trying to smoke away the premonition of doom, of incomprehensible death by urine.

It started happening a couple days earlier, out of the blue. I was recovering from the worst cold I could remember, a cold that choked off my breath with gobs of mucous and gave me terrible headaches. It wasn't long after I'd passed the stage of coughing up thick gunk when the parched throat and the unquenchable thirst began. Then the inexorable demands of the bladder. I got edgy, irritated and started raising my voice at Satomi, finally yelling at her to stop blaming me for her misery and acting like a spoiled teenager. It was as if she believed I'd dragged her home to America against her will. She was beautiful, funny and extraordinarily talented and I still loved her very deeply, but how can you live with someone who does everything she can to make you give up on her? I had to find a way to get her out of my house, as gently and compassionately as possible. I had to get free of the oppressive burden of responsibility for her. I had to get rid of this terrible, virulent cold. I had to take a piss. Then drink.

As I turned out of the white zone I decided I'd tell Yellow I was sick and needed time off. I knew they'd say they couldn't guarantee I'd get a regular shift when I got back, but I had to let the pressure out. I remembered seeing an old movie about the first ever brain operation, where a nineteenth-century surgeon innovated the technique of drilling a hole through the skull to release the pressure on the brain. Something trapped inside the patient's head whistled out like some sort of evil gas escaping after the surgeon lanced a cerebral boil. Evidently the procedure worked and the patient stood up, weeping with relief, his agony lifted. I wondered whether I needed to sign up for something like that as I squirmed behind the wheel of my cab. The torture had to stop. Then the answer came to me. I needed to find the cure in the mountains and the waters of the Sierra. I'd go backpacking and hike into the high country until I returned to peace.

Satomi had a friend from her ESL class at City College who expressed interest in going backpacking during a recent dinner. He was French, as were a number of Satomi's friends. She was an artist and had somehow tapped into a vein of French expatriates in San Francisco. Diderot and his annoying American wife were among them. He was a caricature of the lugubrious French intellectual, a man who seemed like the last person who'd want to go along on a camping trip. The two of us never hit it off – it was if we intuitively decided not to like each other. But I owe my life to Diderot.

My day was an unmitigated disaster already, and I was halfway through my shift without earning enough to make my gates and gas. At that rate I'd end up paying the company for the privilege of driving a cab. I was snared in a hellish Sisyphean trap: Immediately after stopping at the Chinese restaurant to urinate I was thirsty again, and knew drinking more fluid would make me need to flush it out in no time. I was resentful and angry with my passengers, who disrupted my haywire metabolic rhythm. I yelled at a poor old lady who must have been in her late 80s. She wore a heavy black wool coat in the summer heat and demanded I drive her three blocks up Nob Hill. She forced me to stop before the meter passed the $2.90 drop and she demanded her ten cents in change in a surly voice.

I didn't use to hate my passengers. I was able to tolerate the cloying tourists looking for postcard locales. I was able to restrain my contempt when I ferried pompous men in designer suits from the financial district to overpriced restaurants and they insisted I take nonsensical wrong-way routes to their destinations, smug carpetbaggers from New York who either thought they knew the City better than the natives or suspected I was ripping them off on the meter by taking the long way around. I was entertained by all the local characters, drunks and lunatics who hopped into the back of my cab, telling me absurd stories about lost loves or encounters with the law. On the night shift I prospered thanks to gay men who talked about taking poppers in the back seat as I shuttled them between Polk Street and the Castro to the baths south of Market. They were the most generous tippers and always surprised me by speaking to me kindly and with respect and sympathy, as if struggling taxi drivers like me were kindred sprits in a cruel world. I was young and ignorant about the ways of city life, and driving the cab gave me a crash education in the grubby reality of the world. I eavesdropped on intimate conversations between men and women and listened to the sounds of heavy petting and moaning in the back seat, wondering whether I was invisible to them or a crucial audience as they put on their show.

Today, I loathed all my passengers. Disaster was near. It suddenly occurred to me, in my heightened state of misery, that I hadn't had a bowel movement for four days, and things started to make sense. My colon was putting mighty pressure on my bladder, causing all these problems. Backpacking in the Sierras was bound to be the ultimate laxative that would cure my urban distress.

I drove directly into a traffic trap on Mason Street, the kind of trick corner that more experienced drivers had learned to avoid. I was in the correct lane to turn left onto a one-way street, but I didn't see the little sign that said No Left Turn Allowed. When I rolled around the corner a motorcycle cop was waiting for me. He wore leather riding breeches and he didn't waste any time in thrusting a $20 ticket in my face and saying, "sign this, sir." I was already furious at the curse of my bladder, and now lost control of my wits, swearing at him as I handed him back the ticket in indignation. I was stupid enough to get out of the car and face off with the cop, yelling about deceit and entrapment. I will not sign this fucking ticket, I shouted. There was a little flap of skin on my neck that I scratched now and it started bleeding. The police officer stood motionless, like a mountain, and calmly informed me that I was under arrest and that he would escort me down to the Hall of Justice where I might cool off with an evening in jail, a guest of the City. "I've had enough of cabbies like you," he said in a low tone. His hand was touching the hilt of his gun.

It all caved in on me at that moment. I watched myself in horror as I bowed before the cop apologizing in tears as I said please, please, I've been sick, I can't stop pissing and it's driving me mad. I lost my head and I'm sorry. He handed back the ticket, which I signed and said thank you, thank you. Then he dismounted, approached me and leaned his head toward my face. I was confused. After all this he now suspected me of drunk driving. "I can smell it, the sweet breath," he said, his growl softening. "You'd better check your blood sugar, buddy. And your ketones. My daughter has it too."

What the hell was he talking about, I thought. What does he mean by blood sugar? What the hell are ketones?

The cop roared off on his bike. I got in my cursed taxicab and tried to think of a strategy to find a place with a bathroom where I could also pick up a coke and maybe a fare. Cold and shaking, I turned the vehicle around and headed to the St. Francis Hotel. I resolved to call Satomi's French friend when I got home. We're going to the mountains.

———

The coroner realized he needed to visit the bathroom himself and quench his own thirst with a tall glass of water. He could also use a dose of Tennessee whiskey to clear the cache of his mental circuitry. Barlow's crisis had him rattled him. What a fool that man is, rutting around in his own misery and stepping deeper and deeper into it.

The coroner returned to the desk and turned the page to the next section.

———

The Stone Woman

I had my first hard lesson in the folly of immortality when I started hiking up an unforgiving mountain trail. My prickly French companion, Diderot, bitched all the way on the long drive past Sacramento and up Route 108 to the Kennedy Meadows trailhead in the Emigrant Wilderness. I had to get out and fiddle with the carburetor every half hour or so when my feeble 1964 VW bus slowed down, gasping for air and fuel. I did a respectable job rebuilding the engine using the Dummies repair manual, but never got the carburetor quite right. Diderot probably didn't notice I was taking advantage of the carburetor stops to water the weeds by the shoulder of the road. We arrived late at night and pitched the tent at the campground on Deadman Creek, prepared to start hiking early in the morning. The plan was to hike up the grueling switchbacks about three miles to Relief Reservoir, break there for an early lunch and then head south on the Summit

Creek trail. We'd see how far up the mountain we got, then head back on the third day. I'd never backpacked in the Emigrant Wilderness area, so this was going to be all new to me.

Waking up early wasn't a problem because I was up most of the night slipping out of the tent to piss on a nearby pine. My companion was a sound sleeper and difficult to rouse, but once he put on his boots he was happy to start hiking. I was exhausted after sleeping in thirty-minute spurts and, so I dragged my feet on the trail, but he didn't seem to mind walking far ahead to spare us forced conversation. The Frenchman was in far better shape than I'd sized him up to be. Mid-morning, he waited until I caught up, and we stopped to snack on peanut butter and Ak-Mak without exchanging a word. I studied the contrast of sunlight and shadow in the trees, remembering what Gerb, my summer camp marksmanship instructor, told me, to focus on the green to soothe my eyes and calm my mind. We looked over the topo map and agreed to meet again where the trail went flat and turned westerly on its descent toward the banks of the reservoir.

Diderot started up the trail before I finished packing up the peanut butter. I knew that if I kept up a steady rhythm at my own pace, sooner or later I'd loosen up my bowels, and after relieving myself of the heavy rock in my entrails I could start climbing at a decent clip, maybe even catch up with Diderot. Heaving deeply, I lumbered up a switchback and noticed a man resting motionless on a boulder by the trail holding a weathered staff fashioned from a tree limb, shirtless, watching hikers go by like an observant lion. When he called out to me I was struck by the unnatural red-orange tint in the skin of his hairless chest.

"I noticed you way down there," he said, pointing across the tops of the trees to an exposed section of trail on the other side of the ravine. "Are you all right? You looked like you were really struggling."

"I'm fine, thanks," I said, nodding, grateful for the excuse to take another breather. "Just moving a little slowly today on account of the lack of sleep and a bad headache."

"I'm taking it easy too. I got to watch my blood sugar, which is running a *sukosh* low right now," he said. "But, I have plenty of glucose tablets with me, enough to get me to Nevada and back. I just started out a little too gung ho this morning."

I had no idea what he was talking about. It didn't sound good, whatever it was, and there was something about the guy that didn't seem quite right – his voice was slurred and he seemed agitated.

"Are you sure you're okay?" I said. "Do you need help?"

"No, no, everything's under control," he said. "When you know your limits and respect them you're in control."

I was about to push on and find the next secluded tree to piss on, but I gave in to my curiosity.

"So what's going on? What do you mean by low blood sugar?"

"Oh, right, sorry, I always forget a lot of people don't know much about diabetes," he said. "You see, if a diabetic takes too much insulin and doesn't eat enough to match it with carbohydrates he gets a little woozy and confused, particularly when exercising like this. But I'm all right . . . been a diabetic since I was seven, and I know how to stay out of serous trouble. It's no big deal, really, unless you do something stupid and your blood sugar goes so low, or so high, you pass out and put yourself into a coma. It can be managed."

I felt insensitive and ignorant. I'd been healthy all my life and took it for granted, never really giving much thought to less fortunate people, maybe even turning away because they made me uncomfortable. Then I remembered Jeff, a wiry and talkative friend who said he was diabetic, but never explained it to me. The only unusual thing I noticed about him was that he'd get sudden urges to run out for ice cream. He was always in a big hurry to dash up 24th Street to Bud's. I thought it was just one of his idiosyncrasies.

"I have a friend who's diabetic," I said. "He eats an awful lot of ice cream, but I don't suppose that's the right thing to do."

"Hell no, that's not a good idea," he laughed. "But I sneak it now and then. The point is to keep your metabolism balanced, then you can do just about anything."

To prove his point, he sprang up from the rock and tossed a huge backpack over his shoulders like a feather pillow. He was some ten years older than me, which would make him about thirty-five, and he had the stocky physique of a wrestler, meaty biceps and rippled abdomen. He exuded vigor that was incongruous with his orange -hued skin. I said "Happy trails to you," and he turned and smiled before bounding up the next switchback. I wondered if I'd ever catch up with him.

Diderot would be waiting, contemptuously, so I got a move on. It was strange, though, how the conversation with this stranger relaxed me and lightened my load. It was as if I had a drink of spring water, so pure that it didn't make me want to piss it away as soon as it hit the bottom of my stomach. But the spell didn't last long.

Trying to scramble on enervated legs, slowing down and halting when I was too exhausted or too thirsty or too bloated to keep up my pace, I finally reached the reconnaissance spot and found Diderot sitting on a log, face expressionless. We had a terse conversation and agreed I wasn't going to move much further up the trail until I got a good rest. He'd go ahead and scout out a good place to stop for lunch. I hiked on until I scaled to a high point to see a hazy blue range of granite looming high on my left. The mountains were bluish gray, more blue than gray in my blurry vision. How extraordinary, I thought. I took off my sunglasses to see if the tint was distorting the color. The brightness of the gray cast silver highlights interspersed by commanding blue shadows. I could make out a sliver of the reservoir far over the treetops to my right, shimmering like a mirage. "Eons of mountains and waters," I heard myself say, but I had no idea what that meant or why I said it. Suddenly I had a desperate urge to dive into the cool waters of the reservoir and swim to the far shore, but I couldn't take another step. I sat down in a shady grove that sheltered me from the July sun. I freed myself from the pack and sat down in the umbrage of a massive, ancient sugar pine, then sprawled out on a bed of the blue-green needles that poked my neck when I stirred.

I was surprised to see a sugar pine growing so close to the tree line. It seemed strangely aware, as if it detected my presence and uttered soothing reassurance at a pitch below the range of human hearing. In my years of study in Japan I'd learned about animism, the belief that regards rocks, trees and rivers as sentient, having souls or even consciousness. In Japan, tradition-bound people still worship the *kami* of sacred places. A waterfall or an ancient cypress can be a god sanctified in its own shrine, bestowing fecundity on local farmers who have for centuries celebrated the *kami* with seasonal rites and offerings of *sake* and glutinous rice cakes. I imagined this pine was a *kami* offering me refuge. I heard the robust boot steps of hikers tromping past me on the trail and imagined them looking down in amusement at the out-of-shape city dude taking a nap in the shade. I heard a scurrying sound and out of the corner of my ground-level eye caught sight of an impetuous Douglas squirrel darting from tree to tree. It froze in its tracks for one long instant to examine me with round eyes that were hugely out of proportion to its little body, accentuated by stripes of white mascara against the gray-brown fur on his brow. Before flitting away, the squirrel released a shrill cry, as if were alerting the forest of my incapacitation. I wondered if I seemed threatening or pitiful lying quietly there, bug eyed and breathing heavily from exhaustion.

Sleep was seductive, irresistible, and terrifying. The pain in my gut dissolved into a warm glow, my thirst slackened. It felt as though my whole body was gloved in numbness and suspended half an inch off the ground. When I realized my arms and legs were deadened flesh that I couldn't move, a panic set in. The instinct to fight off the trance was balanced by a sensation of acquiescence, a sense of allowing myself to be carried away, and then the instinct to resist, floating loose and then willing myself to stay rooted to the spot. I had a vision of a woman, a tall woman with green eyes and long black hair, wearing a white dress, who seemed very familiar, an apparition either from the past or of the future, I thought in bewilderment. If I'd met her before she certainly would have made a lasting impression—she was so strikingly beautiful. It seemed as though the woman was drawing me into her bosom and at the same time repelling me, beckoning and warning me to go away. With graceful flowing arms she gestured for me to go back down to the trailhead, to leave the hazy blue-gray mountains. Hallucinating, I suppose, I swear I heard her say: *"Go home, Raul, you don't belong here, it's not time yet."*

I woke in confusion and bolted upright, raising my head above water to gulp fresh air. My throat was bone-dry. I pushed myself to my feet and made it to the back side of the sugar pine just in time to unbutton my fly, but I could not save myself from the total disgrace of pissing on my boots. Luckily there weren't any hikers in sight to watch this humiliating act. I nearly keeled over when I heaved the backpack **on** my shoulders. When I looked back I noticed a stack of small rocks nestled in the bed of pine needles. The rocks had been carefully placed on top of each other: One wide and horizontal stone served as the base, with a plump stone at the next layer, shaped like a woman's hips, followed by a round thin one, and topped by a craggy little granite egg. The pile was solid in its construction, weighted to the earth to defy the wind, rain and squirrels. The form was animated, as alive as the pine tree. A chill raced down my spine.

On the way to the reservoir, the trail was lit by dappled sunlight through the high branches of Douglass fir. Rounding the bend on the final descent, the scene opened up to an expanse of glassy water, and I could see tents lining the shore. I found Diderot sitting on the bank with his bare feet cooling off in the water, thumbing over the map to demonstrate his disappointment. We'd made pathetic progress that morning; it was already two p.m. He'd eaten without me, but I wasn't hungry anyway. What if my problem wasn't simple constipation after all but something far worse, a giant gallstone? A growing tumor that had planted itself in the colon, blocking traffic? The experience was far too ominous to be explained so easily.

We got back on the trail, both of us determined to make better progress, until I collapsed to my knees about a half-mile ahead. Diderot was seething with anger now, and when I said we ought to go back to the reservoir and pitch camp for the night, promising I'd be better in the morning after a good night's sleep, he spit out the word *merde*.

He saw through the lie, and I didn't fool myself into thinking I'd be revived in the morning either. I was buying time, clinging to irrational hope. I knew in my gut that I must not let myself sleep that night no matter how exhausted I was, because it would mean surrendering to a dark sinkhole. The woman in my dream warned me of this destination, a place so comfortable it would free me from my anguish, a place from which I'd never return.

I went a respectable distance into the trees and fashioned a latrine, by scraping a hole in the hard dirt and suspending a thick fir branch over two mossy logs, praying to the *kami* of shit.

Diderot was cooking dehydrated rice and curry paste on the Gaz burner when I returned from the woods. The smell made me sick to my stomach, and when I tried to eat more of the dried prunes I'd been swallowing for the for the past several days they wouldn't go down. I tried to eat Diderot's dinner out of courtesy but it stopped in my throat and rebounded up my nasal cavity with the taste of bile. It was the longest night in my life, battling the urge to sleep, the urge to urinate, the urge to scream and double up into the fetal position. I stayed outside the tent far enough away to spare Diderot from my contortions, and preoccupied myself with drinking water from the reservoir and visiting my makeshift latrine. I tried to stay on my feet and paced around. I leaned against trees to stay upright. When I crumpled to the ground I made myself count to ten before uncurling and pushing myself upright. I kept myself busy turning my flashlight on and off, refilling my canteen and guzzling it down, pissing, walking, falling, doubling up, crawling to my feet. I watched the dark surface of the reservoir grow to lighter shades of gray, then blue gray, and with ecstatic relief I heard the peeping of digital-watch alarms and the stirrings of campers in nearby tents as dawn broke.

After I'd curled up again in the snail posture a man touched my shoulder. "You look like you're in serious trouble, mate," he said. "You've been keeping me up all night with your scurrying around and moaning. Are you alone or do you have a friend who can help you?"

I pointed to the miserable orange tent where Diderot was sleeping and my eyes followed the man as he shook the flap and called out in his Australian accent: "Wake up, now. I need you to wake up. Now!" I saw anger in the groggy face that emerged from the tent. I heard the backpacker tell Diderot he was a member of the Sierra Club and had been hiking these trails for years. With authority in his voice he told Diderot there was a ranger station with a radio on a fire road about two miles down off the main trail and he'd better go there to get help. I was prostrate, hyperventilating and soaked in sweat, and the only relief I felt was a cool breeze on my cheek. I looked up and saw the two men standing over me. Diderot had his arms crossed, but he wore an expression of genuine concern now, the Gallic irritation missing from his eyes.

"I'll go," he told the man without hesitation. Looking down at me he sad, "I'm going to get the ranger, Raul. Don't worry, I'll be back right away. Try to breathe more slowly. Drink water." He took my sleeping bag out of the tent and placed it over me, gently like a nurse, then ran to the shore and filled both our canteens, putting them by my side before taking off down the trail at a fast trot. I drifted off for I don't know how long until I was dimly aware of muffled voices and the scuffing of boots in the dirt around me. I tasted the mawkish sugary film on my tongue and palate that had grown increasingly pasty since I first noticed and dismissed signs of it in my taxi. I smelled the stench from the crotch of my wet jeans. It was forever before I heard the whirring of helicopter blades on the far shore of the reservoir and looked up to see two men in uniforms paddling a boat to shore. Diderot was standing over me, guarding me like a sentry, back straight, stolid, expressionless.

I didn't realize how delirious I was until I tried to speak to my rescuers as they strapped me onto a stretcher. Nothing came out but whiny vowel sounds over a thick tongue. They checked my pulse, looked into my eyes. "Smell the breath," one of the men said to his partner. "It's stinking sweet. We're lucky we caught him before the coma." The other man grunted. "What the hell was he doing up here in the first place?" he said, glowering at Diderot, who shrugged as though he didn't really know me. "See if you can find the insulin in his pack while I radio the pilot." Diderot returned empty handed. The flying EMT looked down at me sternly. "You're a damn fool for coming up here without your insulin and you're damn lucky we were in the neighborhood."

I couldn't understand any of this. I heard myself babble at him in protest, but wasn't sure the words came out. "I'm fine, I'm really okay,"

I tried to say. "I'm just really plugged up. All I need is a laxative or something. You guys have an enema on board?"

They wouldn't let me drink during the choppy flight to Modesto, but they allowed me to soak my grimy bandana with water from my canteen and suck on it. They put a bedpan by my side and I thanked them profusely.

———

The coroner dragged his feet to the bathroom, borrowed a few more pills from the medicine cabinet and washed them down with a generous snort from the bottle of bourbon on Barlow's kitchen counter. Technically it was not bourbon, having been distilled in Tennessee instead of Kentucky, but he preferred the brand, and apparently so did Barlow.

Maybe there is something in the cardboard box that is not about disease, he wondered. A man is more than a sum total of his ailments. Yet he supposed it was possible that there was nothing at all in the story other than disease, or in his own or anyone's life, a state of being that begs for mercy, forgiveness, dispensation and cure. It begs for freedom from the body, freedom from greed and delusion, freedom from time. The coroner knew this all along, but only below the surface, and now awakening in his Jack Daniel's mind.

Fifteen

The coroner picked out a thin notebook marked Par Three. It appeared to be about golf, a sport he never understood. He would be surprised if Barlow ever played it. It was out of character for a man he was just beginning to know.

———

Par Three

It was a timeless afternoon that sweltered under a hazy prairie sun with low barometric pressure that sucked air out of your lungs, with sweaty tee-shirts that didn't dry, with all the omens of a big thunderstorm coming. It was the worst and the best part of a summer cycle of unbearable humidity broken by stupendous rain, when I sat in the screened-in porch thrilled by the wild energy and counted the seconds between the flash and the boom, one one-thousand, two one-thousand, the time quickening as the ferocity of the storm drew near.

Thundering drums and thin bolts of fire made you wince and scream in ecstasy until the count got longer and the sensational entertainment moved on toward the horizon, leaving in its wake a cleansing sweetness. The others laughed when I mentioned the exhilarating smell in the air minutes after the storm was gone. It was another thirty years before I had a name for it: Ozone. It was the good atmospheric ozone not the stinking man-made ozone I would encounter late in life.

Good ozone smelled like innocence. It heralded relief and it accentuated a crystal clean resolution of verdant lawns and white houses. Bad ozone, the kind emitted by a medical cyclotron, reeked of death.

My summers in suburban Chicago were filled with sensational moments like this, interlaced with utter boredom. I lived in a space where old whistle-stop villages radiated from the city into farmland along rail lines wedging undeveloped fields of long grass and rows of corn that spread across the prairie as far as the eye could see. My boyhood friend Ralph and I went exploring in the canopy of elms and oaks in a vestigial forest preserve nearby. One day we crawled through culverts under the toll road to uncharted terrain. "Don't be afraid, Cowie," Ralph said, using the nickname I acquired after gaining weight in the fourth grade. It was a different world, beyond our imagination, a mile away from home. The neighborhood on the other side had dilapidated houses with peeling paint, abandoned brick storehouses, a shabby, discolored school without a grass lawn, only a concrete yard with basketball hoops missing their nets. The residential streets were not sheltered by the tall trees we took for granted on our side of the highway. We met real black people who sat on their front stoops and smiled at us graciously and said hello.

We did stupid things. We arranged elaborate battle scenes with plastic Civil War soldiers and made it realistic by setting them on fire with lighter fluid and watching them blacken, melt, and die. Ralph always took command of the heroic rebels in gray, I was left with the blue ones, Ralph liked fire. "Cowie, watch this!" he said as he dropped a burning match on a patch of weeds in the empty lots down the street from his house. He bragged that he once set fire to the tall dry grass on the banks of the toll road to see how far it would burn before the fire truck came. We were 10, in the prime of our childhood.

That afternoon before the rain came I had a plan laid out to ride my bike to the village center where I would hang out at the toy store a while, buy a couple comic books and a Hershey's bar at the News Agency and loiter on the benches of the train depot. It was a ritual I practiced alone, without Ralph or any one of my other friends. But just as I was ready to bike to the village center my father summoned me to his den. I wondered why I was in trouble, but he said he was going to take me to Par Three, a little nine-hole golf course a few miles away where you could duff around without worrying too much about making divots and it was okay to cheat when the balls went astray. Unlike the families of many of my friends, we didn't belong to the town's prestigious golf club, for reasons I didn't understand. I was invited there for lunch once by a friend and had to listen to him brag about the sauna in the oak-paneled, brass-railed men's locker room. He told me in a confidential whisper: "Jews aren't allowed to join the club."

I didn't get it. This was a few years before I become aware that my father was Jewish – he described himself as a "devout atheist." My mother was a half-hearted Christian who made me go to Sunday school. It all seemed normal to me. To explain why we didn't belong to the Hinsdale Golf Club my father said it was too expensive and he was a "lousy gawlfer" anyway. He never liked the game, but he feigned interest when he took my brothers and me to Par Three to learn the game. "It will serve you well in life," he said.

As tension rose in the prelude to the storm, I would have much more preferred the solace of Marvel Comics. I could see that my father wanted to step out of character and spend some rare personal time with me on a Saturday when he wasn't on call. His motives seemed pure and I was grateful for his attention even as I felt a rising sense of foreboding. I figured there was a fifty-fifty chance he'd call it off at the last minute so he could make a house call or visit a patient in the hospital, yet another promise to be broken. But my negative expectations were unfounded. We loaded the clubs in the trunk of his second-hand Mercedes coupe and I enjoyed a rare chance to sit in the passenger seat. I didn't have to squeeze into the narrow shelf behind the seats, which I always had to do when one of my older brothers was on board. This was supposed to be a special occasion.

He read my sullen mood and pulled one of his old tricks, the rubber face. He stretched his neck and looked down at me at an angle and contorted his mouth and nose. I always surrendered to helpless laughter and he would snort triumphantly and pat my head. He always won.

On the golf course my father struggled. It was muggy and he was sweating profusely in the creepy warm wind. The game stalled on the sixth hole when he got stuck trying to blast his way off a fairly tame sand trap, using what even I could see was the wrong club. I suggest a nine-iron. He wouldn't hear of it, taking advice from a "snotty-nosed little boy." I understood this term was intended to be a term of endearment, cast in one of his classic attempts at sarcasm, but this time it was spoken in desperation to mask his embarrassment and frustration. He was a proud man and he had a tendency to puff up his ego by belittling his sons.

I don't recall ever hearing him use the f-word or say "shit!" He preferred to bark out such phrases as "Jesus Christ Almighty" or Dammit to hell!" Now, after six or seven tries to whack the ball into the air and onto the green he spewed a succession of unrestrained epithets. Without looking in my direction he finally relented and pulled the nine iron out of his cart. Again, he drove the ball further into the sand. In a fulminating rage my father climbed out the shallow pit, waved the club in the air and swung it like baseball bat at the cart. He hit it again and again until the nine iron was bent in a 12-degree angle. He didn't notice when I stepped back, tripped and crawled away from him while he stood there dumbstruck at the sight of his mangled golf club. Sweat dripped down from his balding, sunburned head, drenching the collar of his only informal weekend shirt. Luckily, there were no other golfers within viewing range, sparing him from utter mortification. I was thinking what a hilarious scene it was until I saw how helpless and vulnerable he was, and that frightened me. He quickly regained his composure, picked up the ball and placed on the edge of the green and sank it with a single putt.

We played on in silence, as if nothing unusual had happened, We were to "play to the bitter end," a phrase he often used that I took to mean that persevering under absurd circumstances was a manly way to live life. When I grew older I understood what he meant.

As we crunched gravel under the wheels of our carts on the way to the car, we approached the old man who owned the golf course, one of my father's long-time patients, who always insisted we play for free.

My father had treated the man's wife, who was dying of breast cancer, with great compassion, the way he did all his patients. They were all completely devoted to their Jewish doctor. Ever since I could remember, his patients would recognize me and stop me on the sidewalk or in a store to tell me how much they loved my father for the way he took care of them. I'd smile and nod my head politely, choking down the feeling that their doctor was not the father I knew. My mother used to call it his other persona, the one with the bedside manner. I didn't fully understand what she meant until that afternoon when I watched him switch in an instant from a frightening ogre into a gentle healer.

He told me I should thank the man for allowing us to play and say something nice to console him about the passing of his wife, who just died on Tuesday. When I protested that I had no idea what to say, he spoke softly into my ear, so close I could smell the mixture of men's cologne and greasy sweat on his neck. His voice seemed to be coming from the gravel under our feet.

"Just speak from your heart. Raul," he said. "At times like this a man is hurting very deeply and he needs to be touched. Keep it simple, speak sincerely from your heart."

I can't remember what I said but I worked up the courage to mumble something that worked. The man bowed his head as his lips moved in a silent thank you. Then he put his hand on my shoulder to draw me near and he whispered: "Son, you should be proud of your father. He is a saint."

I wanted to get away from there as quickly as possible, to wriggle out of the heat, to go home and drink cold soda in the cool basement of our stone house. My father was a Jewish saint and I was a chubby little boy whose best friends, affectionately, called me Cowie.

That evening I sat alone on the screened-in porch, listening to the booming of thunder approach, waiting for the clouds to burst and the lightning to flash. And I hungered for the coming of unnamable ozone.

Sixteen

O ne more story before I try again to crack the laptop, he told himself, one more notebook. He chose a notebook of the sort he used when he visited Japan for a conference six years earlier, before Alice died. The cover bore its brand name, Campus Note, on a pale blue background. He remembered the quality of the notebook, bound by stitches and featuring thick pages with thin lines. The Japanese excel at craftsmanship, he recalled thinking, even in their stationery supplies. The coroner had sketched out the time differences between Osaka and San Francisco on its inside cover so he could call Alice without waking her up. She was sick and he called her every day until she told him to stop wasting money.

The first entry in the small, ruled "Campus Note" pad was titled It Ain't Necessarily So.

———

It was a cool evening in October, I believe, and we went to see a production of "Porgy and Bess" in a tent they'd thrown up in a parking lot somewhere in the labyrinth of narrow alleyways west of Shibuya Station. She dragged me out of the bureau early to see a visiting troupe from Harlem staging the play. Inside the tent a small crowd of urbane Tokyoites sat politely in rows of folding chairs. I waited with a certain amount of anxiety for the invisible curtain to rise because Mayumi and her mother were sitting across the aisle, too close for comfort. My fiancée always bristled when Mayumi was around. She read my body language, she noticed how I reacted to her at press receptions; she knew things about how I felt for Mayumi I didn't know myself. This is the problem with women. They have X-ray vision.

We exchanged hesitant little waves and tight smiles. Her mother, a poker-faced aristocratic lady, turned her head away and stared at the empty stage. I was another one of her daughter's shabby journalist friends. To avoid further embarrassment I put my nose into the playbill and read the biographies of the Gershwin brothers. I stopped at the parenthetical reference to George's death from brain cancer, a deadly glioblastoma, at the thirty-eight. The line spooked me. I was thirty-eight. How odd, I thought, and I reread the words several times until it sank in. What a terrible thing to happen so early in his brilliant career. I didn't know why this clutched my attention. My career had been a mediocre one. I was struggling to keep pace with smarter and more experienced correspondents in Tokyo. Language skills and an intuitive feel for the local culture I got from years of studying in Japan couldn't compensate for my inexperience and limited ability to make snap news judgments. I didn't known why I identified so strongly with the great composer. There wasn't anything in my life so dramatic as brain cancer, just plain vanilla diabetes. It may have something to do with the encounter with Mayumi. She used to tell me how much she admired me for managing diabetes under difficult circumstances. I never knew whether the comment was intended to attract or repel. She probably didn't know herself.

All I know is that for the next several weeks I couldn't get Porgy's bass-baritone lament over lost love out of my head, but pretty soon I couldn't remember the tune and I forgot all about George's tumor.

———

The coroner sighed as he tossed the notebook back into the box. Barlow's journals, however intriguing, made his head throb and it took the pain in his tooth to a new magnitude of nausea. He must go home now and get to sleep before dawn. He would come back here in the early afternoon. The laptop would have to wait for now. He would shower and shave and stop off at the It's Tops Coffee Shop on Market for some eggs, hash browns and strong coffee.

He tried to make sense of what he had learned so far by reading the testimony of the man in his morgue who, unlike any other corpse, demanded comprehension. He was not the only body whose life was cut short before realizing its greatest desire, but he was the first to make him share the yearning and the grief. The coroner knew he had crossed the line. He was a voyeur, not a medical examiner now, cutting into the cadaver's mind instead of tissue.

He stood up and lost his balance, barely saving himself from falling by grabbing the back of Barlow's couch, swaying in delirium, cursing himself for his clumsiness. The sight of the bottle on the kitchen counter reminded him he should refill his flask, just in case, before sneaking out the back door of the bungalow. "Can't take it with you," he said aloud in an affected slur, saluting the bottle.

Then he saw for the first time an open wallet by the sink, presumably the one Barlow did not have on his person when he stepped out for his stroll. It contained a driver's license with his face but a different address, suggesting he moved to Dolores Heights within the past five years, before he had to renew it. There were the usual credit cards in his name, a Kaiser card, a Neptune Society card and an AAA road service card. The wallet was stuffed with faded receipts, scraps of paper with illegible handwriting, and two crisp twenty-dollar bills.

He decided he had better preserve the evidence before a corrupt law enforcement official got to it and hid it in the silverware drawer. Pain radiated from the back molar on the lower left side of his jaw. It must be abscessed, because he tasted a tinge of tooth rot in his mouth. The whiskey made it sting.

Robbing a dead man of his whiskey, he reflected, is a despicable act. Barlow would not mind, however. Barlow would want his personal medical examiner to make himself at home.

He slipped out the rear, leaving the kitchen door unlocked so he could easily sneak back into the house that afternoon without fumbling with the key in plain sight at the front door. He did not want an old man walking a Yorkshire terrier named Shorty to report suspicious activity in the neighborhood. Barlow's house appeared more dilapidated from the rear than it did from front. The dark redwood frame had the generous dimensions of a home built in the early 20th century, before two-by-fours were whittled down to 1-3/4 by 3-1/2 inches by an economizing lumber industry. The tiny patch of a back yard was tangled with tall weeds. He followed the walkway to a sagging gate and crept to the sidewalk.

He looked up and down the street, trying to find his humpback Volvo, until he remembered parking it down the hill somewhere near the death scene. He wondered whether Barlow's car was one of those parked along the curb. Several Subaru Outbacks lined the street, including a dark green one that looked familiar, but there were so many used green Subarus like that one buzzing around the Bay Area that he dismissed his feeling of *déjà vu*. What kind of car would Barlow drive? He thought he knew enough about the man already to plot out the rough lines of a personality profile. Divorced, seemingly unemployed, the father of at least one daughter, living alone with only one toothbrush in the bathroom and without the scent of a woman in his house. Someone with women in his past, one of whom just contacted him, an old lover he was both excited and ambivalent about seeing. Or so it seemed.

The neighborhood was blurred, harder to bring into focus than it was when he trudged up the hill from the south earlier in the night. He reached up to check that his glasses were still hung on his face. His eyes must be tired from reading Barlow's handwriting. His instincts told him to go north, away from the Liberty Street gully and over the crest of the hill. He recalled that in his youth he drank at an ancient Irish bar in that direction, down the hill and a few blocks to the east near Guerrero Street. He lived in a Spartan studio apartment in the neighborhood when he was an impoverished medical resident. His watch said twenty minutes to six o'clock. The pub would be open by the time he got there. He would sit down on a stool and drink a preliminary breakfast of stout to clear his cognitive faculties before coming back to look for his car. The exercise would do him good. Then he would go home and sleep it off, free of any hint of insomnia.

He thought he heard footsteps behind him, faint ones that came from rubber soles. When he turned to look he saw the outline of a man in a porkpie hat across the dark street who stopped and faced away as if to tie his shoes. The silhouette was familiar. *"Don't mind me. You need a drink,"* he heard someone say in a hoarse voice, a distant voice he recognized as his own.

In moments of disequilibrium he had a deeply ingrained habit of patting himself down to confirm that certain essential items were still in place. He would touch the bridge of his nose to make sure his glasses were intact, slap the top of his right thigh to hear the keys jingle in his pants pocket, and probe the area of his left rump until he was satisfied he had not lost his wallet. So there was a long moment of confusion bordering on panic when he performed this nervous-tic ritual on his way down the hill. His glasses were there, but he felt only a single house key in his pocket, and an empty left rear pocket where his wallet should be. He calmed down after he concluded he must have left these items in Barlow's house, and he shivered with relief when he found the flask in his jacket and a wad of bills in his pants pocket.

"This is why God invented pockets," he heard a voice say. *"To help you conceal things from yourself."*

Seventeen

He woke to find himself sprawled out on a luminous green lawn with the sun blazing down on his neck. He raised his head to get up when a wave of nausea washed over him, forcing him to collapse onto his knees to see the carpet of grass opening up beneath him. His head spun, his eyes crossed and twittered. The only escape was to dive into the earth. He tasted salty blades of grass and smelled what earthworms must smell when they burrow into moist soil. He breathed deeply, slowly, to hold terror at bay. The pain in his head was furry and diffuse.

Labyrinthitis was his diagnosis, the worst episode in years. After several minutes pressing himself to the ground he rolled over and assumed the corpse position, a relaxation technique he learned when he dabbled in metaphysics before embracing hard science as his religion. It was a yoga pose where you lie limp on your back with your arms at your side, palms up, heels touching, breathing like there was a feather on his belly gently floating and dropping. The feeling of helplessness soon passed, and when he sat up he found himself perched on a slope with an unobstructed view of the skyline to the northeast, grayish brown structures that poked at a cloudless sky. A light breeze cooled the greasy sweat on his face and neck.

The sun had crawled across the sky to the west, far enough to establish that it was mid-afternoon. He checked his watch. It was twenty-seven after three. He had been doing something he could not remember since dawn.

The palm trees looked familiar, and when he saw the large edifice with a Spanish tile roof he recognized it as the high school fronting Dolores Park. He had not traveled all that far from Barlow's house, whatever he had done all morning. Maybe he went home to Russian Hill and returned, but that seemed improbable, because he was neither shaved nor showered. He vaguely recalled entering a playground, swaying on a swing and humming a tune, but was not certain whether that was a recent memory or one from his childhood. To regain his bearings he looked instinctively for the Good Karma Café, which would give him a definitive landmark. He stopped there regularly for spicy chai tea and carob muffins when he lived in the neighborhood and slaved away as a resident at Pacific Medical Center. How many decades ago was that? He was too groggy to calculate it, but the absence of the Good Karma was conspicuous as his eyes swept across the landscape. A new establishment took its place across from the northeast corner of the park, displaying the same large plate-glass windows, trimmed now in bright chrome and black lacquer. The sign said "Java."

"What the hell, I wouldn't mind some java," he croaked.

In an effort to restore his dignity, the coroner righted himself and straightened the knot of his necktie, pressed his palms over his breast and thighs to smooth out his rumpled brown suit, and brushed off the grass. He checked to see if his fly was zipped and his scuffed wingtips were tied before plodding down the slope.

At the sidewalk he encountered a coven of men hovering with Safeway carts. The vehicles were laden with black plastic bags that might be filled with anything – their best clothing, photos of loved ones, meaningful found items, or cans and bottles to redeem for a nickel a pop. Folded cardboard boxes wedged between the bags suggested shelter for sleeping in the rough.

One of the three, a tall black man who wore his hair in dreadlocks and sported a short grizzled beard, whom he judged to be approximately forty-five years old, looked up and offered him an infectious grin. The man had three teeth, two on top and one on the bottom that did not come close to meshing. The lack of dentistry did not lessen the man's air of dignity and the strength of a face that could be described as strong-jawed and ruggedly handsome. He waved and beckoned, and the coroner found his legs moving in that direction.

"You're new, aren't you, my brother. I haven't seen you around, have I? Welcome to Dolores Village, the green ghetto." He spoke with the clipped English diction of an old boy from Eaton, which the coroner could not determine was genuine or theatrical. "My name is Rolly. You must be the false Messiah."

Rolly puffed up his chest and erupted into baritone howls of laughter. The other two men eyed the coroner with deep suspicion and shook their heads. They had seen Rolly invite strangers into their space and put on this show many times before. Evidently they were not amused, and it was clear they did like the looks of the latest guest.

He noted that Rolly's torso was draped with a patch of blue polyester fabric that displayed a large "S" insignia on a golden shield. A little red cape attached to his neck fluttered in the breeze. He guessed that Rolly found the remnants of a child's Halloween costume discarded in a trashcan as he foraged for items of value.

It was then he realized how foul and disheveled he appeared, bad enough to be mistaken for a fellow traveler. He found himself responding by instinct with the refined manners he affected when meeting new colleagues at a conference of forensic pathologists, wishing to show respect and minimize the hostility of Rolly's comrades before moving on.

"Very pleased to meet you, Rolly, and friends," he said with a nod. "I'm Dr. Bacigalupi, but you can call me Leo. I live up on Russian Hill." He quickly realized that was the wrong thing to say. What if they wanted his money? He went for the laugh line. "But I'm not Russian."

Rolly inspected the coroner like a punter checking out a horse on the paddock before the third race at Golden Gate Fields. "You're Italian, and you come from North Beach or Sausalito, lower middle class, educated on scholarships. Am I not right? It's obvious," he said.

"Close enough," the coroner said, amazed at how the homeless man read him with such accuracy. His brain was slowly adapting to the man's sharp wit. "My parents were from Milan. I grew up in Larkspur, and my dad worked as a janitor at an elementary school. I got through med school by selling my body to lonely widows. Let me guess, now, you are from Britain, or the Islands. You are an English lord, perhaps. A pretender to the throne?

"Yes, I come from nobility indeed," Rolly said. His pals shifted their feet and turned their faces away from the scene, bored and impatient, waiting for the right moment to roll their carts down the sidewalk.

"Honest, decent hog farmers in the kingdom of southern Arkansas. I speak in many tongues and accents and I wear disguises so I can carry out my mission without being detected. Somebody must save the planet from greed, suffering and delusion, and that is me." He lowered his voice to a confidential whisper. "When I got fired by the post office the doctors said I'm a schizophrenic, but little do they know of my true nature and my destiny."

The coroner shrugged in sympathy, wondering how long Rolly had been off his meds.

"Look, I'm feeling a little disoriented here, like I'm just waking up from a bad dream. Can any of you tell me what happened to the Good Karma Café? It's missing, gone. It used to be right there."

One of Rolly's comrades suddenly showed interest in the conversation, a burly old man with white hair. "Ain't nothin' but bad karma 'round here these days. You must of just crawled out from under some rock, doctor Bachigahoopy," he said with an ironic hoot. "You tell me where the good karma is and I can get me a fine suit like the one you wearing at the Salvation Army, and maybe some of that macrobiotic food they used to serve over there." The third man nodded demonstratively, rocking on his heels.

The old man continued in a wistful tone. "A bunch of hippies ran it back in the day, before young Rolly here was even born. They used to give me leftover bread when I came around at closing time. It was brown and dry and tasted like dirt, but it was better than nothing at all. The motherfuckers that run Java's don't give a shit. They kick you out on your ass if you don't smell right and threaten to call the police if you hang around, even when you got good money to buy their coffee. You see, we're bad for business."

"That's right," Rolly piped in, "we're *baaad*."

The coroner was tempted to pass around his flask in commiseration but thought better of it.

"How about I give it a try," he said, reaching into the inside breast pocket of his brown suit for the thin leather wallet. "I have credentials."

There was a frightening moment when he found the pocket empty. Then he calmed himself with the thought that he must have left his CME identification in the car after visiting Buck Pomeroy at Mission Emergency. "My investigator's license is back in the car, but don't worry. I know how to boss my way around without it."

"You're a cop! I knew if from the start. Undercover. Your dirty suit gives you away." Rolly said. He stood his ground while his friends started to shrink away, ready to bolt.

"Wait, no, don't jump to conclusions. I'm not a cop, I'm just a medical examiner. I have a county commission to investigate the dead, not the living. I use the ID to get into crime scenes. I don't shake people down."

"Where's your stinking gun?" Rolly said. "Most cops I know use the Beretta 96D. Forty caliber. I know because I've had them pointed at my nose several times on suspicion of walking while black. What kind of gun do you carry?"

The coroner raised his palms to indicate he was unarmed as he turned and walked across the street with a wobbly strut. "Stay here and I'll get us some go juice."

Where did he leave his Walther PPK, he wondered. Probably still in the spring-loaded catch under the dashboard of the Volvo where he always kept it. He had not taken it out and cleaned it or even looked at it in years.

His daze of nostalgia for the old Good Karma dissipated as soon after he entered the establishment. The oversized green chalkboard that once listed organic broccoli soup, brown rice curry pilaf and nutmeg tofu stir-fry was no longer hanging on the wall. Gone was the sweet redolence of a coarse wheat bread baking in the ovens. No battered wooden tables covered with thick shellac. No bulletin board papered with flyers for new age masseurs and Maoist study groups.

The chrome and black lacquer motif updated the premises to a clean cold contemporary look. It reminded him of the morgue.

He wondered if the shopping cart detail would still be at the park when he returned with a cardboard tray carrying four large "*café grand*" coffees du jour. He wanted to buy the "*café géant*" size, but a surly young barista told him that the super sized cups wouldn't fit into the tray. He noted with amusement that the woman had green vine tattoos etched on her arms and gold pins and rings impaled on her lips, her nose, cheeks and forehead. He tipped her an extra dollar. The counter culture lives, he thought. Long live the revolution!

The guys were waiting and he gave them each a coffees and a thin paper sack containing a raspberry walnut scone, which as far as he could tell were identical to pastry baked at the same factory served at every coffee house in the City. He put a fourth scone in his pocket.

"Thank you, doctor, but I take cream and two cubes of sugar," Rolly said through a three-toothed grin. "Actually I prefer Earl Gray and crumpets." Rolly seemed to think his remark was uproariously funny; the others scowled.

Eighteen

The coroner scaled the eastern flank of Dolores Heights while sucking on the plastic nipple lid and burning his tongue on the hot coffee. His head rattled with much more than a simple hangover. Sweaty and heaving for breath, he reentered the bungalow from the rear yard after darting around the neighborhood to make sure he was undetected. It was just as he left it. He dropped into Barlow's chair, careful not to spill his Grand-sized Ethiopian roast. The bag with his scone slipped out of his fingers. He bent over to pick it up and dropped it again as he sat up. He decided to leave it on the floor, where it seemed to belong, until he got hungry.

Where to go now? It was Sunday afternoon already, and he had barely scratched the surface of the mountain of documentary evidence in Barlow's sanctum. The thought entered his mind that he should call Wilson to share the discovery of the corpse's true identity and get him working on Raul Barlow's background with the full name and correct DOB. There was not much, however, that the *diener* could do before the shop opened Monday morning. He would be back at the morgue then, and guide the research better by learning what he could here. He was certain to find the next of kin by plowing through the man's written record, and find out more about Christina, the mystery lover. Then he remembered the MedicAlert bracelet. Wilson's top priority would have to be calling the people in Modesto and getting them to cough up the old profile that he could not obtain the night before. That was bound to have critical information. Wilson may get a breakthrough on the case while he made an end run around Du Goyle and appealed directly to the Chief ME for permission to do the autopsy on his very own corpse. He must collect himself now and investigate.

The computer was the first challenge. He admonished himself for giving in to the fear of frustration and computer rage and not concentrating on this elementary task before getting sucked into the box of notebooks. He had to find a way to unlock the machine somehow. The email account would be the most expedient way of finding the woman and the family and all the people Barlow was in contact with, unraveling the man's social life and leading him to a host of circumstantial evidence. If anyone who knew Barlow suspected that he was deeply depressed or suicidal, for instance, that would turn the hit-and-run scenario on its head.

In a flash of inspiration he remembered the book, the secret red book on the shelf that contained nothing in the hole hollowed out inside. He tried the words redhorse, redhorsehill, secret, confidential, and hidden in the password box to no avail. Then he tapped out "nothing," because there was nothing inside *Red Horse Hill.*

"Open sesame!" he yelped and slammed his thumb on the space bar. Two icons popped up on the desktop. One was a large blue B and the other bore double exclamation marks on a yellow background. B was a dead link sending him to a page that said, "This page in not available at this time. Contact your Internet service provider for more information." Yes, but who would be the provider to contact? The coroner put that sort of information on files inside his computer and thought that might also be the case with Barlow.

The *!!* icon took him to the Bamboozlemail sign-on site. Progress, he thought, but every word and combination of words he associated with Barlow came up dry when he typed them into the password box. Most likely there was a combination of letters, numbers and symbols that were not random but personal to Barlow, yet finding it was beyond his imagination. Wilson could do it. The morgue assistant was a genius criminal hacker when he was a mere child and he could easily crack it open with one of his algorithms, but for some strange reason he did not want the young man to trespass on Barlow's sanctuary at this critical time. He vowed to try again later, and if he could not find the password himself he would have no choice but to impound the machine and bring it back to the lab for a forensic examination Monday.

He turned to the cardboard box at his feet. Barlow was not just a journalist, he concluded, the man was also a compulsive journalizer.

"Hello there, scone," he said to the pastry. "Just wait, I'll deal with you later."

The notebooks were of different sizes, bindings and colors. Many of them had titles, but there were very few dates on the covers so it was impossible to read them in chronological order. It would have to be a fishing expedition. He stirred the contents of the box until he saw the title "Robert's Dream."

—

Robert's Dream

I have nightmares, recurring dreams about this kid I used to know at Oak School. It was back in second grade. His name was Robert Reuss and I didn't like him at all. I hated him because he was painfully shy and strange, very much out of kilter.

Robert was skinny, and the navy blue pants he wore every day were far too short, prominently displaying white socks. He wore scuffed black dress shoes that were a size too large for his feet, and he buttoned the top button of his shirt, failing to comprehend that all normal boys kept their collars open. The problem with Robert wasn't just his hand-me-down clothing – the mark of alien frugality amidst pampered white suburban children – it was his awkward social skills that identified him as "mental." I'm sure he was of sound mind and normal, probably much higher than normal in intelligence, but that didn't matter because the boy kept buttoning his top button. His parents emigrated from Estonia when he was six years old and he retained a very slight Baltic accent, I recall. He didn't have what it took to joke around or play kickball. We smelled his weakness like baby vultures and we pecked at him mercilessly. It might have been different if Robert called himself Rob or Bob, but the poor guy was clueless.

His only friend was Rachel, a feisty redheaded girl I used to idolize in first grade. Rachel and I sat next to each other in our flip-top wooden combo chair-desks and I was inspired by her zany subversive ways. She was the trickster, constantly playing pranks on other kids, acting up in class, and fomenting disorder. She'd put pencils in her nose to get laughs when the teacher had her back to us. Rachel had a mischievous child's charisma and I couldn't resist falling in with her to break the boredom of a curriculum designed for kids who hadn't learned to read yet, insipid exercises and stories that droned on all day. I started disrupting class myself by making dumb comments and shouting out annoying questions without raising my hand. Miss Archey eventually punished the two of us by separating our desks way across the classroom, with the redheaded ringleader in the front row so she could be watched. I was banished to the back, away from the spotlight, and forced to sit next to Robert.

It was the worst punishment imaginable. But the teacher couldn't keep Rachel and me apart during recess. We hatched a plot to blow her to smithereens. I called the poor woman "Miss Ouchy" because I couldn't say R very well back then. That's how my name became Chucky instead of "Wa-ool." Rachel was one of the few kids who didn't tease me about my speech impediment. Fßor all her troublemaking she had the gift of empathy. We built the bomb out of a Band-Aid tin, stuffed it with lethal rubber bands and pieces of broken chalk. At the last minute we added scraps of red construction paper, because there would be blood involved in our cartoon fantasy. When our teacher sat down on the improvised explosive device after lunch break she jumped up like a jack-in-the-box and shouted "Shit!"

Miss Archey knew immediately who did it. Our sentence was to endure the torture of sitting silently all afternoon on the "marble bench," the seat of ultimate shame across the hall from the principal's door, which he kept open to cast an evil eye on us. If we talked, he made a veiled threat to phone our mothers, or worse.

Those were innocent days. Seven-year-olds didn't bring loaded revolvers to school for show-and-tell, junior high students didn't watch pornography on the Internet and high school students didn't smoke pot under the football field bleachers in the early 1960s. But we elementary school kids did our best to be bad with available means.

My devotion to Rachel started to fray in third grade after I helped my friends beat up Robert for no particular reason. I had adopted the aversion for girls that young boys affected. I learned how to say R but didn't use my first name because it sounded foreign and would attract suspicion. Rachel was next-door-neighbors with Robert and the two spent a lot of time together, the outcast and the rebel. It became well known that Rachel frequently went to Robert's house after school to play chess. Rachel persuaded me to join them one day and I agreed out of lingering puppy love, only to be slaughtered in a match with Robert. I hated chess, a game for idiots as far as I was concerned.

My little gang of bullies never gave Robert a chance. We all rode Sting Rays, small-framed bikes with chopper handlebars and banana seats that were designed to pull wheelies, make quick turns, and terrify small pedestrians. We went out of our way to razz him and one day it got completely out of hand. We dismounted our Sting Rays bikes and chased him in circles on the blacktop and hounded him across the school lawn before tackling him in what we used to call a "nigger pile," in the spirit of our racist redlined suburban culture. Thatch started it by slugging him in the gut after we disentangled and when Robert wouldn't fight back the other boys pounced on him. After a moment of hesitation I jumped into the one-sided fray. We were on Robert like a pack of baby wolves going for third-grade blood. He curled up into a snail posture wailing with snot all over his face and we kept hitting him until the bell rang announcing the end of recess.

Everyone took off except me. I didn't know why, but I stopped in my tracks and I looked over my shoulder to see him lying there whimpering, not so much out of physical pain but from a bottomless empty hurt I recognized at once as my own.

I knelt down beside Robert and, touched his shoulder with a trembling hand and tried to comfort him. I said I was so sorry, really sorry and when he didn't respond I dug into my pocket, pulled out a dime I'd been saving and offered it to him out of desperation, almost terror at what we'd done. He struck my arm away with shocking strength, hitting me so hard it hurt my wrist and sent the dime flying into the grass where it would never be found again. "Go away Chucky, just leave me alone," he shouted. "Go away!" So I stood up and turned my back on him and skulked off, leaving Robert sobbing with his face buried in the spring grass. Then I saw Rachel lingering at the school door watching this and nearly lost my balance when she brushed past me running to her friend.

Robert's parents put him in another school in a neighboring town and I haven't seen or heard about him since. We cowardly boys went unpunished, leaving me with cowardly memories. It would have been better to be whipped with a strap than to go free as if nothing serious had occurred.

It wasn't long before I started dreaming about Robert, recurring nightmares that haunt me to this day – forty years later. It's always late afternoon, and I see Robert balancing on top of a chain link fence, teetering side to side. Suddenly he falls and lands his head on the pavement so hard I hear it crack. I rush to help him and see that a bloody square hatch has broken off from the left side of his skull revealing ghoulish white brain tissue about to spill out on the side-walk. Frantically I pick the piece of skull off the ground and try to stick it back on his head, but it keeps falling off. I'm helpless. Robert whimpers.

As a teenager Rachel bloomed into a tall and beautiful young woman with wavy red hair and fleshy breasts. But she was darkly aloof, a wearer of ungainly eyeglasses who had a reputation for being odd and unsociable. She was rumored to be the school's best source for mescaline mushrooms. After years of not thinking twice about the girl who had shunned me since third grade I suddenly felt surrounded by her, fascinated by her powerful brooding silence and the way she inhabited an entirely different world from mine, barely tolerating the fools around her, fools like me. Whenever I approached her to talk she met my eyes only fleetingly, then looked away, acting as if she didn't remember who I was.

This went on until the semester when Rachel and I sat next to each other at a biology lab bench, a situation that only heightened my misery. She didn't speak to me unless it was about a Bunsen burner or a dead frog and outside the classroom she avoided me.

Eventually I worked up the courage break the ice. I was no longer the fat little boy called Cowie in grade school, but a gaunt high school wrestler named Chuck who worked hard to build self-respect and confidence. I trapped her in a corner of the hallway and asked her if she wanted to go the park and take a walk, maybe talk about things, go out for pizza, ice cream, a movie. I don't remember what I said, but the effect was completely humiliating, as I half expected it was going to be. Her eyes scoffed at me playfully, gently, kindly, and she didn't bother to say a word in response. But the next morning my cruel lab partner caught me completely off guard.

"Hey Raul," she said. "Have you ever been on top of the junior high school roof?" I was flummoxed, still feeling foolish from the previous day's encounter. She spoke to me intimately, as if we'd been the closest of friends all along. I was shocked when she said Raul. Nobody called me Raul anymore except my father – I was Chuck to everyone else. Rachel disarmed me by invoking the name I couldn't pronounce when we were in first grade. I took a long breath and said, "Rachel, no, I haven't. I thought about it but it looked too hairy. I heard people went up there but I couldn't see how they could do it." I did my best to affect nonchalance. "How the hell do you get to the roof without breaking your neck?"

"I'll show you. I'll take you there," she said, furrowing her brow and lowering her voice to a sultry conspiratorial tone. The Band-Aid tin bomb again. "It's the new moon tonight, totally dark, and the view will be grand. Are you coming with me?"

We met at 11:30 pm behind the old gothic three-story school on Garfield Street near the village center, a pile of dark stone and black mortar built in 1911 with faux turrets and belcast eaves. She showed me where to squeeze through the chain-link fence in the back by the dumpster and how to pull down the fire escape ladder, to scale the side of the stone wall, to belly-crawl over the eaves and shimmy up the crest of the pitched roof. Barefoot and wearing burgundy corduroy jeans and a baggy brown sweater, she scampered up the roof like a cat as

I clambered up behind her, thrilled at the sight of the fleshy fullness of her bottom and thighs, just so. The lights from the city sparkled like Christmas tree bulbs in the east. It was so close I couldn't believe my eyes, a sight you couldn't imagine seeing with your feet stuck to the flat prairie floor encircled by the tree-shrouded suburban horizon. I wanted to fly, holding her in my arms, to look down from space. I became aware of the geo-location of my home town for the first time, my spot on the planet near a huge city with whistle-stop towns radiating westward in orbit around a magical place crowned by a cluster of ethereal light. The night was soundless.

She took out a thin slip of paper from her pocket, shook some loose leaves on it from a plastic bag, rolled it, licked, lit it on fire, and passed it to me. Rachel slipped a hand softly between my thighs and pointed with the other into the light. "Look, Raul, you can see the Sears Tower."

Nineteen

He thought about his raspberry scone. He had an urgent desire to eat it now, before things got too complicated. "Come here, little fellow," he said as he bent down to fetch it.

He hurt, he ached, he searched for the bottom of his ravaged heart and found the source of the pain. He grieved. Alice had red hair. It erupted into wild snakes of dancing color against the sun when she released it from her ponytail.

The notebook had another entry, a long one, which he read eating the scone.

———

Peaches

I got out of bed late this morning and dragged myself to the kitchen to boil water for coffee. My tired old Capresso was beyond cleansing with vinegar and it brewed a bitter sludge that made my stomach burn, so it will be hand-drip until I get around to replacing the machine. Waiting for the kettle to whistle I was shocked by a powerful fragrance that overtook the aroma of freshly ground beans. It came from a paper bag on the counter where I squirreled away five yellow peaches to let them ripen shaded from sunlight after inspecting and buying them at the fruit vendor on 24th Street earlier this week. I've had too many peaches rot on me before I had a chance to eat them. I'm stalking

these ones, waiting for the perfect moment to eat all five at once leaning over the sink. Peaches require a certain suchness to attain their full
flavor and once you are under the spell of their scent you are helpless.
I found myself in Modesto.

I'd been released from the hospital that morning after recovering
from ketoacidosis. They instructed me on the rudimentary tasks of
using needles and checking my urine to control the disease, and they
didn't waste any time sending me on my way because it didn't appear
I had health insurance. I was basically an indigent cab driver from
a distant city where who knew what would happen to me. Friendly
farm-girl nurses gave me a few vials of insulin, a package of syringes,
and a phone number to call a clinic at UCSF Medical Center where
they could train me how to live with my new chronic, incurable disease. "Things will be different for the rest of your life," said a very kind
Indian doctor who reeked of men's cologne. "You must change your
lifestyle now, Raul. Cut down on anything with sugar in it. Reduce the
stress, get good exercise. Absolutely no smoking."

I checked out of the hospital with a yawn of resignation that I faced
a future of pissing on little sticks to test for sugar levels and taking
shots before meals, and if I managed it all well it wouldn't kill me, it
would only put me at high risk for a litany of grave diseases that might
shorten my life if I wasn't conscientious. I wasn't frightened about the
future because I believed I was invincible, but the exit from Modesto
was more than anti-climactic. Diabetes was going to be a tedious disease, one of scrupulous attention to detail.

Three days earlier I'd checked into Modesto General Hospital in
a flurry of excitement after an interminable helicopter flight from
the reservoir, a bumpy ride that had been annoyingly interrupted by
a stop in Yosemite to pick up a man who got bucked from a horse and
landed skull-first on a large rock. The flying EMTs were shouting to
each through the roar of the helicopter blades and they told me to
be patient because before I got out of the craft they had to wheel the
horseman straight into the bboperating room. I was in a stupor, moaning deliriously for water and a urinal, still behind the wheel of the cab
looking for hotel lobbies. Those bastards hadn't let me drink water

on the flight, but they let me suck on the wet bandana I'd used to get through the night, dipping and re-dipping it in the reservoir. When I came to my senses I was strapped to a gurney in the emergency room with IV tubes in my arm, one dripping insulin and the other delivering saline solution for dehydration, they explained. They had to stabilize me and flush me out, they said. I wasn't going to argue because I felt more comfortable attached to these tubes than I'd been in weeks. Safe.

"Your blood sugar was over 700," a tall nurse snapped. "The keto-acidosis might have killed you! What in God's name made you think you could go backpacking up there without your insulin!"

She changed her tone when I told her I was confused. "What do you mean, insulin?"

In a gentler tone she gave me the shorthand on the disease, the technical part that the stranger on the trail didn't explain. Your pancreas stopped producing insulin, and without insulin you can't break down the sugar in your bloodstream and use it to feed your body after you eat. Without sugar your body starts metabolizing the fat and then your own muscle tissue. That releases an acidic byproduct. That's what was poisoning you.

"Your body tells you to flush it out and you pee until you're thirsty, you pee and you drink and you pee and you drink and eventually you can go into a coma," she said. "You don't know how lucky you are."

I wondered how long it would take before my skin turned reddish orange.

They handed me a telephone and told me to call my family. I was surprised I remembered my parents' number in Chicago – I'd never called them without looking at my address book since they sold the old house and withdrew into their gated community. The line was busy. I gave the phone back and told them the number, and when they finally got through to my mother she was apparently too hysterical to talk. They managed to extract from her the number to my father's medical school office. When he called back I could see the emergency room doctor gesturing in frustration behind a glass partition before they finally handed me the phone.

There was impatient silence at the other end of the line.

"They tell me I have diabetes, Dad." I said. "I don't know how this happened, but I'm okay now. Tell Mom not to worry." I could hear him breathing laboriously until the line went dead, then crackled. "No Raul, you don't have diabetes. That's not possible. You don't know what you're talking about," he said. His brusque tone turned tender. "You're going to be fine, son. We'll take care of this. Now put that idiot doctor back on the line."

He was going to use sheer determination and willpower to change the diagnosis. Then everything would be fine. It was the only way he knew how to love me.

As soon as my oldest brother learned of my calamity he phoned, asking if there was anything he could do. He was ready to miss work and jump on a shuttle from Los Angeles. I told him I'd be okay. My other brother, a medical student, called later. "Don't worry Ralo," he said. "It's not life threatening. It's chronic. You just have to give yourself shots and you'll be all right."

My mother recovered her senses that evening and booked the next flight to San Francisco. I begged her not to come, told her I was in good hands and didn't need help, but I could see that she needed to be needed. I was irritated at first and didn't understand her. I thought, unkindly, that she saw this as her moment on the stage, a rare chance to come to the rescue of her helpless child. Dramatic sequences such as this are hard-wired in the brains of all mothers, bundled up with the involuntary command to feed and protect offspring. Now that I'm a father I fully understand. But sometimes my mother took the drama to the point of absurdity. Her greatest show of this heroic urge came twenty years later when she obtained a Chinese tourist visa and a plane ticket to Beijing in preparation for her rescue operation. She was ready to swoop in and save her son the foreign correspondent from mayhem when I was reporting on the Tiananmen student uprising, having been all worked up watching live coverage of the tragedy on CNN.

She didn't need a visa for Modesto. When she arrived that morning she neglected to pick up my girlfriend on her way from the airport to Modesto, an act that was insulting to me but not surprising. She wouldn't have wanted to share the stage. Yet I was also somewhat relieved at the slight, because she'd have humiliated Satomi with condescension, further poisoning what was left of our fragile relationship. I'd had enough ketoacidosis already.

To her credit, her hysterical impulse did involve bravery: She was an inexperienced traveler and this was the first time in her life she'd gotten on a plane by herself. She depended on her worldly husband to take charge, so this was a moment of true liberation and empowerment for her. In her burst of adrenaline she rented a car, drove ninety miles and found the hospital. I can only imagine how frightened she was. My illness presented an opportunity and a turning point for her as well as me.

She turned out to be very helpful, despite my wariness that she'd be a burden, not a care-giver. She drove me in her rental car to my broken-down VW bus, left where Diderot had abandoned it in disgust about a mile away from the hospital when he couldn't get the carburetor working. We knew where to find it because the ill-tempered Frenchman stopped by the hospital to drop off the keys and a rough map at the admissions desk without taking the trouble to visit my room.

I drove home praying the carburetor wouldn't act up. It was 1980. "Whip It," "Hungry Heart," and "Another Brick In the Wall" played on the radio. My mother trailed in her rental car and followed my hand signals when I pulled over to a roadside fruit stand. I bought a crate of perfect peaches and put it in the bus, keeping two of them to wash. We found shade under a walnut tree and ate the fruit together in silence. It was one of the very few times I can remember when she didn't feel the need to the fill the empty spaces of a conversation. She was just there, sitting under a tree with me. We didn't need to say anything at all. It was probably the greatest expression of love she's ever given me in my adult life. Just sitting there, off stage, eating a peach.

She looked on, curious, scared and uncomprehending when I took my first shot of insulin in the real world outside of the hospital. Two units ought to do for one peach, I guessed, starting out on my new journey. From that point on I would be defined in terms of ill health by anyone who knew me well. But I learned how to hide illness, to defy illness, and to use it as a vault that took me to places I didn't even know existed.

I never knew how Diderot got back to San Francisco, whether he took a Greyhound Bus or hitchhiked. We met only once after that, when he demanded the plastic travel mug and a pair of dirty woolen socks he'd left behind in the back of the offending vehicle. I tried to apologize and express my appreciation for his help. And when I explained that I honestly did not know I had diabetes when we started the backpacking trip, he scoffed in disbelief. The Frenchman who saved my life was far more than irritated with me now, he reviled me.

Before leaving the hospital I asked the nurses about the horseman from Yosemite, was he going to be all right? They shook their heads slightly with sadness in their eyes and tried their best to put on their professional nurse faces. I asked what had happened. They shook their heads again and made themselves busy.

Twenty

The coroner was intrigued by the title of the next notebook in his hands. "The Salty Lagoon."

What was this, he thought. A primordial swamp, another bog of memory? A veil of salty damp wind when he plummeted from the rails of the bridge? Some of Barlow's notebooks were markedly older than the others, cardboard covers smeared and bent, paper thin and wrinkled with time, the wire-coil binding on the steno pads twisted out of their holes. This one stood out from the rest, but not for its age. It was sea-weathered and sandy and distinguished by the boldness of the words tattooed on its cover. There was a single, short entry. The rest of the pages were blank.

———

The Salty Lagoon

I know the date and the evening hour of her conception and I honor the place where the lovemaking began, this pristine beach with the magical lagoon. I returned today to see it in its full noontime glory. It's already been ten months since I met the girl for the first time and confirmed my paternity with a single glance in her eyes.

I see her mother and me in a mirror of sand, an image perfectly preserved in time. But when I walked away toward the little wooden bridge to the trail and back to my car, I stopped to look over my shoulder to see my footprints fill with sand and vanish.

It's a simple story. We went on an outing with friends to this place in the Point Reyes National Seashore, taking the mile hike from the road to the beach. It was a scorching hot Saturday afternoon in late August and the sand was so hot we dug our toes beneath the surface to find the cool moist layer underneath. The others walked away, trudging down the expansive shoreline past the massive black tidepool rocks that jutted into the beach. They disappeared from sight in the hazy veil of heat and bright sunlight. We stayed behind and after testing the frigid water's edge retreated to the lagoon, where we settled behind a low dune and gazed at each other through dark glasses. Wordlessly we watched grebes and coots skim the surface of the lagoon for their supper. For the longest time we watched the surf rise and crest in frothy white, heard it roar and felt it pound on the shore with the broken rhythm of a delirious heart. We waded in the lagoon and anointed each other in brine. We reclined next to one another on hot towels and faced a scorching sun, moved closer and kissed for the first time. We laughed about the sting of our sunburned lips as we tangled reddened arms and legs and breathed in unison as if we shared a single breath. We sat up and collapsed in a salty, sand-basted pretzel and froze that way, not knowing or caring what would happen when we returned to the city that night.

I've tried to find her since then, hoping to learn whether the seeds were from me or the other man in her mother's life. I've been back to Abbott's Lagoon many times in the past twenty-seven years and always wondered who she might be, always feeling a blue tinge of confusion and guilt, grief and sorrow. But I've met her now and know she's real. I'm trying to find the right words to tell her this: Despite all the hardships and loneliness she must have endured she was born from sacred love, fleeting but pure. Yet we don't need any words, do we? It's enough just to know.

———

Barlow is quite capable of purple prose, among his other talents, the coroner thought. I suppose this is why we all need editors, but even the best editor cannot change fate. Most diarists who write for other eyes are liars and confidence tricksters, but some can be unstintingly loyal to the truth while they are lying. Where did Barlow's craft reside?

After thinking it over, he believed in the Salty Lagoon. Barlow spoke from his heart in this passage, better for the lack of an editor.

He decided he should go for a walk. He worried that the amount of whiskey he had been borrowing from Barlow's kitchen counter, however modest, threatened to cloud not clarify his mind. Fresh air would invigorate him. He suddenly craved tobacco, which was ridiculous and mystifying because he had not smoked a cigarette in thirty years, and he coughed and gagged when someone nearby lit up. Now, however, he remembered the forbidden taste, the nicotine rush, the vapors that wafted up, stinging the sinuses, emitting a sweet bitter aroma on their way through the nose. He missed the scent of saltpeter when he struck the match, the convenience of having something to do with his hands when he would otherwise fidget, the ritual totem of being lost in thought. The diagnosis of oral fixation was far too simplistic. It was the pleasure of toxicity, of tiny sips of suicide. Reading Barlow made him want a cigarette. Perhaps it would cure his headache.

He did not know why but he thought it would be a good idea to check the voicemail on his home phone before he left, despite the desire to remain sequestered and avoid any distraction that might impinge on his work. He turned the dial on Barlow's Bakelite rotary phone with his thumb and heard his outgoing message: "Leo here. I am not available and please do not call my cell phone if it isn't urgent. You can leave a message and I might get back to you. Call my office if you are dead and wish to schedule an appointment."

There were five new messages, three from Wilson asking where he was and why he was not answering his cell phone. The thing must have turned itself off when its battery got too low, he realized. He decided to leave it as it was. Another message was from his sister-in-law, his self-appointed guardian angel who for the third time this week scolded him for not enrolling in a detox program as Alice would have wanted him to do. The other was from Jake, his long-time friend, a plumber and a member of his small scraggly cadre of drinking mates. Jake had wanted to go out for a few shots at Specs' Saturday night. The coroner tried to delete the messages by dialing seven but the analogue pulse was too slow. It was a day too late to return Jake's call even if he wanted to take a break from his labors, but the idea of making a quick visit to a local pub was very appealing. Perhaps he would violate the taboo on tobacco while he was at it.

Walking downhill can be more difficult than going up, he remembered as he descended past the death scene to Twenty-fourth Street. The tug of gravity made him feel unsteady and the torn lateral meniscus he tolerated for three decades without surgery jabbed his left knee in contempt. Perhaps Barlow was on his way to the all-night supermarket down the street, where he could buy ingredients for the breakfast he planned to serve his visitor in the morning. What would he have purchased with the $33.49 wadded up in his pocket? Milk, eggs, bacon and Jarlsberg cheese for the omelets? English muffins? How sophisticated were Barlow's tastes, he wondered.

In the daytime Noe Valley was unremarkable, a small neighborhood commercial strip yawning with 1950s mediocrity, but in recent years it had been updated with a modest nod to contemporary retail chic, which made it all the more mediocre. It closed its shutters early on a Sunday evening. After dark its nature changed, however, with a hollowness of shadow and gray that was a negative filmstrip of the innocence of daylight. This would be the perfect street, he thought, on which to have your throat slit. Nary a soul would be around to witness the act.

At the intersection the windows of the shuttered liquor store on the corner glowed in amber light. The bar to his left, which identified itself as Dubliners, emitted a faint clinking of glasses and muffled laughter. "A rude imposter," he said under his breath, teeth clenched. "The genuine Irish bar on this street is Finnegan's Wake."

The windows of the bakery and the breakfast joint across the street, and the *shibui* boutiques and gift shops down the block to the west were all dark. He walked toward the lights of Bell Market and wondered if the grocery store was open twenty-four hours to sell Barlow the ingredients of his ill-fated breakfast. Noe Valley was a district of three-quarter sized Victorian homes built for the Irish working class at the beginning of the last century, now housing a predominately white upper-caste of stroller-pushing young professionals who could afford to buy homes here during the dot-com real estate boom.

The coroner continued west looking for evidence of nocturnal street life. He was shocked to see that Finnegan's Wake, the raucous pub he frequented in his youth, had vanished from the spot. Dubliners would have to do, a pale substitute that lacked the cigar smoke and drunken poets. He turned back in an easterly direction, and when he stepped off the curb at Noe Street a late model Plymouth came whipping down the hill with bright lights glaring and screeched to a halt, its front bumper two inches from the coroner's bad knee, and the driver laid on the horn. "Asshole!" the driver screamed. "Get the fuck out of the street when a car's coming! You're going to get your sorry ass killed!"

The coroner froze on the spot, heart racing and legs shaking. He thought of various ripostes he might use to address the motorist, such as "There's a stop sign here, you moron" or "I got the fucking right of way in the crosswalk," punctuated by a display of his middle finger, but his mouth would not open and he scuttled across the street like a frightened beetle. At that point he noticed a vaguely familiar shape watching him furtively from down the block, possibly alerted by the screech and the shouting. The shadow wore a flat cap, the sort favored by the British working class, and it paused before sidestepping into the Bell Market parking lot. A hack job of surveillance if I ever saw one, he thought, before shrugging off the spook as a figment of his jagged nervous system.

He found a stool and sipped on a double shot of Locke's Single Malt, nearly spilling the whiskey with his shaking right hand, mindful of an attractive young woman sitting by herself at a table across the room. She was dressed in white and reminded him vaguely of the sobbing woman he saw when he first climbed the hill to Barlow's the night before. He felt shame because he let that woman run off, obviously disconsolate and in need of comfort, while he did not possess the conviction to intervene. The woman in the bar glanced at him but he could tell she wanted to be left alone by the way she quickly cast her eyes downward, by the way she hunched her shoulders and crossed her arms in a posture of defense. She did not appear to be a prostitute because she was wearing running shoes instead of stiletto heels. She was not waiting, she was not going anywhere. She was planted in melancholy discontent with her body saying, "Don't touch." The girl would not have lasted five minutes without being charmed by one of the lads at Finnegan's Wake, he mused. He left a generous tip for the Chinese bartender and abandoned the hum of barely audible conversation in the bar.

On his way up the hill he thought about his lost car, gritting his teeth. He wondered whether he had been careless enough to park near the death scene without regard to blocking driveways, red curbs and fire hydrants, which he usually ignored on official business. He walked two long blocks up the hill, rather briskly for a man in his condition, and saw to his dismay that his car was nowhere in sight. Probably towed away. Tracking it down and retrieving the vehicle from the yard would have to wait until morning. He walked slowly, stopping frequently to catch his breath, up and over the crest of the hill to Liberty Street.

Twenty-One

The light was off in the kitchen when he reentered the bungalow, and after struggling with the various switches by the door he looked down at his watch. It was quarter after nine, time to get back to work. His eyes were dry and tired after straining to read Barlow's handwriting, so he decided to inspect the premises. There was the filing cabinet that indubitably would offer up bank records, utility bills, insurance policies and all the paper minutiae of a person's life. Someone would have to go through that before he was finished with his inquest, but it did not seem urgent. Wilson could do this, and plumb the man's public record, in the morning while he was leisurely eating breakfast.

He was more interested in the corpse's personal record. His house had the stale ambience of a bachelor hermit, without a trace of a woman's scent in its crevices. He took a look at the bedrooms. One was crammed with dusty old furniture and cardboard boxes, giving the impression Barlow moved in hurriedly years earlier but never finished unpacking.

The master bedroom, if that is what you could call it, was masculine in its disorder, piles of clothing in a corner chair, a dresser top cluttered with magazines, rubber bands, coins and dirty coffee cups. The bed was unmade. Winding blue sheets and a clipboard on top that on further inspection held a sheath of crossword puzzles from the back page of the Chronicle's Datebook section. None of them was completed. He did his crosswords in pen, and the puzzles were a mess of smudged ink, scratch outs and overwriting, perhaps a testament to a struggle with lost words. A sparse collection of clothes hung on the pole in the closet: Six shirts, four pairs of pants, a tan poplin suit, and one Jerry Garcia tie, light blue with a touch of gray. A new pair of Levi jeans hung on a hook, button fly 501s, size 32/30. It was the wardrobe of someone who had few occasions to wear formal clothing, or possibly a small portion of a larger wardrobe from a previous life stored away in boxes in the other bedroom or donated to the Salvation Army. If a woman had visited this room in recent history she left no ponytail bands on the floor, no lipstick on the coffee mugs, no strands of hair on the bed. What would Christina's scent be?

The main room, dusty as it was, showed evidence of a hasty attempt to tidy up. The open cardboard boxes with papers spilling over the rims were arranged in a clean line, the afghan blanket on the couch was folded and smoothed out. A broom and dustpan hid in a corner. Perhaps he planned to return and make his bedroom respectable before she arrived. He could not have been so clueless about women as to leave his bedroom in such a sorry state of disarray while he waited for a lost love to ring his doorbell. Maybe he was on his way to the supermarket to shop for cleaning supplies as well as food.

"Another notebook," he announced to all who would listen in Barlow's bungalow, the termites chewing in the timbers, the spiders weaving their webs, the mice tap-dancing in the attic.

—

Raul the House Wrecker

I never regretted going on a rampage that afternoon. It was inevitable, and I'm glad I got it done sooner rather than later when the consequences might have been more serious. All I did was destroy my own bedroom. I felt better afterwards.

I was flat broke and not ready to get back behind the wheel of a cab just yet, maybe never. My parents sent me a check for $230 – the price of a month's rent – to tide me over, and I was too proud to ask them for more. I applied for food stamps and was waiting for them to come in the mail. I needed to see doctors, but the stickers on my Medi-Cal benefits sheet ran out and I wasn't qualified for another month because I still owned a motor vehicle. There was no dispensation for broken carburetors. Medi-Cal coverage was a fluke in the first place – somehow I qualified when I went to get my fifth wisdom tooth extracted by students at the Pacific Dental School. I was under the false impression their services would be free but they told me I had to apply for the program. I don't recall why, but the city's social service agency determined I was an indigent cab driver before changing its mind the next month. I used up the rest of my stickers for the co-pay at the hospital in Modesto.

Earlier in the day I had a scary moment driving down hill on San Jose Avenue on my way to Dolores Street when my brakes failed. I thumped on the pedal but my wretched 1962 VW bus kept gliding down hill toward a red light and I could see the panorama of impending doom through the wide windshield that Volkswagen designed without the protection of a dashboard so the driver and front-seat passenger could catapult through broken glass in a collision. I was thinking about this when my survival instincts took over and told me to cut a sharp left turn, thread through horn-blasting traffic in the intersection and careen uphill on a side street, where the vehicle came to rest with a jerk of the hand brake and a slide backwards into the curb. My heart was racing and my hands were shaking so badly I had to lie back in the seat and breathe deeply until I could open the door. It turned out the brake fluid had completely leaked out of the reservoir.

I knew from my hare-brained trip to the Sierras that anything can happen. I had auto insurance but no health insurance to protect myself from the next disaster. My quick reaction time and stunt man taxi driving skills saved me this time, but the hubris of invincibility, already in tatters, was frightened out of my system. I only had seven more cat lives left.

I had a can of brake fluid in the back of the bus, and after I cautiously and timidly drove home I went right to the Yellow Pages and flipped to the section on health insurance. I circled the ones that looked promising and began dialing. I got lucky on the first try because

I reached a very nice woman who tried to be helpful, but her message was not reassuring: Blue Cross can't cover you because you are an individual with a "disqualifying pre-existing condition." The curse of diabetes began.

She thought I might have better luck with other companies, but it was the same message from each provider in the phone book. The voices on the other end of the line were different, ranging from impatient to insolent to practically scornful, but the message was the same. They scoffed when I asked questions, and I could hear them getting ready to hang up soon as they heard me say the dirty word "diabetes."

I had no idea this was the way the world worked, that if you don't already have a health insurance policy you couldn't get covered unless you're in perfect health. Get into a group policy, some of them said, get a job.

Then the frustration and the rage took over. I watched myself helplessly as I ripped the telephone out of its socket and hurled it against the wall. I bellowed at the top of my lungs as I set about systematically wrecking everything within reach. I hoisted my plywood desk into the air with supernatural strength and crashed it upside down on the hardwood floor, I smashed my gooseneck lamp on the bedpost, and I heaved my typewriter at a shelf, sending books flying across the room. When it was over I sat down cross-legged, with dread burning in my stomach, and stared into space for an hour, ignoring my roommates' voices and their tenuous knocking on the door. I must have terrified Satomi because I heard her calling me plaintively from the corridor, "Raruuru! Raruuru! Daijobu ka?" Robin broke the lock and yanked open the door, barging in with a pint of Jim Beam and two shot glasses in his hand. Robin's one of my oldest and best friends. He knew what to do.

"Time for a snort," he said. "Once you cool down we're going to North Beach, you and me, get some Italian food and cheap Chianti at the US Restaurant and stop off at Specs. You're a real mess, man. You're practically foaming at the mouth."

When I was a young child I threw tantrums when I was very frustrated, and occasionally threw things around. In recognition of my temperament, and amusement of it, my father gave me a pint-sized carpenter's apron with a loop for the hammer and pockets for nails. The lettering on the front of the apron said: "Raul the House Wrecker."

The immediate solution to healthcare was to volunteer for a clinical trial on diabetic alcohol tolerance at UCSF Medical Center in exchange for consultations by a prominent endocrinologist and his residents. Then I hatched the plan that launched my career. I'd go back to school, because universities offer healthcare to students. I'd study journalism, then find a job as a reporter, because newspaper companies provide group health insurance to employees, and writing was about the only thing I could think of to make a living at the time. I couldn't imagine myself working in an office. I thought I'd try journalism for a few years to get stable, then figure out what I really wanted to do in the future. Someday I'd get a real job.

———

Barlow got stuck, the coroner mused, but eventually landed a job he was born to do.

Now, another notebook, another story. He could not stop himself, and since he was inspired by the bourbon that rescued Raul the House Wrecker he'd help himself to another shot from the bottle on the kitchen counter. He opened the new journal and saw it was dated ten years after the previous story. He would have to find out later what happened in the intervening years.

———

Yamato

Falling and picking myself up off the ground and falling once more, only to claw my way back onto my feet again. That pattern defines my life. I learned how to trip and fall and roll to break the impact and rise smoothly to a fighting stance when I practiced martial arts, giving me a certain amount of dignity under duress. Sometimes I trip over a curb or miss a step on a staircase and when I hit the ground I spring back to my feet, then raise my hands and say *tada!* It's a circus trick that calms onlookers before they get a chance to say, "Oh my God, are you okay?" I do it all the time, I tell people, this is what I am.

Before being afflicted with brain cancer there were signs portending disaster, but I didn't recognize them at the time. Over a period of about six to eight months I became increasingly stressed and dispirited. I gained a considerable amount of weight, as though my metabolism was preparing for a long winter of scarcity. I started drinking too much, far out of proportion to the rituals of intoxication demanded by my Japanese friend, acquaintances and news sources. I had headaches, searing headaches. I had trouble concentrating and I was developing tongue-tied writer's block. I thought this was very peculiar for someone trained as a wire service reporter. The gears in my mind were slowing down, my interest in my work and the world around me was flagging. I thought I was getting depressed about having lived in Japan too long, nearly ten years if you combined my time as a student and as a correspondent. There was a ready name for this condition: "Japan burnout." That was my self-diagnosis, and the only cure was to leave the best job I would ever have in my life, to bail out of Japan, the land of the rising stress.

I pleaded to my foreign editor and then the executive editor for a reassignment, and they agreed to send me to the Warsaw bureau, which was exactly what I was asking for, to learn about a new culture, study a new language, get a perspective on the world free from the tunnel vision I'd developed in Japan. I resigned myself to the frightening thrill of parachuting out of Poland to cover the war in Bosnia. But I was double-crossed. They decided to swap me with an ambitious reporter in Los Angeles who was agitating for my job in Tokyo. It was an undeserved fall from grace, being forced to leave a prestigious job as a foreign correspondent. Sooner or later it would have to happen, because the paper was rightly committed to rotating its staff to different posts. But being called home was premature and unfair, I thought. It turned out to be a stroke of good luck.

Most correspondents have a sudden burst of attachment when they're about to be transferred out of their countries. Clinging to what expertise they believe they've accumulated, they all want to write the so-called swan-song story, a series of lengthy articles or a magazine piece. The fortunate get time off to write books. In my time as a reporter in Japan I did my best to get under the skin of the place, exploit intimate knowledge of ordinary people I gained as a student in Kyoto years earlier and get deeper into the story, to go beyond the shallow pop sociology that is stock in trade for many correspondents. I took on the mission of debunking myths and stereotypes, and in my final shot I got a magazine assignment to write about the mother lode of civil disobedience and non-conformity in Japan. American readers had been fed for decades with the pabulum about the compliant blind conformity of the Japanese people, the faceless, robotic and inscrutable workers wearing matching coveralls, the universal *sarariman* office workers in dark business suits. These weren't the Japanese I cared much about because they represented only the surface of a complex society.

So I planned to write about the other side of the cultural ethos: Sympathy for the underdog. Most Japanese I knew intimately have a repressed urge to rebel and dissent and sabotage the crushing complacency of group harmony. The most popular song for intoxicated middle-aged men at *karaoke* bars in Japan is Sinatra's "I Did it My Way," revealing the fantasy of what they might have done.

I picked out a cast of remarkable Japanese to profile who had the courage to go against the grain – to be the nail that sticks up and refuses to be hammered down. A human rights lawyer who petitioned for the legal right of married women to use their maiden names, an eminent historian who battled the hide-bound Ministry of Education for an accurate accounting in public textbooks of Japan's wartime military aggression, an independent gasoline station entrepreneur who challenged the fuel distribution monopoly that was trying to put him out of business, and an ultra-nationalist who was able to calmly articulate right-wing views without screaming into a megaphone from a sound truck bedecked with the usual wartime flags and blaring the national anthem.

All were underdogs, heroes in their own right.

One of the experts I sought out for guidance was Yamato Heihachiro, a respected scholar of Japanese intellectual history. I arranged an interview. Here's what happened:

His office, an expansive room at the Tokyo Metropolitan Library, had an odd combination of a pre-war Western aesthetic with dark oak panels and shelving that stood in contrast to a contemporary, pragmatic look with gray steel stacks of shelves in the middle of the room, the kind you see in a middling government bureaucrat's office, cluttered with reports, loose magazines, journals and books in Japanese, English and German. His desk was very large, made of teak, and the items on top were neatly arranged, suggesting a clear and organized mind. Yamato was a husky, graying and sober-faced man whose eyebrows were brooding and quizzical. He moved slowly and deliberately when he greeted me, gesturing for me to sit down. It was a standard set of office furniture, a couch and two armchairs covered in pedestrian black vinyl and arranged around a low coffee table. It struck me as very unusual that he had me sit in one of the chairs facing the door while he sat on the couch with his back to the door in a reverse of traditional seating protocol. Ordinarily the host or superior person sits furthest from the door and the visitor or subordinate sits closest. I always found in countless interviews that the couch, which invariably has its back to the door, offers a disadvantageous seat because it's far more difficult to rise from a couch than an armchair when the meeting is over, allowing the person in the seat of honor to look down on the other at the close of the ritual. Arcane details like this truly matter in Japan, where everyone has his place in the pecking order, but it was my impression that Yamato was beyond caring about it.

He was fluent in English but encouraged me to conduct the interview in Japanese, which meant I had to interpret his words instantaneously as I took notes. This was usually not a problem but when the subject matter was complicated and the vocabulary more specialized I had to concentrate hard and strain to keep up. I had an epiphany of sorts when Yamato explained the obstreperous role of Marxism in post-war academia as one of the few channels for social and political dissent. A bright light went on in my head. Of course! More moderate institutions of civil society had been crushed by the militarists and their civilian successors in power, he went on to say, and the Marxists emerged from prison as the best game in town. My brain was ticking furiously to catch every nuance in Yamato's words and interpret their meaning into English, and my hand was working furiously to get as much of it as I could into a pocket-sized notebook.

Suddenly something strange happened.

In my excitement I was scrambling to write down his answers as I was asking the next question and racing forward in my mind to think of the questions I had to ask after this and how I would say them in Japanese when I noticed my fingers were twitching and splaying and the pen was slipping out of my hand. I heard the pitch of my voice rise and come out in a slur as I searched frantically for the next word. I looked down at my little notebook and saw my handwriting had deteriorated into scribbles and stray lines and ink blotches where I had shoved the pen into paper. In desperation I reached over with my left hand and gripped my wrist to steady the pen. A haze of confusion enveloped my mind as I struggled with my hand and started shaking, feeling my entire arm go numb as I saw it jerk around wildly as though it was controlled by a mad puppeteer. I tried to speak but my tongue was paralyzed. My body was gloved in numbness and I heard the banging of a chair as I slipped to the hard wooden floor. I heard a shout and scurrying shoes and cries of alarm before I blacked out.

———

Memory is, by nature, selective and unreliable, the coroner thought as he set the notebook down and rubbed his burning tired eyes. It is suppressed when it is unpleasant and goosed up in high drama to disguise mundane events. It invokes itself in terms of what it wants to be remembered for and forgets itself for what it wants to hide. It fabricates elaborate stories out of whole cloth.

This particular passage was too copious in detail to be invented, the coroner judged. It rang true. A moment of heightened consciousness in a crisis can etch itself in indelible memory, and he believed every one of Barlow's words. Certain episodes in the coroner's own life had recalled themselves back to laser-lit clarity so intense he knew them to be accurately seared into his hippocampus. The lucid recollection of the seizure in Yamato's office seemed suspended in time and space for Barlow.

Twenty-Two

The coroner was getting sleepy, nodding off while he turned the pages. He slapped his face and resumed his reading.

—

The Bureaucrat's Altar

A brain tumor can ruin your plans.

Our wedding was scheduled for eight days after the seizure in Yamato's office, and it was supposed to be a small and low-key affair with family and a few friends in a small Congregational church in Hanalei on the north coast of Kauai. Invitations went out on mottled beige *washi* paper to family and close friends, those who could afford the cost and time to attend replied yes. We booked rooms at a resort where we planned the reception. It was going to be a beautiful celebration of a romance sparked by love letters between Tokyo and Seoul, where she was assigned, and later, when we lived together in Tokyo, restored by the two kittens I brought home for her as a peace offering after a knock-down drag-out fight.

The seizure left us shell shocked. We cancelled the wedding.

But before we boarded a plane for Chicago to get the kind of thorough diagnosis and a level of treatment we doubted was available in Japan, she did a remarkable thing. Nobody knew my chances of surviving the menacing lump they found in my brain after I was carted out of Yamato's office. I was doing my best to affect stoic calm. I bought a book titled *Essentials of Neurosurgery* and studied all the grim possibilities, searching for the name of the tumor that killed George Gershwin and I found it. The effect was short and sweet. A diagnosis of cancer can be as embarrassing as it is frightening, and I hated the thought that people would gush with sympathy when they knew. The first instinct is to be guarded, closed, selfish.

Getting married under these circumstances was the last thing on my mind when she dragged me to the U.S. Embassy and then to the Minato Ward office for the official paperwork. The diplomat who handled the case so tenderly from behind a bulletproof Plexiglas window was a friend of mine who'd recently survived a massive brain hemorrhage. The bloodless Japanese bureaucrat who put the chop on our marriage certificate without the hint of a smile was a total stranger and he wanted to stay that way. You could say my new bride was a hero. Fifteen years later at the end of our troubled marriage, bad things happened that are too toxic and hurtful to write about. But our hasty civil marriage was her finest hour.

—

The Garden

Kato's garden looked like this: From the living room window you see past a screen of spindly bamboo and the trunks of redwood and cypress trees to a pond banked by myrtle and azalea shrubs, and beyond that to the old *azumaya*, an open-air tea shelter, shaded by a huge live oak.

From the tea shelter, where I would sit in meditation, you can see the four stone-encrusted ponds spanned by little concrete bridges, one of them designed in a zigzag pattern to evade demons in hot pursuit. To the north, a snow lantern stands on an island in the main pond next to a large rock that juts out of the water in a shape suggesting a tortoise, auspicious for its longevity. This pond and its waterfall are guarded by sculptured pines and flanked by a hillock studded with irises and sago palms. A curtain of yew trees backs this tiny universe, and above their tops the San Gabriel Mountains serve as borrowed scenery, framing the upper limits of the garden.

She and I acquired the property on an impulse, instantly seduced by the overgrown and unkempt garden behind the modest bungalow. At first glance, the sorcery of the landscape is moody, contemplative, confusing, but in time it became so familiar I didn't know where my mind left off and the garden began. My home was a Japanese garden with a small house attached. I wouldn't learn for another five years that my brain cancer was statistically cured and in all probability would never come back.

To say the garden was therapeutic misses the point. It was Elmer's glue, keeping me tacked together like pasta shells stuck on construction paper by a four-year-old, until stronger and more permanent bonding made me whole again and I could walk away, no longer needing the garden.

My favorite uncle attempted suicide when I was in college. He gobbled down a handful of sleeping pills, got into his car and drove at a high rate of speed directly into a tree. Uncle Fred summed things up for me when I met him several years later. "Dying is easy, Raul," he said. "It's surviving that's hell."

I'm certifiably alive and I plan to age gracefully with equal parts of joy and sorrow. Life is tantalizing, mysterious, seductive and cruel. It flickered softly in Kato's Garden during my convalescence, and its force has proven to be more resilient than I ever imagined, but a survivor knows that life is fleeting. We don't own our molecules; we just rent them, the same as I never owned Kato's Garden. We were temporary custodians.

The previous owner and the real estate lady who sold us the house related a tale about the origins of the garden in our back yard. They said a master Japanese landscaper who was formerly employed by Imperial Gardens in Tokyo designed it and built it shortly after the turn of the nineteenth century for an eccentric heiress who owned the property as part of a larger estate.

Mr. Kato supposedly signed his work in the concrete at the bottom of the retaining pond that fed the stream. I drained the pond and scraped the putrid muck off the bottom to find the word KATO and the date 1916 scratched faintly into the concrete alongside two mysterious sets of initials, THG and EGO. Anybody could have written that, and the story teetered between credible and apocryphal when I did extensive research on its provenance to unravel part of the puzzle for a magazine article about the garden. I never learned Kato's full name and never found conclusive evidence that he even existed, but, real or imagined, he haunted the enchanted garden. Our nanny said she saw him out there in the dusk several times. I had no reason to disbelieve her, and in time I thought I saw him too, brooding among the pines like a hungry ghost.

―――

Read on, read on, he told himself. The man was trapped, no, he had trapped himself in his illness, and was doing whatever he could to exorcize the beast. Despite his sanguine testimonial, Barlow has not bared the depths of insecurity and self-blame that swim beneath the surface of his words and lurk in Kato's garden.

This is the problem with human beings, the coroner thought. They all suffer, and they allow themselves to dwell on their suffering by seeking mercy in the wrong places, where mercy is transitory at best, where the illusion of personal mercy strips them of the ability to understand the suffering of all humanity. He knew this because he dwelled in a basement morgue and examined the tissue of untold thousands of hungry ghosts. He considered himself an expert on the matter, and when he gesticulated in playful emphasis and appreciation of his own insights he knocked a tumbler of Barlow's whiskey to the floor. "You idiot," the coroner hissed at himself. "You're an oaf!" *Hush . . . stop saying that . . .*

He resumed.

―――

Beethoven

I rediscovered on a backpacking trip with my brother what I suspected all my life: The world is not set in stone; it flows like lava. When I studied history in school I had a very hard time remembering the names and dates of great men and battles but I understood the patterns that rose and fell, created and destroyed, built incredible monuments to glory only to annihilate them in the carnage of war. That's what history is, as far as I'm concerned. Waves of information, not a linear narrative of places, names and dates. Today they would diagnose this as a learning disability.

We were hiking in Kings Canyon National Park, seeing how far we'd get into the high Sierras, when I lagged behind my brother, a serious outdoorsman. Suddenly I heard my voice telling myself that I had to take longer strides. I made better progress up the trail thinking this, repeating it in my mind. I need to take longer strides. But when my thoughts strayed to other images and ideas I abandoned the insight, forgetting to stretch my legs and throw my front boot forward up the trail. Then I remembered to concentrate on my gait, kicking my legs forward until I was a few paces behind him. I need to take longer strides, I thought to myself.

At that exact moment my brother stopped and turned around to face me.

"You need to take longer strides," he said.

I realized this strange sort of pseudo-telepathy between my brother and me had been going on for a long time before I understood it. It wasn't always pleasant, but as time passed we took it for granted as one of life's amazing things. We've gone for long periods of time without seeing or talking to one another, but that's never seemed to matter. He went to medical school, I went to Asia, and it was the same. He became a doctor, and his tremendous gift of empathy makes him beloved by his patients, like his father but without the pent-up fury.

We share an uncanny awareness that 9:15 is the time that occurs most often in the day. I call him or he calls me once in a while on a random basis and more often than not I look at my watch and it's 9:15 p.m.

The most incredible story is the time I parked my car in front of my apartment building and paused a minute before getting out to listen to the crescendo of Beethoven's 5th sympathy playing on the car radio. I'd had a terrible night driving and barely made my gates and gas before the shift was done. I was exhausted and broke when I limped up the front stoop and fished a post card out of the mail box that was addressed to me. There was only one line on the card: "Da da da DAH! – Beethoven." It was from my brother.

My oldest brother couldn't be more different. He's one of the smartest people I've ever known and he is a totally rational creature, so smart he's intimidating and so eccentric in his ways he can be baffling, amusing and maddening. He built primitive computers when he was a teen and became an IT geek in the early 1970s, well before the rest of us could imagine how the micro-processing revolution would change our lives. He was an unbearable know-it-all when we were growing up, but in fact he did know it all, or most of it, because he was and still is a sponge for information. But he spent years wandering through life, unable to hold onto jobs, until he finally found his calling as a hard-nosed public defender. I envy him for that. Despite all his troubles he's remained constant in his loyalty to his family. He's the first to call when I'm in trouble, honest in his concern. Our mother used to tell me I'm a combination of my two brothers. She intended it as flattery but it always made me angry for some reason, maybe because it left open the questions of whether I could ever live up to that standard and who I was in my own right.

—

So we have brothers, do we? The coroner wondered if the first brother knew through intuition or clairvoyance Barlow's state of mind before he absquatulated. Did the other call him on the phone now and notice anything wrong? Could the brothers conjecture how Barlow felt in anticipation of Christina's arrival, if indeed they knew who she was? Did they know whether their brother was dejected, elated, confused or calm on the thirty-first of October? Both evidently had unusual gifts, whoever and wherever they were. Good traits to combine in a single journalist, assuming the journalist with his learning disabilities knew how to take advantage of them. He wondered if the brothers drank the same Tennessee whiskey.

He sat back in the creaking oak chair and touched the space bar, rousing the machine from sleep. The same screen popped up and taunted him, demanding a password again. Had he tried her name before? Misspelled it? Character by character he pecked out Christina. Nothing. Then for the first time he noticed an icon hidden in the lower left corner of the screen. How could he have missed this? Was it there before but unnoticed because the other two icons claimed his full attention? Did it pop up on its own by magic? It called itself Narcmoo alias. "Curiouser and curiouser," he said aloud. He punched it with the cursor.

The screen came to life with a seductive black page that was crisscrossed by lines of white Verdana font and dotted with photographs of a beautiful woman in various scenes and poses. It was one of those web logs he always found to be more annoying than informative, personal diaries, outrageous scandal sheets, online space for intellectually bankrupt newspaper columnists, and soap boxes for unintelligible citizen-journalists.

A bold title read: NARCISSISTIC CHAMELEON MOO.

At the top right corner of the page the sultry face of a black-haired woman with penetrating green eyes looked directly at him. She could have been anywhere between her mid-to -late thirties judging by the knowing furrow in her brow. Under the photo was the name he hoped to find: Christina.

"Bingo!" the coroner exclaimed. In the profile box she wrote a self-introduction: "I'm a jobless geneticist, a lost genome mapper. I've used a lot of IT in my work but I'm a complete idiot when it comes to blogs and social networking, so please indulge me while I figure this out."

The top, most recent entry made him sit up straight.

Thursday, October 31, 2003
Found You!

Oh my God! Call me Raul. I am out of my mind . . . you're alive! The private investigator just phoned me and said he'd found you in San Francisco living alone in the Mission District and I'm so relieved, my worst fears haven't come true. You survived all those terrible diseases and your awful marriage. I don't care whether you want to see me ever again, but that doesn't matter. When I told you to go away and leave me alone I hated you and resolved to forget you forever because you were so self-centered and hopelessly locked into your other life but I don't know why, all the while I wanted to see you anyway to try again. I wanted to see you against my own dignity and self-interests. I don't want to intrude on your messy personal life because I'm not a stalker, I am the one who made you go away, and when I thought about it I hated you all over again. When I tried to find you everything I knew about you was gone, your phone number didn't work, my emails bounced back, your letters came back marked undeliverable. I called your bureau and the guy said you quit and didn't leave a forwarding address. It was like you were lost at sea and on land you totally disappeared from the grid. Damn you Raul, you idiot. You should have known how I really felt. Where have you been hiding for the past three years! I guess I should be happy you didn't reconcile with your wife, or move to China or Africa to start all over as a correspondent, or go out and die on me.

Shit, Raul. The investigator instructed me to wait patiently, he said he'd given you my phone number and Web address for this blog and that the first thing I needed to do is sit back and give you time to react and decide whether to call me or not. As if I was some kind of woman scorned, and planned to slice you up with a kitchen knife. Simply a precaution, he said, because you never know in my trade. I told him when I hired him the truth, that I was the one who threw you out of my life because I felt like a whore being with an older married man who was incapable of making up his mind. And then lately I regretted what I did after thinking about it for a long time so the guy took pity on me and agreed to help. I'm so embarrassed about what I wrote in this blog. If I knew how to erase it I'd make it go away so you wouldn't get the wrong impression about me. I'm not a woman possessed just feeling really bad about what happened and the way it happened, what a waste. I'm starting my life over again and if I don't find you now to tell you this it would haunt me, forever. Please try to understand, you have to understand. Don't judge me by my stupid blog, Raul, it's not what you think. It's not who I really am. I've just been coming out of a long emotional funk and the more I get my balance the more I've been thinking about you. Damn you. You probably haven't thought about me at all so please forgive me if I'm being creepy, Raul. I'm so sorry. I can't help it.

Everything is coming loose all of a sudden. I spilled my guts about this the other night when me and my friend Isabelle when we were getting roaring drunk on tequila at her apartment celebrating the acceptance of my dissertation and talking about how barren my love life has been when I was finishing the fucking research. It's not just that I didn't have time for a man, and there wasn't a lack of prospects. There were guys hitting on me at the lab and Alex was pounding at my door begging to be let back in, but I just haven't been interested. Sometimes I think I'm holding out for someone, maybe it's you. I got to find out, Raul.

Isabelle was adamant that I should hire this private eye she knew to find you. I said no, no, no but she persisted, saying I had to get you out of my system and move on. That's all I'm trying to do Raul. Then I'll leave you alone. It wasn't my idea but you must think I'm a total fool. Holy Christ what have I done? We'll just hate each other all over again.

So now this man says if I don't hear from you within 48 hours he'd stop by with a dossier of photos and information and leave the rest up to me. I'd have to put it deep in a desk drawer to ferment with so many broken fantasies. I'll know then that I made you up out of my own imagination, just as you made me up out of yours.

Call me Raul!

Posted by Christina at 7:45 PM 1 Comments

Where did this woman learn to write? They must not train geneticists in the English language anymore, the coroner thought. He could see that the bottom line of the entry indicated that someone made a comment to Christina. He had a hunch who it was. Flustered, he realized he did not know how to open blog comments and read them. He was so out of touch with this new digital world, however curious he was and how hard he tried, it did not come naturally. He must rise to the occasion now, because that comment could have triggered the chain of events leading to the accident down the hill.

After poking the cursor around the page with trembling index finger and thumb, however, he discovered that simply clicking on the place where it said "comment" opened up the message. "Damn!"

———

Raul said...

Christina, get off the phone! I've been trying to reach you for the past hour and your line is constantly busy. I got a call from a strange guy who said you were looking for me. He was cryptic. He said he couldn't identify himself because the matter was confidential but he gave me your phone number and told me to look at your blog before calling. We've got to talk. I never hated you. I never stopped loving you. I understood you did what you had to do. You can't believe how much I've been thinking about you and worrying it wasn't real, that sacred memories of our time together come from dreams. I never imagined you'd want to hear from me again. I miss you terribly. – Raul

October 31, 2003 9:15 PM

———

She loved him enough to hate him, she saved herself for him like a chaste maiden. She wanted him with all the best intentions, then she lured him down the hill and placed him in front of a speeding automobile.

Christina killed Barlow with her blog.

The coroner was anxious to read the rest of Christina's writings but the screen displayed only that one post. He tried to figure out how to open the rest of the blog but was blinded by confusion.

Then he studied the screen on Barlow's laptop to find the link to his email account. He had to make another attempt to log on so he could find the first page of Christina's email message to Barlow, the one she sent him around midnight. He needed to match it with the second page, found in the dead man's pocket. The screen was blurry and difficult to read but he recognized the little icon on a bar at the top that said B-Mail. Ah hah! When he clicked it the screen filled with a colorful page that said *Welcome to Bamboozle Mail.* The same box popped up calling for a user name and a password. Again, the coroner tried to come up with as many combinations of letters and numbers he thought Barlow might use. He gritted his teeth so hard his abscessed molar wailed in pain. He felt the temperature rise to a boil in his temples, his headache flared, his face was flushed and his hands began to tremble. When he closed his eyes he saw red. The insanity of computer rage was upon him, he recognized immediately. He had to stop before he exploded.

He hated computers with their hard cold text, brutal sophistication and haughty secrets. Rather than dash Barlow's laptop on the floor he collected himself, breathed deeply and reached into the cardboard box for relief. Barlow's truest story, he decided, was in his own sloppy handwriting.

Twenty-Three

He grabbed a thick notebook from the box, folded it and stuck it in his back pocket. His stomach was making all the noise that a stomach could make as he stepped out on the curb. He was surprised how steady he was when he practically goose-stepped down the slope like a character out of an R. Crumb comic, leaning back into the hill and exaggerating the extension of his foot and leg with every stride. He would try to find his car, and if he failed he would hail a cab on 24th Street to go home, sleep, shower, eat the eggs at the It's Tops and drive to the morgue to smite his enemies.

As he walked he felt the cool air, the autumn dampness, and smelled he scent of hidden flowers, then without warning Alice loomed in his mind like a genie uncorked, flowing out of the lamp. The memories of their nighttime strolls together returned in a wave of unbearable sadness. This was the empty pit, and what was missing was not the waning sex life or the edgy, quarrelsome humor in their love, it was simple companionship. It was times when no one felt the need to violate a gentle mood by speaking of mundane things, it was muted happiness, hushed joy: A middle-aged couple meandering across the city's jagged, hilly terrain, cold hands touching and releasing then gripping, wanting nothing more than to grow old together.

"I am the doctor of death, I am the one who escorts the bright lights of the living to their next destination," he announced to the darkened houses and midnight trees, choking out words that held themselves back from a full-throated scream. "But I was powerless when you were dying,

Karl Schoenberger

Alice my love. All I could do was hold your wasting body in my arms and refuse to let you go."

The crazed widower realized he was hallucinating when he saw a silvery sparkler rise from the rose bush to his left, streak to the sky and then vanish, leaving behind a glowing trail. His lost love was a firefly.

The coroner's hump-backed car should have been an easy target to find, but it was not parked where it was supposed to be. Perhaps it was ticketed and towed away. He would have to call his friends downtown in the morning to get that taken care of. There was not a prayer of getting a cab on the deserted street at the bottom of the hill, but he heard a Muni bus growling in the distance, coming his way. He was stranded and hungry. Mission Street was his only option at this late hour so he waited at the bus stop on the corner, watching the moon poke through the clouds in the western sky, one sliver wider than the exact half-orb it had been the night before, the waxing quarter moon. It had been cloudy when he went out for a drink earlier in the evening and now it was a little chilly, with temperatures he guessed in the low 50s Fahrenheit.

The fog was beginning to lift. Fog in Noe Valley was not the same fog that blanketed his neighborhood on Russian Hill. It was not romantic. It was not pea soup. But it was fog nonetheless, that descends from the eastern flank of Twin Peaks and creeps down Dolores Heights into the valley, chilling the air on 24th street and giving the lie to the area's reputation as a warm and sunny pocket of the city. This night's fog seemed relevant to Barlow's death, eerie and forlorn, but it wasn't something he could zip into an evidence bag. He wondered if he was losing his grip as a scientist.

Christina was apparently a scientist, despite the gushing banter in her blog. Perhaps he would get along with her if he got the chance, he thought, perhaps she was much more than a geneticist and might help solve the mysteries of the Barlow case with a woman's intuition. She was the key. He concentrated on counting out the exact change when the bus lurched forward and he fumbled, dropping a quarter on the filthy floor, picking it up then dropping it again until the weary driver waved him to the back.

154

He slipped on the hard plastic seat, and after pulling himself upright with the steel pole, he put on his thinking cap to review the information from the written record he had gathered in Barlow's apartment. I am a man of pure science, not a clown, he reminded himself, impartial and objective in my deduction and analysis of the facts. Or was it the other way around? Was he mixing up his deduction with induction on this woozy MUNI bus?

Barlow and Christina were acquainted, intimate, and had likely committed the act of coitus more than once in an extramarital relationship some three or four years ago. There had been a dispute and the two lovers separated on bad terms. Barlow had been married to an unnamed spouse. There is reason to believe both parties had been seeking each other prior to the planned encounter. In Barlow's case it would have followed his divorce or a separation from his wife; in hers a breakup with a person named Alex, gender uncertain, apparently triggered a response that returned her attention to her previous lover, leading her to take the unusual measure of hiring a private investigator to find him.

It was not clear how these circumstances related to the cause of death, but they raised the possibility of suicide. An intoxicated diabetic man, anguished over his health condition as he prepared to reunite with a much younger and nubile lover, could have consciously or unconsciously feared failure of intimacy to the point of despair. Not likely, perhaps, but it cannot be dismissed. Barlow showed few signs of serious depression in his writings, but his trained professional writer's voice could have cloaked an underlying psychological state consistent with chronic anxiety. Or so it seemed.

Then there was the possibility of murder at the hands of coked-up suburban punks.

The bus screeched to a halt at Mission and he jerked forward, banging his head on the steel pole he was gripping for stability. "Christ!" he snorted, touching the point of impact, feeling for blood. He stumbled down the steps at the exit door and fell when he hit the ground, landing on his shoulder and rolling away from the wheels to save himself from being maimed as the MUNI driver roared into the intersection to catch a yellow light. This was too much to bear, he thought, choking down the epithets in fear he was about to scream like a lunatic. He was a professional, not a foaming-at-the-mouth madman. People on the sidewalk looked away to spare him from humiliation until an elderly Hispanic woman with a painted face and a cane knelt beside him and patted him on the shoulder.

"Hey mister, are you okay? I'll call the doctor." He looked at her more closely to see she was blind. He pushed himself into a kneeling position and rose to his feet and brushed himself off. "Thank you Ma'am, you're very kind but I'm fine. Don't worry about me. I do this all the time. May I help you cross the street?" She said "no, no, no," as though she feared this clumsy stranger would walk her into a car.

He ducked into the first restaurant he could find that provided table service so he could sit and reconnoiter with his bruised body. He considered himself fortunate to land in a place that did not feature the usual grub line at the counter, and was surprised that its menu was sophisticated in its offerings. He ordered a chile relleno and chicken enchilada combination platter with black, not pinto beans and found pleasure in the sensation of Barlow's fat journal still stuck in his back pocket. When he stood to pull it out the blood rushed to his head and his rump and hip ached from his ejection from the bus. "Ouch! Ouch, ouch ouch!" *Hush...* The pain was an excuse to add a Tecate to his order.

It was a cozy place to read, reminiscent of an old-fashioned family-style Mexican restaurant, with permanently out-of-season Christmas tree lights strung on the ceiling and faded travel posters tacked to the walls depicting the pristine beaches and azure skies of Mazatlan and Cozumel. In fact it was a 24-hour dump, but a welcome relief from the ubiquitous take-out establishments with soulless Formica tables where the cashier expects a tip for reaching across the counter and handing the customer a meal in a dripping Styrofoam container.

He remembered the row of spirited down-to-earth Mexican restaurants he once frequented on 24th Street, seven or eight blocks to the east. La Palma and Café Sanchez were still in business. But on his last visit to the neighborhood to execute his grim business, he found that the finest ones, the casual ones, had shut down with the times. The Maoist bookstore that added a touch of eccentricity to the neighborhood, it too was gone. San Francisco caters only to the very rich and the very poor these days, leaving ordinary citizens like him craving for something in the middle offering reasonably priced, honestly good-tasting, genuine food.

This place may have been below his usual standards of hygiene but it was pleasingly quiet; the only other patrons were two elderly Hispanic men drinking in silence at the bar in the rear, one of them morbidly obese, with a thin trimmed moustache and a rump so large it swallowed his stool, the other sitting erect, attentive, dignified, appeared extraordinarily thin sitting next to his drinking mate. He watched the coroner surreptitiously from the corner of his eye.

The coroner spread Barlow's journal on the surface of the wooden table, which was pocked with dings and cigarette burns, oddly comforting. They have been in business for a very long time, he gathered. Perhaps this was once a great restaurant. The cone lamp overhead, cast an amber light on the pages. The room was a little too dim to read comfortably and he wished he had the reading glasses he left on Barlow's desk. This notebook had a title, "Chicago," and contained a great deal of writing to chew on. He moved the little candle close to the journal and squinted.

———

Glioma

All day I'd been wheeled around on gurneys as they conducted more brain scans to define the perimeter of that lump in my left parietal lobe. It was a pain in the ass rather than frightening. There was a shortage of orderlies because of a recent downsizing, my father told me, which explained why I was left alone for more than an hour outside the room where they conducted the encephalogram. I got off the cart and walked back to my ward, upsetting the nurses. Turns out they'd lost me, not forgotten me, in the bowels of the enormous hospital.

I wondered how the test results would get into my chart and inform the neurosurgeon when they couldn't keep track of the patient. I was relieved to be back in my bed, even if there was no tasteless hospital meal waiting, the kind of miserable food you crave until it's delivered and you have to eat it. You crave even more when they say you have to fast before the operation.

My brothers showed up at my bedside in the late afternoon, hiding their grim faces with reassuring smiles. The older one called from Orange County the day I landed at the hospital and said he was coming to Chicago as soon as he could. I didn't hear my middle brother, the doctor, but it turned out he jumped on the red-eye from San Francisco that the previous night and tapped my shoulder on my first morning in the cancer ward. "Hey Ralo," he said. "Wake up, it's 9:15 already."

Early in the evening the surgeon marched into my room, back straight and chest out like a four-star general, and gave me the straight dope. "I get the sense that you'd want to hear this, Raul. You strike me as someone who wants to know what's going on, and I don't believe you're going to flinch when I tell you," he said. A smile of gratitude came to my face.

"I discussed this with your brother just now but I haven't told your father yet, because he's not ready. He's worried out of his mind," he continued, a commanding officer briefing the troops. "We think it's a glioma. I believe you understand what that means." He motioned toward the book on the bedside table, the one I'd brought home from Tokyo and read with sickening fascination. The textbook contained dense text and charts and photos of tumors and other things that can wreck a brain.

I knew what a glioma was. The deadliest of brain tumors, worse than the one that killed George Gershwin.

I once wrote an article about how the dying Emperor Hirohito never leaned, or was never informed, about what was killing him. Cancer was such a taboo in Japan his doctors gave him another benign-sounding name for the illness ravaging his imperial duodenum and his retainers denied him access to the newspapers so he wouldn't learn the truth. I'd learned enough about brain cancer to engage the diagnosticians in brief conversations until they cut it off, saying it was too soon to speculate.

But now I had the comfort of an expert interpretation of the tests and scans, the hard and seemingly irrefutable data.

"The prognosis is not very good, son." He softened the timbre of his voice from hard-nosed to avuncular. "We're hoping it'd be something easier to treat, but I'd say it's about a seventy percent chance you got the bad one. We're going to do everything we can, but we have to dig pretty deep without damaging the good part of your brain. I have to let you know the tumor is nestled right up against the speech center, and I am going to avoid cutting into that if I can. I believe you want to know the worst case scenario because you're a writer and even in the best scenario we're talking about maybe taking some of your words away. There are all kinds of risks in a surgery like this, so we want you to be prepared."

It didn't sound rehearsed. It was the first time someone said anything so completely and truly honest to me in a long, long while, maybe ever. The tension melted like butter. I was grateful.

I sat up in bed that evening and wrote a letter on a yellow legal pad to HR before one of the nurses came in to inject something to make me sleep soundly. I instructed them to change the beneficiaries on my life insurance policy from my two brothers to my new cancer-ward bride. I placed it on the table and waited for something else to think about. I didn't need to write a will, because our civil marriage in Tokyo, translated and certified by the U.S. Embassy, qualified her to inherit what little I had anyway, but I wanted to make things easy on her if she had to deal with bureaucracy at the newspaper.

I tried very hard to think of her face but had trouble conjuring the image. There should have been an upwelling of emotion by now, I thought, a gut feeling of tragic romantic attachment, but my feelings were stripped of the illusions of romance. This must be what love is in the end, I thought, hard-headed, with a lingering feeling of deep gratitude and warm compassion for a best friend, the would-be mother of my future children, the sweet companion I'd planned to live life with. I didn't know how to say this when we kissed each other and held hands until visiting time was over. I didn't want to sound sentimentally morbid. She was already so scared. I couldn't tell her what the neurosurgeon said to me that afternoon. We'd soon find out together after the operation was done, the result would be ours to live with.

My cancer became her story, not just mine, and the same with my parents, it was their story. Loved ones suffer as badly and maybe more than the victims of a fatal disease because they internalize the illness into their own experience, which is natural because everyone suffers from the fear of death, which at its root is a collective fear not an individual experience. The victim can find a way to come to terms with his fate, but the loved ones don't have that choice; what's in control of the victim is out of control for the loved ones. They start mourning privately even before the patient dies because that serves the purpose of surviving the trauma of their own vicarious death. Outwardly they cling to hope, demonstrably, and insist you must also cling to hope, keep your spirits high, chin up, fight the monster for me please. And so the patient plays along and ends up in the role of comforting the healthy ones. But hope and optimism must be borne from within, not swallowed like a dose of medicine. But they mean well. My wife of three days was so wracked with fear that she unwittingly sent out a high-voltage dose of negative energy that made matters much worse for me, even as I knew it masked a nurturing intent.

That was actually okay with me because I might have done the same. I didn't doubt her devotion – it was going to be sickness and health, the sanguine cliché we wrote in the rough draft of our vows. The fact that we never had a chance to speak that phrase before witnesses might have been a bad omen. Years later my deteriorating health, and probably the way I dealt with it, wrecked the marriage. On the eve of the craniotomy I expected I'd want to clutch her in my arms but the urge didn't come, not until the end of marriage, and it only served to drive her further away. We both had secrets we couldn't share with each other, secrets that were set in motion that night. I felt deep sorrow for her but at the same time I knew I had to dispel her troubled energy from my mind. I couldn't think of what I could do for her other than try to spare her some of the onerous paperwork of death. A woman in the HR department later informed me that they had received my letter but could not change my beneficiary status because I didn't submitted the proper form.

The nurses told me they'd wake me at 6:00 am for the surgery. I'd been instructed to wash myself thoroughly in the shower with surgical-grade antibiotic soap, thick red baptismal water in a bottle they left on the bathroom counter. Then to put on the fresh hospital gown sealed in a plastic bag next to the soap. They told me an orderly would escort me in a gurney and that the surgeon's attendant would shave my head. I couldn't help thinking about all the death row scenes in cheesy old black & white movies where the condemned man gets the last sacrament of a haircut to make the electric chair more efficient, and he breaks down, sobbing "I'm innocent! Please, warden, I don't deserve to die." Only in my case they will just shave the left side of the head, I was informed, where the surgeon needed to cut through the skull. It was the resident's turn to cut the tension with black humor: "We'd hate to shave off all your hair. You're going to want to keep as much hair as you can now for later."

That was about the most positive remark I'd heard all day, a suggestion I'd have a chance at living long enough to enjoy the perverse vanity of staples on one side of my head and scrubby brown hair on the other before chemotherapy made it all fall out. We usually call this form of therapy "chemo," but if you look closely there is a "mother" inside the word chemotherapy, extracting the brutal benefits of tough love. An image came to mind of a cheerful young woman I once saw in a dance club wearing a loose scarf that didn't totally conceal her baldness. She was very pretty, even without eyebrows. I remarked on this to my friend's wife, and she said I should ask her to dance. But I didn't have the courage. That's the kind of memory that makes me want to go back in time to fix things.

That night I waited for the terror, but it didn't come.

Was I being cheated out of what you'd think would be one of the most dramatic scenes in the theater of cancer? Why did I feel a tremendous calm wash over me, warmth that delighted and amused despite the dire situation? They hadn't given me any medication, so this wasn't drug induced. There's time to pray when you know something bad is coming, but I hadn't prayed myself into an altered state of consciousness, and I wouldn't have known who or what to pray to anyway.

A few days after losing consciousness with my tumor-induced petit mal seizure in Tokyo, I remembered that I felt the presence of a higher being when I collapsed. For lack of a better explanation, I associated it with my vaguely Christian upbringing. It felt as though Jesus was there, forgiving me, and Yamato was was the agent of some strange divinity. In Kennedy Meadows, where I narrowly escaped slipping away into a potentially lethal diabetic coma, it was the spiritual hum of the mountains, trees and rocks that embraced me. But that evening neither the Lord's Prayer or the Psalms were in the room to comfort me and the Heart Sutra didn't come to mind. Nor the ponetry of Kahlil Gibran, Gary Snyder or Robert Frost. I wouldn't have wanted words to violate the absolute stillness of my hospital room as I sat up in the bed alone, hearing softly the melody of Filipina nurses in the corridor, a sweet twittering of songbirds in the background that registered fleetingly on a quiet mind.

I don't know how long I sat there like that. It could have been forty minutes, forty seconds or the flash of a tiny synapse. It was in an eternal moment and the secret and irresistible vapors of self-pity I confronted and wallowed in and fought off since the diagnosis had completely vanished. I wasn't feeling courage or cowardice, anticipation or resignation, happiness or sadness. Just calm, awake and rooted to the spot.

That was seven years ago, and only now can I tell this story to myself. It's the first time I've had the chance to sit down and collect my thoughts and write them down. I've been so preoccupied with getting back on my feet, jumping back into the newsroom with arrogant and consuming ambition. I guess I succumbed to the safety of deep denial, refusing to confront the changes coming in my life that survival brings. I'm in long-term remission, statistically cured, but now know that some of the most damaging repercussions are yet to come. I'm a blind man stumbling over a field of rubble, constantly falling and getting back on my feet, but I gain strength with every fall. You often hear that a grave illness like cancer makes you stronger. That's nonsense. It weakens you, no matter how hard you try to fool yourself into thinking you're cured. The scar doesn't go away. It indelibly changes who you are, how you perceive yourself and how others perceive you. People who survive and say it made them stronger are talking about prevailing over a curse that will always come back to be prevailed over again. It doesn't make you any stronger than you already were, but it tests the power of your faith in life. Am I making any sense? I think that if you're ready to accept your new weakness it helps you tap into something you didn't realize you already had. In my case, it makes me remember how to get up off the ground every time I fall. That's not strength, it's practice. It's a comical way of doing the best I can do with what I have left. There's something big out there that's durably strong, but it can kill me in a single stroke as easily as it can help me flourish. The horse sense of knowing this can be mistaken for strength. Cancer made me better, not stronger, by helping me come to terms with my weakness and my limitations.

I'm lucky. I'm alive. Living with brain damage isn't so bad compared to the alternative, and the experience is hardly unique to me. It doesn't belong to anyone. My brain tumor is an echo of everybody's personal pain, an amulet of common suffering I'm only beginning to understand. Everybody has my tumor. The ravenous emaciated children in sub-Saharan Africa, the mentally ill cast out to live in the streets in the world's richest nation, the victims of viral pandemic, natural disaster, crack cocaine, genocide. My brain trouble is trivial, a tiny drop in an ocean of pain.

———

The coroner's discomfort over Barlow's confession was interrupted by a smiling overweight woman who put the plate of food on his table. Discomfort because the passage struck a nerve in his own grief that he had yet to put into perspective. He needed to get to that place where his own mourning for Alice was succored by a world of common sorrow.

He ordered another beer and resisted the desire to ask for a shot of tequila to chase it down. Tequila always had an awakening effect on him, but he was not sure how it would interact with beer on top of

Tennessee whiskey. He could not afford to compromise his concentration when he was getting deeper and deeper into Barlow's tale. The notebook invited him back.

—

No Ifs, Ands or Buts

When they roused me at 5:00 a.m. they asked me if I had eaten anything or drunk water. It didn't make any sense. How could I eat or drink when I was sound asleep? I dutifully went to the bathroom to shower with the red soap, which didn't lather up very well and had the effect of drying out the skin when I rubbed it in. The more I rubbed, the more the moisture was sucked out of my pores by the red soap. By the time I toweled off and popped the seal on the freshly sanitized hospital gown I was starting to feel nervous about what was going to happen in the long hours I'd be laid out on the operating table. Just a little jittery, trying over and over again to tie the gown behind my back. Brain mapping, they said. I'd have to be awake for the first part of it.

A large blonde nurse was waiting for me by the bed with a syringe. I asked what was in it and she said, "Your insulin, of course. Thirteen units."

"What? Do you mean thirteen units of regular insulin on an empty stomach? I've never taken thirteen units at once, not even before a big meal when my blood sugar was sky high!" My right hand fluttered and started to feel numb. "I'll be fasting during the operation and if you give me that much insulin now it'll kill me!"

She gave a knowing smile as if I was a little boy refusing to swallow my cough medicine. "It's on the chart, honey. Dr. Ringgold wrote thirteen units pre-op, and he knows all about your condition."

I bent over backward to be kind and respectful to the nurses and the hospital staff, partly because my father was on the faculty of this teaching hospital, but more importantly because I wanted to face my fate with dignity and grace. But this was too much. I'd been seen by a half-dozen doctors in the past two days and this Dr. Ringgold was not one of them. He wasn't the kindly endocrinologist, Dr. Nelson, who went over my diabetes management in detail the day before. I asked to the see the chart and it was as she explained. A lethal dose of insulin.

"Put the Goddamned needle away," I barked. "I'm not going to let you put me into a coma on the operating table."

"Now calm down, please," she said, changing the tone of her voice to stern authority. "You've got to take it. It's on your chart."

I got up and walked out of the room to the nursing station and asked to see the attending physician on the ward. In my most arrogant and outraged foreign correspondent's voice I demanded he get my neurosurgeon on the phone. It was an effective outburst. He connected me to the resident on duty, who said she wasn't sure what was on my chart but it was hospital rules that you don't overturn an intern's order. "What! An intern? You're going to let a fucking intern kill me so he can learn from his mistakes!" The conversation that followed was not pleasant, but she finally agreed to patch me through to my four-star neurosurgeon who phoned my father and the endocrinologist, and we brokered a deal. They agreed to give me a basal drip of insulin through an IV and monitor my blood sugar continuously through the operation, and I, in turn, would calm down.

I couldn't believe that I had to jump in and save my own life in an institution that was supposed to heal me. But in eleven years as a diabetic I had learned the hard way to take responsibility for my own health, aggressively if need be. And this Doctor Doogie had taken the Hippocratic Oath that says first, you idiot, do no harm. I was ready to strangle the young man with tufts of his blond hair when he came to my bedside to re-examine the chart, which had been changed moments earlier by the resident. Poor fellow, he had to endure the shame of being overruled by a patient. He left the room, sheepishly, without looking at me or saying a word.

The operation had to be delayed an hour because of my little rebellion, but I was relaxed and ready when they strapped me securely and taped down my head to keep it steady for the saw. I can't recall what the anesthesiologist said he was giving me, but it did exactly what he said it would do: ßNumb my entire body to kill the pain but keep me awake and alert to allow me to hear and speak. I was vaguely aware of what they were doing back there when they sliced open the sheath of skin and muscle covering the bone and peeled it back. It was the most amazing sensation when they started drilling into my head to make four holes where they could insert the router to cut through the skull, stopping precisely at the surface of my brain. I heard the blurry sound of power tools and felt the reverberation of saw on bone that went on for eternity as they carved out a square hatch over the left parietal lobe. It was amusing, not frightening. "Are you all right, Billy? Roger? Is your name Gus? What was your name?" the neurosurgeon said. "Very funny," I replied. "My name is Barlow, Raul Barlow, I take my martinis shaken, not stirred."

Then we played the game of Where's the Tumor? Whack-a-mole with electrodes. It was all mapped out on the computer and now they were going to map it on the brain itself, probing with electrical stimuli while asking me questions and listening to my responses to see what circuits fired up and when. I was an experimental dog. They kept asking my date of birth and my home address and I'd answer and then they'd ask me again, probing different places in the left parietal lobe where they suspected the tumor was hiding below. Once in a while I'd try to answer but couldn't. I thought the answer but my tongue didn't obey. They'd found a marker. Then they did things that made the fingers on my right hand twitch uncontrollably, then came the backward counting, start at 99 and count backwards, please, and I did so, anxious to please. I'd keep counting and realize my voice didn't accompany the numbers, and then I'd hear it again, 79. 78. 77, and suddenly it would all melt away into total confusion. I wasn't sure where I was but I heard a faint murmuring of conspiratorial voices that reassured me that I was still among the living. Then the fog lifted and I was fully conscious again. They said keep counting, please. "Where was I, 61?" They laughed. And while I continued the counting would slow, then speed up, and I'd mumble like a drunk, slide into confusion, come back. They'd found a trigger in my brain with their electrode stingers and were toying with haywire ganglia, tracing a path to the guilty malignant cells.

The last thing I remember was "No ifs, ands or buts." They asked me to repeat the phrase over and over again until it became a brainteaser, an annoying mantra, tonguing its way in and out of forced articulation.

"Okay, stop." It was the voice of the neurologist, the one with the moustache that made him look like Kurt Vonnegut. I wondered if he had a surgical mask covering his moustache. Of course he did. "Now resume," he said. "No ifs, ands or buts," I'd say, then stop saying, then saying again. It was the strangest conversation I ever had. Then it fell silent, and I knew it was time to start slicing into the tissue where X marked the spot. "You did great, Raul," I heard the surgeon say. "Are you ready?"

Less than a minute later, it seemed, I returned to consciousness. The room was uncompromisingly white, and there was a machine next to me pumping air in and out of plastic sheaths on my legs, kneading my calves. I tried to say hey, it's my brain, not my calves that needs the massage. But the words came out as little dry squeaks from the throat. I looked up to see the neurosurgeon beaming a radiant smile, totally out of character, a smile that said, you're in luck. "I don't think I'm dead, am I?" He couldn't hear me, but he answered anyway. "It's just lymphoma, Raul. We did the biopsy and it's very good news. Malignant, potentially lethal, but we can beat it. Your prognosis is good. Maybe you'll meet your grandchildren, assuming you don't get run over by a car." He nodded and walked off while I thought of something to say in response. Thank you, or that's great, or where am I? The cogs of cognition were turning slowly, trapped in medicated gelatin. I felt giddy. I thought about being run over by a car after going to all the trouble of having my brain fixed, and had to laugh.

I soon discovered where I was, not in a whitewashed heaven but in an intensive care unit, and it was the end of the day. where dusk showed itself in the windows, not the bright morning light I'd imagined. They came in groups of two and three, my wife and my two brothers, my parents, a parade of my father's colleagues, who puzzled over my condition before the operation, all smiling effusively. I wasn't going to expire anytime soon. It seemed I had my visa to the world stamped and renewed. I could live forever or die tomorrow, but it wouldn't have to be on account of mutinous killer T-cells in my left parietal lobe.

They say there are about ten billion cells and one hundred billion neurons in a single brain, plenty to waste, and that the generation and regeneration of each brain cell goes back 550 million years – way before Adam and Eve and the apes and the restless fish who decided to crawl on shore and spawn humankind. The first brain cells belonged to flatworms. Whatever is left in my brain can't be measured or counted, but the odds are I'm going to have to make do with less. I'm not asking for much. I'd still be happy with forty or fifty billion neurons. I'm not greedy. My hematologist told a great story about a patient of hers who had an MRI taken after complaining of headaches, and the scan revealed a very small brain – about twenty percent the size of a normal brain – tucked into a corner of his skull. The rest was salt water. Other than size, it was a healthy and perfectly functional brain. The man went to law school, passed the rigorous California Bar exam and prospered as a high-powered attorney, but he couldn't accept the fact that he accomplished all this with such a small brain. Size doesn't matter, the doctor told him, but he was so angry he went off to seek a second opinion and presumably the rest of his missing brain, never to be seen again.

—

The coroner came up for air. He resumed drinking his forgotten Tecate and noticed the thin man at the bar watching with steely eyes, as though he was prepared to draw a knife and slash his throat if he made the wrong move. Maybe it is about time I should leave, he thought, even I am imagining malice out of my own paranoia. I will read to the end of the notebook and finish this last beer before nodding in respect to the men at the bar and departing this sanctuary, its odors of spices, carnitas and refried beans, and the glow of its quiet light.

—

Penmanship

I woke from a foggy nap on a thickly starched white hospital sheet and assessed the damage, the words that didn't come to mind, the weakness in my right hand, the tremors. I picked up the notebook on the nightstand, the one I'd brought to the hospital three days earlier when I checked in, expecting I'd keep a log of the medical adventure.

But I couldn't hold a pencil in my hand, let alone write with it. Writing my journals would now become physical therapy, not just mythology. I worked with a lump of yellow clay the nurse gave me to strengthen the numb right hand that was neurologically compromised when they cut out the tumor – how badly, I didn't know. It was more than a matter of muscle control. I had to rebuild the pathways of confused motor neurons before I could write anything legible on the page. I had to start retrieving words and learn to write again or I would go mad.

I started simply with the alphabet, lines and lines of letters that didn't take on any distinguishing shape or sequential order until I hummed the ABC song like a child. It took willpower to fish letters out of the dark, connect my thoughts to my right hand, and make my hand obey. I worked at this for days in secret, too embarrassed to let my wife or anyone else see how I was struggling to regain sloppy second-grade penmanship. I drew comfort from thinking back to the time Rachel and I had amused ourselves by drawing silly looping and increasingly ridiculous letters in our cursive workbooks to battle the stultifying boredom of the classroom. It was if Rachel's ghost sat on a visitor's chair behind me in my room at Rush University Medical Center, teasing me. *"Nobody's going to be able to read that, Raul. You've got to open it up with flourish, make people laugh, then they'll be interested in what your handwriting is trying say."* Where is that girl now, I wonder, still somewhere around Chicago, still building bombs? I can't recall her telling me where she was going, and I'm a fool for not not wanting to find her again.

Twenty years since Rachel and I parted ways, I have to move my hand slowly and deliberately, concentrating on every stroke, or the handwriting deteriorates into jumbled shaky glyphs. Even now I tend to leap over dropped words, leaving gaping holes in the sentence. The rest of my life it'll be like this, maybe worse; I'm a professional writer who will forever search for lost words and struggle to write them down.

Illegible handwriting is a sloppy mirror to other secret afflictions. Very few people I interact with realize how blind I am, literally and figuratively. Thanks to the curative and crippling powers of radiation I live and survive partially blind in one eye and sighted in the other, two partners seeking parallax. A gifted doctor saved my vision with aggressive laser surgery, but the laser beams singed my rods and cones and compromised my peripheral vision. I'm resigned to the constant hilarity of bumping into strangers on the street, tripping over small children, stubbing my toes and jabbing my scarred shins on unseen objects, wounding the top of my head by banging it against low thresholds and treacherously open cabinet doors, anything above my field of tunnel vision. But I'm happy because I can still read. I've retained my depth perception and my ability to see clearly large moving objects and judge the speed of their movement well enough to drive safely. With a pair of cheap drug-store reading glasses I can do crossword puzzles and see the sentence I just wrote on this page. I have trouble seeing the stars, which saddens me deeply, but I'm still gifted with enough sight to watch the moon rise over the eastern hills, to study the masquerade of people walking past me on the sidewalk, to see enough of the color spectrum to wonder at glorious sunsets.

I've stopped explaining this to people who assume I'm not trying hard enough to see, even to loved ones who forget, or don't want to remember, my visual disability. It's easier to imagine the world of a totally blind person walking down the street with a white cane than to understand the world of the partially blind, who bump their way around an environment built for 20–20 eyesight. People are offended when I can't always recognize their faces, but how would they know that it's not a lack of remembrance of their features and caring for them but instead a problem with my optic nerve? One of my neurological scars is face blindness – prosopagnosia is the medical term. It's a particularity painful affliction because it hurts the feelings of people

I so desperately want to recognize. I didn't have a name for this at first and tried to compensate for it by looking for other clues to identify people, the outline of their bodies, their hairstyles, sometimes the way they moved. I later learned that the fabled neurologist and storyteller Oliver Sachs has prosopagnosia, a much more severe case than mine. It's reassuring because he didn't allow the disability to undermine his gift of empathy for his patients and all the characters he's brought to life in his literary case studies.

Two other annoying neurological problems arose immediately after my brain surgery. In the same way with my face blindness, I tried to keep quiet about these as well, but they were too obvious to hide. I lost my sense of balance, to the point where I can fall down putting on my boxer shorts when I get dressed. I discovered that I can stay steady on my feet if my arm grazes a solid object like a handrail on a stairway; I don't need to grab it or lean on it, just touch it lightly. The other is my sense of orientation. I'm a former cab driver who no longer can navigate the streets of my home town without getting confused or lost. I've heard these three conditions – face blindness, loss of balance and disorientation – sometimes come as a package in cases of neurological damage, but I haven't gotten around to checking it out because it didn't seem to matter very much. It's the way it is, and I need to focus on how to live with it and take control of it rather than dwell on the loss.

Ironically, a lot of the neurological problems that torture me now weren't caused directly by the brain tumor itself, but rather the treatment that saved my life. I used to tell the friends I know through the Japan experience that I'm a medical *hibakusha*. But not everyone gets the joke, and I reserve the irony for those who are comfortable with my health condition and know about the post-war epidemic of long-term radiation sickness in Hiroshima and Nagasaki. It'd be audacious of me to seriously compare myself to survivors of a nuclear weapon, but we do have something in common. A ghostly translucent mist shows up on the ceiling of my brain on slices of my MRI images, wafting downward and depicting the fallout from radiation treatment. This is the softly mysterious marker of radiological damage to my cognitive function, as well as the black lacuna of scar tissue where the tumor was extracted. The worst effects were delayed, kicking in ten years after the treatment. Suddenly, it's brain damage I have to cope with, and like everything else in life, good or bad, it is what it is.

———

The coroner lifted his face out of the notebook, rubbed his eyes and yawned. He looked around the room and checked to see if the thin man with the moustache was still eyeballing him from the bar, but the man's head was turned away now. He was speaking to his stoolmate in hushed Spanish, studying his hands as though they were not his own. The journal continued with another interesting passage he felt compelled to read.

———

Tattoo

I called them Heckle and Jeckle for lack of a better description, the two technicians I had to trust my life with after being treated at the hands of eminent neurosurgeons, neurologists and hematologists. They operated the equipment that blasted my brain with thousands of rads of radiation to eradicate the remaining scrap of tumor, a pencil eraser-sized clump of malignant cells still festering in my left parietal lobe where surgeons didn't dig deeper out of fear they'd destroy my speech center, should I survive.

During daily outpatient procedures the two of them bantered incessantly with each other about their personal lives, cars, pop music, movies, boyfriends and celebrity scandals, laughing and snorting as though I wasn't in the room. The corpulent blonde talked about going back to school when she was a waitress to take her high school equivalency test so she could enroll in community college in Riverside, where she first learned about vocational training in radiation technology. The freckle-faced man said his cousin told him there was good money in the career. I was a slab of meat strapped in a chair in their eyes, head taped to a brace, a passing stranger hoping to buy a little time before his death sentence was carried out. They had no idea of my prognosis and wouldn't care they did. On the first day, while they were fitting out the lead mask that would protect the area outside the target zone from the shower of gamma rays, they engaged me in one of the few conversations we had during the treatment. They said they were going to tattoo lines on my face to mark the exact position for the mask. They thought it better not to use magic markers because the lines wore off and the traces were hard to see.

I protested. I wasn't going to spend the rest my life with lines tattooed on my face –

permanent burr holes on the top of my stapled half-bald scalp were already enough to advertise my medical condition to the public. This was beyond vanity. It was defiance. My landlords in the Fairfax district were concentration camp survivors with numbers tattooed on their wrists. I wasn't going to let a tattoo brand me as a victim.

Heckle and Jeckle exchanged weary, knowing looks. Another goner, their eyes said, non-compliant and deluded about his chances of surviving brain cancer. They'd have to humor the man with magic markers.

The radiologist was worse. He stopped by once or twice during treatment and said spooky things in a hushed condescending voice like, "We're going to do everything we can to save your life, Raul. I think you have a fair prognosis." In fact, the other doctors on my case told me I'd have a very good chance of surviving, but I couldn't dismiss the possibility that the radiologist knew something I didn't. Toward the end of my treatment, when the round of whole brain treatment was done and they were ready to finish off with a series of localized radiation aimed at the immediate area around the tumor, it became evident that he was trying to scare me into volunteering as a subject in an experimental study using a new, untested technical procedure. He needed more cases for his research. "There are some risks involved, but this could save your life," he said. I'll never know whether that protocol of focal radiation, which is commonplace now, would have prevented some of the neurological damage that afflicts my cognition now. I didn't trust the man, and will have to live with the consequences.

The radiologist's message of doom was poles apart from the story my hematologist told me, that she did a thorough re-examination of the cell biopsy report from Chicago and determined the form of lymphoma that went haywire in my brain was slow growing and highly treatable. I had an excellent prognosis. She happened to be an AIDS expert who had seen scores of patients with similar brain tumors and watched them all die. But in these cases the cancer had metastasized from ravaged internal organs to their last outpost in the brain. I did not have HIV, she confirmed with the third test for the plague. My tumor, for whatever reason, originated in the brain and would not travel south because of the so-called brain blood barrier, which regulates a one-way traffic of blood flow, in to but not out of the central nervous system. My doctor was one of the busiest on-demand doctors I've ever known, her pager constantly buzzing, her nurse entering the examination room every few minutes to tap her on the shoulder when she had to take another urgent call. But she spent hours with me. She was a talented teacher and she explained in minute detail what was going on in my brain, sketching pictures and laughing. She told me the arcane reasons why she changed the treatment protocol when she realized conventional chemotherapy was a waste of time. Intrathecal chemo was the correct approach, which involved inserting long needles between my lower vertebrae to fire the chemical agent AraC directly up the spine and into the brain.

"You're a very interesting case," she said many times, not in dispassionate professional aloofness but in a maternal tone. She hugged her patients. She hugged me with the gentle power of Earth itself. Her unbounded enthusiasm and hope was infectious, and I couldn't resist being swept up by the electromagnetic field of good feeling she cast with her personality. She was a distilled and unadulterated life force. I haven't seen her in twenty years, but she's still my guardian angel.

"Raul, you are a writer, a good one as far as I know," she said during one of my last visits to Norris Cancer Hospital. "You're going to start writing again soon, and you have to keep writing because that's who you are. Do me a favor and write a book about your experience with cancer some day. People need to know."

I'm still working on it. I'm trying. If I live long enough I'll stitch all the little stories together into one tale, but right now I have no idea how to do that. Coping with work and the everyday tasks of living can be overwhelming. The gears are turning slower and slower in my left brain now, and time is speeding by without me. The world doesn't need another cancer memoir, and anyhow I doubt I could write one worth reading. But the doctor's encouragement to write my unfinished story has never left my mind. At dusk, when my spirits sag and my journey pauses, I conjure up the memory of Kato's garden and sometimes see her sitting next to me on the glider in front of the tea shelter, making me laugh about my brain. Now I can look back in amusement at the excruciating pain in my lower back where the needle missed its target and hit bone. She was an expert in the procedure, having performed it countless times without a problem, but my backbone was so tight with muscle contraction compressing my lower vertebrae that even she had difficulty. I think how lucky I was that she insisted on doing it herself instead of relegating the task to one of her interns. It was as if she gave me a lollypop once the fear had passed.

Remembering the pain brings me back to the misery of my first assignment after treatment was done and I foolishly returned to the newsroom too soon. I writhed in agony in the back seat of a rice farmer's car in the Sacramento delta as we toured the harvested fields where the dry rice stalks were stacked in pyres waiting to be burned. I finished the reporting, flew back to LA, and wrote the story, feeling false triumph. The story was poorly researched and written and I see now that it marked the beginning of my decline as a journalist. But I never gave up hope that I'd return to the quality of work I attained in Tokyo. Dr. Levine bolstered me with a transmission of improbable hope and the knowledge that the power to sustain hope comes from within. Without saying a word about it, she made me realize that in death there is no such thing as darkness, that survival is not dumb luck but another word for grace, that illness is our birthright and that illness is the cure.

Twenty-Four

There were no cabs in sight and the buses had all but stopped running. The coroner considered his next move as he let the door of the restaurant jingle closed behind him. He could wait an hour for a bus that may never come. Or he could walk back to Barlow's burrow and sleep on the couch, because getting back home to Leavenworth tonight was not in the cards. Even if he did have enough cash in his pocket to pay the taxi fare, he could not remember with certainty whether he put the spare key under the loose brick on the steps the last time he used it.

Across the street he saw a man loitering in the dark by the shuttered BART station entrance who covered his head with a handsome Australian akubra hat and gazed in his direction as though he was surveying the outback. He could not help being unnerved by the apparition in millinery disguise – perhaps a private investigator Du Goyle put on his tail, or a spook from Homeland Security looking into Barlow's dated primer on the use of dead baby records for false identities. The coroner crossed the intersection to confront the man and caught him by the arm before he could flit away into the shadow around the corner.

"Who the hell are you and why are you following me," the coroner said, attempting to speak in his most authoritative voice without slurring.

"I beg your pardon," the man said in an English accent that sounded false. "I think it's a case of mistaken identity. I was hired by this woman down south to find a fellow, but you know it's a needle in a haystack in a place like San Francisco, where it's easy to disappear, even though I already found him once, before. My name is Tremain, Gus Tremain. Here's my card in case you ever require my services. I'm licensed. Very sorry to have bothered you, sir."

The name was familiar, but the coroner could not place it. Ordinarily he would call up the name of someone he had met, whether the person was important or just a passer-by, but tonight there was too much to process.

"Do me a favor and get rid of those ridiculous hats," the coroner said. "I have employed a number of private Dicks in my day but I have never known them to use cheap gimmicks like false beards or hats."

Gus Tremain bolted across the street and disappeared from sight.

The walk up the hill to Barlow's house will sober me up, he thought, it will do me a world of good. My evening constitutional. He developed a habit of taking long, lonely midnight walks since becoming a widower. Alice could no longer accompany him. He made it a point to use different routes than they took together, traversing Russian hill the roundabout way to North Beach, where he would stop at Specs' for a bourbon when he was in the mood. The steep incline up 24th Street to Noe Valley and the ascent to Dolores Heights would not pose a problem because he was a good strong walker in relative cardiac fitness despite his slovenly habits. The surfeit of alcohol in his bloodstream would burn off like gasoline.

He had been cooped up indoors for hours and hours reading documents, and he was enervated by the weight of it all, so now was a good time to focus on his own physical well being, he declared to himself. He would borrow Barlow's shower, get a few solid hours of sleep on the couch, and march to his doom in the morning. First, however, he needed to get Wilson thinking clearly about what they had to accomplish tomorrow at the office. He drew his cell phone and punched seven, the speed dial number for Wilson's home.

"Young man! This is my vengeance, a wake-up call for you," he said to the *diener* when a doped-up voice came on the line. "We have business to attend to early in the aye yem. Listen to me closely, boy."

"Leo, you're drunk, and it's after two in the morning. What do you want from me? Not another anonymous corpse, please," he said. "You're not supposed to be on duty tonight, unless you're freaking crazy."

"Certainly not, Wilson. I'm as sober as a judge and I am walking the mean streets of San Francisco to prove it."

The coroner wondered if he was giving himself away by slurring. Hell with it.

"I have Barlow's full name, son, he's the other one, the Raul guy, do you fully understand? I need you to do a complete rundown on Raul Charles Barlow soon as you get your ass into the office. Before seven, before Du Goyle pokes his acne-scarred nose around. The corpse is more alive than I had ever imagined. And Jesus, go online and check out Narcissistic Chameleon something, Moo. That is her blog, Wilson. Her last name appears to be Gudebski, a nice Polish girl, or maybe Russian. Check her on the flight records Saturday morning. I also have a medical tag number you need to follow up on. I have the ID and numbers somewhere, which I will give to you as soon as I find out where I put my memo pad. The number has a Modesto area code. If I think of anything else I will call to interrupt your little REM state again."

"Where the heck are you, Leo? I've been trying to call you all day."

"Not of importance. I have spoken and you shall obey," he said, affecting an imperious nasal tone. He flipped the phone closed on the words "But Leo ..." and turned it off so Wilson could not annoy him by calling back with questions about the inquest.

He walked on the north side of 24th Street, marveling at how quiet it was, even for a Sunday night. The ladies of the night had retired early, and there were no schizophrenic vagrants wandering the streets. No danger. Or so it seemed.

Shoe by shoe, he progressed in a westerly direction, past Valencia and Guerrero, trudging slowly uphill before reaching the necklace of palm trees on Dolores. That was where he heard it coming, the deep growling of an automobile approaching from behind, the menacing sound of a classic muscle car gaining on him, then slowing to keep pace with his accelerating frightened stride. He heard sick peals of laughter and gleeful shouts of "there's one" and "road kill!" He bolted up Dolores and stumbled on the uneven sidewalk, scraping his face. He got on his hands and knees, feeling gastric juices rise to his throat, and he crawled to the grassy median strip behind the trunk of a scaly palm to hide from the voices pursuing him.

It was a feeble escape. They set upon him taunting and kicking and laughing. "You fucking filthy scum of the earth," said a shaven-pate young man.

Not again, do I really look so bad they take me for a bum, he asked himself as he shielded his face from the blows and curled up like a snail without a shell. A hard-toed boot connected with his ribs and he felt excruciating pain racing through his body. They grabbed his hair and lifted his face and ground it into the median curb. They turned him over and slammed hard fists on his temples and brow, then dropped a rock on his forehead, hooting cries of jubilation. I am going to die, he thought, this is my time. The beating intensified and he was on the verge of losing consciousness when he heard a voice that was so shrill and piercing that it jolted him to a red galaxy of pure distilled fear. It was a mighty war whoop. The final blow was coming.

Heart racing, he managed to raise his head in determination to face his killer. He saw the shadow of a tall demon twirling a long club in the air like a medieval mace. The coroner squeezed his eyes shut when his attacker released a primordial scream. Time melted into blueness and stopped and waited. "Alice!" *Shhh* . . . "No, Alice please!" He felt no pain.

Through throbbing hot temples and muffled ears he heard someone screaming in agony beside him, and he turned to see one of his attackers crash on the ground holding his head and rocking back and forth. Someone yanked the boy to his feet and dragged him away. He heard fleeing boot steps, a big engine thundering to life and the screeching of tires.

They were gone. Utterly confused and soaked in sweat, the coroner pulled himself up sideways to a sitting position, shivering in fear. He saw the silhouette of a tall man with one hand on his hip, the other wielding a section of two-by-four aloft in triumph. The coroner could barely make out the golden S shield on the man's breast, the little red rag that served as his cape and the jagged pumpkin-mouthed grin.

"It is Rolly, sir, I'm here to the rescue. And don't you worry, you're going to be okay." He had abandoned his improbable British accent in favor of a high-toned Ebonic elocution. "Damn, those muthafuckas really fucked...you...up!"

Stooping to one knee he gently placed his giant hand on the coroner's neck with his index finger pressed lightly on the jugular. "Your ass is still alive, thank God almighty. Your heart is ticking, you're not bleeding to death," Rolly said. "Good thing I was on patrol around here tonight. Do you got a cell phone? Let me have it and I'll dial 911, get an ambulance out here. They beat you to a pulp, my brother. You need medical attention."

"No, I am okay, I am okay," the coroner said. "It is not as bad as it looks." The two men studied each other's faces. "Just a flesh wound." The coroner exhaled in a burst of guttural laughter that made his ribs yelp with pain. Rolly joined in before hoisting the doctor to his feet to get him walking back and forth. "Not as if they kicked me in the balls or broke my nose. I was mostly all curled up."

"Did you show them your badge?"

"Very funny," said the coroner, who touched a gash on his forehead and examined the smudge of blood on his fingertips to confirm the wound was not bleeding profusely. He found a pair of mangled eyeglasses still hanging on his nose.

"I do my best. There's not much to laugh about out here so I try to keep a little humor in the situation, you know what I mean?"

"I know what you mean."

He was aware of being ushered into a yellow sedan that had been summoned out of thin air. He slumped on the back seat and saw Rolly pull dollar bills from his pocket one by one until he had counted out eighteen and handed them ceremoniously to a turbaned cabbie, whose bland expression said he had ferried passengers in much worse shape than the miserable lump in the rear.

"Take the good doctor home, please," he said, returning to the affectation of his nasal British voice. "And keep the change."

The coroner wracked his brain to retrieve his own address on Russian Hill but information was lost. He directed the driver to Liberty and Sanchez where he could take refuge for the night and nurse his wounds without any objections from the homeowner. He thought he would take a bath to soothe himself, then patch himself up with the gauze and tape and the Tiger Balm he had seen in Barlow's medicine cabinet. Then sleep.

Twenty-Five

He tried to fend off the blast of sunlight that knifed into his cheek from a gap in the matchstick blinds, demanding him to rise from the carpet, but to no avail. His nose was congealed by dried blood, hard snot and dust, making it difficult to breathe. The clock on Barlow's kitchen wall was an angry chronometer prodding him into a cross-legged slump. He made a delirious assessment of the damage, much as he would with a fresh body waiting for him at the morgue. Head throbbing beyond reason, abscessed tooth shrieking and starting to smell of rot, lower left ribs yowling for relief that he estimated would not come until the cracks mended in another seven weeks. Painfully he leaned to his side for a view of the obstreperous clock in order to understand what it was trying to tell him. Eleven twenty four. "Christ!" He was late, irreparably late, so late he did not need to bother going into the office. Whatever notion he might have had of saving his skin and somehow keeping his job was dashed. The black masked executioner now waited for him in certain fury, ready to demand his resignation.

He reeled when he stood, as though he just stepped off the Giant Dipper at the Santa Cruz Boardwalk. He had to brace himself. Barlow's over-the-counter ache-killers were useless against the agony of his bruised and battered body. He needed opiates. He felt like finding a pair of pliers and yanking the sadistic tooth from his jaw. He needed ice, bags of ice to put on his head and inside his shirt over his ribs, a bowl of ice to feed a tumbler of bourbon to medicate the monstrosity of his gray-and-white matter. Perhaps he should stop at the emergency room on his way to the office. No, he would have to follow to Plan B: Forget the job and delve further into Barlow's archive.

He drew a bath and stripped off his pathetic brown suit and tie and ragged underwear to be assaulted by the rank odor of unwashed private parts. It was an old-fashioned porcelain tub, long, deep and roomy and supported by four clawed feet, a magical animal poised to spirit him away to another world. He submerged himself in its steamy foam and cringed as the hot water stung the abrasions and lacerations on his nose, cheeks and hands. Once afloat, he grabbed the washcloth on the rim and soaped up. More hot stinging and jagged burning, but he noted the soothing affects of the water on the contusions moaning across his thighs and rump. The tight muscles around the cracked ribs relaxed somewhat. The wound on his forehead sizzled. Wishing he had Epsom salt to pour in, he sank deeper into the water, allowing the warmth to lap at the steel cables in the nape of his neck until the water turned cold. He toggled the drain and when all the water had been sucked away he found himself plastered to the bottom of the tub in the mighty grip of gravity, making it extremely difficult to vault himself upward. Barlow's towel was mildewed but on the scale of smells it was acceptable, and he decided not to traipse across the house dripping wet while looking for the linen closet.

He helped himself to a clean set of clothing from Barlow's wardrobe. A black **tee-shirt** that emitted a faint scent of laundry soap and a pair of baggy khaki pants. Then he hobbled to the front room to reignite his cell phone. He had to call in.

"Leo, you sound like death warmed over. Are you all right and where the hell are you? This is more than a hangover. What happened?"

"Never been better, my boy." The coroner listened to the feedback of his heavy, labored breathing.

"Listen up, Wilson. I have some favors I'd like you to do for me," he said, gently, careful not to upset the *diener*. "Do you remember our conversation last night? The instructions I gave you?"`

"Shit, Leo, you didn't make any sense last night any more than you do now. And you missed your meeting. I tried to cover for you. We've been worried about you. Nicki is going crazy she's so upset, and

Du Goyle is ballistic. I've never seen him this pissed off, Leo, he said he's going to toss you out on your sorry ass for rank insubordination," Wilson said, his voice revealing a rising tone of panic. "The chief's been asking for you too. She called me three times this morning. She was going to sit in on the meeting and I think she's sympathetic, maybe even on your side. You got to check in with her. She might be able to fix things."

"Can't fix something that's been broken and broken all over again, son, and bound to break again. And don't believe what the chief says. She is a decent woman but she is also a politician. There comes a time when you just have to suck it in and do things your own way, damn the torpedoes and to hell with the consequences. This is my last case, my last stand, Wilson. My final inquest is of myself, and I'm going to do it right and I need to count on you for your help.

"Pay attention now. Raul Charles fucking Barlow, that's his name as I believe I told you already, a journalist, born whenever, divorced, in love, a ruined man. Did I give you the number on his dog tag already? You must call Modesto. Get Medic Alert to open all his records, find the doctors on file, find his next of kin, find Christina, find *Moo*. Then we can cut him up secretly and respectfully and cremate him with dignity and hand his ashes over to the one who loves him most. Then I can die for the night and wake up human again."

"You're talking nonsense, Leo. This isn't like you. You're worse than drunk this time. Where are you hiding out? I demand to know – you owe me that. I'm coming to get you right now," he said. "Tell me where you are and I'll be there in a minute. I know you're not at home because I phoned and pounded on your door to wake you up on time for the meeting. I had to sneak through your back window to see if you were dead. Dammit, Leo. Stop being ridiculous and give me the address. Please!"

"I do not think he meant to die. He tried to live. He loved life. He did not want to worry anyone or hurt anyone," he said. "That is my conclusive diagnosis. I know the manner of his death and I have a reasonable idea about the cause of his death, but now I must find the meaning of his death and in order to do that I need to find the meaning of his life. Wilson, let me tell you a little secret I'm learning about as I continue on this inquest. If you take heaven, hell and metaphysics out of the picture, which are ridiculous anyway, the assumption is that death is final. But that's wrong, very wrong. There is absolutely no finality in death."

"Look, Leo, I'm not interested in philosophy right now. I'm going to put Nicki on the phone. She's frantic about this, way too worked up. Says she has a terrible premonition."

"I am just fine, son. I have a lot of important work to do here and. I cannot tell you where I am right now and I cannot be bothered with the pathological morons who think they rule the San Francisco morgue, my Goddamned morgue," he said. "Do me a favor and be brave, keep working on the Barlow case for me even if you have to do it in stealth. Tell the deputy chief I am taking a sick day even if he did not authorize the absence. I will be in tomorrow to rip the heart out of his chest, no, take that back. He has no heart so I shall rip his lungs out. And tell Nicki to be calm and that I would give her my most affectionate hug if I could. If only it was not for what I have become. Tell her not to worry about me because I was saved by Superman last night. No doubt about it. It was Superman himself."

Wilson was shouting when he cut off the call.

He found a brown bag of ground Chain Café coffee and a round quart of Bud's Kona Chip in Barlow's freezer. Sustenance. He spooned the ice cream right out of the container while the coffee was dripping, and he propped himself on the counter for a view out the back window of Barlow's yard, overgrown with tall milkweed and grass under a dome of gray clouds that veiled the sun while he was taking his bath. Standing by the gate he saw a forlorn lemon tree with thick tar-painted stumps where its lower branches should be. The clouds had taken command of the sky, their pigment graduating in the gray scale from comfortably soft heather to the color of burnt gristle. He saw a pair of finches flitting around the bird feeder on Barlow's fence and heard the cheeping of their flirtatious song.

"I will slip out later and find my way to It's Tops for some eggs, bacon and hash browns," someone said aloud, maybe him, addressing the ambivalent sky. "If it does not rain." *Hush . . . Shut up! Before you lose your mind.*

At the desk he knew there was no choice but to summon up the courage to do battle with Barlow's laptop. He tried again to crack the password to the email program but came up dry. Then he fumbled around with the Start button in the hopes of finding some way to circumnavigate the security wall. He stumbled onto a list of documents. Not bad, Leo, he congratulated himself for his persistence after so many failures. He scrolled the list of files, hunting for stories buried in the long queue of electronic chaff. This would be more rational than trawling for notebooks in the cardboard box, and it would spare him the need to squint in order to catch the meaning in Barlow's post-tumorous handwriting. He came across a file titled "essential vocabulary" and opened it to see a disorganized tableau of words and definitions crammed together in different fonts and sizes, suggesting a disorderly mind had cut and pasted them from online sources when he saw something he once knew. *Malversation, ligature, ipso facto.* Barlow was an addled harvester of lost words, he thought, a writer who was so terrified of losing the cherished vocabulary he had absorbed over a lifetime that he was driven to rescue them. *Rhabditeda, krakowiak, schadenfreude.* He made it his business to pin them on a board like butterflies before they flew away. The man had a serious problem with aphasia, the coroner deduced, which requires the kind of toil people with brain damage are condemned to perform until they can toil no more.

He moved along the list of dot-docs until he found a file name that intrigued him. Was Barlow going blind?

——

Braille

My only moment of total horror following brain surgery was at the records department waiting room at the USC's Doheny Eye Institute, where an esteemed ophthalmologist failed to diagnose the symptoms of accelerating radiation retinopathy. Six months after brushing off my complaints of foggy vision he finally got around to doing a thorough exam of my retinae and when he saw the damage he ordered a fluoroscopy. He was shocked to see the extent of neovascularization, a condition where the tiny veins feeding the retina go haywire and poke their way into the vitreous gel looking for a source of fresh oxygen. It's a common cause of blindness in diabetics. In my case it was triggered prematurely by the whole brain radiation therapy that zapped my retinas while saving my life. In a state of agitation he told me the bad news. I'd have to undergo extensive laser surgery to save my sight, and even if that was successful I'd still lose a lot of vision, particularly in the peripheral field. I asked him why he didn't catch this six months earlier and he answered with a nervous shrug, then told me he would schedule laser surgery for that afternoon. I had no confidence in the man. I didn't trust him with my eyes.

Days later I was sitting on one of those stiff waiting-room chairs, anxious to collect a batch of medical records I would take to UCLA Medical Center for a second opinion. I noticed an interesting magazine on the pile to my left. It had a wonderful brown texture on the cover, much like the mottled hand-made *washi* paper I'd occasionally used for personal notes in Japan to express my thoughts with the earthy aesthetic of folk art. I touched the magazine gently with my fingers before picking it up. It had bumps. A pattern of bumps. It took me a few moments to realize what it was. Braille. And for the first and last time during my illness and convalescence I felt deep and inconsolable fear and sorrow for myself, and I broke down, sobbing, doubled up, heaving wails of anguish like a dam inside me finally burst. I had made a pathetic scene in a waiting room where real blind people were sitting patiently in silence like Buddhas listening to a grown man blubber. With snot and tears on my face and in utter humiliation I picked up the medical records from a woman at the reception desk whose face betrayed annoyance bordering on disgust.

On my way out the door I felt a soft touch on my arm and turned to see a coffee-colored hand. It belonged to an elderly woman who wore a fashionable red hat and projected a regal bearing as she held her cane. The beauty of her expressive face wasn't diminished at all by sunken eye sockets. She was beaming.

"Don't be afraid. Losing your vision doesn't mean you can't see anymore, my child," she said. "You don't need eyesight to rejoice in the wondrous world that surrounds us. Praise the Lord!"

I later learned how right she was. A skilled and experienced retinal specialist at UCLA medical center saved most of my sight by making dozens of precision laser burns across both retinas. The laser treatment extracted a price in terms of limiting peripheral vision and causing near-sightedness that can't be fully corrected by eyeglasses. I have a hard time distinguishing colors indoors away from ultraviolet light. But I've learned that a visual disability opens other gifts of perception and animates senses that I'd taken for granted. My ears can detect high pitched sounds emitted by lamps and electric clocks in the room, and the whispering of trees and faraway sounds. My nose assails me when I smell the stench of rotting teeth across the room, just as I can be jolted with ecstatic awareness of the faint scent of lilac in a woman's hair when she passes by. I think I have a more delicate palate. People laugh when I say I taste the difference in municipal waters in neighboring towns. As the sensations become more acute, so do the memories they trigger. It can be splendid, soothing as well as bitter and sometimes overwhelmingly confusing.

———

The body is warming up, he thought, starting to come to life on the page. Did the corpse feel it when he probed him during his cursory physical examination Saturday? Can a dead brain hear the buzz of fluorescent lights? What happens to consciousness in the twilight – does it sputter and gasp? What about the sensorium. Does it linger past rigor mortis or flame out at the moment he signs the death certificate? He had no time for metaphysical ruminations when he practiced his trade, but Barlow changed the rules. The coroner felt free from his professional strictures, but he did not know whether that was a good thing.

He scrolled around and found the cursor traveling toward the bottom of the list, where he saw another file that grabbed his attention.

———

The Town I Loved So Well

The YMCA in Kowloon is the poor man's Peninsula Hotel. As a matter of fact, they are a block away from each other, both affording a spectacular view of Hong Kong Harbor if you're in the right room, but the Y doesn't have any Bentleys parked out front with motors purring in wait for the next eminent passenger. That's where it happened, in a humble room, the cheapest I could reserve, in a hard narrow bed pushed against a chalky wall bordering a utility closet containing a loudly snoring hot water heater. I was spoiled by some of the fancy hotels I stayed at when I traveled around Asia as a foreign correspondent. More often I stayed in modest yet comfortable lodgings, and I camped out in local dumps when the experience was part of the story. But this time I was on my own dime in Hong Kong as a civilian doing research for a book. I no longer worked for a heralded newspaper based in Tokyo or the iconic business magazine in Hong Kong. I was flying solo without the security of a major news organization for the first time in Asia. The experience was strange and disorienting. I wasn't sure what I hoped to accomplish by coming back. I was writing a book that required me to visit sweatshops in China's Pearl River Delta.

On my second day in Hong Kong I was jolted awake deep in the night by a chunk of cadaverous tissue on the mattress next to me, a big, cold freakish thing touching my side. I was terrified. My first thought was nightmare, I'm dreaming about being trapped in a horror movie with zombies, but no, I was fully awake and the thing was still there. I tried to push the thing out of the bed and when it wouldn't move I punched it hard with my left fist, but it was attached to me. I sat up and looked at it and saw my right arm in the dark. It was lifeless, heavy and unfeeling, an appendage of dead meat hanging from the sleeve of my tee shirt.

I said "Oh Shit!" But there was no sound coming out of my mouth. I was as if I were under water, helpless and mute.

It took an hour of deep-tissue *shiatsu* massage to bring the arm back to life. I spoke out loud to test my larynx: "No ifs, ands or buts," said a quavering voice.

By dawn I was fine. The arm was normal again and I got in the shower and sang the song I often sing to call up bravery when it's needed. It's an Irish folk song from the troubles that my colleague Jim Flannigan introduced to me while he grieved over his dying wife. *In my memories I will always see, the town that I loved, that I loved so well.* I decided that no one needed to know about this bizarre episode with my arm because I knew no one would believe me. *Now the army's installed, by that old gas yard wall, and the damned barbed wire gets higher and higher.* My singing is best in the shower when my throat opens to the warm water.

You were dreaming, they would say, or your arm was pinched and a nerve got cut off making it seem paralyzed. I wondered if an arm could fall asleep when you're already sleeping. And why did I lose my ability to speak? I thought about all the possible explanations and nothing came close to making sense.

The gruesome arm haunted me as I crossed the Chinese border that morning to follow some leads in my high-minded search for despicable labor abuse. The assistant manager at a giant sneaker factory in Shenzhen greeted me with beady eyes. "We comply with all the health and safety codes of conduct. Look, we have it posted there on the wall for all to see," he said through an interpreter, reciting a familiar script. The sign was in English, and I asked him how many of the young farm girls stooping over the assembly lines could read it. He was visibly insulted by the question.

The building reeked of noxious fumes from the industrial shoe-goo the girls were applying to rubber soles. When my nostrils flared and I pinched my nose in a sign of revulsion, the assistant manager could plainly see I wasn't a prospective wholesale buyer for a big American chain store. After a few more probative questions he lost his temper and chased me out of the factory, yelling without his interpreter that I was a "damn human rights guy" whose aim was to make China's right to develop its economy look bad. I dashed out the door to the abandoned street and when I saw a stocky man from the factory chasing me I got scared. The thought entered my mind that he was a goon and he intended to beat the nosey human-rights-guy to a pulp.

The man pointed menacingly at my racing heart. "Your badge, your badge!" he shouted. "I'm very sorry, sir, but you didn't sign out and return your visitor's badge."

My arm tingled.

And the townspeople? *Their spirits are bruised, never broken. They can never forget, but their hearts are set, on peace and hope once again.*

——

The coroner was familiar with the brave Irish tune that Barlow sang in the shower, but it struck him that courage was, at best, situational. It was a song of determination and lament that he recalled hearing for the first time at Finnegan's Wake, sung spontaneously in a coarse voice through a haze of tobacco smoke.

Twenty-Six

The coroner did not feel like going back to the top of the queue to read the files alphabetically in an effort to be orderly, because the list was bound to be laden with inconsequential and irrelevant information. He continued trawling for the most interesting titles. Barlow's computer files were most likely random, just like the notebooks in his cardboard box, concealing thoughts and memories that didn't necessarily tie together.

He stopped the spinning wheel of the mouse on an item named Fireworks. This should be revealing, the thought, because fireworks are celebratory and trigger amazement and emotion like no other form of entertainment. He saw a curious note at the top of the file: Move this to the vault. "What the hell is the vault?" he said aloud. Barlow intended to hide this somewhere in a deep chamber away from prying eyes like his, the coroner realized.

———

Fireworks

Being chronically ill, at least in my case, causes the mind to obsess over certain abstract ideas, familiar notions that have speckled my consciousness without earnest examination, not since the all-night bouts of drinking and bullshitting with motley friends during my twenties. Once you think you have a pretty good hold on the big questions curiosity wanes and ideas become rigid. But there's nothing like brain damage to dislodge all the assumptions that once made me comfortable with reality. The subject of immortality is cheapened by a mother lode of hackneyed ideas, but it's the one that bugs me above all others and I suppose it's the same for many survivors.

I think I've made my peace already with the inevitability of death, but I can't help wondering what will keep me alive after I die.

Dragonflies, maybe?

Soon after my operation, but before my initial round of chemotherapy, my new wife got the idea in her head that all the toxins they were going to pump into my veins would render me impotent if I lived to the time we were ready to have babies. I resented the idea, but she insisted on driving to a sperm bank in Chicago several times to take "samples," which would be put on ice for a not inconsiderable sum of money until we were ready to plant the seeds. It turned out to be a ridiculous experience. It was way too soon to do this while I was doped up on medication and the photos of beautiful young women in the Playboys stacked on the table in the antiseptic little collection room nauseated me. I tried to work myself into arousal. I thought I should say to myself, "Just look at those big boobs," or "I'd sure would like to fuck that 19-year-old bimbo," but the erotic pictures left me cold in my weakened state. Masturbating is a very private matter, but when there are people waiting for results on the other side of the door it becomes a public act. I felt like I was on a surveillance camera with punters placing bets on whether I would vomit or ejaculate on the magazines. That's what I had to do instead of carrying my bride across the threshold of a luxury room at a resort in Hawaii. At last I managed to have miserable sex with a busty blonde named Crystal and to made make humiliating love to a sultry nymph from Kansas whose vital statistics were 38-24-36.

Despite the degradation of obligatory libido, putting sperm in the bank gave me a certain kind of immortality. I could die from cancer in two months and still father a child in two years or twenty years, provided someone kept up the payments.

Sometimes sitting on the bench in Kato's Garden made me think of existential matters in a logical, not spiritual, way. I don't know why but I recalled reading a story about the blind hope, the sustaining hope, of a man who went home every day expecting to find a hot turkey dinner waiting for him. Was it Kierkegaard? I wasn't sure whether it was something I read or a distorted memory from a classroom assignment or whether they even had turkeys in Denmark. But I wasn't about to go to the library to find the Kierkegaard book I read when I was 18 to fact-check the allusion. It was a perfect metaphor for a cancer survivor and I didn't want to ruin the thought.

My wife and I both worked at the newspaper in Los Angeles. She was doing research for an article on alternative birth control and she started to test out the rhythm method, which we practiced with great precision, until I woke one morning to hear her vomiting in the bathroom.

We hadn't planned on this. We were blown away with surprise and I had to wonder whether we accomplished this out of subconscious dare or out of sheer luck. The question about my potency was still unresolved and I had ruled out having children until I was in solid remission with the cancer and statistically cured. But there was absolutely no question about our choice to welcome her into the world. We didn't have to say a word about it. We wept with joy. The baby was nothing short of a miracle.

Life has major turning points and it has points of no return. I had some catastrophic experiences that nearly killed me, but they don't come close to the eternal drama of bringing a child into this world. I can't imagine anything more stunning and sanctified than watching her being tugged out of the birth canal and listening to her wail in utter surprise at the bright light, at the doctor's slap on the rump, at the cool air rushing into her lungs.

Seeing her bawling herself to life in the warmth of the incubator, swaddled in a tiny white blanket and looking like a baby Buddha in a white cap, that was a moment of boundless joy. Then something remarkable happened that's not supposed to happen with newborns. She looked up to see me grinning across the room and for a long moment she stopped squirming and focused on my eyes with a riveting gaze that spoke a silent incantation announcing her arrival. Newborns aren't supposed to see past their noses at that stage but our eyes locked. There was an unmistakable and sublime transmission. I knew at that very moment I would survive brain cancer to watch over her. As the years passed she revealed an extraordinary gift of vision, way beyond 20-20 eyesight. She has a quickness to her optic nerve that allows her to see things first, before anyone around her can catch the image.

Kato's Garden was best in the morning when the sun rose to about 20 degrees from the horizon and peeked over the roofline of the house, illuminating the sculptured trees and lily pond in soft color. I tried whenever I could to catch that moment, sitting on the glider by the ramshackle *azumaya*, drinking my coffee and wading through the morning's *Los Angeles Times*. Japanese gardens are designed to express the evanescence of life, with the turning colors of the baby maple and the fleeting buoyancy of falling cherry petals. When you open your heart to the garden you taste a delicious melancholy that anchors you to unspoken wonder.

It wasn't long before the garden turned playful. As soon as she could walk my daughter took to exploring the magic terrain in the backyard. She was a curious thrill-seeker traversing the dangerous bridge over the pond without fear, trudging up the stream in pursuit of dragonflies and digging her fingers into the moss for bugs and worms. The garden watched over my child.

And then the garden watched us fall into deep despair. After the second miscarriage, my wife was very upset that I'd closed the account at the sperm bank after our first child was born. She imagined I didn't share the pain and anguish of losing a baby, and I couldn't say anything to make her understand how deeply I was hurting too. This was when it started, by my reckoning, the waning of intimacy that eventually deflated our marriage. After we moved to Hong Kong the third miscarriage came, and we repeated the horrible mistake of grieving separately, drifting further apart. Then out of the blue our second daughter was conceived, and she stuck to the womb tenaciously, the first manifestation of the indomitable fighting spirit that has defined her character ever since. She demanded to be born, popping out of the birth canal at the beginning of labor as though she was in a hurry to stomp on the ground and raise her arms and declare her divine nature. Heavens above, heavens below, I am the Buddha! Then she got down to the business of vigorously suckling milk and soiling diapers.

She was four months old when we had to break camp and prepare to leave Hong Kong on account of an untenable dispute with egomaniacal editors at the magazine in New York, pathologically insecure men who took perverse delight in crushing my spirit when I was vulnerable, giving me a debilitating case of writer's block. Before we left town we witnessed the pompous celebration of the handover of the British colony to Chinese sovereignty. It was a scripted and anticlimactic event, the only value of which was the two spectacular firework displays, one staged by the new masters from Beijing, the other by the retreating Redcoats. In my mind they dedicated the fireworks to my two miraculous children, because these girls gave me the strength and resolution to face the unknown of joblessness when we returned to the United States.

The Chinese invented gunpowder in 850 AD and soon started applying the new technology to the art of making firecrackers. But, like so many other innovations, it was the Japanese who perfected modern fireworks 900 years later. On miserably hot and humid summer nights, the Shogunate put on fireworks displays on the banks of the Sumida River in the heart of Edo's downtown area to entertain and calm, if not cool, the restless urban poor. The concept of *Hanabi Taikai,* or dueling fireworks, was born on the Sumida with two clans of fireworks craftsmen duking it out in the air to put on the better, most spectacular show.

Popular history may remember the July 1997 Hong Kong handover not for its important global-strategic paradigm shift but for one of the greatest Hanabi Taikai in the twentieth century. The outgoing British colonial government staged a fireworks extravaganza over the harbor on the eve of the change in sovereignty, which we watched in amazement through the window of our room in the Excelsior Hotel. The following evening we left the girls in the care of their soon-to-be unemployed Filipina nanny to watch the Chinese fireworks display lying face up on the deck of a sampan: Bursting stars and rocket trails, scattering red and blue buckshot, balls of yellow fire that exploded into smaller balls of yellow fire, a breathtaking kaleidoscope of brightly colored flowers that lit the black sky for what seemed hours. Everybody knew China would win in the duel just as I knew I would prevail over the implosion of my cursed magazine job, a disaster that threatened to ruin my career and pushed my frazzled marriage to the limit. I knew I would find a way to provide for my daughters.

—

He must tell Wilson to make a priority of finding the daughters. No, they would be too young still and probably in the custody of his ex-wife. Contacting them all before the next of kin might be a dicey proposition, he thought. Was it the older dragonfly daughter who wrote the letter he found on the floor? Still too young. How very odd, he thought. Perhaps there was a third, older daughter from a previous marriage? The coroner remembered the Salty Lagoon. The man has a past, he thought, dating back to before his path to illness. Nevertheless, the coroner resolved to find the girlfriend first, because she might hold all the answers. He would try to crack his way back into her blog for clues before calling Wilson to get the phone number on the back of the email printout, which he foolishly left behind at the morgue. He needed to find the vault, whatever it was, before he abandoned Barlow's house. He went to the kitchen and saw, to his chagrin, that he had already drained the bottle on the counter. Leaning against the wall, he massaged his head before drawing the phone out of its plastic holster like a wounded gunslinger.

"Wilson, find the daughters, check the schools, find their mother but hold off, don't contact them yet," he shouted at the handset. "Two young daughters, grade school and middle school age. And he's got two brothers. Parents may still be living. You find them, son, and if we can piece it all together, we can lay Barlow to rest."

"Okay Leo, shut up for a minute, cut the crap. And don't be so condescending to me anymore. I've had enough of your bullshit. Tell me where you are so I can help you save your own ass," he said.

"You're not Wilson. Patch me through to Wilson. I need his help."

"I am Wilson, Leo. Have you lost your mind? And what daughters are you talking about? You have names?"

"Okay, Wilson, I found them before he put the evidence in the vault, but no names yet. I will keep sniffing around and you put some ingenuity into the task. It should not be hard. Have you followed up on the dog tag information like I told you? You might find the ex, if she wasn't etched out completely from the past iterations of his dog tag profile already. Get to work, son."

He cut the line and turned off the phone before the *diener* could protest. He wondered if Du Goyle had a tap on Wilson's phone and was listening in and if he had the technical ability to trace the call. It occurred to him he forgot to ask Wilson for the number on the email printout. Oh well, first things first.

"Hi ho, hi ho, it's off to work we go," he sang as he plunked his fingers on the keyboard to reopen Christina's solo blog post. This time with greater clarity of mind he searched for a way to navigate from the segment to the entire site. He was determined to explore the plaintive exchange between the living and the dead. He had not noticed the faint text on the right side of the page beneath the subtitle, Blog Archive, listing previous posts. He chose the top item.

Tuesday, October 14, 2003
Sex, Brain and Belly

I don't know what I'm going to do, probably give it up before it turns into an unhealthy obsession. The trail is dry. It started out of idle curiosity but then became an old-fashioned mystery story, and I was the lady detective, but I realize what I've really been wasting my time.

It's too late, and what would he say to me if I found him anyway? "Nice to hear from you but you're a bitch. Goodbye."

At least then I'd know and get out of this trap. I know the scientific name for it: Synaptic Rutting. It's when your brain is involuntarily locked into neuro-pathways that trigger bodily habits or a psychological pattern. It's soft wired compulsion. I've got to break the sequence and stop imagining that Raul might forgive me for driving him back to San Francisco. I've got to stop thinking I'm an idiot for letting a foolish man make me feel this way. I need to stop it now before it eats me up.

My therapist says it's because I'm confused and disoriented by the emotional strain of hacking away at writing my dissertation, and it's natural to feel abandoned by the writing teacher who was there at the beginning. She knows all about Raul and doesn't have a very high opinion of him. She knows all about Alex and the seduction of his cameras, but is more sympathetic to him. How curious that they're both older men, she says. I'm looking to the past for answers, she says, instead of moving forward. It's a pattern, she says, a repeat of the time I broke off the relationship with Alex and ended up seeking affirmation from Raul, taking refuge instead of standing up on my own. "It's the chameleon in me," I tell her, and she says "A very good observation, Christina," in a maternal voice bordering on condescension. But what does she know? During one session I feel like I'm choking on Freudian mumbo-jumbo and I scream. "Leave my father out of this!" I'd read Freud, extensively, and regard him as a pretty good trial-and-error scientist, not the god of human psychology.

I knew Raul was not a father figure and I was not fucking my dad when we made love. I'm glad I finally got that off my chest because she doesn't get Freudian on me again. I think my relationships with men tend to be disastrous because I'm a very strong-willed and independent chameleon and I'm far too demanding. It's always that way, I suppose because I don't know what I'm looking for and when I get close to finding it I reject it. "Fear of intimacy?" she'd ask. This makes me think about what is so unique about Raul. His intimacy is unscripted and he makes me feel there wasn't a fear in the world. "It's not romantic love, it's belly love," I tell her, and she nods as though she understands. I like my therapist a lot but wonder if she knows me at all. She listens, and I suppose that's what good therapists are paid to do.

I don't know, maybe I'm going beyond the point of no return and it's too late to stop looking for the man. I thought I was being brave when I cut it off with Raul because it was unbearable and I had the good sense to protect myself. He couldn't make up his mind, he needed time, he had to protect his children. He wrote beautiful letters saying how much he loved me, explaining it all from his point of view and imagining, with deadly accuracy, how I felt about the situation. He pleaded with me to wait until he solved the problems with his family, but I didn't buy it. I used the shredder at the lab to turn the letters into strings of nonsense. I took the shreds home to burn in my fireplace, to purify the memories that cause such pain and sadness, but I stopped before lighting the match. I felt the urge to paste them back together again. They're in a sandalwood box under my bed now, and I think I'll keep them there until I find Raul, which may be never.

I'm so glad I made this stupid blog private instead of broadcasting my gushy soul to the public. I limited access to just a few of my closest friends and they all think I'm nuts. My ancient dowager mother definitely will never see it. If Raul found it he'd think I was a self-indulgent hypocrite. God damn you Raul. Go to hell. Stay with that ball-breaking wife of yours – those were the words you used to describe her, not mine. Forget all about me and I'll forget about you. I must take a rational approach to this whole matter. I'm a trained scientist. I need data. But what are the metrics of love?

Posted by Christina at 3:47 AM 0 Comments

———

The coroner rolled his eyes. "Oh Jesus," he said under his breath. "Who is this woman? I think I like her already." She had illustrated the post at the top with the image of a Nancy Drew book cover showing the teen sleuth in a plaid skirt holding a magnifying glass over tire tracks on the road. Hmm, evidence. The book bore the title: The Quest of the Missing Map." Below this image was a photo of a fashion model wearing a luminous cobalt dress, posing on the ramp with a haughty expression on her face, half angry, half flirtatious. She had black hair and green eyes.

He scrolled down the blog, stopping and skipping over entries, deciding he would go back and read them all later. Each entry had photos of tall women with hair changing colors, lengths, and styles that all looked similar but at once so very different from one another, laughing, pouting, scowling and brooding. The color of her irises gave her away. That was one thing the chameleon could not change. Then he saw a black-and-white drawing of a large bird. He could not resist.

———

Monday, August 4, 2003

Today I feel like a Raven.

It's late Monday morning and I need to get going and dance through a long list of chores and phone calls and errands and paper-work and job applications that make the life of an aging unemployed post-doc and aspiring junior scientist hell. Life seemed so much simpler when I was slaving away on my dissertation in graduate school. I didn't have time to busy myself with this level of minutiae – things just seemed to get done. Having no partner in the last couple of years probably helped in terms of efficiency. I think I'm much happier alone and abandoned. I can't imagine another serious relationship, with one exception, and I've already ruined everything with him. What I didn't ruin he ruined back at me, both of us singed by ill-fated passion. I don't even know where he is and it's better that way. Better to imagine how it could've been and fantasize how it might be rather than let reality interfere.

I don't exactly know where this raven sensation comes from but I have a few ideas. I wake up this morning half-dreaming about the bird and can't get her out of my fuzzy mind while I shower and drink a bowl of coffee, dress and half-listen to NPR say something about the evil war we've starting in Iraq.

It isn't a Poe-poem raven perched on my shoulder with intimations of premature death. It's a beautiful raven, a darkly glamorous raven, a raucous, ebullient lover of life and freedom. I feel it arising from my breast, tingling softly, with cool, glossy feathers. My friend Raul used to tell me I had raven hair, which struck me as a rather wonderful complement because I never really liked my thick and unmanageable hair. Even the stylists couldn't tame it for very long. I thought seriously once or twice about letting it tangle into dreadlocks or shaving it clean from my scalp. Raul and I didn't work out. It breaks my heart to think about it. One morning in a cloud of feather quilts he holds my face close to his and says he can see tiny flecks of brown in my green eyes. No one had seen them before. I thought they were my secret.

Nobody's perfect," I say. "You can't judge a woman by her irises."

"Oh yes you can," he says, "and yours are sensational. There's chocolate in there, little flecks from a Godiva bar, which is why they taste good when I look into them. Your eyes have mutated into mint chocolate chip ice cream. You should do your dissertation about this, not your little mice."

Raul and I were meant for each other, but it seems we're also meant not to be together. He's arrogant, self-centered and self-defeating, always saying he was too old and too poor to deserve someone like me. He's not what you'd call a catch. He isn't handsome except in a melancholy way, as if he used to be serviceably good looking and kept a trace of it on the path to middle age, through misfortune and morbid disease and nagging regret over all the wrong decisions he'd made in his early years. "I'm learning how to live in the present," he says when the topic comes up, "and you're my teacher." I say: "you're full of bullshit, Raul. I'm just a prostitute, soothing your damaged ego." Then he smiles.

He has strangely splayed eyes, but when he looks at me it's as if I was the only living thing in the world in that moment. The intensity is hard to get used to. I'm always the first to blink and look away, but sometimes our eyes dock in a kind of a vapor lock and we exchange unspoken bytes of ourselves before the gaze breaks and we float away. Now and then I wish it could have lasted forever but there's no such thing as a perfect match and ours is jinxed by things outside of our control. It's stupid, stupid, stupid on my part to get involved with a married man. I'd like to forget but the memories are so vivid it's like they're glued on, enduring disproportionately to the short time we spent together, just a year, and much of that in harmless friendship until it plunged quietly into passion. When we broke the rules and he was no longer my teacher and I not his student, when he stopped being the faithful unhappy husband and I became his happy home-wrecker . . . I really shouldn't finish that sentence. Let's just say I have an indelible memory of Raul Barlow sliding his fingers through my hair, my raven's hair.

I can be a Raven without Raul, or without Alex and his Hasselblads or any other lover. My chameleon essence allows me to be any animal and my hair can be any feathers or rabbit fur if I want. Ravens are basically larger and more intelligent than crows, as I recall. But *corvus christina* does not feel like a big crow – there's no glamour or grace in ordinary crow consciousness. I don't see crows wearing satin gowns to the ball but ravens could do that on the flip of a wing. We ravens fly more fluidly than crows, with aerodynamic long loping wings, and our cries are more sophisticated and far more euphonious than the metallic caw-caw of the common black pest. Plaintive, yes, but not irritating, maybe even dignified. You don't hear about Scare Ravens protecting the farmer's cornfields. Crows are pesky; ravens are alluring, with their luscious darkness. Poe did not understand ravens at all. He mistook them for omens of death and overlooked their dusky lust for life. You just have to look past the carrion in their diet.

If you're a little too tall, like me, you identify with the larger variation of any species. With dimension there has to be a change in elemental nature, something that can't be understood by measurement. Oh God, please, give me a long vacation from the tyranny of scientific metrics and the icy precision of the human genome, from the fruit flies and rodents I've violated by splitting their genes into tiny mutant life forms. I'm free from my father, the exalted astrophysicist who had such great expectations for me and was terribly disappointed in me up to the day he died. Free from the fear of turning thirty-six in two

months. Right now I am a bird of passion, not a little animal pecking away in competition with brilliant cohorts for a coveted post in
Berkeley or Cambridge. I am a dark-breasted raven with a golden beak
and green eyes, five feet-eleven and five-eighths inches, plus a few mil-
limeters, tall, and I have blue-black raven feathers and bird's eyes the
color green. It says so on my driver's license. A raven flying solo who
belongs only to herself, who doesn't need to divulge her age to prospective employers or make excuses for the seven-year gap in her curriculum vitae. The raven feels no shame in rejecting Alex when he calls
persistently begging me to take him back. A raven is not a photo slut
who is easily seduced by the lens of a camera. A raven does not make
her living off fickle style and ephemeral beauty, she uses her brains.
Feeding on carrion may seem distasteful, yes, but we are born oppor-
tunists and smart enough to let others do the killing. Oh my God,
that's sick! What am I talking about? Stop! End of raven metaphor.

All I have to do now is clear my mind of the last lingering feelings
for a disappearing man named Raul. I have no idea why I'm still thinking about him. It's long over. But I wonder where he is. Is he finally
divorced? Has he fallen into the arms of another lover? What does he
think of me? I've got to know. Dammit! Come home, Raul! Does it matter whether I banished you or you abandoned me? Just find your way
home, Raul, back to where you belong.

Shit, girl! I can't believe you're letting yourself say all this. It
must sound like I'm a total fool living in a fantasy world. Christina in
Wonderland? Time to stop.

Posted by Christina at 1:54 AM 0 Comments

———

Who the hell is this Christina anyway? A mad woman? What is this
man named Alex? Is he a parasite to a smart rich girl with maturing
depth and beauty? I am missing something, the coroner thought as he
continued skipping around the blog. Maybe there is no coherence in
her story at all. It seemed a blog could be an ideal canvas for a diary
you can easily revise and manipulate to reinvent your personal history,

a Petri dish for a geneticist like Christina or a writer like Barlow to incubate phantoms. He wondered if Barlow had a blog in addition to his box of notebooks and the stories in his vault, whatever the vault was supposed to be, wherever it was hidden away. Perhaps the vault was alive in his irradiated hippocampus, not in a hatch in the wall or a storage unit out in the desert.

Twenty-Seven

The coroner dropped the blog and went back to Barlow's My Documents folder where he selected a short item called "Expiation" to read. This too had the note at the top *move to vault.*

———

We'd stand in the kitchen yelling at each other over petty infractions. She'd blame me for a myriad of transgressions in absolute terms. "You always do this." The marriage counselor called this "global" accusation, which is apparently not helpful in the art of communication. I'd get angry and shoot back with a knee-jerk response, "you do it too!" The counselor said this response was childish and just made things worse. "It's not helpful," she'd say to just about everything. It didn't matter what the subject of the dispute was, breaking promises, shirking child-care, failing to fold the laundry and put it away. I pleaded no contest to the charge of forgetting to remove the lint from the dryer. "You always leave lint in the dryer." I'd say "No I don't." She conceded that she committed the sin of putting empty ice trays back in the freezer, but dismissed that as unimportant. I'd point out that refilling them and putting them back in the freezer was a lot more work for me than removing lint from the dryer and besides we wouldn't have ice when we needed it. She'd say "so what." The counselor would say, "This is not helpful." I'd grit my teeth and get sarcastic, complaining that she loaded the toilet paper on the spool the wrong way with the end coming up from the bottom instead of rolling over the top. "Haven't you ever stayed at a hotel? Over the top is the correct way, the only way." She'd say, "you're always sarcastic." (I since changed my mind on toilet paper positing; rolling it under is correct but never in my dying days would I admit that to her.) I suppose sarcasm was my default defense, a conversation stopper when I got fed up. She'd leave the room in fury. "Sarcasm isn't helpful," the counselor would say. You're not helpful yourself, you charlatan pop-psych bimbo, I wanted to spit back, but I didn't.

It was a bad sitcom without a laugh track.

Our trust in each other hit bottom when she'd get legalistic and recite verbatim conversations we'd supposedly had days earlier as incriminating evidence of my major errors. I'd protest that her accuracy was flawed, saying she had the delusions of mnemonic infallibility, a new diagnostic category I made up on the spot one day and made it a stock retort. She'd blame the problem on my selective memory, an accusation that was probably true a lot of the time, though I never gave her points for it. I knew my short-term memory deficit was worsening gradually before it plateaued toward the end of the marriage, but I deeply resented the inference that cognitive dysfunction was a character flaw. I'd fight back with my tools of cynicism and armchair psychology by saying she was subconsciously mistaking me for her deadbeat father and hated men. Fathers are always good material for marital feuds, and she countered with her analysis of the affect effect my father's abusive nature had on me. She was the martyr and I was the perpetrator; I was the martyr and she was the perpetrator. The counselor was aghast at our behavior, but eventually she tilted her bias, with great subtlety, toward siding with my wife. I became the "identified patient," the term of art in the trade, meaning my psychological state was the primary source of the problem. My troubles at work, my various diseases, my sarcasm. It was only half the picture, of course, but it became the title page. It wasn't very helpful.

My parents probably should have split up when I was a teenager. But they came to an accommodation that kept them together for another 44 years, fighting and bickering, blaming and harboring bitterness for each other until he was on his deathbed, when things lightened up. They loved each other by way of symbiotic dependence that was their saving grace, twisted, perverse but genuine love. I believe that in their minds they sacrificed their personal freedom to keep their dysfunctional family together in a confused and conflicted gift to my brothers and me. Along the way, long after their sons didn't need them any more, they cemented an endurable bond. This was hardly a model for marriage I wanted to emulate, but the jagged tolerance they constructed for each other left a deep impression. I can't imagine waking up in the morning and not seeing my two young children, not sharing in their lives every day from the time we rouse them awake to the time we read them to sleep at night. They're getting older now and the dynamic is changing. But I want them both to know that I fought like a determined fool to preserve this life even while I knew deep inside such an accommodation with their mother could not last.

When I was a hard-hearted, sullen and aloof sixteen-year-old, things got so bad between my parents that my father was preparing to move out and rent an apartment in downtown Chicago. Leaving behind a bitter wife wasn't the whole story, I could see. He was preparing to escape the humiliation he endured as a Jewish doctor in a quietly anti-Semitic suburban town. I believe the community's admiration and appreciation for his dedication was sincere, but I was old enough to understand that even though my parents socialized congenially with the town's elite, he was shut out of their inner circles. My angry father was deeply wounded by his craving for acceptance in a barren place. I loved him as much as I hated him, and it broke my heart to see him suffering so. I didn't know how much I loved him until one day in autumn when, to my surprise, he picked me up after school – for the first time in my memory. He stopped the car outside the football field fence and turned to me with agony in his face.

"Raul," he said, his voice cracking and heaving with sadness. "I want to tell you something very important. It's gotten so bad between your mother and me we can't live together any more, and I'm thinking about moving to Chicago until things cool down. I'm going to give up my medical practice in town and get back into my academic research work at the medical school. You could visit me on weekends, any time you want. Tell me what you feel about this, son. I don't want to hurt you. I know I haven't been a very good father to you and your brothers, but I never meant to hurt you and I don't want to hurt you now. Tell me what you think about this. Be honest."

At first I was bewildered by this rare show of emotion. I didn't know how to respond to this arrogant man who was now humbled and in despair, expressing a deep yearning to be needed and loved. I remembered the advice he gave me one summer afternoon years earlier after a miserable game of golf, advice that would influence me all my life, even when I was too bound up to use it. Comfort the old man as he grieves. Speak from your heart.

The sun was sinking into the distant cornfields on the flat horizon, casting a sorrowful November glow. Indian summer had come and gone. Soon the football season would end and dark evenings, bitter cold and snow would come.

"I don't want to visit you in Chicago, Dad," I said. "I need to see you every day."

When I was in my mother's womb my father was dying of polio. He was in the final stage, nearing the point when he would go into the iron lung and never come out. But a miracle happed. He did the improbable and recovered, the doctors said, by sheer willpower. He was too stubborn to let go. His third son was on his way, kicking furiously at his mother's belly. He defied polio.

A close colleague of his was involved in his redemption, a friend from medical school who came to visit him at the hospital nearly every day during the bleakest moments. The friend's name was Raul.

That afternoon we drove home from the high school in silence. My father didn't move to Chicago. He stayed.

I once listened to an interview on public radio with some expert who'd just written a best-selling book on divorce and its impact on children. My wife hadn't given me the final ultimatum of divorce at that time, but it was coming. She'd been furious with me for years and she was, rightly or wrongly, exasperated by a litany of my many shortcomings and failures. The core issue was whether I was being responsible about taking care of my own health problems, which for me was a blind measure; she was justifiably correct in one aspect but devoid of understanding in another. The divorce guru on the radio said something I'll never forget. "You can't love your children without loving their mother." What was that supposed to mean, was my initial reaction. It's a trap.

I'll love my children completely and unconditionally until I stop breathing, but beneath the surface, their mother's and my story simmers in a cauldron of mutual mistrust and unresolved bitterness. We agreed to maintain amicable civility in order to spare the kids from further emotional wreckage, but it didn't take long for them to see through the ruse. I've been meditating for a long time on what it means to love their mother under the circumstances. I suppose Christina gave me the key to understanding this. Her brand of fury is tempestuous, it is triggered by something that is visibly tied to the moment and it results a total release of scorching white heat that is quickly followed by self-awareness, contrition and affection. It's exhausting, but things are clear and out in the open. I actually grew fond of her tantrums after I realized that's just who she is. She's not going to change. My children's mother had her own brand of fury, bottled up inside her for weeks or months, or decades, then, without warning, blowing like a volcano. Then the anger would simmer and ferment anew, never resolved. I now understand this is just who she is, the sum total of a terrible experience she can't talk about and a struggle with her dampened brilliance – there was never a doubt that she has an extraordinary mind. I was aware of this before we married, but I was truly in love with the woman and I suppose I still am.

The lesson for me is that grownup people are at the mercy of themselves. I think the answer to the riddle posed by the divorce expert on the radio is this: It's possible to feel sympathy and compassion for someone you have good reasons to resent. To accept the fact that most people are incapable of being anyone else but who they are. All they can do is learn how to be nice about it. I hope this is the path to making my children feel loved. I keep thinking of it in terms of the old Smokey Robinson song: "I don't like you, but I love you."

Divorce is like a death in the family. No matter how much I secretly begged for freedom, I find myself grieving over the loss. I should be feeling great relief, but now that she's gone it's as if I have a phantom limb, a perverse attachment to something that isn't good for me and shouldn't be there anymore. I miss her, I feel sorrow for her pain, and I mourn the destruction of our marriage. And I'm trying my best to forgive her.

—

The coroner marched to the kitchen, wondering why he was on the verge of sniffling and cursing at the same time. He looked for a cabinet where Barlow might have stowed his liquor. It was time already. Fifteen minutes past nine. His fingers were trembling when he reached for the unopened bottle of Stolichnaya that was waiting for him. "Poor miserable dead bastard," he said aloud, not caring who listened. He didn't get a chance to defy the odds and protect his children, to see them flower into beautiful young women, to walk them down the aisle, to meet his grandchildren. Could any man die without grasping and grieving for the loved ones he leaves behind? The repose of the dead hides the whole story, the coroner thought. It fools the medical examiner, the funeral director, the survivors and the obituary writer at the local rag. No one will write a biography of Raul Barlow in the future. The story will vanish in the furnace unless it is captured first. Christina was all of the above and she will disappear as well unless he can find her.

The coroner found it increasingly difficult to keep up the pretense of professional detachment. His Vulcan nature, he thought, must resist having his emotions get sucked into the tragic relationships between the living and the dead. The finality of death in many of his cases at the morgue had been a soft and peaceful release of life force, but the rest had cruel endings. He made it a point of pride to mete out his sympathy to the bereaved with equanimity. He would have been callous and inhumane had he no compassion for the victims and kinfolk, yet he always stopped short of sharing emotions. The tasteless black humor he and his colleagues engaged in at the morgue was a coping mechanism for the mundane horrors of their work, not an abjuration of decency. No matter what the imbeciles in the county administration did to disgrace the institution of the Chief Medical Examiner's Office, he always regarded his job as honorable public service in the highest sense of duty. Barlow's case broke down that edifice of discernment, however, and, in the end, the coroner knew it was bound to end his career.

Tomorrow, should he sober up and return to the office wearing a fresh white shirt and the spare brown suit he had dry-cleaned last week, it was almost certain he would be summarily executed before he had the opportunity to rip open Barlow's rib cage for the autopsy. He had already defied the authority of the firing squad waiting to pounce on him at his performance review meeting, presided over by Horse's-Ass Du Goyle and the ugly HR woman who glared at him in every encounter with blood lust in her eyes. "We are very concerned about your job performance, Dr. Bacigalupi," the woman said when she cornered him in the hallway the previous week. "The functional aptitude metrics in your dossier, as reported by your supervisors, has shown a marked decline in recent years." She was enjoying herself.

The grounds for termination? Insubordination, violation of department protocol, failure to submit autopsy reports in a timely manner, spending too much time with individual cases, taking long lunch hours. There were rumors he secreted a bottle of vodka in his credenza. He was reprimanded for taking off more days than he was allowed on the policy for bereavement leave. He had been warned about this many times before and shrugged it off as bunk, but this time he was at the end of his rope.

He knew his most grievous crime was unvarnished arrogance combined with growing older, slower, and sloppier. His seniority and the merit raises for excellent service he earned earlier in his career made him the highest paid Assistant Chief Medical Examiner in the State. Du Goyle had once shoved a compensation chart in his face, frothing with contempt, and threatened to reduce his salary, which of course he did not have the power to do. The coroner suspected he might be earning more than Du Goyle himself.

The coroner was ready to go down with dignity. He would solve this politically unimportant case, which had become so vitally important to him for reasons he did not comprehend. He would talk to Christina and find Barlow's ex-wife and the daughters and brothers and anyone else who might keep memories of the man alive. All the information he needed was concealed in the dog-tag files, in the computer he was cracking, in the notebooks he was plowing through, in that filing cabinet he was neglecting, and in the vault that had yet to be found and penetrated. His final duty as an officer of the City and County of San Francisco would be to reunite Barlow's ghost with the mysterious Christina. He would preside over a love story, not an inquest. He would determine whether it was murder, suicide, an accident, or pure fantasy. He must tell Christina what happened.

"Look here!" There was something taped onto Barlow's desk that he had noticed peripherally before but had dismissed. Now it stood out like a blinking billboard. "How the hell did I miss this? It said: "Drink me," followed by tiny script.

On close inspection it was a line of fifteen letters, numbers and keyboard symbols that was way too long to be a password for an email account. He reckoned it had to be a code that unlocked Barlow's vault, whatever that was supposed to be. It would provide access to forbidden files, just what he was hoping to unearth.

It was slipshod security to paste it on his desk for trespassing eyes like his to see, but he suspected this might be an important facet of Barlow's character, fastidious and at the same time sloppy. The code promised an opportunity for the coroner if he could figure out how to use it. Wilson once explained during one of their erratic computer lessons that the toughest security walls require complicated encryption keys, not just conventional passwords. He could not summon Wilson to Barlow's sanctuary now without spoiling the privacy of his inquest. He double-checked his cell phone to make certain it was turned off lest the *diener* intrude. So he would have to try to do this himself. The reformed juvenile delinquent hacker said that the longer the chain of keystrokes, the more challenging it would be to hack into a system.

Wilson's inflection when he said the word "challenging" suggested a naughty adrenaline rush, the coroner recalled.

In this instance, however, he had the key but not the gate to unlock. He was reasonably certain this was the code to open Barlow's "vault," but had no idea what shape or form that would take. It was the same with the house key in the fifth pocket of the man's tattered Levi's jeans when he was presumed homeless. He had to find the house that fit the key before the key was any use.

The long snake of code made him dizzy. binkP<red85l#hors@ hil8oTxw.

The archive had to be lurking somewhere in Barlow's laptop, and the coroner was determined to find it. He began the laborious chore of sliding the cursor down the list of documents, looking for a likely file to open, perhaps an item marked *vault* or *secret* or *confidential* or *QT*. It seemed consistent with Barlow's character to hide something in plain sight. He started trawling again, this time from the bottom up. There was a file labeled *himitsu*, whatever that meant – some Japanese tale perhaps – but nothing marked *secret*. Wary of his predilection for computer rage, the coroner reached instinctively for his flask to brace himself against spiraling frustration, for if he punted the laptop across the room all would be lost. He pulled his hand back, however, when an idea occurred to him. Wilson said if you ever lose track of a file or program, you could find it with "search." He strained to remember how to do that. Of course, he had to go back to the Start button that had led him serendipitously to the list of documents. There, he should click Search, and above the little bouncy dog he would see an arrow pointing to All Files and Programs. Enter a name. He tried the obvious words he could not find on the documents list, and was ready to give up when the right side of his aching brain spoke up. *Why not enter the code as a file name?* He started with the first few letters: "bink."

Indeed, his needle in the haystack was sandwiched in the random flow of file names: "Binkus.org - Social Justice Security System." He slammed his thumb on the return key triumphantly to see a tan window open with a keypad of numbers and alphabetically arranged letters, upper and lower case, and a row of symbols. It said enter your password. Stroke by stroke he punched each character on a keypad to no avail. He struck out three times, slowly reentered the code key, on guard for typos and case-sensitive characters. Yet Binkus mocked him with its impenetrable security wall. Out of frustration the coroner entered the grawlix of profanity, "@#$%&!" Binkus responded to the coded epithet by rejecting the intruder with a beeping alarm, then turned itself off.

He kept his hands away from the laptop, fearing he would whack it with his palm until it obeyed him. He calmed himself and studied the encryption key once again, hoping to find clues. There it was, "red." Interspersed among the following characters were fragments, hors and hil. He shot up from Barlow's oak chair and stumbled to the bookcase to grab the red book with the hollow core. Inside he saw one tiny shred of paper wedged among the other sheds lining the cavity, which he failed to notice the first time he inspected *Red Horse Hill*. He pincered it out with finger and thumb nails and examined it closely to see the miniscule script: *P<chris915#teen@hil8oTxw*. When he rushed back to the desk and tapped out the revised code he paused to say "*abraca-dabra!*" before slapping the Enter key. A list of files streamed down the screen like black magic, astonishing him with their crisp Arial font. He had managed to penetrate the dead man's chamber of secrets. "Jesus fucking Christ!" he hollered, "God almighty I'm home!"

Twenty-Eight

A note above the list of documents said the files had to be retrieved from a secure proxy server before they could be opened, meaning the vault was not hidden in Barlow's own computer but locked away in a cloud of digits somewhere off the Internet. Barlow's intent, he wondered, might have been to take his secrets to the crematorium. He did not anticipate that he, Leo Bacigalupi, the dogged pathology investigator, would be on the case. Why, he wondered, would a dead man want to conceal himself like this? It was dumb luck that he stumbled onto the red book and this trove of stories. Were these the unvarnished memories that arise in the panicky mind of the proverbial bridge-jumper seconds before his impact on the choppy current of the Golden Gate? The coroner feared he would betray Barlow's wishes to seal the vault after his demise. No, he thought, that is not true. Barlow's eyes asked him to open the vault and eavesdrop. He gave in to the flask now, but in celebration instead of vexation. He drained the remaining ounce of vodka, thinking he could always replenish it when the appropriate time came. Sooner or later he would get his eggs, bacon and hash browns and go home to sleep.

He opened the most recent file in the vault.

———

October 31, 2003
Christina

She found me. I'm in a daze. All I can think about is how my desperation in wanting her all this time is contorted by a feeling of apprehension and inadequacy, that I might never live up to her hopes, or to an idealized and distorted remembrance of how it all happened in a particular place in a particular time relegated to the past tense. I've got to be totally honest with myself to recognize how ambivalent I feel about seeing her again, scared to the point of paralysis, and knowing the danger of falling in love all over again with an indescribably beautiful phantom of womanly art and science, whom I never deserved to love or be loved by in the first place. I'm still sixteen years older than her and she's no doubt blossomed into graceful maturity while I've aged ingloriously these past three years. No matter how hard I've tried to regain the vigor of my youth, I recognize I'm hovering on the brink of decline. What do I have to offer a woman whose future has boundless potential while mine is under a cloud? I'm a writer laboring under the delusion of beating the odds to gain a scrap of distinction some day – a bad match for Christina.

I have to go back and try to understand how the magic entanglement happened in the first place. I have to consider some sort of transference, the phenomenon whereby patients are sexually attracted to their therapists, political pages to their senators, models to their photographers – and students to their teachers. It's where a man or a woman, with or without intention, casts a spell on someone who's vulnerable to an unconscious attraction to the beguiling power authority. Could there be more than a dash of Oedipus and Electra involved? Whatever it is, it's ancient. I've seen it all around me and I've seen in myself. It can be the toxic seed of sexual abuse just as it can be the catalyst to enduring love.

For a brief period, an accident in time, Christina was my student and I was her teacher. I honestly don't think she'd have taken a second look at me outside the classroom. I was in awe of her and never looked down on her as inferior, and I believe she was too self-confident to look up to me as superior, yet I suspect now that there was more than simple attraction going on. I tempered my feeling with the admonishment "look, don't touch."

The restraints didn't last long. There was a subversive attraction that fermented and cooked until we eventually confessed that we felt unusually at ease in each other's presence. There was the feeling of tacit understanding that evolved over time from long conversations, harmless flirtation and gentle teasing before we began grazing and touching shoulders and exchanging timid social hugs. I can't help feeling that when she looks at me now the spell will be long gone. There's no foundation for a lasting love, and it wouldn't matter that I'm no longer shackled to a bad marriage, that my children and I are safe and live nearby, that I'm over the worst of my writing block. Chances are, Christina and I would end up recreating the same cruel and hurtful parting we had in Los Angeles. I don't believe I'm wallowing in feelings of inadequacy here, just coming to terms with the facts, the almost certainty, not the probability, the result of an honest appraisal. I'm not stupid.

I have no illusions about what's going to happen when we meet in the morning. She'll take a good look at me and, come to her senses and realize we can't go back. We'll kiss in a warm and compassionate way and join in a melancholy sigh. She'll be kind-hearted. She'll probably insist on making me breakfast before she finds an excuse to rush home to the Southland. We'll leave off where we started, a pure state of fantasy.

How will I stop myself making a fool out of myself tomorrow by leaking what's in my heart, the fear that I might reunite with the love of my life only to lose her again? What would she think if I told her I haven't been able to chase her from my mind all this time, that she's in my thoughts constantly, that like an idiot I'm sometimes convinced she's in bed with me at night and I escort her into my dreams?

Would she believe me if I told her I met an apparition named Aurora on BART who kissed with your mouth and your lips and made me feel as though the world was about to end? When I grit my teeth in rush hour traffic, I talk to Christina instead of shouting at reckless drivers, and she calms me. She's right next to me when I sit on the bench in meditation, where I try to end the delusion of desiring her past the point of distraction.

"You're not real," I tell her so I can dismiss the hallucination. "No, no, you made me real, Raul, by loving me so much," she responds. "You said so yourself one night. That I'm your Velveteen Rabbit."

Whoever you are, I want you as my first and only lover, Christina, my closest friend, my greatest companion. I want to spar with you and allow you to knock me out, to possess you and submit to you, to release you and wait for you to return. To argue and agree with you, please you and disappoint you, enter you and be released. To entertain you, disgust you, nurture you, embarrass you, lift you from dark moments and burden you with my despair. I want to wear you like a sweaty tee shirt and feel you seep into the pores on my back. Let me marvel at your shining mind, your mysterious heart and your stunning passion for life. Accept me for what I am, Christina, as I'm learning to accept myself. Knock on my front door tomorrow morning and take me home. Tell me you're real, please, that this is all true and not the product of a yearning so great that I cooked you up in my mind.

—

The coroner stood up and clenched his fists. The blood rushed to his head and his knees wobbled before he dropped on his rump in Barlow's oak captain's chair with a heavy thud. The vault sat open on the screen like a mirror, inviting him to hop through the glass.

So this is what was in Barlow's mind, the manner of his death, not the cause of it.

He noticed the item below was dated the same day as the sketch of his meeting Christine's double on the train, the one in the notebook the coroner found open on Barlow's desk when he first stole into the house.

—

The Geneticist

Meeting that woman on the train today brought home a cascade of sensations I wasn't ready to feel. I couldn't get it all down in the journal. It will take me a lifetime of writing to understand Christina, the parts that are her and the parts I suppose I've imagined because I was only beginning to know her.

I don't trust myself expressing myself on the computer – the cold type is better suited to my left brain, my journalist's brain, the expository writing brain where the damage lies. But I'm growing more and more impatient with my handwriting. It exhausts me far more than the keyboard because it takes so much effort to control my right hand.

Right now, I've got to clear my mind, no matter what medium I have to use.

I was on a newsroom sabbatical when I met Christina. I took a year off do a journalist-in-residence fellowship at UCLA – it was an experiment, and I was their first and last one. We encountered each other shortly after my arrival at the beginning of the first semester. I was casting about for a course I might teach to break the monotony of doing research for my ill-fated crime novel, but the head of the undergraduate journalism program said she didn't need me. I didn't fit into the curriculum because I wasn't a broadcast journalist, just print, and newspaper people were a dime-a-dozen with so many of my former colleagues at the local newspaper begging to teach for free.

I was affiliated with the School of Public Affairs, so I approached the dean with a proposal to teach a seminar on the Japanese media, which fell on deaf ears. Finally the dean approached me with the idea of teaching a writing workshop for graduate students. We discussed this and he said his aim was to give some remedial English training for PhD candidates struggling with their dissertations. Atrocious writing is pandemic among these scholars, and he thought the craft of a journalist's writing could sharpen their prose and help them better organize their ideas. I reluctantly agreed and slapped together a syllabus for a two-unit seminar I called "Having Fun while Writing Good." Not a single student signed up during early registration. You can't force them to enroll, I told the dean, but he had another idea: How about an enticement, like calling it Creative Writing for PhD Dummies? The result would be the same, he said. You edit them mercilessly and they'll learn sentence structure and a cohesive narrative whether they like it or not. A spoon full of sugar . . .

The dean is brilliant, I thought.

Seventeen students showed up on the first day of class, most of them very young, shopping around for easy credits and checking me out. I scared away as many as I could by telling them how hard they'd have to work to get an A. We spent fifteen minutes going around the horse-shoe table introducing ourselves while I peppered them with intrusive questions about their writing backgrounds and personal motivations. I told them that if they weren't ready to read their stories aloud and have them critiqued by fellow students – and suffer my intimidating margin notes – they didn't belong in the seminar. One of them, a comparatively older woman in a baggy gray sweatshirt, asked me if the class was open to graduate students in the sciences without any writing experience. "You're perfect," I said. I didn't pay much attention to her until it was her turn in the round of self-introductions. She described herself as a "late bloomer" working on her PhD in genetics. Her name was Christina, she said. Our eyes locked for a shy moment until I had to lower my gaze for fear of making her as uncomfortable as I was. She was shockingly beautiful.

There were six students waiting at the table when I entered the classroom the following week and I was happy to see she was one of them. I had asked those who wanted to commit to the seminar to bring in some of their writing, a short story, a newspaper article or a poem, and if they didn't have anything of their own to bring any short piece of writing by someone they admired. Christina presented an article from the New Yorker by Calvin Trillin on the subject of barbequed back ribs. She read a section of it and told us how much she liked good food and that Trillin's food writing made her salivate. She got a ripple of laughter from the other students with that. Then she explained the biochemical basis of salivation, the sensory stimulation of the taste and smell receptor cells on the tongue and palate that trigged the involuntary response from the glands, "I want to write like Calvin," she said. "Make my dissertation committee hungry."

I suppose I was dumbstruck. I studied her closely and noticed there was something remarkably different about this woman. While the others read their presentations, it was everything I could do to take my eyes off of her, to dismiss her tangled black hair tied up in a careless knot on the top of her head. She was a striking woman who looked to be anywhere between her early to mid-thirties. She must have done something interesting for a while and returned to school with a goal in mind, I thought. The movement of her hands was fluid, and I was impressed by the way she sat in her chair with her back softly tilting as if she were bringing her ear closer to listen in total concentration as the other students read aloud, awkward and uncomfortable. I got the feeling that her presence calmed them and encouraged them. She was doing my job for me. I lamented my limited peripheral vision, because I wanted to drink in the sight of her the whole fifty minutes. I allowed myself only a few passing glances, that's all, because I didn't want her to think I was ogling her. She must have been accustomed to the effect she had on men, I thought. It was the first meeting of the class and I was already breaking the taboo against teachers seeing their students as sex objects, but this woman was exceptional in every way. I suppose I'm more susceptible than I'd realized, still shell-shocked by the separation from my wife and kids, trying to work out the ambiguity of being married but without a real partner, feeling adrift and scorned, facing the prospects of seeing my daughters only on weekends. I already missed them miserably and it's only been a little more than two weeks since I left San Francisco.

—

The coroner made a note to himself to return to Christina's blog later to see what her initial impression was of Barlow. He wanted to triangulate the lovers' tales with a baseline of probability, to apply science to romanticism. There had to be some sort of incubation for the relationship to reach the point of intensity that each lover described. Great love stories don't reach their frenzied crescendo right away. They ferment until they seethe with deep desire and madness, then they come down to earth and either blossom into reality or implode on impact. He was not a literary man, the coroner admitted, but he knew how people behaved as a keen observer of the human condition. He was one of the lucky ones who knew what a lasting love is, and he was one of the unlucky ones who had it cut short.

He resumed reading Barlow's tale of the geneticist.

———

She was born to wealth. Her mother was a third-generation Californian whose family made a great fortune speculating in real estate in the late 1800s. Her father, the son of a postman in Peoria, Illinois, had been nominated for the Nobel Prize in physics when he was a young man, but he was passed over in favor of an older and more established genius. They were Pasadena people, the kind who took pride in pronouncing Los Angeles with a hard "G" as a shibboleth for class, distinguishing themselves from the riff-raff out west, the Jews in Hollywood and the nouveau riche in Malibu. It didn't surprise me when Christina described herself as a spoiled and rebellious only child. She loathed the ballet lessons and theater camps for gifted children that her mother, a great patron of the arts, forced her to attend. She boasted about sneaking out of her stately Green & Green house after midnight to go cruising with older, verboten friends. She incited her father's rage by skipping school to hang out in Westwood or go surfing at Hermosa Beach. She was arrested at a rave. One summer she got thrown out of the house for bringing home a boy named Bobby Bullard and smoking pot in her bedroom. Her mother changed her mind and used her connections to have the county sheriff bring her home when she heard Christina was auditioning for suspicious modeling jobs at second-rate agencies. "I was a naughty child," she confessed, "but I still got straight A's, so they couldn't disown me."

She told me this during our first encounter outside the classroom when we met over lunch at Hamburger Hamlet to discuss an ingenious short story she'd written about talking houseplants. The Boston ferns and spider plants gossiped among themselves about the psychotic people who watered them. It ended with a double herbicide.

I met with the other students over lunch to give them one-on-one help with their writing, so there was nothing out of the ordinary about my first few meetings with Christine. But soon we were getting together regularly and discreetly at a quiet coffee house in Santa Monica. She was the one who initiated these meetings, always asking for help with her stories because she was a "neurotic perfectionist" and never finished rewriting them. I was thrilled. I could tell she was exceptionally bright because she knew how to ask questions, relentlessly, and threw herself into the joy of learning new things. The craft of writing become her new passion and she couldn't help herself from wanting to excel in the way she excelled at everything else she ever did.

Eventually the conversation got more personal. She told me she was cutting off a romantic involvement with a photographer she used to work with years ago. Their professional relationship turned romantic the previous year, but now it was falling apart because she spent so much of her time in the lab and the library working on her dissertation. The problem got even worse now that she was writing stories for my class, which she thought made him jealous for no reason. Alex was his name, and he was adamant in telling her that creative writing was a big distraction and a waste of time. He was bossy and manipulative in the way some of the best photographers are on a shoot, she said, but that didn't work in real life. She hated being told what to do.

"He was like a big brother to me," she said. "And then we started having ... well, you know what I mean, I think it ruined the friendship. That sounds like a cliché."

"Sometimes clichés are true, Christina," I said. "That's how they got to be clichés in the first place. They're fractured metaphors repeated so often we get sick of them. They're the stuff of lazy thinkers who use them for cheap rhetoric but sometimes they can be the best way to describe things. Also saying this about clichés is a cliché in and of itself – I've heard it said that said so many times before it's hackneyed. Ha ha. Am I getting too convoluted?"

"Your bullshit meter is rising, if that's what you mean," she said. "Why don't you come over here and whisper some sweet platitudes in my ear, professor."

"Okay, just let me complete the thought. In my writing I sometimes like to play with clichés by inverting them or twisting them around by their snouts. Excessive alliteration is good, but I try to avoid gratuitous portmanteau words. It's a joke between me and the reader, who either gets it or not but doesn't have to choke on it. The meaning jumps out when you play with words because the reader has to stop and think twice. You have to throw out an anchor."

"I'm working on a story about my cliché with Alex. I think it's scintillating and sad."

"I wouldn't start writing your memoir just yet, not until you're a great scientist. You're not done aging like a fine wine," I said. "Now there's good cliché for you. Incidentally, I'd like you to tell me what you were doing with a photographer in your past life, and what you're doing in the lab of yours that's so important."

"The past is the past, Raul, and none of your beeswax. Besides, you'd get the wrong impression of me," she said. "I finally listened to my daddy – he was right about me all along. I got my GED, went to Berkeley, dropped out of medical school, and found salvation in genetics. It's been a long journey and I'm no spring chicken anymore. Alex is the last figment of my previous life."

She looked up from her hands and nailed me with her oversized eyes. "Just think of me as a junior geneticist in a frumpy white coat," she said. "I'll tell you what we're doing at the lab. It's no secret. We're working on human genome stuff, looking at the DNA that makes you unique and we try ßto figure out where you came from."

She took a breath. "I kill a lot of mice. I'm mouse-o-cidal. That's the entertaining part, but mostly it's a lot of tedious work, spending a lot of time on the computer, crunching data."

"I'm intrigued, fascinated. What do you suppose my genome is? Could you take a swab of DNA from my tongue now and l tell me what it looks like? I've always wanted to know where I came from."

"Stop sticking your tongue out, Raul – it's undignified for a man of your station," she said with an exaggerated frown. "It's more than complicated. Your DNA is about one terabyte of meatloaf and I'd need a grant and a lot of time to study all your mutations. Leave the DNA to your forensic pathologist, if you have one yet. Besides, only about four percent of your DNA is uniquely human, you know. The rest is bonobo. If you don't know what a bonobo is, I can tell you."

"Tell me what a bonobo is."

"They're cousins of the chimpanzees but they're matriarchal and very affectionate with each other. They're physical about it, demonstrative. Downright promiscuous, doing it all day long. No kidding, that's what the latest research tells us, but I'm embarrassing myself. It's not polite conversation. But I suppose most people would rather be a bonobo than a nasty little chimp."

Christina could be both sober and flirtatious at the same time and the combination was deadly. She was eloquent in her use of foul language and she also knew how to be overbearingly prim and proper. She was irresistible. I tried not to betray my reckless infatuation with her, and if she knew, it probably didn't matter a whole lot to her. She was in control. Her writing was terrible at first but soon her sloppy love of language revealed itself and her imagination ran wild. I still don't know exactly what she did in front of a camera in her past life but I was pretty sure it wasn't boring. It had something to do with her troubled beauty and the vanity she struggled to overcome.

Twenty-Nine

The coroner sucked air between his teeth as he continued his scrolling though the vault. He wanted to follow the progression of the affair, from its coy twenty-question chatter to its culmination in lusty passion, but there were too many titles in the vault to sort out. He would have to jump around to find a strike, just like fishing in the cardboard box of hand-written notebooks. He saw a file that looked like the answer to the mystery of the eldest child, the one who possibly slipped that note under Barlow's door. It is a digression, but it will be useful in establishing his emotional landscape, he thought.

———

Miracle Three

Houston was visiting from Maine, staying with me at the dilapidated, pre-earthquake goat-herder's shack I rented for a song on the flank of Diamond Heights. We were getting drunk on a magnum of cheap sh ch one night out in the patch of front yard, admiring the unobstructed view of the lights on the Bay Bridge. I'd gotten to know Houston when I was studying in Kyoto and we were the best of friends, especially when we were drinking and philosophizing. We were sitting on the sloped front yard, surrounded by tall weeds, wild California poppies and night-blooming jasmine. We talked endlessly about nothing at all until I finally got it off my chest, something I'd been struggling with for the past two years.

"I haven't shared this with anyone, Hu, not even Satomi," I said. "I think I might have a daughter out there, somewhere."

"What do you mean 'out there?' You can't have a child without a mother," Houston said. "Who is she? One of the *kawaiiko-chans* you messed around with in Japan? Feeling a pang of guilt?"

"No, it's even worse than that. She's right here in the Bay Area. You remember me telling you about the social worker job I had in Oakland before coming to Japan, with Vietnamese boat people? There was a beautiful girl working there. I was smitten. She had another boyfriend and she never made it clear who the father was before I left, and she said it didn't matter. She wanted to have the baby her own way."

"Sounds like a half-assed Madame Butterfly story to me," he said. "In reverse."

"Cut the crap," I said. "This is serious. I can't run from it any longer. I need to know whether it's my child or not because the ambivalence is killing me. The other guy in the triangle was older and had a solid job and she said he was participating in her Lamaze pre-natal classes. But it didn't sound right somehow. There was something in her voice. She sent me a baby picture not long after I landed in Japan, very matter-of-factly, sort of like, 'Hello, how are you? Here's a picture of my baby.' It was hard to tell who she looked like. I wanted to find some kind of clue, but it wasn't there."

"Go out and find the mother," he said. "Ask her."

"What if she's happily married to this other guy? It'd be an unwanted intrusion on their lives and I'd make a mess of things"

The following day I was scanning the job listings from my college's employment center and saw a listing for my old position at the social services agency in Oakland. I knew what I had to do. It was going to be humiliating to apply for the same job I'd already failed at, and I had no intention of taking it should they be desperate enough to offer it to me, but it was a sure way of getting the information I needed. If she was still working there I'd know by looking into her eyes. If she wasn't,

I'd be able to sound out my former colleagues on what happened after I left for Japan without intruding directly on her privacy. Maybe she'd hear through the grapevine I was back in town and know why I was nosing around at the agency. Houston said I had to do it, giving me the push I needed.

I was operating under the assumption that my former co-workers had no idea about the office fling, but Mike, my old boss, saw right through me. He pretended not to know why I was there and he had the sensitivity and alacrity to avoid putting me on the spot. Mike got the message across by telling me about a really wild wedding party he'd attended a few weekends earlier where there was a lot of drinking and dancing. The bride married a dentist in San Jose, a great guy who was going to adopt her two-year old child. "You remember her, don't you?" Mike said, with a raised eyebrow suggesting conspiracy. "The pretty blonde who used to work here?"

I never stopped wondering, brooding, hoping for a definitive answer. After I began my career as a journalist I held out the hope that the wife of the San Jose dentist would somehow see my byline, contact me, and mercifully put an end to the anguish that never stopped quietly festering in my soul. In the end, when I took the job in San Jose, I was certain she would see the email and phone number at the bottom of my articles and, if she wanted to, call me.

I had no idea the family had moved to Susanville, on the far side of the Sierra Nevada Mountains. The woman had divorced and moved to Oregon by the time she finally phoned me out of the blue, ending twenty-seven years of doubt and confusion. I was speechless. She spoke casually, as if we'd been chatting amicably all these years. She explained that her daughter was going to have an operation and the doctor wanted to know the medical history of her biological father. I sat down in a stupor and told her to take out pen and a pad of paper because the story of my health was long and complicated.

My bio-daughter came out of the operation without serious problems. We met at the Berkeley Marina, and when our eyes met it was like looking into a mirror. The pain and guilt of more than two decades melted away. It's been nothing but boundless joy ever since. She invited me to her upcoming wedding on the spot. Her family welcomed me into the fold and my children fell madly in love with their half-sister at first sight. It was a miracle.

One day she told me that her mother had recorded the other man's name as the father on her birth certificate, but that she'd told her that her real father was a writer named Raul Barlow. This man, the mother said, wasn't aware he had a daughter. "She said you didn't know I existed." I don't know how I held it together until that night when I locked myself in the bedroom, pushed my face into a pillow and bawled like a newborn gasping for air.

—

The coroner did not know what to think or how to feel about this. That last line epitomized Barlow's penchant for schlocky sentimentalism when the emotional level of his writing passed a certain threshold of melancholia. Yet the depth of his sentiments survived his maudlin prose. It triggered the recollection of his and Alice's ache after their nine-year-old son was killed on his way to school by a drunk driver. The coroner had no heirs, only an insufferable S.O.B. of a nephew he had taken out of his will, but he sometimes imagined he had a biological offspring out in the world looking for him. We should have tried to conceive again, we should have adopted, he told himself over and over again, before it was too late.

Back to Barlow. This is his story, not mine, he thought, snapping to attention. He feared there were too many items in the vault for him to read and comprehend without confusing the story and eroding his mental acuity, so he decided to pick them out selectively. He spotted one called Seizures, which struck him as good ore for a pathologist to mine and highly relevant to his inquest. He clicked it open and found a strange new title at the top of the text.

—

The Useless Tree

With shrinking ad revenue and declining profit margins, the paper is getting ready for another round of buyouts, and, this time, layoffs. They are preparing to fire me. My supervisors have hounded me about my sub-sub-standard performance for the past year and they're right; I've more than lost my edge. The gears are moving slower and slower. The prophecy of neurotoxicity has finally caught up with me. They've threatened me with termination if I don't meet their new quota of bylines and front-page stories.

I'm hanging in by a thread. I can't think straight in the buzz of the newsroom anymore and I'm paralyzed with writer's block. No, that's the wrong term. I'm too confused, too slow, too exhausted to write in the afternoons; I freeze on deadline. Their hostility doesn't help, it only heightens the stress and deepens the funk.

When I was an AP reporter at the beginning of my career I could pick up a phone at the scene of a fire and dictate the story to the desk while flipping through my notebook, composing the rough draft in my head. When I was a newspaper correspondent in Japan I was able to crank out a 3,000-word story in a few hours after a long day of reporting and meet my deadline at 3:00 AM Tokyo time. Now I struggle with a simple 400-word story. I lose track of what I'm trying to say. I can't do the math for business stories. My reporting is riddled with humiliating factual errors and my writing is unacceptably dirty, full of typos, dropped words and illogical transitions. I get drowsy on deadline and it gets worse day by day. I've made excuses for myself, claiming my problems are caused by the side effects of anti-seizure medication. They don't buy that. They've made up their minds that I'm some sort of slacker, a prima donna ex-foreign hack, a liar. I wish I could attribute this entirely to my own paranoia because that's something I might have the power to overcome, but in my rational mind I can see clearly what's happening around me. They're truly closing in for the kill, and probably for sound reasons.

Two decades ago, the Associated Press let me go because I refused to serve another four-week stint on the overnight shift in the Philadelphia bureau. The dislocation of my biological clock made it all but impossible to control my blood sugar when I worked for extended periods overnight. The glucose numbers went haywire, running so high I had short bouts of ketoacidosis, the condition that threatened to kill me in the Sierras five years earlier. These were followed by numbers that would plummet to seriously low levels of hypoglycemia in the middle of the night when I was alone in the bureau. After eating in panic to correct the problem the numbers on my glucose meter bounced up again to outrageously high peaks during the daylight hours. When it was my turn again for the graveyard shift on the next rotation I refused. The bureau chief told me that was not acceptable and gave me two weeks notice, and when I appealed to the executive news editor in New York he lied to me, saying there were no jobs in the AP system that didn't require overnight duty. I was powerless to fight back because I was still on probation and wasn't protected by the union. My two years as a "local hire" in the Tokyo bureau didn't count in the domestic service. The Americans with Disability Act hadn't been enacted yet, and they unceremoniously sacked me. The shock has never worn off.

Now, twenty years later, I see it happening all over again. I'm the loser in another calamity that pits illness against employment and I know I'm only delaying the final reckoning by going on temporary disability leave. I'm disgracing myself by saying things and writing angry emails that are compulsive and irrational. I'm undermining my own dignity by lashing out at authority instead of negotiating with it, by blaming others instead of taking responsibility for my sluggish cognition, by losing control over the unrelenting stress of terminating my ruined marriage. I've already lost Christina. In the newsroom I've turned into a pariah and an asshole – I can see it in the eyes of my colleagues. This is not who I really am, I want to tell them. But it's too late to apologize. I've trapped myself.

I consulted a labor lawyer who told me the ADA has proved toothless in most employment litigation, and it would bankrupt me to sue a newspaper owned by the nation's second-largest media chain and armed with a phalanx of corporate lawyers. These are hard-nosed people who have to cut staff to appease obstreperous shareholders complaining about declining profit margins. It's strange, but I sympathize with the executive editor. She's a skilled journalist with incisive news judgment, but her fate was to preside over a collapsing newspaper. She has no choice but to cut back a costly staff, and she has to start with closing sections and cutting out the deadwood. Nothing personal. But the aggressive style and hostility of her sub-editors is abusive and humiliating. There's no excuse for that.

I'm covered by a long-term disability policy and that's an option, but it makes me sick to think about it. It will ruin my reputation and wreck my career as a journalist. I don't know how to do anything else than write for a living, and at this point I can't write professionally because I get so exhausted when I can't make my brain take on intellectual tasks toward the end of the day. I get woozy and have to resist falling asleep on my keyboard. At night my mind is mired in a cognitive bog and I can only write piecemeal and excruciatingly slowly, as I'm doing now. I can tuck the results into my Binkus vault where no one will be embarrassed for me by reading them. I can write about Christina without reserve in this sanctum. I can be as hard or as easy on myself as I reflect on my predicament and slowly move the words further down the page.

Several years ago my oncologist told me there were new studies in the medical literature about a particular kind of brain damage called neurological toxicity in patients who'd had a combination of high-dose radiation and chemotherapy to treat brain cancer. The evidence pointed to delayed symptoms of early dementia, he said, and this condition generally kicks in around eight to ten years after remission of the cancer itself. This was radiation poisoning, I thought, with consequences far beyond simply losing my hair.

"They haven't done studies on younger brain cancer survivors near your age," the oncologist said as if to reassure me. "It's not clear what might happen – I just thought you'd want to know so you keep an eye out for it."

The news was upsetting but I was grateful he told me, because it explained things already going on even back then that I refused to accept.

After my craniotomy they treated me first with a daily, then weekly blast of brain radiation that added up to 5,000 rad (50,000 milisievert), then they administered a painful round of intrathecal chemotherapy, which involved sticking a long needle into my spinal cord and sending the toxic chemicals straight to my brain. The treatment saved my life, but now it holds a lien on my cognition. The idea that sooner or later the true price of survival will catch up with me is a nasty pill to swallow. Over the past several years I guess I've been in denial about the neurological problems I'm experiencing, even as I've consciously tried to compensate for them and mask them from others. I haven't really talked about it, not even with my wife, my brothers and my closest friends – and definitely not with Christina.

Long ago I had a martial arts teacher who gave me solemn advice. "Never reveal your weakness," said Oka Sensei, the deadpan kickboxing master who occasionally took me out on drinking binges after training in the dojo. By day he was a car salesman who knew all the bars in Kyoto from entertaining his customers, and when he got drunk he never showed a hint of incapacitation. He maintained a straight-backed posture and the appearance of an alert tiger with a tumbler of Suntory whisky in hand, ready to strike if provoked. "If you show your adversary where your weaknesses lie," he said in clipped and precise Japanese, "you've already lost. You've defeated yourself."

It was good counsel for a freshly-minted black belt, perhaps, but probably bad advice for someone under siege by radiation poisoning. The delusion of machismo has made me weak, not strong.

I shared a lot of secrets with Christina, but not this one. She knew my medical history and she never stopped asking about it. I didn't mind the prying curiosity because it was her nature to explore, and the way she asked questions was intelligent and cogent, not the usual platitudes friends used when they couldn't think of other words. Her style was smart, never gooey, midway between the scientist and the empathetic companion she was. She kept asking about my abandoned novel and I told her it was a jinx to talk about a work in progress, even it is stillborn. She demanded to read the draft but even if I had wanted to

I couldn't show her. I put it on a thumb drive and deleted all the files on my laptop. Now I can't remember where I put the thumb drive. I finally relented and told her the gist of it. A man jumps off the Golden Gate Bridge and sees his life go by on his way down. A fruitless investigation of his death. A Grim Reaper in white. An ambivalent happy ending. "It's trash," I said. "It'll never see the light of day."

But I never let her in all the way about my medical problems. I thought I was still capable of passing as fairly normal, but at the same time I feared the whole truth would ruin any chance of a lasting relationship with this incredible woman. I ruined everything by shutting her out because ßI think she intuited the wall when she finally sent me away, and I failed to wrestle with her fury and open my heart completely. Instead I retreated to San Francisco – not just to follow the hard-wired instinct to protect my children, but also to protect the both of us from the curse of my illness. She might have understood and accepted me as I was, but it would have been devastating if that weren't the case. My ex-wife shrank away from me, knowing the depth of my incapacity, and I lacked the courage to risk that happening again. I spoiled my chance of sharing the greatest intimacy that a man and a woman can share.

I started hiding secrets from Christina soon after we first fell into the confidence of new lovers – pillow talk, if that's not too cute an expression for a hushed conversation that follows lovemaking as the tension of a lifetime dissolves. That moody time when lovers in the cinema light cigarettes and sigh. Neither of us smoked, but we sighed a lot. Christina knew how to nuzzle and she knew how to disarm me as she waltzed into forbidden territory. On our first time she came close to cracking the safe.

"You're releasing something painful," she said. "A lot of bad air, and I think now you're breathing in the good but I can still smell the bad. You're sighing away something wrong."

"I'll go brush my teeth, if you want me to. Can I use your toothbrush?"

"Oh shut up silly," she said. "Let me in. There's something wrong deep inside you that hurts you, and now it's hurting me."

"Okay, okay. It's just that this is like detox for me," I said. "Healing. You can't imagine how hungry I've been for a simple touch. It's been years, and maybe I've never known a touch like yours. "

"That sounds awful, Raul. How could someone not touch you? I don't understand," she said. "Even if you're fighting with her all the time, there had to be something . . . "

"It's not so easy to explain, sweet Christina. She won't let me touch her and she doesn't want to be touched. She flinches and shrinks away as if I'm hurting her. She says it's no good anymore. She says touching doesn't work. It's all bound up in sickness, hers and mine."

"I'm touching you now. But you're being very cryptic. Raul, tell me what's going on in there. The pain is back in your face and I want to make it go away. Tell me."

She caressed my left temple and ran her fingers through the mousey gray hair covering the burr holes in my skull. She pressed her finger gently on the burr hole on the top of my skull by the balding hairline, the one people can see, probing into the archeology of anguish. I wanted to tell her. I wanted to trust her with my weakness and air out the depths of my self-doubt. But I couldn't.

"Hush, Christina, hush," was all I could say. "You don't need to know because you're already the cure."

—

The coroner realized how little he understood Barlow. He could speak his mind here in the vault but he couldn't say it to the woman he loved: He could express passion but not candor. The words he left unsaid to Christina were the little lights in the dead man's eyes that gave the coroner the distinct impression when he first examined the corpse that Barlow had unfinished business to attend to.

—

The oncologist's warning came home shortly before I joined the newspaper in San Jose. I started having very brief petit mal seizures.

The right hand that I taught how to write the alphabet after brain surgery would go numb, then the arm would freeze and hang limp from my shoulder like a useless shank of meat. Finally, I'd lose my ability to speak. At first the episodes lasted for a few minutes at a time, but when they happened more often and lasted longer I knew I was in trouble. I associated seizures with hypoglycemia at first and would guzzle orange juice until I felt my fingers. I kept it all to myself.

Then one morning the seizure didn't stop. I checked my blood sugar and it was too high, not too low. The seizures faded and then came back, each time more intense until I thought maybe I was careening into my first full-blown grand mal seizure, with the shaking, gagging, teeth-grinding and incontinence before blacking out. The other possibility was a stroke, I thought, somehow making my weakest synapses go haywire. My wife was in the kitchen with me at the time, but when I tried to explain what was going on the words didn't come out. My mind was crystal clear but my body was beyond my control. I found a piece of paper on the kitchen counter and with my left hand picked up a pen and forced it into my right and saw it drop to the floor.

The seizure subsided for a moment, long enough to say *"th't . . . thtwo . . . thtwo . . . ku, ku, ku. Thtwo . . ."*

"You mean you're choking?" She was getting ready to perform the Heimlich when I danced away.

"Do, do, thwe, thwee . . . thwoh." The situation was becoming comical, but when I started laughing I don't think any sounds came out of my mouth – I was mute again. I tried to pantomime with one arm, hopping around the kitchen like a ridiculously frustrated circus monkey. I tried to cough and salivate until my tongue loosened up enough for me to say: *"Stwoook. Thwejar, emrrrrg, eeh rrrr!ß"*

She said, "stroke?" I nodded.

At the emergency room it was a mistake to ask the attending doctor whether I was having a stroke because he made up his mind within minutes that I was experiencing transient ischemic attacks, mini-strokes that warned of something worse to come. When I could articulate more clearly I asked whether these mini-strokes could actually be mini-seizures related to my brain tumor, similar to the one that knocked me out in Tokyo ten years earlier. The tumor pressed against the cerebral white matter that controlled my speech and right-hand motor control. "Maybe the synapses are misfiring in there again," I asked. The doctor was a neurologist, and I thought he'd understand what I was talking about, but he dismissed that possibility. He put me in the hospital overnight for observation, but he didn't observe me. I had several more seizures that afternoon, one of them so long and severe we asked the nurses to fetch the neurologist. He was right outside my room doing paperwork at the nurse's station, but said he was too busy to examine me.

The next morning my wife woke me up with an urgent phone call and said, "Don't turn on the TV. You've got too much going on to worry about the news, just rest."

I found the remote control immediately and fired it at the hospital TV hanging high on the wall to see incomprehensible images of a passenger jet flying directly into a skyscraper. At first I thought it was computer animation. It couldn't be real. My situation in the hospital couldn't be real either. It was a razor sharp moment of disbelief, a cruel dream on another plane of reality.

They discharged me with a prescription for Coumadin, a powerful blood-thinner used to treat stroke victims. My brother refused to let me take the script to the pharmacy. "It could cause a brain hemorrhage and kill you," he said. He made the correct diagnosis that the seizures were caused by the scar tissue around the old tumor that was interrupting neurotransmission. The idea of mini-strokes didn't make sense, he said. The neurologist I saw for a second opinion at UCSF also agreed and put me on an anticonvulsive medication, telling me I'd need to get a lot of extra sleep – no less than nine hours a day – and take the anti-seizure drug for the rest of my life. Sleep has ruled my life like a merciless despot since that moment in time, punishing me with exhaustion and delirium when I disobey, rewarding me with mornings of energy and crisp intelligence when I comply, then betraying me with afternoons and evenings of sluggishness, aphasia and disequilibrium, no matter what I do.

A few months later I went to see a neurologist who was sanctioned by my health insurance company as one of the few "in-network" doctors in the area. I'd examined his credentials on the Internet: Board-certified in all the right fields and evidently quite experienced. He was a very interesting man, a former neurosurgeon who walked with a limp, spine bent, and he twisted his craggy asymmetrical face when he smiled. He was also a gifted raconteur who regaled me with bizarre tales from in and out of the operating theater. He never seemed to be in a hurry. Indeed, there were hardly any patients in his waiting room, which gave me pause, but I had no reason to doubt his expertise.

I described to him all the problems I'd been experiencing with memory, cognition and intellectual stamina. I described how the seizures mirrored the damage the tumor inflicted to my brain. I told him what was happening to me on the job, that I was sucker-punched with exhaustion and confusion every afternoon on deadline and that my competence was in disrepute. I asked him the question I'd dreaded since the day my oncologist mentioned the words neurological toxicity years before. Was it finally happening? Was I already starting to slip into post-radiation dementia? How could I fight it? Where will it go from now, what would it do to my ability to think, read, write and to engage in the kind of intellectual work I needed to do to earn a living? To maintain my sense of self?

"How will I know whether it's going to completely incapacitate me?"

He waved his hand in a playful dismissive gesture.

"No need to worry," Dr. Garang said. "You won't feel a thing. You won't know when you have it but you'll like it." His crooked mien was unnervingly comical. "Once you stop worrying about it you won't have a care in the world. You'll be in bliss."

I found another neurologist. The new doctor specialized in treating severe cases of multiple sclerosis, and the symptoms I presented must have been trivial in her eyes. She had the bedside manner to make me feel as important as all her other patients, but she has occasionally betrayed skepticism about the severity of the symptoms I described, as though I had a touch of hypochondria, or the problem was caused by depression not hard wiring. She changed her tone after I asked her to refer me to a neuropsychologist for cognitive testing. I'd had this done five years earlier at the suggestion of my oncologist to establish base-line, and at the time I was found to be within the range of normal. I had to know where I'd traveled since then, to get an objective measure of the long-term effects – not from the brain tumor itself but from the repercussions of its cure.

The exam went on for hours and was conducted over two days. Each test was timed: Counting and mathematical tasks, memorizing and reciting streams of numbers and words, picking up little rings and washers and putting them in the right place on a peg board, listening to stories and then repeating them, copying a geometrical diagram and drawing it again from memory thirty minutes later. I was so frus-trated I nearly broke down at the part of the test where she said a number and I had to subtract five from that number and she'd spit back another number, over and over, the whole thing in rapid fire suc-cession, grinding my brain. We took a break when she could see I was on the verge of tears. Then we moved on to the next test.

The results were devastating. I was below average in almost every measure. My short-term memory was pitiful. The speed of my mental processing had descended into the 30 percentile range. The only sav-ing grace was that my verbal aptitude was still above average, but I needed to accept the fact that the cogs of my cognition were turning very slowly. Mental agility was never to be my forte again.

I'm still passionate about language despite the menace of apha-sia, when my memory fails to fish up precious words from the depths, when I call up the wrong words, when I forget how to pronounce them or spell them, and at the worst of moments, when I'm seriously sleep deprived and exhausted, I can't quite lock in on to what they mean. But in the mornings, after a good night's sleep I find I can still write. This morning I'm in fairly good shape because I got my nine hours overnight and caught up with my compounding sleep debt yesterday by taking a very long nap in the afternoon. I sleep, I wake, I write. Therefore I'm what?

I've gradually learned to open up about this to a degree, making an effort to talk cautiously to people I trust. But when I share part of my story of vexation with others, they can't begin to understand what's wrong with me, even if they can plainly see my affect is off base. When I try to explain in greater depth they find it difficult to pay attention. Sometimes I think I should keep quiet after all and concede that the martial arts car salesman master was right all along about silent stoicism. These people don't necessarily exploit my weakness. They aren't my enemies, they're my friends. Yet they just don't get it. They don't want to hear it. My elderly parents go deaf if I make a remark about it; it scares them. They turn off their hearing aids. When I confide jokingly with close friends that I raise my car keys and try to open my front door with the electronic fob, they tell me they have senior moments too, like walking into a room and forgetting what they were going to do there. It's hard to tell whether they are condescending, commiserating or casually dismissing my problem as normal aging, incapable of imagining my experience. I don't bother to tell them that I don't need to go to another room. On my bad brain days I can stand in one place stupidly trying to remember what I was about to do, all day long. My children can't quite understand why I get dimwitted and confused when I look at a busy computer screen while they try to show me how to do something new, why I repeat myself so often, why I take so many naps, and why I ask them to slow down and repeat hurried sentences I can't quite grasp. Brain damage changes your personality – I've heard this described by other people who've sustained serious head injuries. It makes me irritable, short tempered and impatient, traits my children will easily recognize.

Maybe some day when they're older I'll open this vault and let them know what progressive brain damage is like from the inside out. I want to tell them how sorry I am for confusing and embarrassing them all these years. How much I've loved them for standing by me, and how much my love for them and their love for me has kept me sane.

On the scale of things, my affliction is petty compared to the MS patients my neurologist treats. But what's maddening to me is realizing things could get a lot worse and there will be nothing I can do about it. Crossword puzzles, meditation, strenuous physical exercise and prodigious amounts of sleep can keep me stable today, but what about two or three years from now?

I occasionally allow myself to be furious after banging the top of my head on a cabinet door for the third time that morning or knocking another cup of coffee to the floor because I can't sense objects in the immediate periphery of my clumsy body. My shins are scarred by all the collisions they've had with immovable low-lying objects. I grind my teeth and yell at myself for being such an idiot. I spew things like "what the fuck are you doing to yourself?" and "Stop it, stop it, STOP IT!" I'm never sure whether I'm screaming at myself or venting my rage at a higher power – God, the government, the corporate health-industrial complex, the ones who deserve blame, not me. Then I take a deep breath and I laugh at my idiocy. How ridiculous this is, not just me but the play I'm going to have to act in for as long as I live.

Last year I went out and bought a little electric chain saw to take revenge on a malicious lemon tree in the back yard that has been clobbering me on the head with its thick lower branches every time I stoop to pass beneath from one side of the yard to the other. *Bad lemon tree, very bad.* The tree is very old and its tangled limbs are the size of baseball bats and probably hadn't been pruned in thirty years. This tree produces a bumper crop of Meyer lemons, incredibly sweet, but it was fallow for the season after I violated it with the little chain saw; the once powerful fragrance of its blossoms was barely detectable in the fall. The battle with my lemon tree isn't funny anymore.

On my worst days I slam the front door behind me in the middle of the night and walk in meaningless circles around the neighborhood, up and down hills. I chew pack after pack of Wintergreen gum to stop me from grinding my teeth. I pull over to the side of the road to recline the seat in my car, turn the radio down to a soft white noise and resuscitate myself with a long catnap. In the shower I yodel and ululate at the top of my lungs and belt out remnants of ridiculous songs from summer camp in the Quetico wilderness: *"Give me some men who are stout-hearted men who will fight for the rights they adore!"*

About seven million people die of cancer around the world every year. But the statistics don't hit home for me until I think about three friends who died after fighting heroically to beat the odds, three of the finest people I've known, who could have been me just as I could have been them.

Far more people die of heart disease than cancer in the United States. I looked it up. Worldwide, when you take into account poverty-stricken developing nations, cancer ranks seventh as a cause of death, way behind dysentery and AIDS. But cancer has a mythical element that casts terror because the disease has many names and it strikes at random, usually without a knowable cause. We all understand that smoking cigarettes causes lung cancer and overexposure to the sun causes melanoma, but what was it that gave Doug his liver cancer, struck down Nell with breast cancer and punished Nancy with deadly stomach cancer?

Science and mythology are entangled in the effort to explain the *why* for cancer. Exposure to carcinogens in the environment is a prevalent cause but too often the link is impossible to prove. A persistent and malignant myth blames victims for causing their own cancer by being unable to control their anxiety and stress, without a scintilla of scientific proof. Cancer festers in the "occult," which is a medical term that means you generally can't see the malignant cells before they start killing you. In the occult of cancer lies the mystery of why the cells mutate in your body and not someone else's when you're both exposed to the same amount of benzene or tetrachloroethylene. There's a genetic predisposition, and there's the simple roll of the dice. But the worst myth about cancer is the belief that a diagnosis is a death sentence. Most cases are treatable, as we survivors know. Even when the treatment comes at a price, and survival, as joyous and strengthening to the character as it may be, can take a toll on the faith that life is fair. Survival should be celebrated but never be taken for granted.

When I was in high school one of my favorite authors was William Faulkner. I read practically every book he wrote and unsuccessfully tried to emulated his impossibly perfect run-on sentences. "Gibberish," my English teacher wrote in the margin of an ambitious short story. While I can't claim to have grasped the depth of meaning in his novels, Faulkner's Nobel acceptance speech was so simple it rang with powerful clarity, especially the unforgettable line: "I believe that man will not merely endure: he will prevail." It has all the more meaning to me now. It speaks of rock-solid hope.

When I was in college I studied Eastern philosophy and learned about the "Useless Tree," a metaphor used by the Taoist sage Chuang Tzu. It poses a riddle: What value could there be in a tree whose branches were so gnarled and twisted they do not yield lumber? It bore no fruit. Its leaves were too meager to provide shade on a hot afternoon. Its limbs were so fragile a child couldn't climb up for a better view of the rocky landscape. It was so scraggly and strange even the crows wouldn't light on it. It was useless. But there's great value in its uselessness. I think I understand the riddle. The tree may be useless but it is by no means worthless, simply because it perseveres. It's perseverance, in my interpretation, is founded on rock-solid hope.

The tree I wanted to become when I was a young man was a towering redwood reaching for the sun, ambitious and arrogant in its grandeur. Then I acquired a chronic disease and lowered my sights to a mighty Douglas fir, vowing that no illness would stop me from attaining my goals. When sickness struck again I resigned myself to be a respectable pine. And now that the complications of diabetes and the downwind effects of radiation have pulled the forest floor out from under my feet. I'm content to be a red-barked manzanita, still sturdy and clinging tenaciously to the rocky hillside, perhaps useless but always grateful for the ephemeral gift of life.

Brain damage is a humbling thing, jabbing, teaching, and awakening me. But I will never allow myself to succumb to the demented bliss prophesized by Dr. Garang, the prankster neurologist. Someday, I know, I'll have to let go peacefully and surrender myself, but I'm going down fighting when dementia starts to snuff out my life force. I'll rage against the bliss.

—

The coroner stood and raised his hands, trying to say something but nothing came out. *"Nothing!"* he managed to hiss at last. Did the attitude of the manzanita rule out suicide as the manner of Barlow's death? Not if you consider the position of the corpse he inspected at the death scene. He might have seen the headlights coming and stepped off the curb to confront the bliss of his decaying brain. It was not the peaceful demise that he intended to accept once the fight was over, however, and there was every indication that Barlow still had his wits about him when he left his bungalow before dawn Saturday morning. The coroner had to take into account the possibility that Barlow's musings in the vault were disingenuous, perhaps a cover story for inner doubts he couldn't admit to himself, even in secret. Taking it at face value, however, the dead man was talking about a passage he alone would control before losing the power to control it, not a living will but the will to live, in peace and at war with his afflictions. Barlow stood his ground to defy his creator and his destroyer, to prevail in his last moment clenching his fists while he was sprawled out face up on the pavement.

Thirty

The coroner looked longingly at the empty flask before poking the X in the little box to close the confidential document. "The writer has a touch for gushy sentimentality, but I'll allow that," he said to his scuffed brown wingtips. "After all, he was an Ink-stained Wretch." The coroner heard this term spoken in jest among graying reporters during his drinking bouts at the M&M bar. It seemed to be a connotation of a cheap hack past his prime who didn't mind getting dirty in pursuit of a good story. He used it for Barlow as a term of endearment for the writer, and he imagined Barlow would have used it to describe himself in a self-depreciating way, just as he himself, the incomparable Leo Bacigalupi, reckoned he was just a drunken county coroner. "The damned cadaver and I are joined at the hip," he said aloud.

The words pierced the humming cotton-in-the-ears silence that padded the walls of the room. He cringed when he heard a tiny voice ringing in his head that said: *"Hush!"*

What does it matter, he thought. I have already crossed the line. I can be as irreverent and as sarcastic as I want and the dead man will not hear me. He debated what he had to do next. After making a detour to the kitchen, where he replenished the flask and found a box of Ak-Mak crackers that would do just fine lining his gullet. It was growing late. If he were going to make himself presentable for his postponed execution in the morning, he must quit this house, go home and get a decent night's sleep in his own bed. The disappearance of his car from the death scene was a minor inconvenience. He could call a taxi. He would report to the morgue and turn himself in.

No, he could not do that. He would have to return to Barlow's lair in the morning to read until he came to a definitive stopping point. He would take a long hot shower to soothe his throbbing ribs and the map of small wounds on his body. He would see what was in the refrigerator and if it was bare he could check the cabinet by the sink for a can of tuna fish or New England clam chowder, widower's food. Actually he would be wiser to go to It's Tops for eggs, bacon and hash brown potatoes. He would set two alarm clocks. He might call Wilson to brief him on what he had discovered and gather intelligence about the ME's office that the lad had accumulated in his absence.

A foghorn blasted a warning that ripped through the pall of Barlow's house. Moaning in sorrow, it reverberated in the floorboards under his feet. He went to the window and lifted the matchstick blinds to see a gossamer fabric of white vapors snaking along Liberty Street, lifting, floating and sinking as though it were looking for human bones to chill. Death is dressed in white, it occurred to him, not black.

He had dismissed the memory of Saturday night's foghorn calls until now. This time he applied his best empirical skills to unravel the mystery. I am hearing a foghorn in Dolores Heights. One does not hear foghorns in this part of the city. I do not recall seeing much fog up here or down the hill in the flats of Noe Valley, but I never lived here and would not know. However, tonight is different, he concluded, as the sound faded into the distance and gradually became inaudible until it rose and beckoned again. There has to be a reason why this is happening. He could only draw one conclusion, that the horn was telling him it was time to go home. The coroner bargained for more time. He would stay for a little while longer before going out to hail a cab down the hill. If he waited, perhaps the foghorn would shut up.

Then he asked himself whether he was afraid to go out into the darkness and leave the comfort of Barlow's home. He shook his head. No, it is more frightening to stay. The clock on the kitchen wall above the sink made its presence known with assertive ticking, louder than he could remember ever hearing from a cheap plastic wall clock. It was a noisy metronome now with a barely detectable slowing pace, as though its AA-battery were running low.

Should he cheer himself up with another bite out of Narcissistic Chameleon Moo or stay the course mining secrets out of Barlow's crypt? His fingers did the talking now and led him back to Christina.

—

Thursday February 12, 2003
The Gardener

I don' know why I got interested in him in the first place. I'm propped up by an assortment of pillows on the couch wearing my freshly laundered fleece pajamas and my hair is still damp from a long hot shower. I'm feeling the warm glow of contentment. But I have to ask myself why I have no one to share the moment with. *With whom to share the moment?* Mister Barlow told me it was perfectly okay to break the rules when writing in the informal voice, despite what Sister Higgins, my crabby third grade teacher at St, Mary's, drilled into me. She tried to make me her teacher's pet, but I detested her. And here I am, clearing my writing throat, trying to level my lap so the laptop doesn't slip off again and crash on the floor.

Alex was at it again this afternoon calling and leaving messages on my phone saying he wanted to take me out for dinner, just as friends. I know what he's after. He says he'll leave his cameras home and it would be just him and me, and that if dinner wasn't good how about lunch or breakfast or just coffee? I haven't had dinner or slept with him since I met Raul, but he's been annoyingly persistent. When he found out about my breakup with Raul he swooped in like a vulture and begged me to take him back. I make the big mistake of trying to be kind and tell him gently that I was so busy at the lab I didn't have time for him or any man in my life. He apparently took that as a maybe, and every so often he approaches me and asks me if I'm still unattached and why wouldn't I go out for dinner. Dinner to Alex means sleeping together. It's been like this for three solid years.

He stopped sending me flowers, thank God, but he emails me with jpegs of old photos from his dossier that he digitized. I open them to see images of a woman I can hardly recognize anymore. I uploaded some of them to this stupid blog because they proved the point that I am an incorrigibly vain creature, trying to her best to shed her skin. He doesn't have access to my blog, but still he got the wrong message and he keeps sending more of them trying to woo me like a damned fool and it got so bad I now report them as spam.

After today's barrage of voice mails I've made up my mind to call the phone company tomorrow and get a new number and make sure it's unlisted. I don't think he quite fits the profile of a stalker but he won't take no for an answer. I'm not a bitch. I feel sorry for the man because he's so lonely it's pathetic. Practically all men are pathetic now as far as I'm concerned. They strut their testosterone like peacocks and expect me to swoon because I'm evidently a good target to prey on, unmarried and approaching forty, a trust-fund baby and someone who looks like she'd still be good in the sack I hate that.

Raul was so different. He didn't think he deserved me, but he wasn't belittling himself, he was putting me on a pedestal. He had it backward. I needed him and I'm afraid I used him up.

I took Raul home to meet my insufferable mother one Saturday afternoon midway through the fall semester. He and I hadn't become lovers yet but we were hovering in that tentative space between being sweet intimate friends and slaves to lust. What? That's a ridiculous way of putting it. He tucked in his shirt and wore a tie for the occasion. My ingeniously manipulative mother could tell how deeply involved I'd gotten in my writing class because I'd brought it up so often in during our phone conversations and she approved of it because she always considered me as a creative artist at heart and couldn't understand why I was devoted to that "dreary research on people's chromosomes." She told me one evening, to my great surprise, she'd like to meet my teacher. It was very weird, but it made sense when you consider her extraordinary sixth-sense, the kind a mother has when she sniffs the trace of a man in her teenager's laundry. She always made it clear she thought Alex is a lout and I should break it off before he ruined me.

I knew she was right, even if I could never give her credit for the insight. Now she had a new specimen to inspect. I told her repeatedly that Raul and I were just friends but she said she was *so curious* about the teacher I spoke of in such glowing terms.

She loved the idea of my being in a writing seminar. "You wrote such adorable stories when you were a little bug in Montessori." I cringed when told me she kept them all in a file, along with my third-grade poems.

But she hated *Mr. Barlow* on first sight. She knew on the spot where it was going and she did not approve one iota. After a painful attempt at exchanging pleasantries over tea and crumpets, served with her second-best silver teapot and platter, I knew poor Raul was done for. In his awkward attempt to be polite to this spry little wrinkled bird of a dowager he said ma'am too many times. Not long ago Mother complained that a UPS deliveryman had addressed her as ma'am and that made her feel very old. She'd long forbidden the maid and the cook to use the word, instructing them to address her only as Mrs. Wagner. She pointed out to me that *ma'am* is what (*bleep*) servants say. *Ma'am, ma'am, ma'am,* she said. "Then they steal from you." She's entering the early stages of dementia and says awful things she never would have spoken aloud before.

During our tea she launched into a haughty soliloquy about how tasteless La Brea Bakery's crumpets and scones have become these days. Eventually Raul lowered his head and with raised eyebrows looked at me with his eyes at the tops of their sockets, giving me the signal. We excused ourselves, went home to my little yellow house and made love for the first time.

Late that night my mother called me and in the sweetest of her confidential girly voices said: "Honey, I don't understand how you can be interested in a shabby little journalist like that man. He's uncouth. He spilled crumbs all over my silk carpet and made crude noises with his tea. He's much too old and he's an inch shorter than you, darling. Did you see he's wearing a wedding ring, a cheap one?" Her voice turned sharp and disdainful: "I don't know why you're degrading yourself like this . . . why, he's worse than that creepy photographer friend of yours! Is Barlow some sort of a Hispanic name? Maybe we can have him do our lawn. Moreover, I suspect he's Jewish. They can be both, you know."

I hung up on her and laughed until I doubled up and tears came to my eyes and I needed to pee. Poor Mother. At 84 she is what she is and always will be. I thought I should wake up Raul to tell him about this because he'd find it hilarious after his afternoon with the dragon lady, but I let him sleep. He looked so peaceful in my bed.

Posted by Christina at 3:16 AM 1 Comments

———

The coroner was piecing together Barlow's jigsaw puzzle at last. "I'm not far," he sad out loud with no shame in the triumphant voice he heard ricochet back from the wall behind him. "She's out there somewhere, and it now it's just a matter of tracking her down. Where in tarnation is that little yellow house!"

Instinctively, he turned back to the vault. An item marked "Pinky's" popped up before his eyes like a clown's head on a spring and he raced to open it before it went back into its box.

———

10:13:2000, Gazos Creek

I hoped and I worried it would lead to this.

I'm looking over a precipice at a point of no return. This girl has slowly drawn me into the sticky silk strands of her web with every gesture, flinging her hair from her ears with long delicate fingers, arching her back to yawn, sitting like a child with her knees pressed together and her feet splayed to the sides. There is no other woman in the world like this. The way she bends her nearly perfect asymmetrical face to make it more naturally alluringly imperfect, the way she accentuates a provocative remark by freezing her body in a provocative pose, the way she explains dense scientific matters to me as though she were an enthusiastic curator at the art museum or a guide at the Wild Animal

Park. In fact, we did go to the park on a trip to San Diego and rode the tram three times around the outback. She was so excited she nearly fell off the tram, pointing at the creatures and chattering about their sizes, diets, habitats and mating rituals. "Did you know a giraffe's tongue is eighteen inches long?" How did she know all this?

I tried my best to play the game of enchantment by using the landscape that inspired me. Early in our relationship I persuaded her to sneak to San Francisco with me and explore my personal natural habitats. I took her to Pinky's, the long rough beach south of Half Moon Bay where the surf thunders ashore and slams on the beach in winter with such great energy that it makes my bones tingle. I told her on the approach that this was a three-layer beach, not a sunscreen beach like the ones that ditzy blondes populate down in the Southland. "There you go again with your Northern California prejudice again," she said. "You San Franciscans are so smug, specifically the aging balding retrohippies ones like you, with your psychedelic Jerry Garcia neckties."

"How did you know about my Jerry Garcia tie? It's not psychedelic, it's high design."

"You wore it to my mother's house, dodo. You seemed very proud of it," she said. Don't worry, I like it. When I was a little girl I was a hippie for Halloween once. My mother disapproved."

We took the long trek down the beach to where the big black rocks of the tide pools jutted bravely into the sea, saying *so what* to the whitecaps and their furious spray. We hopped around the rocks in our bare feet and I stumbled twice, landing on my ass and hearing peals of laughter followed by "are you okay?" I wasn't surprised when she shouted over the roar of the surf to give me a running commentary on the creatures in the tide pools – the mussels, hermit crabs and snails. She shrieked when she spotted a starfish on a nearby rock and moaned when she saw it was too dangerous to get a closer look. I never saw the thing, but pretended I did.

Wet and freezing, we took shelter in a pocket in a sand dune where the wind wasn't so bad. "It's too cold to take off our clothes and mate like elephant seals," she observed. "It's maybe around 47 degrees in the wet wind."

"Nah," I said. "It's not a degree below 52. But wait until we get back to our rent-a-car. We can crank up the heat and tilt the seats back like teenagers. Steamy windows will give us privacy."

"Raul," she whispered so the ocean couldn't hear. "Did you bring, you know, one of our little pills?" Then she giggled. From our first night together she understood, she waited, she coaxed, and she healed. I had no choice but to fall in love with this woman, even though I had no reason to expect she'd love me in return. My defenses dropped. It seemed safe. "You're a sassy little girl, Christina," I said. "But I think we could learn to get along."

———

The coroner had a very strange feeling about this scene. It was too perfect, too good to be true. He had to put on his skeptic's hat and consider whether Barlow made it up out of whole cloth. Perhaps he wanted a woman like Christina so badly he invented her, or at least embellished on the facts. There was compelling evidence that he had at one point a flesh-and-blood lover named Christina, and that the poor man had been introduced to her domineering mother. Yet the two seemed wedded in fantasy, if not one fantasy, then two separate fantasies that fed upon each other. It had gotten to the point where nothing could be taken at face value, not the flighty banter in Christina's blog nor the sentimental drippings in Barlow's vault. The coroner was perplexed. His head told him one thing, his gut told him another and in the final assessment he believed every word of it. "There is truth in this pile of horse manure," he uttered beneath his breath as he bent his nose closer to the screen.

———

Infidelity

Now what do I do? I'm barricaded in my den feeling the lingering warmth of the mobile phone in my hand after saying good night to her and falling to earth from the thrill of our hushed conversation. Her voice stripped away the layers of the thick skin that has grown thicker every minute since I landed at SFO until I felt encased in rhino hide. Where do I go now? The air is totally still here in the tent of midnight silence, where I can linger in the sound of her voice and her scent on my body. Once I stand and leave the room I'll have to go down the hallway leading to the kitchen where I'll be trapped and forced to endure the excretion of blistering rage from a woman who's made it clear she reviles me. I'll sleep on the couch again tonight and get up early to make a meal of pancakes and breakfast sausages for the girls and watch them eat it, praying they're oblivious to the madness of their parents.

My kids and I took a trip to Oregon last summer to visit my lost daughter, their half-sister. We saw "Romeo and Juliet" in Ashland, picked raspberries and fed the chickens on her farm, and went on an afternoon outing to the banks of the Rogue River, where we took in the sun and splashed around in the stingingly frigid water. I saw an outcropping on the other bank of the river that was stained black and gray by the shadows of the trees. It was as though a Chinese ink brush painting were calling out and luring me to come near. Overtaken by the desire to climb the rocks across the river I plunged into the water and came up gasping and shivering, it was so cold. I started to swim toward my goal but the Chinese boulders started moving upstream and away from me as the Rogue's mighty current took control of my body. Realizing I'd never make it across the river I turned and started swimming toward the safety of the beach, but I was carried farther and farther away with every stroke. I knew immediately I was in serious trouble. I flailed my arms and kicked like a madman, struggling to keep my head above water. My arms and legs and lungs were exhausted as I fought the powerful torrent of water that just minutes earlier seemed so placid. The Velcro strap on one of the sandals I wore into the river was coming loose and the sandal was about to be carried away, which for a moment gave me crazed thoughts about the potential for keeping the sandal and drowning or abandoning it and surviving. I barely managed get enough air to shout: "I need help! I need help!" Panic set in when it was clear nobody could hear me. I saw my daughters skipping rocks on the water's edge, oblivious to my predicament. Then a man in a kayak came out of nowhere, threw me a line, and towed me to shore. "You're the third one I pulled in this morning," he said. When I staggered out of the boat I nearly tripped over the sandal dangling from my foot.

There's no point in surviving the big things if you put your life in jeopardy by not paying attention to the little hazards. But it's not a life worth living if you shrink away from all the signs of danger that clutter your path. In my infatuation with Christina it was like that.

I'm not sure how this came to be. If I had to find a single reason it would be breakfast.

She and I shared an avid interest in greasy spoon diners and the little family breakfast joints scattered around LA, most of them on the verge of being run out of business by the chain restaurants or shut down by the county health department. She knew most of them, which was an idea that titillated my interest in her. She was an aficionado of mushroom and Swiss cheese omelets, sourdough toast and home fries that were never crispy enough. I tried to convince myself that we were merely into an innocent ritual, a very rare and special and unspoiled friendship. I tried to warn myself against the dangers of fantasizing it was more than that, but one day, to my surprise and awe, our breakfast courtship skipped lunch and went directly to dinner. We started talking over the phone every night, saying things that are best said in the safety of distance without the distraction of sight and smell, extracting and revealing intimate details of each other's lives. I think we fooled ourselves into believing there was nothing serious going on, just the platonic circle dance of breakfast mates.

I guess you could say Christina is highly idiosyncratic, meaning that she's safely this side of neurosis but with very odd quirks and faults. She tends to get easily distracted and lets her mind hop about until it locks in total concentration on something. It's the same whether it's momentous or trivial. She invited me home for dinner – still in the harmless stage – and I watched her take out a stack of newspapers to the recycling bin outside the kitchen door only to stop and read a news article that caught her eye. Then she sat down on the lawn and read the entire paper. She is tempestuous by nature with a vein of anger, which I later learned would erupt now and then to sear everything in sight until she calmed down and returned to genuine sweetness. The anger crops up in her writing as well – I used to tease her, saying she had a "livid imagination." She loves that description of herself.

On the day before Halloween, Christina slipped a note across the table while a fellow student was droning on, reading his mangled prose. The note said: "Okay, okay. Stop it! Stop making me feel this. It's stupid. Go away, leave me alone."

We stopped phoning each other for a few days, then she invited me to visit her mother's for a Saturday afternoon tea. The woman lived in one of those huge Craftsman houses in Pasadena, where we settled into our chairs in the corner of the great room with its slit art-deco windows carved into the dark oak-paneled walls, red Persian carpets flung on the mottled hardwood floor, and a stone fireplace that seemed to hoist up the beams and keep the roof from collapsing on top of me. Her mother had light skin across her sculpted face and she made me feel as though I was a lame racehorse being inspected on the paddock at Santa Anita. Christina and I played footsy under the table until she made excuses and we retreated to her yellow house.

My heart was breaking when we kissed for the first time, exhaling a burst of relief before we breathed deeply into each other's mouths, drawing warm air in and out of each other's lungs. We got dizzy and came up gasping for air laughing.

I spoiled the moment with a spasm of worry.

"Wait, Christina," I said before we drifted to her bedroom to taste the thrill and delight of adultery. "Wait a little longer for me until I work this out," I said. "This is going to tear my family apart and hurt my children. I can't hurt them. They need me at home. I have to protect my daughters."

"Protect them from what, Raul," she said. "From your wife? From yourself?"

"From feeling abandoned."

"Raul, I think your kids are going to be fine," she said, leading me to the bedroom with the light touch of her fingertips. "Children are resilient. They're tougher than you think. They'll love you forever even if they don't know it, and they'll love you even more once they learn to know you for who you really are."

We crossed the Rogue River that evening. We climbed up the rocks on the other bank into the gray wash of the ink-brush painting. We were together at last.

"Steamy," the coroner said, aroused to the point of blushing at the thought of having sex with a woman like Christina. He had a vague memory of an asphyxiating kiss like the one Barlow described, but he could not remember when or with whom. He could taste it, however, and feel the elation. He wanted to watch more scenes of Christina's seduction. It was important data for his inquest, he told himself. So he moved further along the trail of empirical voyeurism by opening the next item on the list. There was a hiatus in Barlow's secret narrative, skipping several months.

Sylvia's Café

Time crawled in a lovers' dream, then time shot forward at warp speed, and before I knew it time stood still.

It was late spring, a Saturday afternoon, when Christina was helping me grade papers at our favorite Internet café. She never stopped chiding me, playfully, for giving her a final B-plus grade in the writing course. I did it so her classmates couldn't complain of favoritism – our secret was so obvious – and she understood the reasoning at the time. But when she saw me awarding A's to some of the spring-semester students whose work was terrible, her latent resentment surfaced with a peculiar vengeance. She'd read and critiqued all the stories and she couldn't conceal her indignation. She made disparaging remarks that were uncharacteristic and lacking the charity she'd shown to her classmates in the fall.

"Of course these guys can't write their way out of a plastic bag," I said. "But it's E for effort. They're all PhD geeks, and they came into my class not knowing the difference between a diphthong and a dipstick. The ones who showed up and had something to read in class got A's.

"Okay, I see. They're like disadvantaged children," she said. "You're helping them build confidence, not learn to write." The look on her face betrayed more than cynicism, and at that point it dawned on me: Christina had never received a grade lower than an A in her entire life. She couldn't help herself from being obsessively competitive.

"It's just a two-unit seminar, Christina. Nobody will give a damn about the grade and it won't hurt your chances of getting the McArthur Award."

"You just don't get it, do you, Raul. You're not listening," she said, slamming her coffee cup on the table so hard it sprayed cappuccino foam on her favorite tee shirt, the red one with the image of Mr. Spock on the front. "It's not about your fucking writing course. It's about you!"

The other patrons in the room peeked over their laptops but pretended not to notice the outburst as she dashed off to the ladies' room to clean herself up. I could plainly see that competition had nothing to do with the PhD candidates or their grades. That would have been illogical.

When she returned to the table her face was a mess with smudges on her cheeks from makeup I hadn't even noticed she was wearing.

"I'm turning thirty-six next month," she said in a seething hushed tone, "and I'm sick and tired of pleasing people and waiting for them to tell me it's okay, just pose naturally and be yourself, to be your own image and expression of what you imagine you'd want to be." She raised her voice. "I want to rip out my hair and see if people still think I'm pretty. I want to tell everyone that mutant genes in the human genome are breaking my heart. I want to have children, dammit! I want to strangle your horrible wife so she can't hurt you anymore!"

I leaned over the table to cradle her face in my hands and gave her a long slobbery kiss. The audience at Sylvia's Café rose to their feet and cheered.

I wish it were always that easy to respond to Christina's emotional rollercoaster. She was a force of nature and there was little I could do to assuage her when her indomitable passions turned sour. I was naive to think I could return to San Francisco and continue our trysts without resolving my indecision and taking care of her need for clarity and commitment. I wanted desperately to stay with her, but I was caught in a state of dissonance that would make the damage irreparable. I'm falling into a sinkhole somewhere between Los Angeles and San Francisco on Highway 101, maybe near San Luis Obispo.

In early May the fellowship was over, the novel I hoped to finish was lost in a missing thumb drive, and my relationship with Christina was stressed to the breaking point after weeks of talking in circles about what I intended to do. She was angry; I was getting ever more confused.

One morning when we were in Christina's sleigh bed covered by Christina's extra puffy quilt in Christina's yellow house, I noticed something that made me feel miserable.

"Oh, no, you're crying, Christina," I said.

"No I'm not."

"You're about to cry then, I can see little tiny droplets glistening in the corners of your eyes, ready to drip. What's wrong? What did I say to upset you so?"

"Nothing, Raul. You don't know what you're talking about. I am not crying," she said. "Tear ducts are designed to do other things, you know. They clean and lubricate your eyes periodically and they wash away dust and other particulate matter to protect the surface of your cornea." She tilted her neck so the hair draped over her eyes then she turned away from me.

"Sounds like crying to me," I said. "Maybe it's the sandman. I hear the sandman really loves green eyes. He probably put sand in your eyes to make you sleepy. It's time for your morning nap, little Christina . . . then you'll feel better. Come here and put your head on my lap. No questions asked."

The hair protecting her face was damp.

"Oh, shut up, Raul. It's not logical," she said. "I am not crying."

The following morning she threw me out of her house. She was enraged that I made coffee and served myself without bringing a cup to her bedside.

"You were still sleeping," I said. "There's a whole pot left, so come and get it yourself, you grouch. No, no. I didn't mean to say that. It's coming, knock, knock, room service . . . "

"You're such an insensitive bastard, Raul. I've been vomiting all morning and you've been lying there snoring like a hog. Then you don't have the kindness to bring me coffee. I always bring you coffee when I wake up first but you never do. I've had it up to here. Get out of my goddamned house, right now!" she said. "Nothing personal, but I never want to see you again."

In the late afternoon she phoned me and asked casually where I was going to take her to dinner that evening. "Somewhere special," she said.

"Oh, yes, of course. This is all perfectly logical. Is this what happens with, what do you call it, PMS? BPD? OCD? Seems you got an advanced case of whatever, but I can't help loving you anyway."

"No, Raul, just a scare. I must have gotten food poisoning from that Mexican dump you dragged me to last night," she said. "A girl can vomit in the morning for all kinds of reasons but I eliminated one hypothesis by picking up a little test kit at Walgreens, and by the time I got home I didn't need to use it because a girl thing happened. I'm all better now. My tummy is fine. There's nothing to worry about, period."

It took me a few moments to digest the information. "Look, Christina, it wouldn't matter anyway. I'd be prepared to . . . you know I'd never let that happen again . . . "

"Shut up, Raul," she broke in. "I know you better than you know yourself. You'd take a month or two to decide what to do." Then, in her lowest whisper of a confidential voice she said: "Tonight we can raise a glass to Carl Djerassi and his great gift to womankind."

I had to look up the name later on the Internet to get the joke.

Worrying about all of this is exhausting. The memories are mixed up and all out of order, rationally, chronologically, alphabetically, emotionally – it's all crashing down on me tonight. I'll have to take a few shots of Gentleman Jack before I go to sleep and hope the memories won't haunt me until dawn.

———

Barlow was a trapped rat, the coroner could see. Perhaps a better metaphor would be that the man had boxed himself into a corner. He could not go forward and he could not go back. The coroner was a medical examiner, not a literary critic, he reminded himself, but he wracked his brains for the correct classification of this love story. It was not necessarily a tragedy because in the end, Christina became a raven. Barlow emerged with a greater appreciation of his limitations and a better understanding of the transience of time and memory. That is no small achievement for a man whose ego and self-doubt crimped his mind and incapacitated him for so long. It was neither a comedy nor a farce, despite the absurdity of Barlow's tales. Could one call it an illusory soap opera?

"There is no hard science in love," he said aloud. "And no literary form that can do it justice."

He waited for the little voice to heckle him again, but the annoying guardian of sanity must have been so disappointed it was unable to chime in. The room was locked in an ethereal vacuum. He held his breath, afraid to disturb this strange moment. He looked at the clock on Barlow's kitchen wall anticipating that in a few seconds the long hand would click to the next minute mark. He sat there for an eternity, waiting, until there was a single tock.

He would not go to the morgue in the morning to see the once nameless, homeless lovesick Barlow lying in quietus. Du Goyle could go to hell. Wilson and Nicki – they were his only family now – they could go to hell, too.

It occurred to him then that perhaps he had been deceived entirely by the corpse all along, that Barlow was lying about his love, that Christina and all the rest, his children, brothers, parents and former wife and past lovers were figments of the gyre in his hippocampus. A lonely man can conjure up as many imagined companions as he wants. After serious reflection, however, the idea did not seem right with him because it was too simple. Life is messy and it is not possible to separate truth from prevarication, because the two depend on each other in an elaborate web of perception. There was no doubt in his mind that Christina is flesh and blood just as Barlow was, but he had to question how much they overlaid reality with make-believe.

Thinking these thoughts, the inquisitor fixed himself a drink, slumped on Barlow's Hopi-blanketed couch and expelled pain with his foul breath. After two or three rather theatrical hypnic-jerks he allowed his eyes to shut.

Thirty-One

Barlow hopped off the curb into the blare of high beams careening around the corner and bearing down on him so fast he did not have time to be frightened, just angry. The coroner's body snapped awake at seeing this image, then after a confusing moment he drifted back to sleep. Next, he felt a firm hand push him off the curb into the path of an oncoming car and for a split second he could see the shadow of his assailant cast in the meager glow of the street lamp. The coroner saw a speeding slide show of flashing images shot in black and white projected on his retina. He felt the boots digging into his ribs and the blunt corner of the stone curb banging his forehead. He calmly observed all the big and small incidents of a lifetime as he plummeted toward churning black water.

The coroner broke into a greasy sweat trying to wrestle awake, but he was trapped in a gelatin of fear watching the dream cycle repeat itself and expand in ever-rising speed and fury. He saw a man inching like an earthworm up a hill then crawling then rising only to fall to his knees again. The man knew he had to go home because someone was waiting for him, someone in distress. The man clawed the trunk of a camphor tree to hoist himself back on his feet and hobble up the hill feeling delirious until he collapsed on the steps of his house. He pulled himself up on the rail, fished the key out of his fifth pocket, opened his front door, entered and bolted the lock before following the path to his bedroom, where he dropped to the floor and settled into a pure state where there was no color, no sound, no smell, no taste, no touch and no object of mind. He was conscious of the truth that he had to die before he could live. Then the man vanished altogether when the coroner fell off the couch, out of breath, febrile and baffled. The dream chilled his whole body, as if he had just wolfed down a quart of ice cream in the middle of a cold night, barefoot and buck-naked. He had entered the very mind he was stalking, the mind that spoke to him from the slab, the pages of paper, the digits on the screen, and the confessionals in the vault.

"I've had a vision," he declared in the groggiest of voices, with his neck craned toward the ceiling. "And it doesn't make any goddamned sense."

He righted himself and climbed back on the couch.

"I've got to tell the girl about this right away," he said. "She deserves to know, she's the only one who can unravel it all!" *Quiet, Leo, get a grip on yourself... You're losing it . . .*

He shrugged off the *tisk tisk* nuisance nagging at his ear and produced his cell phone. He punched Wilson's number.

"I need your help, my friend. There's a car out there I got to find and you could do me a world of good by doing a reverse search for the license number, you know, go to the DMV records and back-trace the name and address to the car," he said, mustering a voice of authority. "I have to check it out. There are too damn many Subarus around here."

"What the fuck are you talking about, Leo? You got to sober up and get back down to Earth! You sound like you're going mad."

The coroner paused to calculate what he would say next. He could not insult the *diener* and still expect him to cooperate.

"It's okay, Wilson. I respect where you're coming from. Hell, I'd be that way myself under these circumstances but you have to trust me. After all you and I have been through a lot together, you know. How many times did I save your ass after I hired you against everybody's objections and helped you get your feet back on the ground. You owe me this small consideration."

"That's not what it's all about and you know that, Leo. I'm trying to save your ass this time. I'm coming to get you. Just tell me where you are and I can help you. No more bullshit now."

This is not the Wilson I know, he thought. He is strangely different, out of character, and oddly resolute. He's changed before my eyes. Should he be proud of the boy or double-check his identity?

"Whoever you are, I can respect who you are, whatever that is. I'm just asking for one last favor. Wilson, I really need your help now. I can't tell you why. My life has galloped to this point and I don't have a choice anymore. I need to have that tag number before I can finish this investigation. Don't let me down, I can't go back."

"Just what the hell am I supposed to tell them in the morning? Dr. Bacigalupi has lost his mind? People respect you around here like you wouldn't believe, Leo. The fuck with that asshole Du Goyle – the chief told me she wants to get you in and talk to you so she can personally get you back on track. She knows what you've been going through after Alice passed and she knows the office would never be the same without you."

"I find that hard to believe, but I'll have to take your word for it," he said, wondering if Wilson was bullshitting him or urging him down the path of redemption. "Tell you what, let's make a deal. If you find out Barlow's plate number for me I'll tell you where I'm working tonight and you can come and put me in a straitjacket or handcuffs and take me wherever you want. Scout's honor."

"All right, I'll have to trust you on this," he said. "I got the license number right here. I came up with it when I was putting together Barlow's profile like you asked. Got a pen? Five Z like a zebra T like tiger G for, ah, giraffe three seven zero."

"Thanks, son, he must have some wild animals in that car. I'll call you right back and tell you my coordinates soon as I check this out." He turned off his phone before Wilson could say another word.

———

He found Barlow's car parked one dark block up the street. It was unlocked and when he opened the door he was assaulted by the stale odor of bitter coffee with a trace of rotten low-fat milk. He saw three mangled Chain Coffee paper cups decorating the passenger-side floor.

He did not seen car keys in the house and he did not find a key in the ashtray or under a floor mat, but the vehicle looked easy enough to hotwire when he was ready to hit the road. He went back inside and called Wilson to promise he would turn himself in at the office first thing Tuesday morning.

"This is Wilson Dubrovnik," the voice said. "I can't pick up right now but if you leave a message I'll get back to you."

The coroner dialed Wilson's phone again and encountered the same voicemail after seven rings. In disgust he tossed the cell phone on the desk and watched helplessly as it bounced into the air like a trampoline artist and landed with a hard plastic thud on the floor. He retrieved it and confirmed it was not broken before placing it gently on the desk. As soon as he turned his back on the menace it started vibrating and it slipped off the edge onto the hardwood. He hurried to pick it up and slap it open before it started dancing around again.

"Okay Wilson, we're all set," he barked. "The tag number is good and I'm ready to honor my side of the bargain, but with some preconditions. And by the way, tell me why this God damned phone is vibrating! It was bad enough the way it was, shrieking me to death."

"It's me, Leo," she said. "Thank God you picked up at last. I've been trying to reach you all day and I'm worried sick about you. Wilson says you went out on another bender and I can hear it in your voice, you're drunk again, you old fool."

"Ah, Nicole, my sweet Nicki. Everything's fine. I'm going to be all right," he said. "I hope that doesn't mean you've left me seventeen messages, Nicki. It's hard enough to figure out how to turn this damn thing on and off. How do you expect me to manipulate these little keys all the time?"

"I can hardly hear you, try to speak into the bottom of the phone," she shouted. "Why didn't you come in today? You know how much it's only going to hurt you. Where have you been? The answering machine on your home phone says it can't take any more messages because the memory is full, so I swung by the house twice and you weren't there. This isn't like you, Leo. I've never seen you be so irresponsible, even when you're drinking."

"Sorry, my love. Things have been rather sticky here," he said. "I'm not drunk, I'm tired. I've been pushing back the frontiers of forensic pathology. I am performing an autopsy on a man's soul."

"Whatever you say, Leo. Just promise me you'll come in tomorrow. Du Goyle is on a rampage and HR has gone ballistic because you didn't show up for your performance review yesterday. I can't believe all the things they're saying about you, like you're some kind of criminal. It's boiling over."

"Don't worry, it's just politics. They're going to can me when I show up, but they can't press charges for the crimes of being old and arrogant and having a little drink now and then. They can't take away my pension."

"You have friends here, Leo," she said. "Dixon said he's standing up for you and he's circulating a letter for the other AMEs to sign. You may not realize it, but they told me how they have tremendous respect for you. Dixon once told me that you were his mentor and he learned most everything he knows about practicing forensic pathology from you, the Coroner, things they didn't teach in medical school. He meant it. And the CME told me she wants to help get you out of this mess."

"I'm afraid they're just using you to set a trap," he said with great sadness. "The CME is a decent woman but she and I haven't held each other in high esteem since she stopped working for me and became my boss. That's just the way life goes."

"You're getting paranoid; these people are on your side. You're practically a legend in the department. They say you're an institution."

"I have great respect and affection for Dixon but he's only going to get himself marked as a wise ass if he sticks his neck out for me. I'm already a lost cause. If the others are smart they won't sign any letter. Tell him to quit this and hunker down and fight under the radar. Subversion works best underground, not within firing range."

"Never mind all that," she said. "I need to see you. There are some things I have to tell you, feelings for you I never had a nerve to express. You're like an uncle to me, Leo, something like a father figure, and I never told you how much you meant to me."

"Nicki, what are you talking about? You've never hesitated to speak what's on your beautiful mind before, but this isn't credible. I'm not your uncle, I'm just an old fool who's taken a liking to you."

"Stop it. I'm sick and tired of the teasing and flirting shit, Leo. It's not a joke anymore," she said. "I care for you."

He felt honored but also ashamed that he allowed a subliminal lust for her to poison his twisted mind. It was like incest. She was always so flippant and crass when she talked at the morgue, with a wicked sense of humor that he loved to parry with his gruff deadpan sarcasm. She would always win the match with an audacious balestra of wit. They became bonded in a funny way as he watched her grow from a mousey lab assistant into a highly capable serologist. He supposed he cared for Nicki and Wilson like a surrogate father, but he could never express the feeling of personal intimacy because first and foremost they were his subordinates and his colleagues. They were his secret children, and after Alice passed were all he had left in the world to love.

"I don't know what to say, Nicki. I'm touched," he said. "Let me finish some business and get cleaned up, then I'll come in to give you the big avuncular hug that's, forgive me, long overdue. It shouldn't take long, not longer than a day. First I have to fulfill my promise to a dead man."

Reluctantly, his finger pushed the red button.

"What an idiot I am." He spewed these words at the cell phone as he held it aloft like a ritual bone. "I should steal Barlow's car right now and speed to Nicki's house to comfort her, whatever she needs. I've been a lousy boss and a rotten uncle." *Leo, how many times have I told you to zip it up . . .*

"Shut up! Just get out of my face," he said to the whispering angel. "I'll talk out loud as often as I want, so fuck off!"

Thirty-Two

Once he sat down and regained his composure the coroner reconsidered his priorities. Nicki and Wilson can wait. The CME and Du Goyle can wait.

He reopened the vault, wanting to follow the thread of Barlow's love story to its conclusion. The titles of the documents hid the obvious clues, he surmised. His eyes glazed as he slid down the list, spotting nothing of interest. When he started opening the files at random he was disappointed not to find more information about Barlow's relationship with Christina, for that had become the focus of his investigation.

"Bingo, here's one," he exclaimed aloud. *Hush...* He tapped open a file at the top: "Farewell My Lovely." He noted that it was dated eleven days prior to Barlow's encounter with Aurora, Christina's look-alike, on the train.

———

09:15:2003

Living alone has given me too much time to reflect upon, maybe to obsess about, the past, and the unreasonable wish to return to the past and make it right. I'm an unrequited lover and a divorced man without prospects of companionship, licking his wounds and taking succor in the salve of memory. This whole obsession with Christina has gone way too far and today is the day to put it all behind me, exactly three years since she screamed and ranted and shoved me out the door for the last time, throwing my shoes at me, telling me to get the hell out of her life, sending me running from her yellow house like a mangy cur.

What started out last as a desultory effort to find her took on a life of its own, but I have to stop it now. A strange man answered her phone, saying he didn't know any Christians. She didn't respond to my letters. My emails to her old address bounced back with a cruel reply, "Technical details of permanent failure: The email account that you tried to reach does not exist." I couldn't remember the names of her friends. A woman at UCLA's alumni office said their privacy policy forbids releasing personal information. Searching the Internet I found old images of her as young ramp model and several mentions of her name on scientific articles, but nothing that would lead me to current phone numbers or emails. LA county clerk's office didn't have a marriage certificate for her on file. Her professors didn't return my phone calls either. Her mother was dead.

It's best this way. I'm not sure what I would have said to her if I'd found her, or how she'd react if I made the contact. I'm wallowing in the memory of a relationship that was doomed from the start to be short-lived, and I should let it rest as what it was. I should be grateful that it happened at all. It stops now. I won't punish myself any longer.

Since my divorce I've learned there's a big difference between being lonely and being lonesome. A lonely person desperately craves companionship and sinks into despondency when they don't have it. A lonesome person is more self-sufficient, more independent, more at peace with isolation. But being content in lonesomeness doesn't preclude the pleasure of being in the company of true friends. It doesn't stop the yearning for a lost love.

—

That was a short one, he thought, and it left him feeling unfulfilled. Stopping here would not do justice to the deceased. He glanced at the penultimate item in the black box, headlined "Online Dating: An Abomination." Barlow must have struck out on the Internet and loathed himself for trying. He decided not to bother opening that because he already knew what it was going to say. He thought he should probably leave the vault and take another peek at Christina's blog to break the monotony of Barlow's stilted prose in the vault. Then he would deal with Wilson, which would be tricky, because he had no intention of going to the office the next day or any day.

He heard the roar of a motorcycle engine stopping at the curb in front of the house. The rider stomped up the steps and pounded on the door like the point man in a SWAT team raid. "Open the door, Leo. I know you're in there,"

As he rose to answer the door he felt a sickening jab under his ribs and a soreness that went so deep into his chest cavity it took his breath away, but he could not help himself from laughing through the pain.

"Okay, okay, don't shoot, Wilson," he yelled in feigned panic. "I'll put down my weapon and come out with my hands on my head."

"Jesus, Leo, what the hell are you doing here. You're a complete mess," Wilson said upon entering.

"I was going to ask you the same question," the coroner said. "Where's your search warrant? Let me see your badge. Oh, and you forgot to say 'the jig's up!'"

"You've gone over the deep end, Leo. You look like someone beat the crap out of you," said Wilson, slack-jawed and confused. "What happened to your face and your forehead? What the fuck are you doing hiding out in the victim's house?"

"It took you long enough to find me. I could have used a second pair of nostrils for sniffing for evidence."

"Once I got the information you gave me from the dog tag I thought you might be here but then it seemed too far-fetched," he said. "I didn't breathe a word about it to Du Goyle. He was ranting about you being AWOL and said he was going call the cops if I didn't find you. He's going for blood Leo, yours and mine too."

"Don't you worry over that pink puffery with a moustache, lad. I may look like death warmed over but I'm flying high and I am in total command of the situation," the coroner said, hoping he sounded authoritative.

"Wilson, why don't you sit down on the couch here and I'll tell you a good story. All I need from you at this point is a little technical help, but first, listen."

"You need help but not the kind I can give you any more," Wilson said. "But for now let's say I take you to my house where we can lay low for a while and you can tell me all the stories you want, before the police show up here and nab you for breaking and entering. They can't touch you there. I'll bandage you up and get Nicki to come over to make chicken soup and I'll make a pot of coffee to sober you up. Come on, let's go. Make it easier on all of us. You're drunk, you don't have the judgment . . ."

"I'm skunker than a drunk, but this time I'm drunk on knowledge, son, and I need to put it to good use," the coroner shot back. "I need to set something to rights here, something confidential you don't have to know and you wouldn't understand. And it wasn't breaking and entering. Barlow loaned me his key."

"My bike's outside, Leo. Let's go," Wilson said like a parent speaking to a stubborn child.

"You're not going to drive me anywhere on your Moped. You think I'm crazy? You're the one with the death wish, riding that thing in open traffic."

"It's not a Moped, Leo, it's a Ducati Multistrada, and I brought an extra helmet for you," he said. "It's way safer than that old pile-of-bolts Volvo you drive."

"Okay, let's be reasonable. I have some things to tidy here before I leave, things you wouldn't know how to help with, but consider me your prisoner. You go home and put a kettle on the stove and I will follow in a taxi. You leave me to my own recognizance, out on bail, and I'll get there soon as I can. You have to trust me, son. I know what I'm doing."

Wilson took the bait.

The coroner picked up after himself. In the kitchen he put things back in place and cleaned the counter after reloading his flask and returning the bottle to the cupboard. He took his soiled and torn suit off the bathroom floor and stuffed it into a flimsy plastic shopping bag he found under the sink, . He took a clean white tee-shirt from Barlow's dresser drawer and used it to wipe down all the surfaces in the house that might host his fingerprints: The doorknobs, the faucets, the towel racks, bottles and tumblers. He fetched a spray bottle of glass cleaner and a roll of paper towels from the kitchen to take on the most difficult task, wiping down the computer.

He plopped down on Barlow's oak captain's chair for the last time, groaning as he swiveled counter-clockwise to face the machine. Before cleaning the keyboard and walking away he would obey his desire to look at Narcissistic Chameleon Moo. What did the "Moo" mean, he wondered? A cow's voice? A philosophical code word? Perhaps it meant nothing, simply nothing.

When he opened the blog he was jolted by the appearance of a new item at the top, posted less than an hour earlier. "She's speaking to me," he said. "She knows about the dream." *Hush...*

———

Monday, November 3, 2003
Lunacy

This is going to be my last entry in this mirror-mirror on the wall fucking blog, forever. I should delete it all right now but first I have to get this out of my system because the whole gushing of feelings and deepest thoughts has been getting far too focused on an imaginary man, someone who I was making up and discovering as I wrote and I wanted him so badly I actually believed he was real and divorced and alive in San Francisco waiting for me to knock on his door Saturday morning. I constructed this man in my mind with all the attributes I wanted to find in a man, strength, dependability, honesty, empathy, compassion, affection and constancy. Most of all, affection. Now I know what I've known all along, that he is weak and cowardly, he is afraid of intimacy, he is self-centered in the lies he uses to hide himself, his failing health, his flagging vigor. He betrayed me twice and I'm crushed and lost and degraded, humiliating myself into believing he was genuine.

Hello? Okay, I'm back on this pathetic blog now after a little diversion, getting the package of Oreos from the pantry. It's sinful but I need them now more than ever. Raul had a seven-step process for eating Oreos, but fuck him.

I knew something was very wrong when I called him from the airport and he didn't answer and when I took the taxi to his house and he wasn't there. He broke his promise again. Like an idiot I expected him to open the door and open his heart. I thought I heard him say he forgave me and still loved me under his breath on the phone Friday night in his sandy voice. He was inviting me. It was awkward and strained, then I guess my little neuro-ramparts started softening and caving in one by one until all the tension slipped away and I sighed a deep sigh, not from sadness or grief or even joy, but from a sensation of relief and release that washed down through my breast to my abdomen and it righted me on dry land for the first time in years. It wasn't sexual and not romantic but I was overwhelmed by the desire just to see him again. I must have frightened him away. He must have told himself he wasn't ready for an intrusion from the past – maybe he hasn't gotten over his divorce and maybe he decided at the last minute he couldn't face me. It didn't matter whether we embraced madly or sat quietly next to each other on a couch drinking tea and breathing quietly. I had to see him and I told him I was going to San Francisco and the tone of his voice said yes, no, yes, guarded and uncertain, trying to contain his excitement I think and at the same time concealing his fear that our encounter would only cause us great pain.

"Yes, Christina, it's been too long," he said. "I think we need to talk, I don't know, I'm sorry. You won't believe it but I've been looking for . . . trying to find . . . hoping this would come and I think I'm ready now." He stopped. I could hear the soft sizzling of static on the line masking a distant sad exhalation. "I'll be waiting, Christina," he said. "I love you."

I'm such a fool for not hearing the undertones of doubt when he gave me his address.

I stood there ringing the bell and pounding on his fucking door. I rapped his window with my keys, louder and louder until I thought

I might break the glass. When there was no response I thought maybe he was sound asleep, dead to the world.

It was seven in the morning after a sleepless night and I was both excited and drained. I'd taken the first shuttle out of Burbank and on arrival I called him on my cell phone and I heard his phone ring and ring and ring. Maybe he went for walk out of nervousness or went shopping for food so he could make a special breakfast for me, one of his mushroom and avocado omelets, to feed me what I didn't realize I've been starving for from the moment I told him to get out of my life. How sweet that idea was, how naive, that breakfast could reunite us somehow. I waited three hours sitting on his porch thinking maybe something really bad had happened to him, something so terrible he couldn't come home and wait for me or call me. Maybe he had a seizure or went into a diabetic coma or anything that could have made him unable to keep his promise. Something to do with his health that made him disappear, made him lost, invisible, that sent him away in retreat from me, and in the end maybe he didn't want to see me at all. Maybe I drove him away again.

I saw an old green Subaru parked under a tree a few houses down the street and thought it might be the same car we drove up Highway One to Big Sur on Easter vacation and if this was the case he must have gone out on a walk, a long walk to think things over not realizing how early I'd arrived. That would be just like Raul, the way he was always conflicted about our deepening attachment and how devoted he was to his daughters, determined to save them from the cataclysm of divorce. He took long brooding walks at night. Sometimes he faded in and out of concentration when we talked intimately toward the end. I had to cut it off. I couldn't waste any more of my energy and my youth on a person who would not allow himself to be happy. I truly wanted to bear his child that morning when I thought I was pregnant but at the same time I knew how foolish that would be and abortion would be the only option. I wouldn't have told him about the abortion because he'd think I was a monster, but it never came to that. We made up over dinner at Campanile and I gorged myself on Pork & Ricotta Ravioli and drank too much Chianti. It was one of our last happiest moments and I remember it like it was yesterday.

Later I wondered if this imaginary man was already dead, as I feared he might be when the letter I wrote in January was returned with the stamp "Addressee Unknown." It was the last of a half-dozen letters I started writing last year and never finished. I was hoping it wasn't too late to respond to the to the love letters he sent soon after we parted. Of course, I know now he moved when they divorced and the postal service only forwards mail for one year. I knew that, but I still dreaded the thought that he wasn't alive to receive his mail, whatever his last address might have been. Now I found him, I spoke to him, I waited forever on his front stoop asking myself how could I ever have allowed myself to fall in love with this stupid man. I went back at night and his house was dark and I heard spooky foghorns in the mist. I gave up waiting for him to appear out of thin air.

Why am I even writing this down? I'm torturing myself, it's just spilling out, gushing from a wound, briny plasma, regret.

I made the big mistake of checking into the Hotel Rex, where Raul and I stayed one weekend when his wife and daughters were out east, where we made tender love, dined at Greens and got drunk at a Mexican dive in the Mission he used to go to when he was young. All I wanted to do was go to bed and wake up in the morning with a clear head, but I simply could not go to sleep. I phoned him in vain and taxied back to his house where I pounded on his door again and again. But he never came home. I ran down the hill through the mist and I felt so stupid sobbing and running so fast I lost my balance and nearly tripped. I heard the heels of my boots making too much of a racket on the sidewalk. I was in a trance, running downhill in a dream that I didn't know was mine or someone else's. Was I dreaming this dream, or was the dream dreaming me?

On Sunday morning I couldn't face going back to the house again but I called all the hospital emergency rooms asking if they'd admitted any Barlows. I called the police who said they had no information on a man fitting his description but they encouraged me to come to the Hall of Justice on Bryant Street to file a missing person's report. I already knew Raul wasn't missing; he escaped. But I had to try everything. The officer at the counter was very kind and he suggested I contact the county morgue behind the main building. A pale, gaunt man in a reception cage said there was no Raul Barlow in their keep, just two young black men, a little tiger boy and a homeless man without an identity. He said their files were backed up because it was the weekend and told me I should call the morgue Monday.

I checked out of the hotel and took the next plane home. They put me in a window seat hemmed in by a morbidly obese woman. As we rose into the air I squished over closer to the window to watch over the Bay, lit and shimmering from the afternoon sun. I studied the salt ponds, soups of brine and mineral muck, white, pink and green squares and rectangles protruding from the marshes along the shoreline. It's the little brine shrimp that give the salt ponds their peculiar pastel colors, you know, tiny ones and less tiny ones, different varieties caught in the retaining walls whose fate it was to be burned up in the refining process that makes delicious sea salt into antiseptic table salt. I know my sodium from too many courses in chemistry and, from too much biology and genetics, I know that humans are creatures of the sea, consisting mainly of brine, and that we ooze toxin-enriched salt through the pores of our skin and spill pure and sacred saline through the ducts of our sorry eyes. I didn't cry on the way home. I just cleansed my eyes.

I was lost, but now that I know I'm lost that means that I'm found. I'm not going to allow myself to pine over him ever again. I am no longer a jelly bag of emotion and I refuse to be a chameleon anymore. That's what this stupid blog is all about, killing the chameleon. I'm going to find work at a cutting-edge research institute where I will explore the wondrous human genome, dry eyed and undistracted by stupid men.

This will be my last thought about Raul Barlow. I hear the echoes of a song, a brave and sorrowful song that gave me goose bumps when he sang it to me on long midnight walks, the same one he said he sang as a bedtime lullaby to his children when they were very young, and he sang through the lingering haze of brain cancer thinking he could not bear the idea of losing them, in life or in death – a song that bound the two of us together for a very short time then tore us apart. It was about a ruined town in Northern Ireland that he'd never visited but loved so well. I remember the song ends like this: *"What's done is done and what's won is won, and what's lost is lost and gone forever."*

Posted by Christina at 11:38 PM 0 Comments

———

The coroner felt woozy again. His ears were stuffed with kapok and he heard the clock make a muffled sound. Was it saying tock-tock or lub dub, dub?

He tried to mouse his way back to the top so he could read the entry again but his hand was frozen and his mouth was dry. This must be what they mean by the word stupefaction, he thought, a state of being stunned and scorched blind by laser-bright light.

There was no time for sentimentality now. He looked down at the scrap of paper where he wrote down Barlow's license plate number and the address of Christina's yellow-housed address in Pasadena. He tried to remember if he had ever been there.

He had to tell her what happened to Barlow but he could not imagine the indecency of breaking the news to her over the telephone. It was his obligation to tell her and the only honorable thing to do was to tell her in person.

"I'm coming," he said.

When he looked around the room as if to say goodbye he noticed for the first time a thin gray book leaning on the edge of a messy shelf. It seemed to be calling out to him. He approached it on tiptoes, picked it up and read the title on the cover: *San Francisco Coroner's Office: A History 1850-1980.* He was astonished. It must be a gift from Barlow, he reasoned. Perhaps by coincidence he had been researching the CME's Office for a crime novel he was working on. He opened the history book and started thumbing through the pages when a chart on page xiii caught his attention. It was a list of "Autopsy Surgeons" and the dates they practiced. The line for 1957 listed L. D. Bacigalupi, MD, underlined in pencil. He read it again to confirm what he saw.

The pile of books next to this one had titles such as Unnatural Death: Confessions of a Medical Examiner, Dance of Death and Forensic Pathology: Principles and Practice. "Now I know I'm going mad," he gasped. "These blasted books are here to mock me and goad me on the trail to Christina's house. There is no other explanation."

Thirty-Three

It took three minutes to hot wire Barlow's Subaru. He found a large flat-headed screwdriver waiting for him in the glove compartment, which he used to pry open the plastic casing on the steering column. He pulled out the ignition wires, stripped them and touched them together to spark the engine to life.

All the pain in the world now swirled around in fury inside Barlow's car and collected in the coroner's abscessed molar so painfully it made him tremor and wince. The tooth became a lightning rod for the searing heat that melted through his jaw and into his cracked ribs. He reached for his flask and quenched the fire, and he gripped the steering wheel like he was throttling a rattlesnake, pumping the pedals until he was safely gliding down Sanchez. "I'm not an alcoholic," he said. "This is not mine alone, it's everybody's liquor." *Quiet down there, you idiot.*

He remembered to turn on the headlights. It came to him all of a sudden that he parked his car four blocks away from the death scene Saturday night because he could not find a closer space. "San Francisco has too many damned cars," he muttered before swerving around the corner, careful not to let his tires squeak. He came to a halt behind his humpbacked sedan and jumped out. When he yanked open the door he saw the gas gauge was close to empty, so he decided to use Barlow's Subaru, which he reasoned was in better condition anyway for the long drive. Before closing the door he reached under the dashboard on the passenger side and released the spring-loaded cache. The gun was still there. He took out the bullets and put them in the cup holder next to the transmission shift handle, then he tucked the Walther PPK under his belt and said good-bye to the old Volvo.

The coroner visualized his route: East on Army Street to 101 then 80 across the Bay Bridge. He passed Dolores, the avenue that was ever more doleful after the merciless beating he took under one of its towering palms. The memory made his ribs throb again as he zigzagged his way to Army, seeing clearly in the dark and enjoying the damp coolness on his cheeks.

At the next crosswalk he slammed on his brakes to avoid clipping a pedestrian wearing a black overcoat who jumped off the curb without looking. These people drive me crazy, he fumed, jay-walking into traffic in the middle of the road as if they owned it.

"You're dangerous," he yelled out the window at the pedestrian. "Watch out or you're going to get yourself killed."

"You're an asshole," the man shouted back. "I've got the right of way here. It's a fucking crosswalk and you're supposed to stop!"

The coroner sped off cursing the imbecile under his breath. He took a detour on the way to the highway and stopped off in Bernal Heights, where he searched for the address, trawling up and down Manchester until he found the house. He leaped from the car and ran to the door to pump the bell with his thumb until finally a light went on the foyer.

Horace Albert Du Goyle opened the door wearing a silk bathrobe and a furious scowl.

"What the hell are you doing at my door in the middle of the fucking night, Leo! Get the hell out of here before I call the police."

"Evening, Horace. I heard you were looking for me today. I though I'd pay you a little courtesy call just to let you know I haven't slipped into the pit, not yet."

The coroner drew the Walther from his waistband and pointed it directly at Du Goyle's third eye, delighting at the expression of absolute terror.

"No., no please, Leo!' he howled. "Please don't do this. Forgive me! Oh God . . . "

Leo pulled the trigger. Du Goyle crumpled to his knees like a floppy doll, wailing and shaking.

"Sorry, Horace. I forgot to load the bullets."

The coroner puffed the tip of the gun barrel before turning on his heels and swaggering back to Barlow's car. His heart raced when he swung back onto Army and grumbled to himself about the name change to Cesar Chavez Street. He had nothing but respect for the labor leader and it was fitting to honor this great man, but he was always irritated by changes in his surroundings because change confused him. That was what he was thinking when he saw the cherry lights spinning and heard the siren moaning behind him. The Subaru was the only car on the road so it had to be the target. How did Du Goyle get the cops on his tail so quickly, he wondered with a sense of dread choking his throat. He watched the officer walk toward him in the side mirror. He buzzed down the window like a good citizen.

"Sir, your brake light is out," the cop said. "Can I see your license and registration please?"

He began to panic. He did not have his driver's license. He could not even remember where he put his wallet. When he looked up at his captor he saw a familiar face.

"Oh. It's you," said the tall black man peering down at him. "Forgive me, Coroner. I didn't recognize you in this car. You usually drive a 1961 humpback Volvo sedan, don't you? Nicely restored and gray in color with a big dent in the right rear fender?"

"Correct, Officer Mahoney," he said with the deepest sigh of relief. "As usual you have a superb command of the details. Did I tell you how much I enjoyed your report on the John Doe case you scrounged up in Noe Valley Saturday? It was a masterpiece of descriptive observation, Ed. The dog's name and all the rest."

"I try to do my best, sir. You're kind to notice," he said. "But tell me, Leo, what are you doing driving around in someone else's car at this time of night. On a case?"

"Oh, I was just heading home after getting a pint or two of Guinness down the road, my lad," he said. "Don't rat on me, Ed. A fine Irishman like you should understand."

"Yeah, but aren't you going the wrong way? You still live on Russian Hill, or did you move out after you lost Alice?"

"As a matter of fact I was just about to make a U-turn."

"Are you sure you're okay? It looks like you're injured . . . what happened to your face? Have you been in brawl or something? Let me take a closer look."

"No, no I'm fine." he protested. "You should've seen the other guy."

"All right then," Mahoney said. "Sorry I busted a senior official, but drive carefully and safely for me. And get the owner of the car to fix that tail light."

Thirty-Four

Feeling the jubilation of an escaped felon he shot up the ramp to northbound 101. He had committed the crimes of grand auto theft, assault with an unloaded deadly weapon, and driving under the influence with a burned-out taillight. Barlow would have approved of his filching the car, but he could hardly believe he had the reckless courage to pull the stunt with the gun. It was a premeditated practical joke, not a spur-of-the-moment gag. Even if there was no intent to harm the man, it was a terroristic threat far out of proportion to the menace that Du Goyle perpetrated toward him. Something had sprung out of his dark side that surprised and now shamed him. "I am not that person," he yelled at the image in the rear-view mirror.

The brake light and the competency of his driving under the influence of all his afflictions would be the hazards to watch out for on the journey, he told himself. A swerving Subaru could invite the dreaded CHP Breathalyzer.

He careened across the bridge unmolested by local law enforcement and without incidents, save the error of lightly grazing the passenger side of the Subaru on a concrete barrier. The aging span groaned beneath him in complaint of the heavy load it must bear day in, day out, its back aching from unrepaired earthquake damage and the insult of its second-fiddle status to its celebrity sister on the other side of the city. When the coroner reached the far shore he marveled at the herd of towering cargo cranes off in the distance to his right, heads cocked like stallions and steel bodies bejeweled by lights to warn off low-flying aircraft. He panicked for a moment when he returned his gaze to the road searching for the lanes that would take him to Interstate 580 and onward to the Southland.

Ordinarily he took Highway 101 to Los Angeles because it was the gentler, greener and more humane route in comparison to the desolate corridor cut by the Interstate 5, which plows in an unwavering straight line down the arid floor of the San Joaquin Valley to the Great Valley choked by peat dust and diesel fumes, the new California. Time was of the essence, however, and he reasoned he could cut two hours off the trip with the inland route.

Cutting through the Oakland Hills on the 580, he concentrated hard to avoid straying across the faded white dashes. He flew past the wind turbines in the Livermore Hills on his starboard, that stood in formation like ghostly green-energy sentries in the dark, some of them with blades loping slow circles in the unusually temperate breeze. He passed the monotonous exurban housing nightmare of the Tracy environs. The exit sign for Highway 130 to Modesto popped up and caught his eye. "Modesto," he said, wearily acknowledging the city's existence. Then the road merged with the mighty Interstate 5, and like a rocket launcher the highway blasted him southwards on Barlow's journey.

Then he heard an annoying violin through the whistling windows and the noisy purr of the engine. It was playing the Flight of the Bumblebee. "Oh God!" he said. "Get that tune out of my head!"

Alcoholics sometimes have auditory hallucinations, not just visions of pink elephants, the coroner knew. Perhaps he was regressing to early childhood. He had to be mindful, at a professional level, about the risks of alcohol in his bloodstream. At a personal level, he had to be respectful of the hideous thumping in his head after the bumblebee quieted down. He became intensely aware of the razor-wire barbs below his rib cage where young men in boots played soccer the night before. Try not to cough, and breathe deeply lest your lungs collapse, he reminded himself. Motoring down the Valley he heard a new sound well up in his eardrums, a soothing drum rhythm smothering the pain. *Dong, dodo tock! dodo tock dodo dodo tocka!*

The rhythm increased in volume as he drove. *Dong, dodo tock! dodo tock dodo dodo tocka! Dong, dodo tock! dodo tock dodo dodo tocka* . . . He buzzed down all four windows to slap cold air on his hot, stinging forehead. *Dong, dodo tock! dodo tock dodo dodo tocka! Dong* .

The rushing wind carried the stench of methane as he passed ranches so vast the offending herds of cattle were out of sight. He watched a sign for the Rastau Rest Area rush by and suddenly became aware of his swollen bladder and parched throat. He had to suppress the urge to take a suicidal U-turn across the concrete median at 80 miles per hour. Clean urinals and artesian drinking fountains would have greeted him there had his reflexes been sharper, he lamented. A cordon of semi-trailer trucks hemmed him into the slow lane and blocked him from passing into safer territory. The coroner was dazed by the trucks' jumbo halogen headlamps until the sound returned and brought him back to his senses. *Dong, dodo tock! dodo tock dodo dodo tocka!* The sound was in synch with his heartbeat.

After seventeen miles of gritting teeth and fighting off the gathering peristalsis of his urinary tract he spied the lights of a roadside oasis, Food, Gas and Lodging at exit 47. The Subaru coasted down the off ramp and into the parking lot of a bright red hamburger outlet where he burst through a door marked Men and rid himself of an odiferous brew of uric acid, ketones and alcoholic by-products.

He washed and dried his hands and saw a puffed red face in the mirror, lacerated and sagging with black tea bags under bloodshot eyes. He rolled up Barlow's borrowed shirtsleeves and splashed the face with cold water. It burned.

"Christ almighty Mother of God I'm a mess," he grunted, wondering if the fellow making noises in the toilet stall could hear him. "Who the hell cares at this point?" *Hush, hush, hush* . . .

It was one of those ubiquitous fast food establishments that served prefabricated food, part of a global network renowned for the uniformity of its dry hamburger patties and larded French fries. He squinted in the bright light and asked the chubby girl behind the counter, adorned with the golden N on her breast and tattoos peeking from her sleeves, for a happy dinner with a large cup of black coffee.

"How many creams?" she asked. "Three, please," he said.

You know you can jumbo-size your meal for another dime," she chirped.

"No thank you," he said. "Most everybody gets the jumbo size," she said with a charming grin that spread ear to ear and displayed shiny blue-colored braces. "It's too late in the night to be so cheerful, Miss," he said. "Please just give me the regular. I'll pay extra for the regular meal if I have to." She giggled in response.

He noticed an emaciated man in a trench coat and fedora sitting at a plastic booth in the rear corner of the restaurant, his eyes sunk deep into their sockets, his thin cheekbones protruding from his blanched face. He was devouring a happy hamburger with one hand and clutching a bouquet of French fries in the long bony fingers of the other. On the glistening red and yellow table three empty hamburger wrappers and bent french-fry cups sat before him. This man is famished, the coroner thought, and he can't get enough to sate his hunger.

On his way out the door he thought he heard the man whisper something that sounded like *"Oh sigh, oh sigh . . . roos."*

What? He shivered away the mournful incantation. Was he trying to say Osiris, the Egyptian god of something he learned in school but forgot? No, the man was another hungry night traveler mumbling incoherently with his mouth full of junk food, but he turned to take one last look at the curious fellow, who suddenly became animated. His blank stare turned attentive, his dark eyes turned to alabaster. "Are you going to Bardot?" he said.

"No sir," the coroner said. "I don't know where Bardot is, never heard of it." He walked backward toward the door, suspecting this hamburger ghost was going to try conning him into a ride. He waited for the man to make his pitch, claiming his car broke down and he desperately needed a lift to a god-forsaken cow town twenty miles off the highway named Bardot.

"You'll pass through it down the road. Everybody does," the man said before turning back to his meal.

The coroner crouched in the front seat of Barlow's car and choked down his own food, leaving the creamed-up coffee for consumption later in the drive. As he started the ignition he tasted bile in the back of his throat. He reached a patch of grass behind the edge of the tidy parking lot just in time and used the happy paper napkins from the burger bag to wipe the vomit off his wingtips.

Then he resumed the journey across his ruined map.

It was an endless wide stripe of highway traveled by reckless sport utility vehicles and a motley caravan of big rigs pulling monstrous trailers the size of ranch houses and double loads of corrugated steel shipping containers, all flashing their high beams and honking their air horns as they passed him. He gripped the steering wheel with purple knuckles not daring to turn his neck and watch the trucks swoosh by. *Dong, dodo tock! dodo tock dodo dodo tocka! Dong, dodo tock! dodo tock dodo dodo tocka!*

The Subaru was obstructing traffic traveling at a mere seventy-eight miles per hour in the slow lane after he engaged cruise control. He noticed the lower rim of the steering wheel was sticky with blood, his own he deduced, but from where? Did he touch his forehead and open a wound when he washed his face? He drank coffee and slapped his thighs to relieve the tense monotony of the road. When he reached down to turn on the radio he caught sight of a white stripe poking out from below the knobs, a cassette tape. He punched it in and the car filled with a quiet pulsating rhythm overlaid by a rippling electronic guitar. The music was a starship, exuding faith and desire, lifting him purposefully off the ground. He recognized the tune and associated it with something good in his early life, but could not call up its title.

Then his mind unpeeled into a reverie. He heard a wall of sound, buzzing, whirring, rising and falling in a shrill, melodic song. He was walking along a familiar road inside a tunnel of elms and oaks, and he was transfixed by the sound and by the crackle of dead cicadas under his feet. He was in the epicenter of a massive brood of 17-year cicadas, the magicicada, which had risen from the ground all across northern Illinois to live a brief life of several weeks, sing, mate, and die. They were not locusts at all, he learned. Locusts are grasshoppers that plagued man by destroying crops when they swarmed down from the sky. The magicicada, however noisy, were harmless, peaceful, uplifting, created to serenade the human species and teach the evanescence of life. It was a blazing hot August afternoon. He was nineteen years old. He remembered watching the Watergate hearings all morning and reading the transcript of one of President Nixon's paranoid exculpatory speeches in the newspaper, and he heard an echo of Gil Scott-Heron rapping *Haldeman, Ehrlichman, Mitchell and Dean, it follows a pattern if you dig what I mean*. He remembered being spellbound by the mating song that showered down upon him. He remembered wondering where he would go on his long walk and how long it would take him to return.

Whose memory is this? The coroner was confounded by the time and place of the story. He could not recall ever visiting or living in northern Illinois but the roaring sound of the cicadas was sharp and clear as though they sang to him sometime in the past year or two. Was it static from the radio? No, the radio was off and the cassette tape was not playing, still in cradle waiting to be replayed. He listened as the sound of cicadas turned into the mesmerizing rough sound of the road, the rumbling truck tires, grinding engines needing repair, the blaring radios and drunken shouts from a muscle car packed with farm kids, the Doppler effect of a purring of sports car passing at 93 miles an hour. The Subaru made its own noises, an irritating wind whistling through the damaged rubber gasket on the passenger side window and the clunking of some loose auto part under the chassis in back. It went on like this for a hundred miles with his eardrums inhaling an overlay of the rhythm, softer now but the metronome was accelerating. *Dong Taka-bodobodo-dum, Dong taka-bodobodo-dum . . . Tah-tah-bodo-bodo-podum, Dong Tah-tah-bodo-bodo-podum . . .*

Then there were no trucks, no menacing high-beam headlights, no road signs for what seemed like an eternity. He sped down a stretch of empty highway and took the opportunity to engage Barlow's cruise control, setting it to a reasonable 73 miles per hour. The highway was so straight he hardly needed to steer toward the vanishing point, freeing his hands to unscrew his flask and wet his throat with vodka. "I'm absolutely alone," he shouted, "going God knows where." *Hush . . .*

Now a dense layer of enchanting tule fog blanketed the road with puffs of swans and demons and daredevil hitchhikers making him swerve to avoid collision with nothing at all. He passed sentient vapors shaped like eels inviting drivers to jump the shoulders of the highway into the milky blackness. *Dong, dodo tock! dodo tock dodo dodo tocka!*

The coroner looked into the rear-view mirror to adjust it and when he leaned in he saw a strange face emerge from the milky fog behind the back window coming into the car and gathering on the tinted glass, a scattering of pixilated features that sharpened into the dead man's face where his own should have been. When he flipped the mirror back from its nighttime position to normal the image of the death mask remained, shaking its head back and forth, mimicking the coroner's own shaking until he slapped the mirror askew and stomped on the gas pedal to flee the vision.

In time he became very drowsy. He slapped his cheek, pinching the back of his neck and screamed like a banshee to ward off the hypnosis of the tule fog. For a split second the windshield turned black and when he reopened his eyes the car swerved across the highway from the left to the right lane and he heard the pebbly sound of the shoulder on Barlow's tires before he was able to swing back onto the road praying that a night truck was not hiding in the fog ready to flatten him. The slip-sliding stopped but he continued to feel exhaustion infecting the pit of his stomach The coroner held his breath and made his abdomen taut to resists the sickness. He bellowed *"RrrAaahhh!"* to fight off the urge to close his eyes, until his larynx was raw.

He searched desperately for something to keep him awake in the tule fog. He squeezed the tendons on his shoulder in a Vulcan grip and pounded the top of his head with his knuckles, which he regretted immediately when the impact fired hot buckshot into his skull. Then it came to him: Pain was the one thing that would keep him alive.

He had urgent business to conduct another hundred fifty miles ahead so he concentrated on the knives in his ribs, the sickeningly sour trumpets in his head making his temples throb, the open scab itchiness on his forehead, and the merciless yowling in his abscessed tooth. Pain is a whetting stone, he observed. *Dong*

Taka-bodobodo-dum, Dong taka-bodobodo-dum... Tah-tah-bodo-bodo-podum, Dong Tah-dah-bodumo-bodo-podum...

He punched the knob on the radio, hungry for loud music or even screeching static between stations to stir him. Not a sound emerged. Did he break it? The fog was snowy, dark and deep. It was blowing laughing ghouls at his windshield when he saw a sign crop up on the roadside ahead, the first he had seen in an hour. He had to squint to read it. "Rt. 915 East, Khertneter Salt Lake, Next Exit." The coroner stepped on the accelerator pedal and sped past the turn-off because he knew if he pulled over to rest now he would never reach his destination.

"I wonder if they know," he said, finding another purpose to stay awake. He overheard them once last year when they were in the staff room speaking in low tones about mysterious deposits of funds in their bank accounts. Listening furtively near the door he could tell neither of them knew the other had been receiving the same anonymous deposits of a thousand dollars a month, which bank officials told them could not be traced to the depositor because they were in cash. The two were baffled when they learned it was happening to both of them.

Next thing he knew he had his mobile phone in hand. He turned it back on and pressed eight, the speed dial number for Wilson, who was exceedingly groggy at four forty-seven in the morning.

"Leo, I'm so glad you called," he said. "I've got incredible news for you. Where the hell have you been?"

"First you have to listen to me, Wilson. I know I've done you wrong. But I got something to tell you if you'll just shut up and listen. I'm taking a little trip and everything is fine so don't worry."

"This is bullshit, Leo. I won't stand by and watch you kill yourself like this! Don't be such a self-centered asshole. Wherever the hell you are, you turn around and come back home, Leo, because the case is solved. You're really pissing me off."

The coroner's eyes brightened and the fog lifted. He could see clearly the painted lane markers dashing their way up the road ahead of him. The wind blew warmly though his windows carrying the spicy scent of juniper trees. He did not comprehend what Wilson just told him. Something about the case. It could wait.

"Okay, just hear me out, son. I want you to go to my desk and open the file drawer on the left side where you will find a folder tagged "Personal and confidential." Got me? There are two envelopes inside, one marked Wilson and the other Nicole. Bearer bonds, seventy thousand each. Promise me you'll get out of the fucking morgue and go back to graduate school, full time, finish your doctorate in EE or whatever the hell it was before you jumped off the cliff and turned yourself into a miserable *diener*. Tell Nicki to move out of that hovel of hers and buy herself a decent house."

"Never mind all that Leo. She called!"

"She what?"

"Christina called the morgue asking about Barlow. Evidently she filed a missing persons report with the police after checking with the morgue Saturday. The dots didn't get connected because of our Monday backup but the cops called her once we officially identified Barlow. She called the morgue, Leo. I talked to her about an hour after I left you at Barlow's house but you ditched me. She was in hysterics, Leo, she kept wailing and cursing. The woman sure knows how to swear."

"Okay, Wilson. I got it under control. I'm heading her way right now.

"You're what? Don't tell me you're driving to LA, that's suicide! Du Goyle got the cops to put out an all-points bulletin for your arrest on attempted homicide charges. What's that all about?"

The coroner tossed his cell phone out the window and watched it skip and bounce in his side mirror.

A giant semi-trailer broke though the black lacquer wall behind him, flashing its halogen search lights through the car's back window and tromboning its air horn until it changed lanes, missing the Subaru's rear fender by inches as it ripped past. He noticed the cola logo on its side and thought he could use a stiff Cuba Libre at that moment to calm his frayed nerves.

Barlow's car was shocked into an unpiloted space craft now flying at warp speed into a shapeless starless tunnel wrapped in velvet and guided only by the flickering reflection of lane markers caught in the car's high beams. *Tah-tah-bodo-bodo-podum, Dong Tah-tah-bodo-bodo-podum* . . . He began to fall asleep again, nodding off and bouncing back to consciousness with each jerk of his floppy neck. He barked like a dog, growled like a lion and hollered oaths so loud it tested the capacity of his lungs and measured the limits of his rib cage to endure pain. The wind, which had been so gentle and warming just minutes earlier, turned freezing cold and made him shiver violently, but he did not dare shut the windows. A sign saying "Bakersfield 37 miles" lit up momentarily and slipped by. He thought he saw the flickering of a sign announcing the town of Weedpatch, then other signs appeared for exits to Sage Brush, Dirt Canyon and Cactus Graveyard. Time went on, indecipherable in its fleeting, slowing, sputtering and quickening pace.

He watched for the enormous Scandinavian furniture store on the right that served as a landmark for the approach to the Grapevine. It should be right here. It's the size of two or three airplane hangars and would be impossible to miss. But it had disappeared from the landscape. Instead, he saw a road sign he did not recall ever seeing before. "Bardot, Next 3 Exits."

He felt a jolt of electricity travel up the his hunched spine, from the coccygeal through the sacral to the lumbar and tingling upward to the thoracic curve and his thinning cervical vertebrae, where it triggered a sharp blast of fire beneath the lower edge of his skull. He nearly lost control of the steering wheel before the pain abated. Then his mind started spinning in a whirling dervish of images, sounds and pungent odors as he approached Bardot.

The first exit was marked "Esperanza Negra Ave., Clear Light Tabernacle." Sounds vaguely Pentecostal or Mormon, he thought, and how very odd it was that he had traveled this highway so many times before and had not noticed the town of Bardot or even heard of the name until the hamburger ghost mentioned it. He would be entering the grapevine soon and billowing his way to the Los Padres National Forest. This must be one of those hellish new bedroom communities springing up everywhere with tracts of huge houses with plastic doors and identical roofs. Bardot's residents must commute two or three hours to their jobs in the city, he supposed, the poor devils.

He finished what remained in his flask, a few drops, to stanch the rising ache of his entire body. The pain mocked him as his inner ears reverberated to the crazed cadence guiding him to the Grapevine. *Dong, dodo tock! dodo tock dodo dodo tocka! Dong, dodo tock! dodo tock dodo dodo tocka! Dong, dodo tock! dodo tock dodo dodo tocka . . .*

'I can do better than that,' he told his muffled ears. He slapped the cassette tape back into its slot to listen to the pulsing rhythm and rising crescendo of an electronic guitar. He suddenly remembered the name of the tune. *"Are you going with me?"*

"Yes," he said, "I am coming, Christina."

The second Bardot sign appeared: "Triesteza Blanca Blvd., Locus Plaza, Next Exit." The coroner thought it might be a good idea to pull off the road here and to get a cup of coffee at the Plaza or at a convenience store that he was certain to find on the Triesteza Blanca strip, but there were no lights in sight and something warned him away, a premonition of dire consequences, a fear that once he entered Bardot he would be unable to get out. The road suddenly filled with semi-trailers and big SUVs with giant wheels as the pitch of the incline threw the car into second gear to catch its purchase on the road. He suddenly noticed that the little nozzle-icon light at the bottom of the gas gauge was flicking on and off, flirting with the empty line. He knew the car would have two or three gallons in reserve when the light went solid, but he worried he might not make it to a gas station at one of the little towns ahead near the mountain pass. A third Bardot sign suddenly manifested itself, reading: "El Camino Dolor, Thodol District Courthouse, Next Exit." He did not want to gamble on the Grapevine so he resigned himself to visit the wretched town of Bardot to fill up on gas and, if he could find a gauge in the glove compartment, check the tire pressure. Turning off the Interstate he thought he saw palm trees beckoning him from the bottom of the ramp, but when he squeezed his eyes shut and opened them they were gone.

The coroner cruised up and down El Camino Dolor, the town's main drag paralleling the freeway, looking for a gas station, finding it very odd that there were none in sight. He was not surprised when he saw there were no cars or people on the street at this time of night, but he was taken aback when he saw no lights and heard no sounds, not even a hum. When he pulled into a side-street named Elm Avenue to turn around and head back to the freeway ramp he was puzzled by the lack of houses and buildings in the dark, no sign of life behind the row of dark shops on El Camino Dolor. Turning back he did a double-take when he saw there were no backs to the buildings facing the avenue, just supporting struts angling down from the rooftops.

"Son of a bitch, these are all false fronts," he exclaimed. "Bardot isn't a bedroom community, it is a clever illusion. But why? It is like a bad movie set, a Potemkin village, a fairyland without fairies."

Back on the highway the Subaru's engine strained to power the vehicle uphill and allow the coroner to merge into traffic and snake up the flank of the Tehachapi Mountain Range. This was the granite barrier separating the vast irrigated desert of the Central Valley, the heartland of California, from the boundless urban sprawl of the Southland. He detected a barely audible voice wafting through the car's rear speakers that was disturbingly out of synch with music from the cassette: "*This you must know of a dying man, the quivering fear, the sputum of lies . . .*

"Pipe down back there," the coroner croaked. "Don't distract me when I'm concentrating on the road." He remembered his father saying that all the time on family trips. It took the air out of their yellow station wagon.

Nearly a minute lapsed before the back-seat death rattle resumed, *the thrill of swimming in the darkening brine . . .*

"Okay, that's enough," he said. "I'm warning you!"

"*. . .A cowering clock, a hobo, a shrine.*"

To hell with this weirdness, he thought. I need to flush it out of my mind like a dirty radiator or I'll lose my way.

Redolence of evergreen filled the Subaru as the transmission bumped from drive to third gear and the car began navigating the loping switchbacks in the ascent of the Grapevine. Black and gray vehicles honked and flashed their high beams in disgust at the choking pace of the Subaru as they veered past. A sluggish sixteen- wheeler shifted into the lowest gear and blocked him from weaving through the strobe lights to the safety of the right lane. The highway turned east then south and west then south and east again, rising up inclines and sinking into gullies and rising again.

The Subaru's boxer engine kept losing its power, with pistons begging for a richer injection of fuel, then it regained its vigor when the transmission lurched into third. He looked down at the gas gauge nervously. There's empty when the panic sets in and there's truly empty when the car sputters to a stop. The coroner wondered if Barlow had a Triple-A membership card in the glove compartment. How far to the next station in the blackness ahead, he wondered. A whimpering halt on the shoulder would give him a fifty-fifty chance of getting crushed under the giant wheels of an unstoppable Mack truck, even if Barlow did have road service insurance.

"Have I come this far just to fail?" The voice said *Hush* . . . The coroner said "Oh shut up yourself, you nasty little twit. For Christ's sake leave me alone in my own misery! It belongs to me, not some babbling nag out of my bloody conscience." *Dong, dodo tock! dodo tock dodo dodo tocka! Dong* . . .

He lightened his foot on the pedal and slowed the chugging little-engine-that-could, coasting in neutral when the road sloped downward to conserve his dwindling supply of gasoline, and when the climbing resumed he reluctantly engaged the transmission to accelerate sparingly uphill. He tried to close his ears to the thunder of horns behind him demanding he go faster . . . *dong, dodo tock! dodo toka dong taka* . . . until the motorcar sputtered through Los Padres National Forest and reached Tejon Pass. He pulled over into a rest area, reclined his seat and napped fitfully until he heard them banging on his windows and scratching the paint on Barlow's fenders and hood with razor claws. Were these creatures the guardians of the forest, or the gate to hell? That was the first thought that came to his febrile mind. No, they were raccoons. Panic, dread and terror were their names.

He leaned on the horn to frighten them away but they did not budge, so brazen was this trio of deranged animals peering into the car through their black masks with sinister human eyes. He locked the doors trying to recall whether raccoons had prehensile thumbs they could use to jimmy their way into the front seat to slice open his throat. Do raccoons live at elevations this high? In the lowland forest they raid your campsites foraging for food, knocking over trashcans and slicing open your tent if you forgot to stow away your PowerBars. In residential areas the bandits sneak into your kitchens and claw their way into the pantry for a meal of Cheerios.

"They are not raccoons, they are bewitched *tanuki* devils," he said, not knowing exactly what a *tanuki* was. He had absorbed the word from a crossword puzzle, seventeen across: Japanese badger dog. "I can't let them stop me here." He had not been this sober and alert in three days and found the courage to spark the ignition wires and slammed the accelerator pedal, sending the beasts flying off the hood. It was worth wasting gasoline to hear them shriek in surprise on his way back to the expressway. Sweating profusely, he wiped his brow with a rag from Barlow's passenger seat. The bleeding had stopped, but not the tender pain.

Maybe they were just protecting their young, he wondered. Warding off an intruder. "Oh no. Did I hurt them?"

The fuel held out until he saw distant lights emanating from the town of Lebec, where four spanking clean self-service gas stations welcomed the Subaru as it sputtered down the off ramp. When he slipped his last three dollar bills into the gas pump his eyes navigated to a darkened wooden house across the road that advertised itself as a Mexican restaurant on its switched-off neon sign. If it had been open, and he had not spent the money, he would have ordered a burrito. For a moment he thought he heard a lilting trill from inside the restaurant, sweet women's voices singing in seductive harmony. He felt a powerful urge to go knock on the door. When he crossed the street, however, the singing turned sour and the harmony broke up into a discordant chorus of feral cats. They scattered in every direction when they heard the coroner approach, hissing and yowling as they disappeared into the trees. "No tortilla scraps for you little vultures tonight," he hissed back at them. The snarling song of the cats still rang like tinnitus in his ears when he replaced the nozzle and wired the engine alive, but it was soon smothered by the driving beat of the tabla. *Dong, dodo tock! dodo*

tock dodo dodo tocka . . . Dong, dodo tock! dodo tock dodo dodo tocka! Dong,
dodo tock! dodo tock dodo dodo tock . . .

Back on the road he felt merciful relief. The dark haze that
shrouded the basin below was pocked with pinpoints of light as he
descended the southern flank of the mountain range, the tail lights
of toy cars commuting to Los Angeles. It was not long before Barlow's
car was snagged by the great city's mighty gravitational pull and taken
prisoner by gridlock. This was a coronary disease that shortsighted
road engineers created and that Angelinos must endure, a vast capillary network of surrounding highways conveying too many vehicles
into the sclerotic arteries. It can be fatal, he knew from his experience
in the morgue. Barlow's Subaru could only slow down, stop and lurch
foreword in frustration when the sea of taillights turned red.

The sun was rising by the time he passed through the San
Fernando Valley and followed his path *Dong, dodo tock!* southeast on
the 210 to Pasadena. After exiting at Fair Oaks and finding his way to
Green Street he was tantalizingly close to his destination. The coroner's mood changed when he smelled burning oil from the Subaru's
weary boxer engine and heard an ominous whirling and a growling,
which continued for another mile until the car was in its death throes.
He had time to pull it over to the curb before it stopped running. He
jumped out and opened the hood to look at the motor with uncomprehending eyes.

Christina's house was three or four blocks away, the coroner reckoned, and so he abandoned ship and started walking, then jogging to
his destination. *Dong, dodo tock! dodo tock dodo dodo tocka . . .* Chest heaving and legs burning, he ran. *Dong, dodo tock! dodo tock dodo dodo tocka!*
Dong, dodo tock! dodo tock dodo dodo tock . . . He ran until he collapsed on
the sidewalk across the street from her yellow house. *Tocka tocka tocka*
tocka . . . tock!

Thirty-Five

Under a canopy of old oak trees the street was empty, the neighborhood silent. Her modest home was painted creamy yellow and surrounded by large-scale Mission Bungalows wrapped in dark brown redwood shingles. It looks so familiar, the coroner was thinking as his legs buckled and dropped him into an undignified sitting position on the sidewalk opposite the house. After ten minutes of calming his wheezing breath he rolled to his knees and pushed himself up to a standing position like a wounded gymnast, his body stiff and soaked with sweat and aching from scalp to toe. His heart fluttering with arrhythmia and his lungs near collapsing, he counted out twenty very deep breaths, inhaling three counts, exhaling four, inhaling three counts, exhaling four. Finally he summoned the strength to hobble across the street and up a pathway lined by rose bushes, which tore his borrowed pants on a cluster of thorns as he brushed by. When he reached down to untangle himself, the branches jabbed his fingers and drew tiny drops of blood. "She will be shocked when sees me," he murmured, "but I must tell her about Barlow's dream no matter how awful I look." *Hush, hush, hush . . .*

The coroner somehow knew the bell did not work so he rapped softly, then increasingly louder with greater determination until she pulled open the door.

They both froze, regarding each other tentatively with their eyes locked in bewilderment. Time halted. The coroner was stunned by the impossible beauty of the woman, her green irises textured by tiny flecks of chocolate and her resplendent raven-black hair. She was visibly frightened at first by the bedraggled man at her doorstep, but her shock turned to familiarity with the battered face and scraggly unshaven jowls. She saw through the cheeks discolored by bruises, smeared bent spectacles, the dried blood rimming a gash on his brow.

"Raul?" she said, tentatively. "Oh Jesus, Raul. It's you! You're alive!" She rushed toward the coroner, arms outstretched. "I can't believe it! You came back!"

The coroner was too flustered and confused to think of someyhing to say that would correct the misunderstanding. After an uncomfortable pause she burst into a scream, "Ra – ool!" She wrapped herself around him with such force they spun and tumbled into the rose bushes and she clutched him as they rolled over the red petals and stinging branches onto the soft grassy lawn. She straddled his upturned belly with her skirt hitched up from the fall and planted slobbering kisses on his ruined face. She ran her fingers though his matted hair. He felt the warmth of her vulva on the skin of his stomach and every fear and every worry melted away.

"What have they done to you, Raul? You're hurt. Your forehead is bleeding, my God you're bleeding, Raul. Talk to me, Raul, tell me what happened to you!"

Thirty-Six

A bright shaft of light woke the coroner in a stranger's bed. Disoriented and sore all over, he sat up to inspect the room, its polished light oak floor and walls papered with a pattern of tiny blue flowers. He saw a basket of potpourri atop a chest of drawers, and tasteful lace curtains. A woman's room. Had he been here before? He reached out to touch the bookshelves by the bed to see a disorderly line of paperback novels and a stack of New Yorker magazines nearly spilling off the edge. The three lower shelves were packed with tomes on microbiology, genetics, and astrophysics. "Where am I?"

He felt warm under a familiar feather quilt, and for the first time in many long years he felt a welling of contentment. *Paradise?* He was naked. His first instinct was to search the room for his brown suit but he quickly remembered it was filthy and stuffed in a plastic bag in the back of Barlow's car.

Then he recalled being stripped and guided by strong slender arms to a bathtub where he soaked in warm water as someone caressed his body with scented soap and shampooed his mousey hair. He heard sweet laughter when he wobbled on his feet and someone dried him off with a thick towel. A red antiseptic stung the cuts on his face and arms as someone cleaned and applied a tincture to his lacerations. Someone dressed his forehead with gauze and tape. A hazy memory flirted with his mind, delicate hands under sheets touching him where no one had touched him in three years. The all-but-forgotten tumescence, the sweet musky scent of her body, the slow and kind rhythm rocking him in a cradle of repose. He remembered being inside her and entangled in her arms and legs and weeping together until they slipped away into a tired release, into the twilight of one single death.

He could hear her now on the other side of the door humming, rattling porcelain plates and clanking pots. He smelled wheat bread baking in the oven. Heels clacked lightly on a tile floor. Classical music wafted across the house and into his ears like thin syrup, Mozart? He never learned to connect the tunes of symphonies to their composers. He imagined Christina, statuesque with braided black hair, in a scarlet apron licking something from the tip of a wooden spoon and smiling at the fine taste. The aroma of coffee erupted and seeped under the bedroom door telling him it was time to rise to his feet. His fever had lifted overnight. The murderous headache was gone. His tooth was quiet. His ribs were only sore.

The coroner put on the boxer shorts, shirt and tan pants that were freshly laundered and stacked neatly on a chair. He searched the room for his cell phone to call Wilson. No, I tossed it out the window on Interstate 5. He saw the black princess phone on the night table and pecked in the number without thinking. He thought he should tell Wilson and Nicki he was all right, that he found the girl and the case was closed as far he was concerned. He reckoned that Dixon had done the autopsy already, but the results were inconsequential. He now embodied the corpse by the agency of Barlow's dream, the one that sped him south.

He wanted to tell Wilson that he was coming out of a three-day fugue and that he was okay and ready to report to the office, or the San Francisco police, to face the consequences of his actions. He could always use the insanity defense, and he could rely on friends at the prosecutor's office to keep him out of prison. He would take early retirement with a generous pension and drive his humpbacked Volvo across America on the back roads, stopping at diners and looking up his county coroner friends he had worked with over the years. He would regale them with the tale of Barlow and Christina.

An unfamiliar voice answered the phone. "ME's office," it said. "What can I do you for?"

"Yes, hello. Can you patch me through to Wilson?"

"Who?"

"Wilson Dubrovnik, you know, the *diener* down in the morgue. You must be new. He's the tall kid with red hair."

"Look, buddy, this *is* the San Francisco morgue and we haven't had anybody called a '*diener*' in decades. And there's nobody here that answers to the name Wilson." The man at the other end of the line hacked a smoker's cough and continued with a raspy wheeze. "Either you got the wrong number or the wrong morgue or this is some kind of hoax. Who the hell are you anyway?"

"This is Leo," he barked in indignation. "Dr. Leonardo Dante Bacigalupi, the senior assistant medical examiner of the City and County of San Francisco. Now tell me who the flying fuck you are."

"My name's Dixon and don't fuck with me, asshole. Leo Bacigalupi died fifteen years ago and if I could grab your throat right now I'd throttle it until you're one of our customers." The man was livid.

"This is a sick joke you're pulling, you bastard, and I won't stand for it," he continued. "Leo Bacigalupi was the finest forensic pathologist this office has ever seen and I'm not going to let an idiot like you dishonor The Coroner's name. He was my mentor. He taught me just about every Goddamned thing I know, so shut up about Leo Bacigalupi."

The man at the morgue slammed down the phone.

The coroner recoiled, befuddled and shaken to the core. This had to be a mistake, he told himself. He probably dialed the wrong office, the wrong city, the wrong parallel universe. It made absolutely no sense. He decided not to call Wilson's cell phone just yet, not until he regained his composure and figured out what was going on. He would call him after the breakfast that awaited him in Christina's kitchen.

The coroner sat down stiffly on her bed to put on Barlow's socks. He did not see his wingtips anywhere in the room. His mind was still reeling from the bizarre phone call and the abuse he received from a stranger at the morgue. Then it dawned on him. It was he who was the victim of a hoax, a very cruel hoax. They were all in cahoots with Du Goyle to destroy him. It was an odious and absurd scheme to rob him of his identity and incapacitate him with mental anguish.

They intended to drive him to the breaking point so they could force him out, taking unfair advantage of his weakness for alcohol, those bastards. He was not going to fall for this. He would go straight to the Chief and appeal, and he would get his friends at City Hall to stand up for him. Du Goyle may be cozy with the mayor, but the coroner had solid contacts with veteran civil servants in city government who wielded far more power than the merry-go-round of politicians. These were the people who make the mayor and the supervisors look good by guiding them on policy. Bitchy political functionaries like Du Goyle did not matter.

The sounds of Christina clinking glassware in the kitchen broke his reverie. Was she pouring fresh orange juice? He had to tell her about Barlow's dream, the one he visited. He could not delay in executing his official duty that had minutes before been maligned by an agent provocateur with a hacking cough who answered the phone at his morgue. He would deliver the message to her over eggs and bacon, discreetly and sincerely. Then he would depart like a gentleman, yes, a man of honor.

The memory of the night he spent in this bed, however, still made his mind spin. How could the woman have mistaken him for her lover, a shabby ruined man like him? He felt he betrayed Barlow somehow by sleeping with Christina, even if it was a borrowed ecstasy. All he did was inhabit the corpse, the body that he made his own by digesting the man's stories, peering into his soul, watching his mind fall from the Golden Gate Bridge onto the pavement in Noe Valley.

He would dismiss it as an illusion if it were not for the lingering scent of jasmine and musk on his body, the echoing sensations of being washed and caressed, the taste of her mouth, the seductive sound of her voice and the sight of compassion in her face. If Christina was not real then nothing in the world was real. If she was truly a mere fantasy then everything he thought solid was a deceitful hologram, a vision so realistic it robbed him of the capacity to separate fact from fiction and fiction from fact.

He had labored three days to plumb the inner world of a stranger who seemed so familiar he could not resist cutting deeper. The secrets in the vault awakened his mind with a mysterious spark of synaptic lightning. The dead man refused to leave the planet if it meant letting go of Christina. He remembered it all, and all the experiences and the illusion, the truths and the lies that defined his life, the mourning and yearning, the hope and regret, the unfinished love for Christina.

Time hushed when he rose from the bed and opened the door like a shy schoolboy. He saw her standing with her back to the window silhouetted by bright morning sunlight. He could not see Christina's face or her breasts and belly. All he could see were soft rays that outlined her lovely torso and her beckoning outstretched arms. Suddenly a powerful jolt of electricity shattered his amnesia.

"I remember now, all of it," he said. "My name is Raul."

"Well, duh!" she said, wagging her nimbus in a teasing way.

"But you can't know who I really am, Christina," he said. "Not until I tell you all the stories and memories in the dream I had in San Francisco. I came here to tell you.'"

"I know you're not a stupid coroner named Leo, if that's what you mean," she said. "Wasn't Leo the name of the protagonist in that book you lost in a thumb drive, the one you told me about? About a guy jumping off the bridge? I think you got knocked out or something and started wandering around like a character in your dumb novel. That's what you called it, my dumb fucking novel. You lost your way inside that book but I don't care because you're alive and you found your way home. I didn't realize how faithful I've been to you and how true to me you've been until you came to my door. Fuck that dream and fuck your fucking coroner, Raul. You came home to me. That's all that matters."

"No, no, that's not completely true, Christina. The coroner took me to you. He was there, real as can be. He examined me, dissected me and drilled all the way to the bottom of the well until he released me. I don't know what he did. He was relentless. I was dead and he brought me back to life by listening to my stories and making wisecracks. I have to tell you about the dream."

"I think I already know all about your dreams, Raul," she said. "I know why you've been hiding, I know who you are."

He felt light-headed. He saw her coming toward him and he felt the warmth of her hand grasping his. She was wearing white, all white, sweater, skirt and tights, except for her red ballet slippers. Barlow saw that her apron was white, not scarlet as he imagined, and it bore a familiar logo and the words "It's Tops Café," one of their favorite diners in The City. His stomach growled.

"Let's eat breakfast and put on your shoes," Christina said. "I want to take you somewhere."

"Where's somewhere? This isn't a trick, is it? I just got here a few minutes ago and I don't want to go anywhere else at the moment. I'm hungry. I want to eat you along with breakfast. Doesn't that apron get dirty? You know, with food and stuff? It's totally white."

"You're being goofy again," she said. "I wear it as a precaution, not as paint rag."

"I'm not Goofy, I'm not a cartoon, I'm Leo the coroner, remember him?" He held the back of her neck softly and drew her face so close their mouths had no choice but to meld together with sad, sloppy lips. A burst of relief fused them and made them fall on the kitchen floor, laughing to wake the dead.

Thirty-Seven

After a fine breakfast of bacon, eggs and hash browns, washed down with the best coffee he ever tasted, Christina revealed her plan.

"I have a surprise for you," she said. "I've gotten to know the couple who lives in your old house in Sierra Madre. They're very nice people. She's a member of the ladies' book club I belong to, and when we were reading Tanizaki's *In Praise of Shadows* she and I got to talking about Japanese aesthetics. She told me she had a genuine Japanese garden in her back yard and I knew immediately it was yours. I told her about you and she invited me to come anytime to visit the garden to pine over you."

"Did she show you the Red Book?"

"With the old pictures? Yes, she showed me the Red Book. She told me about Mr. Kato and the magazine article you wrote about him. So I looked it up online. I didn't know how scared you were of dying."

"I never said anything about dying in that article," Barlow said. "It was about the joy of survival, not dying."

"You didn't say it, you emoted it between the lines. And the garden confirmed it when I saw the thing. I pictured you doing your dreary Zen meditation in the tea shelter. I looked for your ghost and when I couldn't see it I was positive you were still alive. That was before I talked to the fucking morgue last night and they said you were killed in an accident. I was devastated, you bastard, how could you do that to me?"

"It was a homeless man, you know, a case of mistaken identity. If I had my cell phone I would have called you to explain," he said.

"Hah, hah," she said.

"Have you considered the possibility that the ghost in the garden those many years back was actually you, Christina, hiding behind a little pine tree and waiting to pounce? No wonder I was scared. The incredibly beautiful ghosts are the scariest ones of all, you know."

"You got your metaphysical chronology wrong, my love. How could I be a ghost when I'm standing here now trying to get you out the door for some fresh air? Let's go to the garden and play whack-a-mole with our friendly ghosts. It would be fun," she said. "Look at the clock, it's already quarter past nine. It's time. Let's not keep Mr. Kato waiting," she said. "Are you going with me?"

"Before we go I want to emphasize something to you. I am not afraid of dying. I worked hard to take care of that on my deathbed a long time ago," he said, "Letting go saved my life."

"Good," she said, "You nailed it. Because when you aren't afraid of dying anymore you open your mind and you're acutely aware of how you're scared to death of death, and that's when real life begins."

"Nonsense. You're talking in circles Christina," he said. "How would you know that even if it's true? You're too young and too alive to be an expert on death."

She answered with a laser blast of green eyes, a Mona Lisa smile and a gust of silence.

The glider was no longer perched in front of the tea shelter, so they sat cross-legged on the ground to admire the sculptured pines, the zigzag bridge and the lily pond with the glittering colors of the koi swimming aimlessly just beneath the surface. Barlow watched Christina gently place her hands on her knees palms upward, sitting straight backed perfectly still as though time stopped and she turned to stone. Only her long black hair moved, swaying and floating in the light breeze.

Barlow shifted his eyes to examine the little stream. "I'm not afraid of dying, Christina," he said. "You may doubt me, but it's true. Go ahead, sweetheart, smite me. I'm ready any time. Let's go home and make blissful love and perish forever in each other's arms. In the morning it'll be my turn to brew coffee and make breakfast."

He waited for her response without turning to look at her. Nothing. He heard dry leaves rustling next to him, and when his eyes followed the sound she was gone. She must have wandered out into the garden, he thought, but when he scanned the yard she was not there. She could not have gone far, he reckoned. She had vanished momentarily, but he would find her again. They would return to the safety of the yellow house. They were reunited at last in constancy and in grace.

Then he saw it. A flash of a white skirt behind one of the sago palms, like the shimmering trace of a garden fairy. "I get it." The words slipped off his tongue so faintly the lilies and the dragonflies could not hear. "She's playing hide-and-seek with me." That is what she has been doing since the day they met, he realized. She cast her spell on himx then drove him away, only to lure him home again. What a wonderful thing it is to survive brain cancer and to be able to love Christina, his true love, the greatest love of all, the love of his life.

Made in the USA
San Bernardino, CA
10 October 2015